This is an intriguing reimagining of Tudor England and the treacheries of court life." —*Kirkus*

The Boleyn King

Winner of the 2013 RT Book Reviews Reviewers' Choice Awards for Best Historical Fiction

"Andersen's novel, alive with historical flair and drama, satisfies both curious and imaginative Tudor aficionados . . . her multidimensional characters are so real that readers will wish it was history and eagerly await the next in the trilogy." —*Romantic Times* (4.5 stars, Top Pick!)

"A surprising gem and a thoroughly enjoyable read. . . . Andersen has given Anne Boleyn fans the happy ending we desire."
—*Historical Novels Society*

"An absolutely gorgeous manifestation of that urge to bring an intriguing story forward. . . . This is history-plus-more. . . . The first in a trilogy, so brilliantly conceived and richly executed, fans of bold, historical dramas are likely to gobble them up as soon as they appear."
—*January Magazine*

"A glamorous royal drama—but *The Boleyn King* offers a refreshingly offbeat, counterfactual take on the familiar story. . . . The first book in a trilogy that promises to be inventive and entertaining."
—*Shelf Awareness*

"High-court intrigue, romantic passions, and danger surround the four central characters of Andersen's gripping first novel. . . . This first entry in a planned trilogy highly entertains with fine pacing, plot, and detail. Perfect for Philippa Gregory fans."
—*Booklist* (starred review)

"Full of intrigue, conspiracies, and the accurate details so essential to good historical fiction, *The Boleyn King* is the ultimate game of *What if?* Anyone who has even the slightest fascination with the Tudors will want to devour this deletectable novel in a single sitting—and not only to see what might have happened to England had Anne Boleyn kept her head."

—TASHA ALEXANDER, New York Times bestselling author

THE VIRGIN'S DAUGHTER

BY LAURA ANDERSEN

The Boleyn King

The Boleyn Deceit

The Boleyn Reckoning

The Virgin's Daughter

THE VIRGIN'S DAUGHTER

A TUDOR LEGACY NOVEL

Laura Andersen

BALLANTINE BOOKS

NEW YORK

A Ballantine Books Trade Paperback Original

Copyright © 2015 by Laura Andersen
Reading group guide copyright © 2015 by Penguin Random House LLC
Excerpt from *The Virgin's Spy* by Laura Andersen copyright © 2015
by Laura Andersen

Published in the United States by Ballantine Books,
an imprint of Random House, a division of Penguin Random House LLC,
New York.

BALLANTINE and the HOUSE colophon are registered
trademarks of Penguin Random House LLC.
RANDOM HOUSE READER'S CIRCLE & Design is a registered
trademark of Penguin Random House LLC.

This book contains an excerpt from the forthcoming book *The Concubine's Daughter* by
Laura Andersen. This excerpt has been set for this edition only and may not reflect the
final content of the forthcoming edition.

Library of Congress Cataloging-in-Publication Data
Andersen, Laura.
The virgin's daughter : a Tudor legacy novel / Laura Andersen.
pages cm
ISBN 978-0-8041-7936-2 (paperback)—ISBN 978-0-8041-7937-9 (ebook)
1. Elizabeth I, Queen of England, 1533–1603—Fiction.   2. Queens—Great Britain—
Fiction.   3. Inheritance and succession—Fiction.   4. Great Britain—Kings and
rulers—Succession—Fiction.   5. Great Britain—History—Tudors, 1485–1603—
Fiction.   I. Title.   II. Title: Tudor legacy novel.
PS3601.N437V57 2015
813'.6—dc23
2014049230

Printed in the United States of America on acid-free paper

www.randomhousereaderscircle.com

2 4 6 8 9 7 5 3 1

Book design by Caroline Cunningham

For Dee F. Andersen

1931—2014

Husband

Father

Gentleman

Loved

THE VIRGIN'S DAUGHTER

PRELUDE

June 1568

Elizabeth Tudor—Queen of England, Ireland, and France; Supreme Head of the Church of England; estranged wife of King Philip of Spain; warrior savior or bastard heretic depending on one's point of view—walked the grounds of a quiet country manor in company of the woman once her dearest friend, and allowed herself to be at ease.

Or relative ease for, of course, a queen could never entirely unbend. Not when there were so many eager to relieve her of her crown.

But today was not a day for such concerns. Elizabeth would once have linked arms with Minuette Courtenay, Duchess of Exeter, as they walked, but that was many years and even more choices ago. But their steps still matched and so did their thoughts.

"The boy is besotted with you," Elizabeth noted drily.

Minuette's amused laughter rang as clear as childhood. "Julien LeClerc is sixteen years old. He's besotted with every female he lays eyes on."

"Does Dominic take his infatuation as lightly as you do?"

"Are you implying my husband has cause for jealousy?" There was the slightest edge to Minuette's teasing question. She had always been highly protective of Dominic.

"I am implying only that your husband's sense of humour has never been highly developed, least of all where you and other men are concerned."

Even a queen occasionally slipped in her choice of words; a shiver passed between them and Elizabeth was grateful when Minuette neatly changed the subject. "It is good of you to allow Anabel to come this summer, despite our French guests in residence."

Only a handful of people used that particular name, for Anabel was properly Her Royal Highness Anne Isabella, Princess of Wales and only daughter of the Queen of England and the King of Spain. At six years old, Anabel was already a precocious mix of Elizabeth's cleverness and Philip's cold-blooded practicality. She had her own household mainly based at Ashridge, but for the last three summers Elizabeth had sent Anabel to the informal Courtenay household at Wynfield Mote. She wanted her daughter to have some warmth in her childhood, and no one better to provide it than Minuette. It also provided Anabel with friends, for Minuette had four children of her own, including twins born the same month as the young princess.

Elizabeth dismissed her generosity with a wave of one hand. "I owe Renaud LeClerc a debt for his care of you. And I can use every possible ally wherever they are placed. A French general and vicomte is a useful friend for England just now."

They had reached the practice yard, a cleared section of fields by an indolent river where today Dominic and Renaud supervised a training bout of swords between Renaud's sons. Julien, the sixteen-year-old whom Elizabeth had watched turn bright colours every time he looked at Minuette with what he thought was studied non-chalance, was already taller than his eighteen-year-old brother, Nicolas, but he was less disciplined. Julien scored hits more by virtue of luck than skill, something that Renaud pointed out to his younger son in caustic French. The smaller children were ranged round the outside of the yard, cheering indiscriminately both young men, who in age and privileges were almost godlike to those ten years behind them.

Minuette's sons followed every move of the older boys and their swords with rapt attention. Eight-year-old Stephen and six-year-old Kit were as different in temperament as in looks, but they shared an affinity for weapons and tactics. From the boys, Elizabeth's gaze skipped over her daughter hand-in-hand with Kit's twin, Pippa—the girls in nearly matching shades of blue gowns, Anabel's subtly more splendid and artful—and rested where it most often did whenever she saw the Courtenays.

Ten-year-old Lucette Courtenay was the eldest of the younger group, a curious, intelligent girl with dark brown hair underlaid with tones of red. From the time she could walk, Lucie'd had a restless, impatient air, as though she could not drink in the world fast enough.

There was something poignantly familiar about that impatience.

But it was Lucette's eyes that Elizabeth dwelt on. Where Minuette had hazel eyes, and Dominic's were deep green, their eldest daughter surveyed the world from eyes of the brightest sea blue, a stunning combination with her dark hair and pale skin.

"No." Minuette interrupted Elizabeth's musings.

Though they did not even look at one another, Elizabeth knew that Minuette had heard the unasked question. It was the same question—and answer—they had been tossing between them for years.

Have you told her?

"You cannot keep it from her forever," Elizabeth pointed out, as she so often had. "There is no mistaking those blue eyes. When once Lucette is introduced at court—"

"Who says she will come to court?"

"The eldest daughter of the Duke of Exeter? She'll be at court." Elizabeth spoke with the confidence of a monarch accustomed to obedience. "People have long memories, Minuette. And when they see your daughter's eyes, she will hear the stories. Do you not prefer she hear it from you?"

Minuette turned her back, a rudeness that only Elizabeth's oldest friend could get away with. "She is my daughter, and it is not your concern, Your Majesty."

Elizabeth watched her friend walk away and thought, The niece of the Queen of England is very much the queen's concern.

ONE

Nonsuch Palace rang with merriment and music on this long winter night, for 21 February 1580 marked the birth of Anne Isabella, Princess of Wales and Queen Elizabeth's sole heir to the English throne. This year was a particularly grand celebration, for Anabel, as she was known to her intimates, had reached the age of eighteen. The courtyards, ballrooms, and corridors of Henry VIII's delicately wrought Nonsuch Palace bubbled with not only celebration, but speculation. Elizabeth had always kept her daughter closely guarded and at one remove from her court. But now that Anabel was eighteen, surely the queen must begin to give serious thought to her daughter's future consort.

Lucette Courtenay had wished Anabel well earlier in the day and did not feel compelled to fight her way through tonight's flatterers simply to lay particular claim to her childhood friend. Anyway, Pippa and Kit were both at her side. Lucette's twin siblings would be eighteen themselves within the week and they had always taken Anabel as one of their own, a trio adept at going their own way and charming themselves out of trouble when necessary. At twenty-two, Lucette felt herself much more than four years their elder.

Her brother Stephen caught her eye as she turned away. "Leaving already?" he asked, his deep voice so much like Dominic's that it always startled her.

"You know I'm not interested in festivities as such. Besides, I've been summoned."

"A private assignation?" He might have been teasing. "Should I follow at a discreet distance to guard your honour?"

"I'm quite capable of guarding my own honour," she retorted. "Not that Dr. Dee is likely to threaten it."

He laughed softly as she left.

Slipping through palace corridors that became decreasingly populated the farther she moved away from England's royals, Lucette did not bother to wonder why Dr. Dee had sent for her. John Dee had been her tutor and mentor since she was fourteen, and Lucette was accustomed to his unusual demands. He might have anything to say to her tonight: from a debate on whether "algeber" or "algebar" was the correct term for that field of mathematics to a request to sight the stars with him. She hoped it wasn't the latter. It was really very cold outdoors, and not that much warmer in the tower room up the four flights of spiral stairs that she climbed now. She was resigned to nearly anything.

But when Lucette knocked and was told to come in, she found herself very surprised indeed. Dr. Dee awaited her, as expected, but so did another man, one who stood with his back to the fire so that his figure was outlined in hazy light. She knew that figure, as did everyone at England's court and many outside it: Francis Walsingham. Queen Elizabeth's principal secretary and intelligencer.

Severe in his black clothing and somewhat devilish with his pointed beard, Walsingham said, "Welcome, Lady Lucette. And thank you for coming."

"I didn't come for you," she replied, only realizing her rudeness as she spoke. She pressed her lips tightly together, determined not to be shaken.

Amusement ghosted through Walsingham's eyes as John Dee said mildly, "Don't let's stand on ceremony, my dear. Be seated, and hear Sir Francis out."

What else could she do? One did not flout the requests of Francis Walsingham. Besides, she trusted Dr. Dee, as much as she trusted anyone, and knew he would not be involved in subterfuge if he did not think it necessary.

Lucette let her amber-coloured skirts bell around her as she sat. She was accustomed to simpler gowns and adornments, but one could not grow up Minuette Courtenay's daughter without learning how to use even fabric to one's advantage. Not that she had ever acquired her mother's instinctive grace.

"What may I do for you, Master Secretary?" she asked coolly.

"You do not consider that perhaps I may be interested in doing something for you?"

She tilted her head thoughtfully. "You do not engage with those who cannot be useful to you in some way. And as I have never yet done you any favours of which I am aware, then there is nothing that you could owe me."

Walsingham inclined his head, again with that faint air of amusement that managed to highlight his intensity rather than diminish it. "You are your mother's daughter," he murmured.

There had been a time when that would have been the highest praise Lucette craved. But now she heard only the unspoken corollary: *Your father's daughter, on the other hand . . .*

Before she had to ask again, Walsingham sat across from her and proceeded to business. "You have been invited to France by Charlotte Bertran. I would very much like you to accept her invitation."

Now doubly surprised, Lucette said, "I have not even spoken of that at home yet. How did you know?" But the answer was evident. "Ah, because you have read my letters. Is that a long habit of yours?"

"No. But Charlotte Bertran is the daughter of Renaud LeClerc.

And I am, shall we say, interested in anything from that quarter just now."

"Why? Surely you do not expect to turn anyone in the LeClerc household to your service."

"It is your service that interests me."

Lucette's gasp was half laugh, half shock. She looked from Walsingham to John Dee, inscrutable as always in the candlelight, then back. "You want me to turn intelligencer? I am a woman."

John Dee interjected in his quiet, thoughtful manner. "If that is your sole objection, then you should hear Sir Francis out."

She was quick enough to grasp why, and the further shock of it drove her to her feet. "You view the LeClercs as enemies, and think that they will not expect a woman to unearth their secrets."

Walsingham rose more slowly, regarding her with an air of disinterest she did not believe. "Nicolas LeClerc is a widower, and Julien has never married. Charlotte made it clear in her letter that she would like to match you with one of her brothers. Why would they suspect a young woman with such long ties to their family—a woman actually born in their household—of spying?"

"They would not, because I will not do it."

"Even if it were a matter of life and death?"

"Is it?"

"I do not trifle in other than matters of life and death, my lady. I have cause for concern in the LeClerc household and would be as happy to have those concerns dismissed as confirmed. I could approach it in another manner, but it would take longer and be less certain."

"No," Lucette said decisively. "As you called me my mother's daughter, then you know that my family does not meddle in politics."

"Not even at the queen's command?"

"Her Majesty would never command this."

"Are you certain?"

Drawing herself up to her full five and a half feet, Lucette said firmly, and daringly, "If Queen Elizabeth has a request for me, she can ask me herself."

She left without being dismissed, fury at Walsingham's impertinence mixed with a less laudable and less comfortable emotion: curiosity.

It had always been her besetting sin, and as Lucette swept through the freezing corridors of Nonsuch Palace she admitted to herself that her interest had been engaged and she would be a little disappointed if nothing more came of it.

"She declined?" Elizabeth asked, before Walsingham had even finished bowing.

"She did. She has something of her mother's tongue about her, but her temper—"

"I know all about Lucette's temper," Elizabeth interrupted drily. It was Will's temper, which meant it would cool as swiftly as it flared.

"The lady more or less dared you to ask her yourself."

"I told you it would come to that." The queen waved away an attendant offering an array of sweets and gestured to Walsingham to sit. "Are you certain involving her is the best course?"

"Absolutely." Walsingham was accustomed to the queen revisiting decisions already made, and he listed his arguments succinctly once more. "No one will think twice about Lucette Courtenay visiting her family's longtime friends in France, especially considering that she was born there. Charlotte is clearly anxious to match the girl with one of her brothers, so Lucette will have every reason and opportunity to get close to both of them."

"You have not told her why, or that you have a particular interest in Julien LeClerc?"

"I will not tell her why until she agrees—and about Julien, I will tell her nothing at all. I need her to make up her own mind."

Elizabeth drummed her fingers on the tabletop, tempted to delay but knowing that another opportunity so perfect might never present itself. "Then I suppose it's time to exercise my royal prerogative and see how far Lucette will allow herself to be commanded."

"Your Majesty will keep in mind the delicacy of the situation."

"A French plot to assassinate me? I am every day aware of the delicacy of the situation, Walsingham. It is why the Princess of Wales will leave court within the week. It would not do to keep her too accessible."

"The princess is not, I take it, in agreement with that plan?" Walsingham asked disingenuously, for those at court who had not heard Anne's outrage for themselves had quickly been apprised by those who had. Elizabeth knew her daughter to have been named well, for she had every single bit of her Boleyn grandmother's temper and quickness to take offense.

"Princess Anne will do as she must, as she was born to do. She may blame me for her position, but I do not think she is in a hurry to give up its privileges. Until Philip accepts the inevitable and divorces me, there is no chance of him having another heir and Anne will continue to be a pawn in Spanish politics."

Walsingham eyed her narrowly, and Elizabeth stared him down, daring him to accuse her of delaying the divorce herself. But he merely cleared his throat and said, "The sooner we have eyes in the LeClerc household, the better."

"Consider it accomplished," Elizabeth said. "I know how to bring Lucette to heel."

But there was a slight hollow inside when she pondered the girl's features in memory—though not really a girl any longer, she mused. Twenty-two. Bright and stubborn and wary and innately generous . . . and with those wide blue eyes that had the power to unsettle the Queen of England more than she had ever allowed anyone to know.

Though Lucette had known Her Majesty, Elizabeth, Queen of England, Ireland, and France as long as she could remember, to be in her presence was to be intimately aware of power. Who had it, and who didn't.

Lucette had been waiting in the queen's privy chamber for a quarter hour when the queen swept in, snapping her fingers at her attendants to leave them. Lucette curtsied, eyes lowered so that all she could see was the bottom few inches of the queen's sapphire and gold gown, intricately wrought with embroidered scallops and whirls.

"Rise," Elizabeth said, "and join me."

Lucette perched on the edge of a seat and waited warily. The queen rested her expressive hands on the gilded chair arms, and pondered Lucette with a remote expression that might have concealed anything from curiosity to disdain.

Tall and slender, the pale-skinned, red-haired queen never seemed to age. Save for the fine lines around her eyes and mouth, Elizabeth looked much younger than her forty-six years. Even if the paleness of her skin owed something to art, and even though her glorious hair was more often a wig these days than not, the Queen of England seemed almost a mythical figure: a fairy queen of boundless youth and wisdom.

Elizabeth's tone was all exaggerated patience. "Walsingham tells me you are disinclined to aid the crown. Might your monarch know why?"

"I am disinclined to repay friendship with betrayal, Your Majesty. To pretend that I am angling for a husband while following the path of mere rumours—"

"It is not rumour," Elizabeth said flatly. "Not this time. Three men were arrested last week in Calais, attempting to cross to England. They carried coded letters that my government deciphered. A most definite plot is under way, aimed not merely at my throne but at my life."

Lucette hesitated. "Might I ask why the government suspects the LeClerc household? I can think of no more honourable man than Renaud LeClerc, or one less likely to be embroiled in secret plots."

"Except perhaps the Duke of Exeter?" Elizabeth asked with a touch of humour. "I agree. It is not Renaud himself we suspect."

"Surely if one of his boys were involved in anything so dangerous, their father would know it."

"His sons are not boys, Lucette, as you are no longer a child yourself. They are men, full-grown and tested in the service of a Catholic government. Give over any childish romantic fantasies you have and consider the matter logically!"

"Is that why you want me, for my logic? Or is it not simply because I am a woman who will not be suspected and can . . . what? Seduce the brothers into spilling their secrets?" She asked it plainly enough, but wondered briefly how exactly one went about seducing secrets.

Elizabeth stood up and, from a coffer on a side table, took a sheet of parchment that she handed over. "Look at this list, Lucette. Take your time. Study each word and phrase, and when you are ready, tell me what you see."

Reluctantly, Lucette accepted the parchment, densely scrawled with distinctive handwriting that she recognized as Walsingham's, and did as she'd been bidden. It was not an especially coherent document, nothing so useful as a complete sentence, just names and phrases and dates compiled without apparent rhyme or reason.

Despite her reluctance, Lucette's mind began to work. She was incapable of refusing a puzzle, and John Dee had used just such apparently chaotic collections in order to teach her how to order information. How to separate the important from the useless and the critical from the merely important. Patterns were instinctive to her way of viewing the world, as natural to her as breathing, and so her eyes skimmed lightly over the sheet, hardly knowing that her breathing slowed and her attention became so inward that she appeared almost to be in a trance. In that manner, the words and phrases rearranged themselves.

"Oh, yes," she murmured, hardly aware of speaking aloud. "There it is."

The queen's voice pulled her forcefully back into the physical world. "There what is?"

"The pattern that has Your Majesty and Walsingham so worried. The flashpoint of trouble that you set me looking for although you have already discerned it."

The queen did not dispute that this had been a test of some sort, but merely raised a cool eyebrow in that smooth, white face. "And?"

"Mary Stuart and Princess Anne. France and Spain. Two foreign interests dangerous enough in themselves, but exponentially more devastating if combined in one threat. It looks very much as though a narrow web is being woven between those two interests."

Lucette laid aside the sheet and proceeded to speak honestly; there were some privileges of the queen's insistence on their blood relationship. "And you did not need me to tell you that. So why am I here, Your Majesty?"

She did not miss the small smile, though the queen spoke matter-of-factly. "You are here because it took Walsingham a solid week to see the pattern that you just uncovered in three minutes. A pattern that has disclosed something called the Nightingale Plot."

"I knew that I was looking for a pattern, and all the information was gathered in one place. Much simpler than sifting through scores of seemingly unrelated letters and documents."

"That list includes unrelated documentary material. I am quite sure you could sift out crucial information . . . in the field, as it were."

"Your Majesty, with all respect, I am not suited for such an endeavour. I will be happy to consider any information you care to pass along, but I wouldn't have the faintest idea how to go about sifting intelligence as I go. People are beyond my skills."

"Not these particular people."

Lucette wasn't sure if the pounding in her head was from apprehension or excitement. It was one thing to hear such a proposal from Francis Walsingham, quite another to hear the Queen of England seriously suggest that she turn intelligencer. Spying was a job for men like Walsingham and those he employed. Men of doubtful loyalty, men of easy conscience, men who could move unnoticed . . .

In short, men.

Attempting indifference, Lucette asked, "Why does Walsingham believe the LeClercs are involved? Surely he is not swayed by mere rumour."

"Among the coded letters carried by the Catholic Englishmen last week, Walsingham encountered a name, a single name of great concern. One that is not on the list you just studied."

Lucette raised her eyebrows in query, knowing she did not do so half as smoothly as her monarch.

Elizabeth spoke the single name. "Blanclair."

It was all she had to say, for Lucette knew that name as well as she knew that of Wynfield Mote or Tiverton. For Chateau Blanclair was the lovely Loire Valley home of Renaud LeClerc, who had sheltered Minuette Courtenay when she'd been driven out of England by the late king's rage, and it was at Blanclair that Lucette had been born and passed nearly the first year of her life.

Though she had never been back, her mother and Dominic had been to France twice in her lifetime, and the Courtenay family had maintained close epistolary ties with the LeClercs. Lucette herself wrote to Charlotte LeClerc at least twice a month; hence Charlotte's latest plea to come to France and see her. Lucette had not discussed the proposal with her family yet, nor had she made up her mind as to her response.

It appeared Elizabeth had preempted her.

"So that is why you want me," Lucette answered. "Not for my mind or my skill in seeing patterns, but because I am a woman and, unlike others of Walsingham's employ, can be sent to seduce men of their secrets."

The queen looked amused. "I hear that both Nicolas and Julien LeClerc are fine men. Seduction would not be such a trial."

"Your Majesty—"

"Do not take the high moral ground on the basis of your sex, Lucette." The queen was not angry—yet—but the warning of it was in her voice. "I am a woman and I do not scorn to make use of it against those weak enough to be so used. For all that, do you find anything lacking in the strength of my mind or the force of my will?"

Lucette pressed her lips tight so as not to lose her temper with royalty.

And then the queen, as she always did, chose precisely the right tone; one of wistful remembrance, tugging on loyalties formed before Lucette was even born. "I need you. England needs you. Body, mind, spirit—you can go where none other I trust half so well can go. You can enter the very heart of a home and family that evidence suggests may be a threat to us. I do not order you to a certain conclusion—I ask you only to bring me the truth, wherever it may lie. Chateau Blanclair and the LeClerc family may be innocently on the fringes of involvement, but a fringe can lead one deeper. If France and Spain combine against me, how long before an assassin gets lucky and my half-Spanish daughter is handed into Philip's control? How long before England is left to be squabbled over by Catholics and Protestants once more? What are the niceties of your conscience against such a threat?"

Even as Lucette recognized the manipulation of Elizabeth's passionate appeal, she was also moved by it.

She offered one last—expected—resistance. "If my father knew what you were asking . . ."

Clearly she was more rattled than she'd thought, or that would not have been her wording. The queen pounced on that slip. "Don't let's be coy, Lucette. If your 'father' were alive to know it, then I would not be queen and my life would not be in danger."

And just when Lucette was prepared to almost hate the queen for her manipulation and self-righteous power, the facade opened a crack and there was Elizabeth—her mother's friend, herself once a clever girl who no doubt could easily have seduced half the secrets of Europe out of any man she liked—and that warm, playful girl smiled out of the wary woman's eyes.

"Ah, Lucie," she said, "you were going to say yes before ever you came in here, whether you admit it or not, because there is no dare you will not take. You want people to think you restrained and modest and demure, but you are aching to live in this world and use the gifts God has granted you. And I like to think that you have a little affection for me, niece, and would rather not see me dead if you can help it."

Fighting against the smile wringing its way out of her, Lucette said, "You truly believe I can help it?"

"Walsingham believes so, as does Dr. Dee. And yes, Lucie, I believe you can do it. Not because you are my niece, but because you are Minuette's daughter. I never knew a woman more able to accomplish her own ends than your mother, and I believe she has passed that to you."

Lucette rose from her seat and made her submission, feeling the wings of panic and pleasure combine in an exhilarating mixture. "I will serve you in this, Your Majesty."

TWO

If Lucette had worried about the reception her impending visit to France would have at home, she needn't have bothered. For her brother Stephen had news of his own to impart upon the Courtenay family's return to Tiverton: namely, that he had been tasked with joining the English royal guard attendant upon Mary Stuart of Scotland. He delivered the news with his customary calmness at dinner, always using as few words as possible to explain himself, and waited for his father's reaction.

One usually had to wait some time for a reaction from Dominic Courtenay. The Duke of Exeter was a man of even fewer words than his eldest son, and only long study and familiarity allowed Lucette and her siblings to read any sign in his countenance. She caught the twitch along his jaw, and then her mother intervened.

"Not quite the posting you had hoped for, Stephen, but at least it is not a dangerous one."

Kit, at eighteen two years younger than Stephen, joined in. "Not dangerous? Tell that to the Duke of Norfolk!"

"Dangerous, then, only to men of little conscience and less intelligence," Minuette Courtenay answered tartly.

Finally, Dominic spoke. "Neither of which applies to you, Stephen. Not that I like the thought of you caught in the tangled web that is Mary Stuart's life. But," he added wryly, "I don't suppose the queen asked so much as commanded."

"I am glad to go, Father," Stephen replied. "And I am not afraid of political tangles."

"You should be," Dominic warned flatly. "You are yourself an earl, which makes you equal rank with Shrewsbury. Do you know how far into debt the Talbots have been driven in their guardianship of Mary Stuart? You'd best hope the queen does not intend to replace Shrewsbury with you as her chief jailer."

"I'm hardly Shrewsbury's equal, Father. My title derives as secondary to yours, not of my own account, and George Talbot is more than twice my age. My purpose at Tutbury has nothing to do with changing Mary's prison or keeper."

That almost sounded as though there *were* a distinct purpose for Stephen's presence at Tutbury, Lucette thought. But before anyone could continue, her sister, Pippa, sent the conversation in an entirely new direction. "Lucette, is it true you have been invited to go to Paris with Dr. Dee?"

Coming from anyone else, this knowledge would have shocked Lucette and sent her wondering furiously how it had been obtained. But Pippa always knew far more than she should. Far more than was good for her. And not always from old-fashioned gossip or eavesdropping. There was a hint of the mystic to Pippa, times when her green eyes seemed to see far more than the world around her. Some of the village folk were superstitious about the single streak of black in her dark blonde hair. *Touched by the faeries,* some whispered.

So Pippa knew—somehow—of the cover story concocted by Walsingham to explain her trip to France. For now, how Pippa knew was less important than that she had opened her mouth and now her mother and Dominic were looking at Lucette, obviously expecting an explanation.

She breathed deep and let it out, prepared with her mix of truth and lie. "Charlotte is pressing me to visit. She wants me to meet her husband, Andry, and her daughters. Dr. Dee is planning a trip to Paris in late May to spend some weeks in consultation with scholars and in search of old manuscripts. He has offered himself as guardian and companion to France and back. If it's agreeable to you," she added disingenuously, looking at her mother. Though Dominic's would be the final word, it was Minuette he would listen to.

Her mother's eyes were narrowed as though seeing beneath Lucette's easy flow of lies to the truth. "What else does Charlotte want?" she asked shrewdly.

"She thought I might like to visit Blanclair."

"And would you?"

For the first time, Lucette considered what she would feel if this were simply a personal visit and not a royal assignment. "I think . . ." She hesitated, always careful about letting her composure slip. "Yes, I think I would."

"We could go with you." It was Dominic who offered, his voice low and curiously rough.

"There's no need." Lucette hoped she sounded cool and indifferent, though the thought of attempting to spy while in their company was horrifying. "Dr. Dee will travel with royal guards and I'm hardly a child myself. I shall be quite safe."

"Going to come back with a French husband?" Kit, Pippa's twin, teased.

"Leave her be," Stephen interceded. He was always quick to take Lucette's side, if only to oppose Kit. The brothers, of the same mettle beneath their differences, seemed to relish opposing one another. Kit because he was younger and envied Stephen's title; Stephen because Kit was everything he was not—impulsive, lighthearted, and just a bit dangerous. Not that they wouldn't turn just as fiercely on anyone from the outside who dared insult the other.

"Boys." The single word from their mother was enough to silence them. Minuette looked at her husband and then her daughter. "We needn't decide today," she said finally. "We will consider it."

Lucette bit back the urge to snap that it was *her* decision, not theirs, and was surprised at her resentment. Of course they could stop her, or try to, but then the queen would become involved, and the last thing Lucette wanted was a power struggle between her parents and the queen, with herself in the balance.

But knowing that her parents might try to stop her from going to France finally convinced her that it was what she truly wanted. If she didn't, would she feel so desolate at the thought of it not coming off?

Mary Stuart had been a queen since she was six days old, and just because she had spent the last twelve years in a curious state of half imprisonment didn't mean she was any less certain of who she was and what was owed her. She behaved with perfect courtesy to her various hosts—currently the Talbots, Earl and Countess of Shrewsbury—appreciative when they were kind but understanding when they were not. They had their own prickly queen to attend to, and everyone knew that Elizabeth Tudor was a difficult woman to please. Mary was quite happy to show herself above the pettiness of personal dislike.

But there were some issues on which Mary Stuart would not bend. Chief among them was her desire to leave England. She had fled Scotland expecting Elizabeth to aid her—as a fellow queen, if not as a cousin—but politics and Elizabeth's stubbornness meant that in twelve years the two women had never been within a hundred miles of each other. But if Elizabeth was not eager to help Mary regain Scotland's throne, there were Catholics aplenty in Europe who would do nearly anything to aid her.

Mary knew how to wait. How to work behind the scenes. And most importantly, how to turn men to her cause.

So she received her newest guard, seconded to her household at Tutbury from Elizabeth's court, with interest. Stephen Courtenay was young, only twenty, but he bowed to her with impeccable courtesy and he met her curious regard with equanimity.

"The Earl of Somerset," Mary said thoughtfully. "Is it not? I have met your father, the Duke of Exeter, years ago in France."

"Yes, Your Majesty. He told me of your grace and beauty."

Did he indeed? Mary wondered. It had been nearly twenty-five years ago, before her marriage to the French dauphin, and she remembered Dominic Courtenay as a serious man who'd had more to think of than the beauty of a young girl. But he'd managed to survive the murderous fury of England's late king, so no doubt he'd learned how to tell useful lies in the interim.

His eldest son had his father's height and broad shoulders and dark colouring, but there was something about the set of his eyes and mouth that spoke to Mary of the lighthearted, joyous girl who had also been in France years ago. "And your mother?" she asked abruptly. "I recall a lady of grace and beauty herself."

"My mother is well, Your Majesty."

"Your family has no concerns about your service here, Lord Somerset?"

"Why would they?"

"I am aware of how close your family is to my dear cousin, Elizabeth."

"And so they rejoice in any service the queen requests."

Mary smiled, thinking that twenty years ago she might have been very taken by this young man. Or possibly not. He had none of Darnley's easy charm, after all, or Bothwell's arrogance. But Mary had lived long enough to learn to respect other qualities in men: steadiness and loyalty were of greater use to her now than flattery.

But fascination still had its uses.

"May I call you Stephen?" she asked with a smile. When the boy nodded, Mary said confidingly, "I take it as a mark of great honour that my cousin Elizabeth has seen fit to send you to me. I know how dearly she holds your family. I hope you will not find your service here . . . unpleasant."

As she was clearly prompting him to do, Stephen Courtenay kissed her hand. His smile was, like everything else about him, reserved. "What greater pleasure can I have than to serve two queens?"

Perhaps not such a boy. For there was a wry intelligence in his eyes that hinted at his understanding of her games.

A worthy companion, then. And one worth cultivating. Certainly those as close to Queen Elizabeth as the Courtenay family were worth cultivating, but Mary thought that Stephen might be almost an enjoyment for her skills. If she could bend him to her uses . . . well, that would be a success worthy of her talents.

Somehow they managed to reach the last week of March without the subject of France arising again at the Courtenay household. After calculating the chances of a refusal, Lucette went ahead and wrote to Charlotte to accept her invitation, making plans to meet in Paris in late May. Then Lucette waited for the confrontation.

There was plenty to keep her occupied in the meantime. The Courtenays were among the wealthiest families in England, thanks to the gifts of two monarchs, and with that wealth came responsibility. Perhaps there were some nobles who did not care overmuch for their estates, save for what riches they could provide, but the Duke of Exeter was not among them.

The family seat was Tiverton Castle in Devon, near the River Exe, with some of the buildings on the estate stretching back four hundred years. Parts of it were grim, indeed, dark stone and brick anchored to the earth against whatever weather the West Country could throw at it. Though it was a Courtenay inheritance, Dominic had not grown up there. His father had been a younger son, who had died in the Tower under suspicion of aiding in the treason against Henry VIII that cost his brother his head. But the last king had overlooked the elder brother's son and restored the estates to Dominic, also increasing the title from Marquess to Duke.

Lucette knew enough of the past to know her father would have been happier without Tiverton and all it came with. But whatever task was set him, he would fulfill to the limits of his ability, and so Tiverton was meticulously run, its tenants prosperous, its soldiers well-trained, and its sometimes unhappy history relieved by the presence of a happy family.

They spent, on average, seven months of the year at Tiverton—from harvest to planting—with the summers passed at Minuette's family home of Wynfield Mote near Stratford-upon-Avon. Lucette preferred Wynfield, with its small manor house and only a dozen tenant farmers to worry about, but Tiverton had its charms. She liked the towers and the bleak half-ruined walls and the corners around which one felt a ghost might be lurking at any moment, and also liked having responsibilities of her own.

When Lucette and her siblings turned fourteen, their parents had gifted each in turn a small manor and farm of their own from the larger estate. They were expected to be good stewards, to know the details of their servants and crops and livestock, to turn a profit to be returned to the upkeep of the manor and farm. To run a manor as though it were a kingdom of its own.

That last might be stretching things, but Minuette had trained her daughters how to run a household and estate of hundreds, and it was no small task. Part of each day, Lucette was expected to help with the necessary mending and sewing for the family and to take turns with Pippa visiting those in need. The rest of the time was hers, for study or sport. The first was generally mathematics or languages—occupied in large part with correspondence between herself and Dr. Dee—and the second was most often hawking or long rides with Pippa.

The girls were always accompanied on their rides by at least two grooms and often by one of their brothers. With Stephen already gone north, Kit offered to ride with them on a chilly Thursday the beginning of April, but Pippa turned her twin away before Lucette could as much as open her mouth.

"Just the grooms, Kit," his twin said. "I know you were set on going into Exeter today."

"Take Matthew along, at least. He won't mind."

No, Lucette thought, Matthew won't mind in the least. The only child of Dominic Courtenay's right-hand man and her mother's closest attendant, Matthew Harrington had been devoted to Pippa since childhood. He was the only person, apart from Kit, who seemed to understand every twist of her sister's mysterious mind.

But Pippa dismissed the idea at once. "Matthew needs to study. Lord Burghley has agreed to take him on in the treasury. He's to go to London next month, I won't have him disturbed."

Perhaps Pippa's insistence on riding without familiar company should have alerted Lucette that she meant to pry. But her little sister always managed to take her by surprise.

"So why are you really going to France, Lucie?" Pippa asked as they walked their matching dappled horses in tandem.

"Why don't you tell me?" She meant to be lighthearted, but thought she sounded suspicious instead.

Pippa's face lit up with the sudden, dazzling smile of their mother. Lucette had always envied her that resemblance, though her eyes were the jewel-green of Dominic's. "What if I said you ended with a French husband after all? Would you stay home?"

"Depends on the husband."

"Poor Julien LeClerc. Why did you so take against him all those years ago?"

How did Pippa know that? They'd all been children then—all right, Julien had been sixteen, but she had been ten years old during that visit and Pippa no more than six.

But then, Pippa always knew far more than anyone should. Except, perhaps, for Dr. Dee.

Why don't you teach my sister? Lucette had asked him once.

She doesn't need me, he'd answered.

Lucette narrowed her eyes now and said crossly, "I promise you that my very last purpose in going to France is to secure a husband."

"I know," Pippa said serenely. "But you are so much fun to tease."

"Are they going to oppose me?" she asked. No need to specify her mother and Dominic.

"Do they ever oppose you?"

No, Lucette thought, not since I was fifteen. Because they were afraid that, pushed to a choice, Lucette would choose court and Elizabeth.

"What will you do this summer?" Lucette asked abruptly. "Other than Anabel's visit to Wynfield Mote."

"I'm not entirely sure Anabel will be allowed at Wynfield Mote this summer. I suppose it depends on how events proceed with King Philip's visit."

"So you will not see her?"

"No, I will. Kit and I will ride on to Pontefract to join her when you leave for court."

They rode a little way in silence, then Pippa said suddenly, "Father fears that if you go to France, you will not come back. He thinks you will choose a French husband simply to avoid having to return home."

"Told you that, did he?" Lucette asked it drily, but could not help the twitch of her eye.

Instead of answering the (admittedly rhetorical) question, Pippa asked instead, "Are you ever going to call him Father again?"

Keeping her face averted and her voice steady, Lucette retorted, "What makes you think he wants me to?"

"Talk to him, Lucie. It's been years since the queen's mischief. Time is only hardening your pride and his fear."

The queen's mischief—a neat if understated phrase for what Elizabeth had wrought on Lucette's fifteenth birthday. When the queen had presented her with an elegant necklace of enameled Tudor roses "because your father would have wished it" and then told Lucette to ask her parents why.

But that had not been the final breach between Lucette and Dominic. No, that she had wrought wholly herself, with only her folly and pride to blame. And that she had never told Pippa.

Not that one had to tell Pippa.

"I have no doubt at all that he will insist on accompanying me to court and Dover when I sail," Lucette said finally. "Perhaps we will talk then."

And perhaps horses would fly her across the Channel to France.

13 April 1580
Pontefract Castle

Dearest Father,

Thank you for the silks. The colours are lovely and will make gowns such as are rarely seen in England. Which was surely your intention.

I look forward to your visit, scarcely able to believe that it has been five years since the last time we saw each other. You will find your cielita much grown since then, but hopefully just as pleasing to you.

The queen has not seen fit to keep me permanently at court yet, but I trust your visit will effect more than one change in my daily habits. I am not certain I am prepared for any but minor changes, however. Eighteen is rather young when one has spent those years in such confined circumstances.

Your loving daughter,
HRH Anne Isabella

Anne, Princess of Wales, was not one to throw tantrums for no reason. Temper was a weapon, and she never wasted her weapons. It had been six weeks now since her household took up residence at Pontefract, and Anabel had channeled her irritation into impeccable studies and furious management of her finances. And all the while she plotted how to get around her mother's plans and weighed how useful her father might be in that endeavour.

The trick being to ensure that Anabel didn't simply trade the Queen of England's suffocating control for that of the King of Spain.

As April drew softly toward May, Lord Burghley paid Anabel a visit. She received the Lord High Treasurer with genuine warmth, but also a hint of calculation as they settled into conversation. She wagered Burghley would only be astonished if she didn't bother to calculate. How else would he be certain she was Elizabeth's daughter?

"You have made the castle most cheerful, Your Highness." Burghley nodded at the tapestries and newly painted paneling in her privy chamber. "I am glad of it."

"You have been here before?" She was surprised, for Pontefract was well off the royal circuit. But then she remembered, and nodded. "Ah, you would naturally have come during the king's last illness."

It was here that King Henry IX—called William by his sister and friends—had died just before his twenty-second birthday. Burghley had been her uncle's Lord Chancellor. Of course he would have come to the king's bedside.

"It is time this castle had some happy memories and bright faces associated with it. How are you finding your days here?"

Long, she wanted to say, *and boring.* But she knew better than to complain. "It is well suited to gathering all my wits and nerves for my father's coming visit. I assume that is why the queen has sent you?"

"The queen is ever mindful of your comfort and care. She wished a firsthand report of how you are faring."

Then why didn't she come herself? Anabel thought. But would never say. "I would fare better if I were certain of the points of discussion between my parents this summer. I assume my future husband will be second in discussion only to the dissolving of their own marriage."

Burghley shook his head, but with a wry look of affection. "Certain it is that you are not afraid to speak your mind, Your Highness."

"Not to you." Anabel smiled with all the charm she had learned at Minuette Courtenay's knee.

"Yes, the topic of your marriage will be foremost in the minds of both Their Majesties. Although not likely to be of the same mind, are they?"

"I don't suppose either of them is interested in my thoughts on the matter?"

"Indeed, the queen would very much like it if you would write to His Majesty, King James of Scotland. On your own account, you understand, as simply another young royal on this island of ours. No need for promises yet."

"Not that I am in a position to make promises, am I? That will be a matter for the queen and her council."

Burghley said gravely, "Yes, Your Highness."

Anabel stood abruptly, hardly noticing as Burghley of necessity did likewise. She stalked to the window and forced herself to linger there as though studying the view, rather than display the full range of her discontent by continued movement. "What does one write to a child, do you think? James may be king, but he has had even less autonomy than I, thanks to his inflexible councilors."

"King James is nearly fourteen, Your Highness, and the protectorship ended this winter. Not so much a child."

Anabel counted to twenty, as Pippa had taught her to do when she longed to lose her temper. Then, with a forced smile of acquiescence, she faced Burghley. "Of course I shall be glad to write to my cousin James. If nothing else, we can commiserate on being surrounded by those determined to live our lives for us."

Burghley might be fond of her, but he was a committed queen's man. And he was far too old—almost sixty—to appreciate how difficult it was to be young and vibrant and yet have every moment of every day decided by someone else. He looked rather like a stern grandfather when he said, "Princess Anne, every man—and woman—is born where God wishes them to be. We have no say in that matter, only in how we adorn the position to which we are called. Do not be so quick to dismiss the responsibilities of your life, for they march in hand with your privileges."

No one other than Burghley could make her feel ashamed . . . except perhaps the Duke of Exeter. Anabel sighed, then said sincerely, "I thank you for your kind counsel."

But don't think I don't resent it at the same time, she thought. For what royal appreciated being told she was wrong?

THREE

J ulien LeClerc threw open the door to his Paris chambers well after midnight, smelling of alcohol and unsavory neighborhoods, and swore once at the sight of the lit candle and the figure sitting calmly in the chamber's only chair.

"Did I startle you?" Nicolas, in the best tradition of older brothers everywhere, managed to look both amused and disapproving.

"Not remotely." And it was mostly true, for Julien had been expecting something of the sort since Charlotte's last letter. He'd known someone would come to try and guilt him personally. He'd even more or less resigned himself to it being Nicolas, for his brother could effortlessly manipulate his guilt to get whatever he wanted.

He had not expected Nicolas to get to his feet and put his hands on Julien's shoulders, studying his unshaven face intently.

"What are you doing?" Julien wrenched away.

"Assessing how drunk you are. I don't want to have this conversation twice."

"How about we don't have this conversation even once?"

With that pitying smile, Nicolas said, "You don't know what I'm going to say."

"Don't I?" Julien retorted. Then, altering his voice to sound more like his brother's, he parodied savagely, "'Please come home, Julien, Charlotte's begging your presence and it's been two years now, long enough for Father to pretend to have forgiven you for not being there when Mother died and how am I to be the saint when I haven't a sinner in residence to play off against?'"

In the stark silence that followed, Nicolas didn't falter. He only said, after a moment too long, "If you're aiming to sound like me, you'll have to pitch your voice somewhat higher."

And just like that, Julien was humbled. "I'm sorry, Nic. I am. It appears I am just drunk enough to be offensive but not drunk enough to be incoherent."

"Well, since you've covered my essential arguments for coming home, there is only one point I can add."

"And that is?"

"We miss you."

Julien heaved a sigh and threw himself onto the bed. Nicolas returned to the chair and they stared at one another for a long minute until Julien had to laugh. "You always were more patient than me."

"Which is why I always get my way. Well, nearly always."

"I suppose if I don't agree, then my next visitor will be Charlotte?"

Nicolas looked around the chamber, at the unmade bed and clothing dropped in heaps and several unwashed piles of crockery. "If Charlotte sees the way you're living, she'll hector you into far more than just one visit home. So if you don't want to be harassed every day for the next year about living somewhere more decent, then come to Blanclair this summer and make everyone happy."

"Everyone?"

"Felix cannot wait to see his uncle again. He has not let go of the short sword you sent him for Christmas. He thinks you are something of a cross between a Crusader and an avenging angel."

"Pity to disappoint him with my presence, then," Julien said, but it was halfhearted. He did want to see his nephew, who was almost eight years old now. "And Father?" he asked, because Nicolas was waiting for him to ask.

"He's lonely. Of course he wants to see you."

Julien scrubbed his hands across his face, feeling the grime that he never seemed able to sluice off entirely in Paris. He thought of Blanclair and its fields and woods and the chateau itself, imbued with childhood and warmth. He rarely let himself think of home because it hurt too much. But maybe Nicolas was right. Maybe it was time.

He ran his hands through his hair and narrowed his eyes at his brother. "What about Charlotte's plan to marry one of us off to the Courtenay girl?" Charlotte thought she was so subtle, but no one knew her better than her brothers. They could sniff out her matchmaking plots in a second.

"Hardly a girl any longer," Nicolas pointed out mildly. "Lucette is twenty-two."

"You know what I mean. You'll not marry again and I'm hardly suitable marriage material. I hope Charlotte hasn't got the girl all in a romantic twitter about one or both of us. Well, you, really. You haven't forgotten how she trailed you around all the weeks we spent in England?"

"Nor have I forgotten how much she disliked you. If Lucette has half as much spirit now as she did when she was ten years old, I think this could be quite an exciting summer."

"Just so she knows from the first that she won't be leaving France with a husband. At least not one from Blanclair."

"No," Nicolas agreed, and there was a note of wistful longing that made Julien want to swear. Or hit someone. "Try to be polite, Julien. Father is quite fond of her, what with her having been born at Blanclair."

Julien's head ached, and it wasn't from the alcohol. "I've said that I'll come, Nic. I'll play the penitent nicely for Charlotte's sake, and for Felix. I will endeavour to be the soul of civility to Lucette Courtenay. Just don't ask me to be other than I am."

"A dissolute drunkard possessed of a wicked reputation with women?" Nicolas stood and reached for his cloak. "That's just a part you play, Julien. I know who you really are."

Julien shut his eyes and heard Nicolas walk out and close the door. His brother had no idea who he really was—and all the better for him.

Nicolas LeClerc hadn't been to Paris for years, and he found to his surprise that he rather enjoyed the city. He'd stayed away so long under the assumption that there would be too many painful memories of his youth. For all Julien's behavior now, it had been Nicolas who had been on the path to being—if not a dissolute drunkard—at least well and truly wicked with women.

Everyone had always assumed Julien was the libertine, because he was younger and lighthearted, with a ready tongue and open heart that won him friends everywhere. But when it came down to it, Julien was a romantic. He believed in things like true love and honour— sometimes Nicolas thought his brother should have been born three hundred years earlier. He was not hardheaded enough for the modern world.

Nicolas, however, knew how to appreciate what was in the world around him, not colour it with what he'd like it to be. And in the real world, he was wealthy, he was handsome, and he'd had girls flocking to his bed from the time he was fourteen. Take, for instance, their visit to England a dozen years ago. He had found plenty of pretty girls willing to welcome the two exotic Frenchmen, but Julien had spent the entire time mooning over the Duchess of Exeter. Not that Nicolas could fault his brother's taste, for she was a truly beautiful woman. But Julien had as much chance of a kiss from Minuette Courtenay as he had of becoming pope—and why waste time dreaming over a woman with a husband as forbidding as Minuette's when there were plenty of girls willing to help you forget?

Nicolas returned to the LeClerc town house on the banks of the Seine in a much more salubrious neighborhood than Julien's. Another example of his brother's mystifying rectitude—he preferred to provide for himself in the gutter rather than make use of their own home. All because he felt guilty: for what he'd done to Nicolas, for the lies he'd told his family these last eight years, for not being at Blanclair when their mother died.

He'd shown up in time for Nicole LeClerc's funeral mass, making no excuses. Nicolas knew where he'd been and what he'd been doing, but he had let Julien hug his guilt to himself. Nicolas had a better use for that information than confronting his brother.

As he had very good use for Lucette Courtenay's impending visit.

Before going to bed he wrote two letters at the mother-of-pearl inlaid desk that had belonged to his mother. The first was to Charlotte, assuring his sister that Julien would come home this summer.

The second was addressed to a man whose name was most certainly not the one by which Nicolas called him. *She is coming*, was all it said.

He smiled to himself. Lucette Courtenay had no idea what she was walking into.

The English court took up residence at Greenwich in mid-May, and it was there that Elizabeth received her onetime closest friends, Dominic and Minuette Courtenay. The Duke and Duchess of Exeter, despite their exalted titles and position, spent very little time at court, and Elizabeth had not tried too hard to change that over the years. It wasn't always comfortable to be around those one had known quite so well in the days before one became queen.

She knew they would come this spring, however, for they had agreed to their daughter's visit to France, and Lucette would depart from Greenwich with Dr. Dee, bound for Dover. Elizabeth braced herself for Minuette's suspicious eyes and wary questions about her daughter's trip, but in the event it was Dominic who asked to speak with the queen. Alone.

When he bowed to her in her privy chamber, Elizabeth felt a moment's déjà vu rush upon her and remembered how William had always been caught between admiration and resentment of his friend. She quite understood her brother's feelings now, for Dominic had a way of looking at you as though he knew every flaw in your character.

But he was, at heart, a gentleman and a loyal subject. "Your Majesty," he said, "you are looking very well."

"Let us hope my husband thinks the same later this summer. I mean to at least make Philip regret the necessity of divorcing me."

"You will not protest?"

"I protest only when there is a reasonable chance of success. I'm afraid Philip and I have reached the end of our mutual usefulness to each other."

"I am sorry for it," Dominic said, and sounded genuinely as though he was sorry for Elizabeth herself, and not just because the ruler of England was losing the partnership of the ruler of Spain.

Disconcerted, Elizabeth said sharply, "Why are you here, Dominic? You never trouble yourself to come to my court unless it is to scold me about something."

"I'm afraid that's the only role I'm familiar with as far as royalty is concerned." There was a shadow to his voice, and Elizabeth knew he was also seeing her brother, William, before him, young and eager and needing Dominic's restraining hand.

Elizabeth refused to follow that painful path. "If you're here to complain about Dr. Dee taking Lucette to France, I'm afraid you've left it rather late. They leave for Dover tomorrow."

"I know. I will ride with them."

Of course you will, she thought. "But you will not cross the sea with Lucette?" That would rather complicate matters, for Dominic's sharp eyes and suspicious mind would be hard for Lucette to blind.

"She does not want me." He said it plainly, almost disinterestedly.

"No, I only wanted your personal assurance that Lucette will be well guarded to and from Renaud LeClerc's hands. There is mischief abroad in Europe these days and some men have long memories. I would not have her hurt merely because she bears my name and the queen's friendship."

Not once in seven years had Dominic spoken to Elizabeth of the revelation she had forced upon his family, never openly acknowledged the eruption that must have followed in his own heart. But confronted with his stern, familiar face, Elizabeth felt something she so rarely did that it took her a moment to identify the emotion: guilt.

Just as Dominic had chosen his vocabulary with care in referring to Lucette, Elizabeth did the same in making her promises. "I swear to you that Lucette's welfare is ever close to my heart. She will be well watched, I promise."

Dominic's voice dropped, to a tone no one ever used with Elizabeth. "If she is hurt in any way, Your Majesty, I shall know where to look."

Only because of their long association—and her own half-told truths—did Elizabeth refrain from sharp correction. But she would not let the implication pass. "Do you think I am unaware of my responsibilities, Lord Exeter? I am well acquainted with the threats offered vulnerable women. But as I have so often entrusted my own daughter to your care, surely you need not fear to do the same. Princess Anne, after all, must surely attract greater threats than Lucette."

"And I would like it to remain that way, Your Majesty. Lucette is her own person, not a pawn in your political games."

Elizabeth smiled with cold fury. "Lucette is most decidedly her own person. Do you honestly believe anyone could persuade that girl to be a pawn of any sort? She knows very well what she is about."

"Or gives that impression. Elizabeth," and it was as though all the intervening years since they were young together dropped away. "I love her dearly. Promise me she will come home safely from France."

She looked at his straight body, the firm, well-balanced figure only slightly marred by the missing left hand, and knew that the last thing she needed in this delicate summer was Dominic Courtenay in a vengeful mood. "I promise, Dominic."

16 May 1580
Greenwich

Dominic spoke with Elizabeth alone last night. He didn't tell me what he said, but I can guess. He is not at all happy about Lucette going to France without him. But he will not protest, for fear of driving her further away.

Sometimes I confess a longing to shake both my husband and my daughter until they come to their senses! But, as I manifestly mishandled telling Lucette the truth, I am not at all confident that I know how to heal this. It was easier when I was the one who was twenty-two—now that I have children old enough to manage their own lives, I find myself praying at odd moments of night and day that they will come through without too many scars.

And yet . . . would I relinquish the scars of my own youth? Good and ill are too tightly wound, we cannot have one without the other. And after all—if Lucette is William's daughter, a truth that only God can ever know for certain—would I wish her never born? No more than Dominic would.

Daughter by blood or not, Lucette has all of Dominic's pride. It is distinct from royal pride, which assumes it is always right. Their pride is a bastion for their fear that if they are not perfect, no one will love them.

I believe I have gentled that fear in my husband over the years. I hope Lucette will find someone to do the same for her.

It had been years since Lucette had spent so much time alone with Dominic. Before her fifteenth birthday, she had loved traveling with him—Dominic would take her to Tiverton ahead of the rest of the family, or let him join him in touring some of his outlying lands in the West. She had always counted herself her father's favorite.

This trip to Dover was an uncomfortable mix of nostalgia and awareness that things were not—and could never again be—the same between them. The easy adoration of a firstborn daughter for her all-powerful, all-wise father had been the dearest casualty of the queen's interference. Sometimes Lucette hated Elizabeth for it, until she remembered that it was not Elizabeth who had created this mess. She had been living in a world of illusion. It was not the queen's fault that disillusion hurt so very much.

For all that, Dominic Courtenay was a fairly simple man to get along with. Lucettte had once overheard her mother complain to him that it was impossible to have a satisfying argument with a man who would not fight back. As she recalled, Dominic had stopped her mother's complaints with a kiss.

For all her promises to Pippa that she would speak to Dominic before leaving England, Lucette found herself nearly as silent as he was on the journey. They were in the company of Dr. Dee and royal guards, it was true, but she did not even attempt to make an effort. Mostly because she did not know, even after all these years, what to say.

I'm sorry I have blue eyes. I'm sorry the king loved your wife. I'm sorry to be a constant reminder of things best forgotten. I'm sorry I gave you all my love when it must have been a daily insult to your feelings to have your wife's bastard calling you Father . . .

Really, far better to keep to neutral matters such as the state of the roads and the likelihood of a smooth Channel crossing.

Which was all well and good, until their final night at Dover Castle. Dominic requested to dine alone with her, and for once he carried the conversation.

"Dr. Dee tells me how much this journey will benefit your studies. He seems to think your primary interest in traveling to France is scholarship rather than courtship."

"Isn't scholarship always my primary interest?"

"Is it?" Dominic asked mildly. "Just as well. Perhaps you'll have less need for a dagger among scholars."

Lucette grinned despite herself. "You've never been in the midst of a scholarly debate, have you? I might very well wish for a dagger."

"Good thing I brought one for you, then." Dominic handed her a silver-chased casket, more than a foot long and half as wide.

Lucette opened it. The dagger Dominic had given her for her fifteenth birthday lay within it, an eight-inch blade inside its beautiful sheath. She could feel the weight of it in her hand, remembered the hours spent learning to use it with Dominic's patient teaching.

"No easily hidden blades for France?" she asked. "The entire household will know what is in this casket before I've been in Blanclair a day."

"Good. I want them knowing you are well armed. Besides, Carrie told me she had already packed a bodice dagger at your request."

Lucette braced herself for questions, but Dominic clearly found nothing unusual in a young woman arming herself before traveling. After all, it was he who had taught her caution.

She swallowed against memories and noted that the dagger was not the sole item in the casket.

"A letter for Renaud LeClerc?" Lucette asked. "Aren't you afraid I might read it before handing it on?"

"You have only to ask if you're interested in its contents."

She hated it when he was reasonable. And Dominic Courtenay was always reasonable. "Unless you're offering to sell me to one of Renaud's sons at a reduced rate, I can't imagine what interest I might have."

"I hope you'll mind your tongue better among those who have no reason to indulge you." Dominic never had to raise his voice to make it bite.

She felt herself flush. "I apologize. Of course whatever you have written to the vicomte is your business. I shall gladly deliver it into his hands, and hope that neither dagger will have need to be used during my sojourn."

With a thrill of nerves, she pondered that weapons might be a much more practical accessory than Dominic had any cause to guess.

This was no intellectual exercise she was walking into. Kingdoms were at stake. Lucette rested her fingertips on the sheathed dagger and wondered. Would her nerve hold if it came to its use? She had never stuck a blade in anything more dangerous than a dead deer.

With a decisive snap, she closed the lid and re-placed the casket on the sideboard. When she moved away, Dominic stopped her with a hand on her shoulder. "Be careful, child. You tend to think that you are indestructible—rather like your mother. But there are men in this world who will not share that view. You have lived protected in England, what with the queen's affections turned your way. Some of that will carry with you, but perhaps not enough. It is time for you to be wise, Lucie, and not simply to trust that others will see you as you see yourself."

And how do I see myself? she nearly asked. For that was the heart of her conundrum, was it not? That she had no fixed point of identity. When one could not be absolutely certain of one's father, how was one supposed to know where she fit in the world?

26 May 1580
Pontefract Castle

To Her Most Gracious Majesty Queen Elizabeth,

> *As befits the first and most humble of your subjects, Your Grace, I send my love and thanks for your gracious care. The days at Pontefract pass with little wit and pleasure, being so far from your glorious court, but I trust my studies are pleasing to Your Grace.*
>
> *As requested, I have enclosed the draft of a letter to His Majesty James VI of Scotland. I trust that it will meet with your approval and that of your government. If there is aught else I can do for Your Grace, no doubt you will inform me in due course.*

Your most loving daughter,
Anne Isabella

Torn between irritation and amusement, Elizabeth tossed Anne's letter on the small table set to the side of her throne and raised an eyebrow at Burghley. "Well," she said drily, "one cannot say the Princess of Wales lacks for spirit."

"One would expect no less from your daughter." Burghley indicated the enclosure, the draft letter to James of Scotland. "And one cannot fault the correctness of her missive to the Scots king."

"No, it is the very model of reserve and maidenly submission. What a shock for James should he indeed make her his wife and discover only afterward my daughter's true character."

"Has King Philip protested your plans toward James of Scotland?"

"Philip has done nothing but protest every plan I have ever made for Anne. I have no doubt I shall hear little but criticism while the Spanish are here this summer. So long as he confines himself to words," she said, with a significant glance at Burghley.

He grunted acknowledgment. "The household guards at Pontefract are on alert, and Walsingham has eyes inside the household. The greatest threat to the princess at present is boredom."

"There will be little time for her to be bored once Philip is here and she returns to court."

"Your Majesty, do you intend to keep her at court after the king's visit? She is of an age to be of some use to you, besides her natural gifts of adornment."

Elizabeth drummed her fingers on the arm of her gilded throne, an outlet for her instinctive displeasure. This was not the first time Burghley had broached the subject. And considered dispassionately, the Lord Treasurer was quite right. At eighteen, she herself had been an active member of her brother's court. But then, her brother had been three years younger, and neither of them had been doing much actual ruling at that age.

Anne, however, was Elizabeth's heir and, in due course of time—a very long course of time, Elizabeth trusted—would herself rule England. The weight of Burghley's arguments rested on the fact that

Anne should be as prepared as possible and not always kept at one remove from the center of government and power.

So why have I resisted so long? Elizabeth asked herself.

She was honest enough to recognize that jealousy played a role—no woman wished to be upstaged by a younger woman—but not so honest as to dwell on that unpleasant fact. So she fixed Burghley with a gimlet eye and said, "The Princess of Wales will serve as she is required. Which for now is to correspond with James of Scotland in order to make her father nervous. It is also for her to be kept safe, for England's security rests wholly on my own life and that of my heir. As you and Walsingham are so quick to remind me."

One reason Burghley had endured so long in royal service was his inability to be offended by his monarch. But almost as important was his ability to remain unruffled in the face of said monarch's displeasure. "The surest way to increase England's security is for your daughter to provide another heir to the Tudor line. And that she cannot do while she remains isolated from your own court. Correspondence alone will not achieve a marriage."

"But it is a necessary first step," Elizabeth countered. "Leave off fretting, Burghley. Anne is quite able to plead her own case, and yes, I do acknowledge the need for her to be more visible. When Philip arrives, Anne will be very visible and very necessary, if only to keep her father and me from each other's throats. I know how to position my daughter for maximum effect."

"So you do have a specific agenda for the Princess of Wales?"

Elizabeth smiled, part amusement and part resignation. "It is not my agenda for Anne you need worry about. My daughter is quite capable of setting her own agenda and doing whatever she thinks necessary to achieve it."

And that, Elizabeth told herself, *is the true reason I keep my daughter on such a tight leash. In order to reduce any damage she might wreak.*

FOUR

Julien cursed himself soundly every day of the spring weeks that led to going home. He also cursed others: Nicolas for preying on his guilt, Charlotte for her irrepressible desire to make him better than he was, and even Lucette Courtenay (who, despite the undeniable passage of years, he still imagined as a bothersome child with sharp eyes and a suspicious nature). He coped by throwing himself into work, which outwardly involved lots of drinking and lots of women.

When he wasn't drinking and womanizing, his work mostly involved hours spent alone ciphering letters and deciphering orders. Intelligence work sounded glamorous, Julien often thought, but was really just a long series of days spent sifting through gossip for fact and passing those facts along without anyone being the wiser. At least the drinking and women killed time.

Nicolas, who so rarely left their chateau near St. Benoir sur Loire, returned to Paris the last week of May in the company of their father. From the family's town home in Paris—rarely used since Nicole LeClerc's death—Renaud sent a brief note to his second son upon their arrival, reminding him that he was expected at a welcome reception being given for Dr. Dee by an English scholar, after which Lucette Courtenay would be formally handed into the LeClercs' hands for the duration of her time in France. Julien swore vividly when he realized he'd be traveling to Blanclair in the company of both his father and brother, though he should have guessed as much. Renaud LeClerc would never leave the girl's safety in any but his own capable hands.

So it was, on this dazzling spring evening, Julien found himself being escorted across a checkerboard marble floor as though he were a guest in his father's home. Fortunately for all the LeClerc men, who might have found this meeting awkward, Charlotte was there before Julien.

Engulfed in a wealth of scarlet satin, Charlotte was the image of their mother: a little short, a trifle plump, with a smile that could summon the birds from the trees. She turned all the power of that smile on Julien, and he felt a moment's pure satisfaction in having pleased his sister.

"Julien!" She flung her arms around him, heedless of her finery, and he wondered with a jolt how long it had been since anyone had touched him in simple affection without wanting anything from him. Long enough that he couldn't remember, at any rate.

Charlotte's overflow of good spirits made it easier for Julien to turn from her welcome to his father. "Sir," he said, and forced himself to stand straight and unflinching while Renaud sized him up. That was something else he could hardly remember—feeling at ease in his father's presence. It hadn't always been that way. The last eight years had left Julien isolated behind his walls, unwilling to let anyone see to the heart of him.

It had been more than a year since he'd seen his father, and he was relieved to note that Renaud looked better now than he had then. The death of his wife two years ago had hit Renaud hard, and Julien had wondered if he might never recover. But his father looked much surer of himself than the last time they'd been together, as though he'd found his feet again and if still mourning was no longer unbalanced by it.

And he had certainly not lost his ability to read his younger son. "You look like a man in need of a drink," Renaud observed, "but who knows better than to dull his wits tonight."

"Parisian society is best enjoyed with dulled wits."

It nearly broke his heart when his father smiled at him. "Then I must conclude that your purpose tonight is not enjoyment."

"Of course Julien will enjoy himself," Charlotte interposed sharply. "We will all enjoy ourselves. Nicolas is determined to, aren't you?"

Nicolas kissed his little sister on the cheek. "For you, *ma chère,* anything. Speaking of enjoyment, why is your husband not with you?"

"Andry will meet us at the reception. He did not want to spoil our family reunion."

"He did not want to risk being forced to express an emotion, you mean." Julien said it out of habit, for he quite liked Charlotte's mild-mannered husband. Andry was ten years older than his second wife, but he adored everything about her and his stability was a good counterpoint to Charlotte's more intense temperament.

Charlotte pulled a face as though she was still ten years old rather than the twenty-five-year-old mother of two young girls. "Just you wait, Julien. I will shake that smug superiority of yours before this summer is out, see if I don't."

I hope not, Julien thought. Because the smug superiority, as she called it, was the defensive wall between his family and the dangers of his professional life. He would not expose them to that for anything in the world.

But he only grinned and said, "Lead on, sister. I promise to flirt with so many women tonight that even you will be pleased."

"I don't believe flirting has ever been your problem, Julien. It's what comes after."

"Dearest sister, whatever do you mean?"

But she was too French to be flustered. "You know exactly what I mean. It's time to grow up, Julien. Find a wife and settle down."

Nicolas, perhaps uncomfortable with the topic of wives, intervened. "If we don't make it to the party, Julien won't even have the opportunity to flirt, let alone marry. Leave him be, Charlotte. I'll see to it that he is the perfectly available gentleman tonight."

The party was being hosted by Edmund Pearce, an expatriate Protestant Englishman with a French Catholic wife. Pearce was a well-known logician and collector of scientific texts who had managed to straddle the uneasy religious divide in both his marriage and his professional life, and Julien knew there would be any number of guests tonight who could harbor secrets he wanted. But he wasn't here to work, he reminded himself. He was here to make his sister happy.

That didn't stop some members of the party from being particularly glad to see him. But those members were mostly in attendance with their husbands, so some measure of discretion prevailed. Julien exchanged several significant bows and followed in Charlotte's wake. He expected they were heading for Andry, wherever he might be, but he should have guessed Charlotte's priorities. They were headed directly for the English guests.

He recognized John Dee from descriptions and from having met him once years ago in England. The doctor was in black robes, a pointed beard lending his face a particular air of scholarship and mysticism. Julien braced himself, knowing his sister well enough to guess that Dee was not her primary aim. He tried to pick out, from the crowd around Dee, Lucette Courtenay. There were half a dozen women of the right age that Julien could see, but none were familiar to him. Her hair had been dark, he remembered—much darker than her mother's honey gold—but beyond that his memories were hazy.

And then one of the women near Dee turned in his direction. She wore a gown of rosy plum, an unusual shade for springtime, and the starched lace ruff at her neck highlighted her elegant pose. He could see even from here that her eyes were blue. She was not French, for he would have remembered seeing her before. But surely life was not so capricious as to turn his heart with the English girl he'd been scoffing at in his head?

Apparently it was exactly that capricious. "Lucie!" Charlotte's voice pealed above the babble and several heads turned their way as the blue-eyed woman returned Charlotte's smile and Julien felt, with a shock of dismay, his own heart turn over in reply.

He did not have the right to fall in love.

From the moment the French coastline came into sight, Lucette had been in a state of acute aliveness. They landed at Calais, once again precariously held by the English after its brief loss in the 1550s to the French. (King Philip had sent Spanish soldiers to retrieve Calais from the French in 1559 and offered the return of the city to Elizabeth as a wedding gift.) They spent one night at the governor's home, then set out on horseback for Paris.

The French countryside was a revelation of colour and scent, though Lucette could imagine her practical brothers asking her what was so different about French grass and flowers. She argued against that practicality in her head, silently assuring them that the green of the Picardy hills was an entirely different shade from that of War-wickshire, and the poppies that edged the roads and fields were a much deeper red than anything seen in England.

The language that surrounded her was a hundred different tones of melody, and the French cheeses were sharp on her tongue. And the wine? Well, everyone knew French wine was superior and Lu-cette enjoyed tasting the different varieties at each meal.

Logically, she knew it for what it was—the rush of excitement at being more or less on her own, at going somewhere wholly for her-self, at having a task before her that would call on all her skills of mind and wit. But she reveled in the rush nonetheless.

They stopped in Amiens to view the cathedral, Dr. Dee pointing

out the 126 pillars that made the nave the largest interior space in
Europe. Although they mostly spoke in French, their group was unmistakably English and there were many curious glances cast at
her—and perhaps a few hostile ones as well. The closer they got to
Paris, the more she began to grasp the reality of European opposition to her queen and country.

She was not officially presented at the French court, for that
would entail a different sort of visit entirely, but when they reached
Paris she and Dr. Dee were invited to a feast at the Louvre. Though
Henri III was not present, nor his formidable mother, Catherine de
Medici, even the edges of Henri's court were brilliant. She thought
herself immune to the trappings of earthly power, made cynical by
her long exposure to Elizabeth's court. But the elegant details of the
dresses, the bold behavior of the women, not to mention the notice-
able presence of many red-cassocked prelates of the Catholic church,
combined to leave Lucette with a hint of unease beneath her pleasure.

In Paris, they were quartered in the luxurious home of Edmund
and Marguerite Pearce, a couple who managed to combine their disparate religions and cultures into a pleasing combination of art and
scholarship. Edmund Pearce and Dr. Dee were longstanding friends
and correspondents and spent many happy hours the first two days
wrangling over books in Pearce's library. Marguerite took Lucette to
Notre Dame (to visit, not worship—it was not nearly as impressive
as Amiens Cathedral) and shopping, which she did not mind as
much as she expected to. And the third night—Lucette's final night
in Paris—the Pearces threw open their doors for a grand reception
in honour of Dr. Dee and Lady Lucette Courtenay.

As one of Marguerite's maids fussed over Lucette's hair, curling
and pinning it into an elaborate piece of art, Lucette braced herself
for the LeClercs. Not Charlotte, whom she loved dearly even if they
had not seen each other for years, nor even Renaud, who troubled
her only because he was Dominic's friend and thus might not think
too highly of her just now. Rumours were not bound by the seas.

Surely they'd heard something in France of Elizabeth's meddling in
Courtenay family affairs and the ensuing strained relationships.

It was the brothers who unsettled her: Nicolas and Julien. And
not simply because Walsingham suspected that one or both of the
young LeClercs might be working against England. That task was
real enough, but so were the memories of herself as a tongue-tied,
impressionable child who had followed Nicolas around like a puppy
and had loathed Julien for pointing it out. She knew they must be
very different after twelve years, but inside she half expected to see
the two tall young men who had overawed her at Wynfield Mote.

By the time Lucette descended, there were already several dozen
members of the Paris intelligentsia who were the natural crowd for
John Dee. But there were nobles as well, the men sharp and watchful
beneath their finery, and the women glittering with a sense of their
own worth. That was not so different from England. Two or three
churchmen moved through the chambers as well, one of them a cardinal in scarlet.

When she heard her name called, she knew Charlotte instantly,
even without the pleasure writ large on her friend's face. It was the
same face of early adolescence, round-cheeked and wide-eyed, and
she gave Lucette an embrace that crushed a great deal of expensive
fabric between them.

But even as she hugged Charlotte, Lucette's mind was turning,
for she had taken in the three LeClerc men and found that she could
name them just as easily as if she'd seen them last week. Renaud, of
course, was silver-haired but otherwise unchanged. Tall, with broad
shoulders and chest, and the bearing of a soldier. Nicolas was nearly
as easy to identify, for he was undeniably his father's son. Though
not, Lucette decided, as imposing. There was something—kinder?
softer?—about him, as though his edges were smoothed away. But he
was still very handsome.

Julien was the shock. He had been taller than his brother even at
sixteen, and now he topped both his father and brother by at least
three inches. He might even be taller than Dominic, she thought

dizzily. His hair was still that wheat-coloured shade, though with streaks of both darker and lighter blond to it. He looked . . . messier than Nicolas, but also more elegant in the way that only Frenchmen can bring off.

His eyes, Lucette noted, when Charlotte stopped hugging her and turned to her brothers, were still unfriendly. And, worst of all, amused. As though he expected her to fawn and blush and fall over her words as she had when she was a child.

He'd be getting no blushes from her.

Renaud, however, was a pure pleasure to greet. His genuine affection nearly brought tears to her eyes. And Nicolas was as gracious as he'd ever been.

"My dear girl," he said in English. "You are every bit as lovely a woman as your childhood promised."

"*Merci*," she said, continuing in rapid French. "And you will do me a favor by letting me speak your language. I need the practice."

"Not at all," he replied, graciously switching. "You have a lovely accent. I do hope you'll do me the honour of dancing with me later. It has been . . . many years since I have so indulged myself."

With that, Lucette remembered his widowhood, how his young wife had died delivering their only son, Felix. How Nicolas had more or less shut himself up at Chateau Blanclair since then. Touched that he had come all the way to Paris to greet her when he could have waited for her to arrive at his home, Lucette smiled. "It has been the purpose of my voyage to dance with you, Nicolas."

She tried to ignore Charlotte's expression—like a cat in the cream—and wondered for the first time what would happen to her investigation if she made the mistake of allowing her childish emotions to get the better of her.

But this was France. Flirting was a game—no more, no less—and she would use it. If she happened to enjoy it, no one need know.

At last she could not avoid greeting Julien without open rudeness. But he had no such scruples. Before she could do more than look his way, he said in rapidly clipped French, "You're not very like your mother, are you?"

In a flood of childhood indignation, Lucette remembered the claim Nicolas had launched at his brother during their trip to Wynfield: *You've been panting after her all summer like a dog in heat.* He had meant Minuette. Whom clearly Julien had found beautiful. And whom he had just casually noted that Lucette was nothing like.

"Enough like her to recognize good manners or the lack thereof," she retorted.

Could it be that she'd stung him? She thought she saw a twitch along his jaw before he said, "That came out rather differently than I intended. I meant only that you are very dark. Your hair, at least. And your eyes—"

"Are blue. I know," she said shortly. Turning to Nicolas, she said, "May I introduce you to Dr. Dee? You'll find him quite an entertaining storyteller while we wait for the dancing to begin."

Charlotte came with them, but Renaud drifted away in conversation with old friends. Julien turned on his heel and melted into the crowd.

And Lucette told herself sternly to remember that liking or disliking had absolutely nothing to do with intelligence work. Just because Julien was as rude as he'd ever been didn't make him an agent against England. It simply meant that her scruples in investigating him were lessened.

Julien walked way from Lucette with his head spinning so much he might as well have been drunk. He could hardly even remember opening his mouth, but somehow he'd managed to insult her very first thing. How had he let his thoughts tumble out of his mouth like that? He never spoke without thinking, for that was likely to get an intelligencer killed.

At least he'd managed not to babble that she was far more beautiful than he remembered even her mother being, that he—who had a specific type of woman, always blonde to some degree and charming and skilled at seduction—had been completely knocked off balance by the contrast of her dark hair and pale skin and sea-blue eyes. *This is ridiculous,* he told himself firmly. *I do not believe in love at first sight.*

He wasn't entirely sure that he believed in love at all. Not any longer.

Best way to get a woman out of one's mind, he knew, was to find another woman. Julien began to scan the crowds to find the best choice for the evening, one whose studied play would demand no more of him than surface expertise. Being Paris, he almost instantly marked three women and decided on the blondest, giggliest, silliest of the lot. He set off toward her and made it five steps before someone laid a restraining hand on his shoulder.

"You're heading for the wrong woman," the familiar voice of Cardinal Ribault said softly. "I thought it was the Englishwoman your sister brought you here to charm."

"Not now," Julien said under his breath. He was in enough turmoil without adding in the quick wits demanded of his work. At least not without warning. What the hell was Cardinal Ribault doing here anyway, at a party designed to welcome an emissary from that most heretic Queen Elizabeth?

Ribault did not leave him long in ignorance. The cleric—short and compact, with flyaway brown hair that curled at the edges of his tonsure—maneuvered Julien into a secluded corner of the chamber and said softly, "Have you really not worked it out? You're slipping, LeClerc. You know about John Dee. He's almost as canny a character as Walsingham, and his scholarly connections are but a thin veil for intelligence activities. He's here to find out what he can about plots against his bastard queen."

"So?" Julien challenged. "What's that to do with me? Unless you want me to abandon my promise to spend the next six weeks at Blanclair and remain here in Paris instead?" He asked it almost with a lift of hope. It would surely infuriate Charlotte, and he could hardly tell his sister the reason why, but then at least he wouldn't have to deal with the profoundly unsettling Lucette.

But Ribault dashed that hope. "You are slipping. It is the girl herself who's the real interest, LeClerc."

He stared dumbly. "Whatever for?"

"Surely you know who she is—or who Elizabeth thinks she is. Those blue eyes?"

Of course there had been rumours, even here. That Lucette's blue eyes were a legacy from her true father, the late king of England. That Elizabeth treated the girl as her niece, whatever the protests of her putative father, the Duke of Exeter. Julien had never thought much about the truth of such rumours, but suddenly he put together their significance. And why the Catholic network was so very interested in her.

"Do you honestly think Walsingham would employ a woman?" Julien asked in disbelief.

"Of course not," came the withering reply. "But that doesn't mean she would not make a very valuable source of information for our cause. Whatever her true relationship to Elizabeth, it is undeniable that the Princess of Wales is extremely close to the Courtenay family and continues to spend her summers at their country home. Whether she will continue that practice this summer is something of a question. A question to which I daresay Lucette Courtenay could provide an answer."

Julien's head spun even more. He was already juggling so many balls, how on earth was he supposed to add this one to the mix? "What do you want?" he asked bluntly.

"What do we ever want? Information."

"And how do you propose I go about it?" He must be rattled, or he would not have posed such a stupid question.

The cardinal, with as much righteous delicacy as possible, said, "I am not aware that you have ever encountered difficulty in gathering information from comely women. Surely you do not need a man of the Church to tell you how."

"Lucette Courtenay is a guest of my family, and I can hardly seduce such a guest in my father's home." Never mind that the thought instantly brought with it irresistible images of seduction, with Lucette in his arms, that dark hair tumbled round her bare shoulders . . .

Heaven above, but he was in trouble.

"I don't care how you do it, LeClerc." Ribault leaned closer, words barely above a whisper that made the threat all the more intense. "This girl is the best chance we have ever had of gaining inside information about the very heart of the heretic's court. Get us what we need to bring us nearer to restoring God's light to the benighted people of England."

The cardinal stalked away in a swirl of crimson robes while Julien cursed inventively and soundlessly. He didn't dare openly disobey. Which meant spending more time with Lucette than was wise for either of them.

If his heart leaped treacherously at the thought, he shoved it firmly away. Lucette was nothing more now than a job. And he was very good at his job.

FIVE

ary Stuart had not been in such a good humour in a very long time. Indeed, she had difficulty remembering when last she'd felt so hopeful. When she'd first married Darnley, she supposed. She had been carried away then both by her passion for the handsome young man and the satisfaction of exercising her royal will, for she had found great pleasure in marrying him despite the vocal protests of her recalcitrant council. Sometimes she wondered if her love had been more about Darnley himself or about getting her own way.

Well, she'd long since learned that lesson. Men were to be used, not trusted. And her satisfactions now depended solely on herself. Much more practical. Not that she minded having handsome men around her. There had been the Duke of Norfolk, of course, though that had ended badly for both of them. (Admittedly, rather the worse for him, since he'd lost his head on her behalf.) Her present guardian, the Earl of Shrewsbury, was attentive enough, certainly polite and careful of her status, and his wife had become a good friend.

Stephen Courtenay, however, the young Earl of Somerset, had made a very welcome addition to Mary's household at Tutbury. Besides being decorative, he was intelligent and astute. A boy of few words, but those few always well-chosen and nicely balanced between loyalty to his own queen and kindness to the imprisoned queen he spent time with.

And such a convenient source of familial information.

"I hear from my friends in Paris that your sister made quite the impression with Dr. Dee," Mary said conversationally one afternoon, as Stephen and she played cards. "It seems everyone in society is highly taken with her beauty and conduct."

"I'm glad to hear it," Stephen said.

"And now she has gone on to . . . Chateau Blanclair, is it?" Mary probed. She knew perfectly well it was; her correspondents were well-informed.

"Yes."

Mary sighed in exasperation. "Really, sir, you could converse with me in more than one syllable words."

"So I could." His quick grin saved the remark from impertinence and moved it into the category—just—of courtly flirting.

Mary laughed. "So what will your parents say if your sister decides to remain in France with a husband? Or more pertinent, perhaps, what would your queen make of the matter?"

Mary naturally knew the gossip, that Elizabeth believed Lucette Courtenay to be her niece. No one spoke of it openly, for the Duke of Exeter was held in high regard and was, besides, a most forbidding man. And the Duchess of Exeter? Well, Mary remembered Minuette Wyatt during her few weeks at the French court. Mary herself had not yet been wed to Francis and had felt a most unusual envy of the older, beautiful, and utterly charming Englishwoman. Had Minuette betrayed her husband with the late king of England? Mary supposed no one living knew that except the woman herself. And what, in the end, did it matter? Elizabeth believed it, and that made it a fact in the murky world of politics and royal intrigue.

And Mary knew very well how to manipulate such facts.

Stephen Courtenay was unusually well-controlled for such a young man; he did not openly rise to the sting of Mary's insinuation. "It would, naturally, be a great sorrow for all of us if my sister chose to live out of England. I must say I do not consider it likely, for none is more attached to my mother's home at Wynfield Mote than Lucette. For one who so deeply loves the essence of the English countryside to give it up for France . . . ?" Stephen shrugged.

Mary was somewhat taken aback by the flood of words, and could only conclude that Stephen was, despite what he said, a little afraid of that very outcome. She knew how to play on that fear. "But love of a person can so easily strike, laying waste to even love of a home. Would you begrudge your sister if she found love in France?"

The hazel eyes that met hers were steady and, despite his youth, unflinching. "Does Your Majesty begrudge the loss of your country for the love of a man?"

She flushed deeply. "You are out of your depth," she spat angrily. "Do not presume on my good nature to insult me."

"I apologize," he said, in the same collected voice that did not sound at all apologetic. "I would never begrudge my sister happiness. But I confess I hope her happiness will be found here, with her family and her religion."

"Ah, so it is the Catholic aspect from which you recoil, as much as the distance." Mary's hauteur conveyed her continued warning to not trespass on her goodwill. "I do not suppose that is a subject on which we could find agreement."

He hesitated, before saying thoughtfully, "I wonder, Your Majesty. Not all minds are as fixed as the fanatics'. And peace is a state greatly to be desired, worth almost any price."

Interesting. Mary pondered that intriguing answer from the young earl for some time afterward. The Courtenays were outwardly devoted Protestants, as befit the dear friends of Elizabeth. She would have expected from them the same disdain that other English Protestants turned on her, considering her Catholic faith primarily an inconvenience that had cost her Scotland as much as her disastrous marriage to Bothwell. But it was her faith that would free her. How could heretics understand the power of truth? Understand it or not, England would be forced to reckon with its undeniable power once the Nightingale Plot released her from the bonds of this hated imprisonment.

And perhaps, in that new England, there would be more families than she could guess ready to grasp any hand that brought peace, whether their faith was devotedly pure or not. She would have to sound Stephen Courtenay on that subject.

But first the Nightingale Plot must advance. She consulted later that evening with her confessor, who was in all her confidences, about the delicate structure of a plot that, this time, must succeed. How could it not? For the first time since her ignominious flight from Scotland in 1568, Mary had more on her side than just her French family. The stars had aligned, and now Catholics in both France and Spain were united in the cause of freeing her from English captivity. What followed her freedom might still be a matter for debate among the competing parties, but Mary was confident in her course.

"And our timing?" Mary asked. "King Philip's visit is definitely set?"

"The Spanish king will arrive in England in late June," her confessor said, "date dependent on the sailing weather. Philip and his entourage will spend three weeks at court, to visit his daughter and to discuss with Queen Elizabeth the marital matters of Princess Anne as well as their own. It is believed the divorce will be finalized before he sets sail for home."

"It had better be," Mary said drily. "We need Philip well and truly separated from Elizabeth to be certain of his support."

"We'll have it," her confessor answered confidently. "The Lord is watching over this endeavour, Your Majesty. There is no need to fear. Righteousness cannot be denied."

But it can often be delayed, Mary thought cynically. And there were any number of wicked men and women who would do whatever it took to keep her in England until she died.

She tried to ignore the fact that one of those wicked opponents might very well be her own son.

25 May 1580
Edinburgh

To Her Royal Highness Anne Isabella,

Your Highness, I thank you for your goodly letter and best wishes. As you say, cousin, is it not reasonable that two young people of similar birth and position should be friends? Sure it is that I wish you well in all your endeavours.

Scotland is most willing for equal friendship with England, and we trust that you and I may have some say in creating that partnership. I look forward to our continued correspondence and wish you well in the coming visit of your royal father, King Philip.

All care from your cousin,
James VI

Anabel studied James's letter with furrowed brow, then tossed it on the table. "So, what do you think? Did James himself have any say in that carefully equivocal letter, or did my cousin merely sign his name to what his council dictated?"

Pippa touched the paper with the fingertips of her right hand and Anabel waited. It was not a common state for the Princess of Wales, but Pippa was always worth waiting for.

If Anabel could order her life entirely the way she wished it, Pippa would always be with her. But the Courtenay family was not hers to order. They would sooner have taken Anabel into their own home than allow their daughter to spend so much time attached, even peripherally, to court. But that had slowly been changing. Now that both girls were eighteen, surely Pippa's own wishes would come into it more.

"James believes that he wrote his own wishes," Pippa answered finally. "But he is not quite fourteen. With no memory of either father or mother, having known only the care of various Lord Protectors, how can James be certain which beliefs are his and which are not?"

"Those carefully chosen words," Anabel mused, "'equal' and 'partnership.' Almost I might be insulted at James's caution in courting me. Clearly he will not have me unless he is certain that Scotland will not be swallowed up by England in the bargain."

"He is four years younger," Pippa reminded her, "and has never met you. Do you want the poor boy to be so madly in love with you that he would simply hand over his country?"

Anabel sniffed. "It would be flattering. But I suppose even he has too much sense—and for certain too much pride—to allow it. There will be a long back and forth before this contract is concluded." She could not keep the note of satisfaction out of her voice.

Pippa, of course, noted it. "Which gives you time to be young and foolish. And to see if you cannot persuade one of your parents into allowing you a different marriage. Or, no, it is not an early marriage you are longing for. What you want is your independence."

Anabel gave a small, secret smile. "I am only eighteen. My mother was not married until she was twenty-six. Why should I be rushed from childhood to marriage bed?"

"As you say, there will be precious little rush about any of this. And really, your mother has shown remarkable restraint in not betrothing you until now. Most future monarchs are matched in the cradle. Not that most of them end by marrying those first matches."

"Like Mary Stuart and my uncle William? Now that is a path for musing: how might the world be different today if England had married Scotland thirty years ago? I would wager Mary Stuart has wondered that. For if she had married my uncle, and if her son had been

William's rather than Lord Darnley's . . . well, then, she would now be Queen of England and her son would rule a united island."

"And you would never have been born," Pippa pointed out caustically.

"I didn't say it was a history I regretted. Only that, on such personal matters as marriage and children do kingdoms rest."

"And that is why your mother will do the dance of royal betrothals for your sake. Because she, not Mary Stuart, is Queen of England, and on her life and yours rests the security of the kingdom."

Anabel sobered. "I know," she said, and those two words were weighted with the knowledge she'd had almost her whole life—that England as an independent and Protestant state depended wholly on the fragile Tudor line. Elizabeth could not afford to keep Anabel single until she was twenty-six. By that age, she needed to have borne at least one son, if not more, to give breathing room to this country she so passionately loved.

Still, she would maneuver for what freedom she could. And being the only child of parents who ruled two different kingdoms meant that she had more pieces of gameplay at her disposal than most royal women. She intended to gamble this summer, but like all good gamblers, she knew that the key to winning was to never wager more than you were willing to lose.

And Anabel would never risk losing England.

"I shall miss you," Lucette said fervently as she hugged Dr. Dee goodbye. He would remain in Paris while she set out for Chateau Blanclair this morning, and she was suddenly much more anxious than she'd ever expected to be at the thought of leaving her last link to the English court.

What if she needed advice? What if she got in over her head? What if she was lonely?

At that last, she drew herself up sharply. *You're not a child,* she lectured herself sternly, *and you're hardly going into battle. All you have to do is keep your eyes and ears open and see if your mind can make a pattern out of anything gleaned.*

And possibly betray Renaud LeClerc's hospitality and Charlotte's friendship by damning someone in their family into the hands of England's spymaster.

Lucette didn't have a clear idea what Walsingham would do if she confirmed the connivance of a LeClerc in the plots against Elizabeth's life, but she was uneasy. Walsingham was not a gentle man where Elizabeth was concerned. And it would be poor repayment of their hospitality to bring ruin to Blanclair.

Dr. Dee held her by the shoulders. "Remember," he said, "I shall be waiting to hear from you at least every other day. Renaud LeClerc will expect no less, for he knows your father well. Keep your missives brief and remember your equations. I shall know how to solve them."

Of course he would, for it was Dee himself who had taught her their idiosyncratic ciphering system based on algebraic equations. Whatever number answered the equation attached to one of their letters would be the number used to decipher the coded message in a seemingly innocuous communication. And it would look like nothing more than a demanding tutor and his apt pupil studying mathematics from afar.

They had also agreed on three key phrases in case she needed to write in a hurry and could not be troubled to create a code: *I am keeping up with my reading in German* meant "all is well." *There is a new argument in Aristotle I am eager to debate with you* meant "I have uncovered evidence." *I long for Wynfield Mote at this time of year* meant simply "get me out of here."

Like any good teacher, Dr. Dee spoke to her deepest fear before she'd even put it into words to herself. "Do not be afraid of making a mistake, Lucette. You are not the only asset Walsingham has attempting to uncover the Nightingale Plot and all its links. It is not on your word alone that any man will be condemned. Trust your instincts and your natural intelligence and you will have no reason to doubt yourself."

"I shall endeavour to do you proud."

"Just come back safely when you're finished. That is all the result I, or anyone who loves you, will ever need."

But for all his comforting words, Lucette was three hours south of Paris before she was able to breathe freely and begin to enjoy her surroundings. The road to Orléans was broad and well-traveled, and Lucette had to admit the company was pleasant. Charlotte was not with them—she and Andry would come on to Blanclair with their children the last week of June, "giving you time to work your charms," Charlotte teased—but Renaud rode beside her all that morning. Their pace was easy and Lucette felt her spirits rising to something close to euphoria the farther they got from Paris and the last remnants of both parental and royal authority.

She was truly on her own now. Time to see what she could do.

They stopped at an inn midday to rest the horses and eat. When they returned to the road afterward, it was Nicolas who maneuvered his horse alongside hers.

Julien called after his brother, "Watch yourself. If Charlotte hears of this, she'll drag a priest in her wake when she comes to Blanclair."

Accustomed to her brothers' (mostly good-natured) bickering, Lucette expected a stinging reply from Nicolas. But Nicolas ignored his brother and turned his attention wholly to her.

And quite heady attention it was. Lucette had certainly had her share of male attention at court, but the Duke of Exeter's fierce reputation—not to mention Queen Elizabeth's close interest—kept such attention extraordinarily formal. And since her disastrous encounter with Brandon Dudley five years ago, Lucette had been content with the formality.

Nicolas, however, was French. And already in his thirties. A widower and father, who was less impressed with Lucette's English network of relationships and comfortable in his own country and his own lands. He was an easy conversationalist, skillfully drawing her out as to her intellectual pursuits.

"I am quite abashed," he said, after Lucette's spirited account of the mathematical equations behind Mercator's cylindrical map. "If that is the level on which your mind operates, I fear you shall quickly grow tired of our quiet life at Blanclair."

"By no means," Lucette replied warmly. "My favorite time of each year is that passed at Wynfield Mote. To ride and read and spend our evenings as a family rather than in grand parties?" She shrugged eloquently. "That has always been a time of great peace."

"I, too, relish peace." Nicolas stared ahead, brooding. "When I was young, I thought I should never wish to live anywhere but Paris and resented the necessary time spent in the country. But these last years, ever since . . ." He trailed off.

Since the death of your wife, Lucette finished. Her name had been Célie, she remembered. A sixteen-year-old married to Nicolas only eleven months when she'd died giving birth to their son, Felix.

Nicolas turned and smiled, a much gentler, warming smile than Julien's challenging one. "To bring such a bright mind from the outside world to the quietness of Blanclair is a great gift. I thank you for it, Lucette."

For the length of several erratic heartbeats, Lucette let herself pretend that she was here for nothing more than to catch the eye of the Blanclair heir. Here there was no queen to intimidate or authority to disapprove—here there was simply a man looking at her as though he liked what he saw. A man she had idolized as a child.

But, being herself, she did not linger in that pleasure. Her responding smile went from genuine to calculated—this much lift to the corners of her mouth to portray shy interest, this much of an angle to her downcast eyes to suggest demure appeal. This much personal exposure in hopes of reeling in someone in Nicolas's family and delivering him to Walsingham.

"The gift," she said, "is entirely your family's doing. It is I who am grateful, sir."

"Nicolas," he insisted.

She tilted her head. "Nicolas."

31 May 1580
Wynfield Mote

We have come home, Dominic and I, for a few weeks' respite before returning to court. It is somewhat unsettling being here without any of the children, but also . . . well, there is a certain headiness to not having to worry who is going to walk around corners and interrupt whatever we may be doing.

I would be happy to remain here all summer, but Elizabeth has requested Dominic's advice on the council that will oversee the dissolution of her marriage to King Philip. I think he would have said no, if it were not that Kit and Pippa will be at court then with Anabel. Elizabeth has pointedly not asked my opinion, but I imagine I will find a way to express it nonetheless. I think she expects me to always be disappointed, as though I have taken the place of her mother in some respects, but her marriage broke down long ago. Better a conscious and careful dissolution than violent recriminations.

Stephen writes twice a week from Tutbury. I wonder if he says any more to Walsingham than he does to us? And Lucette has written dutifully along the road. Last we heard, they were just about to enter Paris. If all has gone to schedule, she will be on her way to Blanclair now.

I wonder if her childhood infatuation for Nicolas LeClerc will be revived. I should be less troubled by that thought than I am—after all, she must marry someone, and who better than Renaud's heir?

But I do not want her to leave England. What a pity children cannot be made to do only what will please their parents!

INTERLUDE

September 1568

L ucette never meant to eavesdrop. Exactly. It was just that she
knew when something was not right in her home, and it would
ring through her almost like pain until she knew what it was. Tension, disagreement, discordance . . . they called to her like the sirens
of ancient Greece, clamouring for her attention.

She fancied she could see those tensions as coloured threads
stretched between various people. Today, those troubled threads
were noticeably woven through all the adults, but reached their
deepest shade—an alarming red—in her parents. Usually they would
talk out any troubles in the rose garden, but after the rider from
London appeared with royal dispatches, Mother and Father shut
themselves up in what had been Grandfather Wyatt's study before
the house was burnt and rebuilt.

But it was a fine warm day for September, and the long windows
of the study were open. Lucette was small enough to fit beneath the
windows and so not be easily seen by anyone inside.

Like most of her eavesdropping, it was more exciting in theory
than in practice. But she had long ago learned that just because she

didn't understand everything she heard didn't mean it wouldn't quiet her mind to know it. So she squirreled away the people and places and concerns of her parents: *Don Carlos . . . starved to death, they say . . . Burghley fears more . . . if Philip was involved . . . Anabel's guards to be tripled . . . already the Catholics fear Mary Stuart will never leave England . . . Philip must press now, for another heir from Elizabeth or else a divorce . . . the weight of two realms resting on a little girl . . .*

And all at once, like fireworks exploding, that collection of names and phrases arranged themselves into a startling, shocking pattern.

It was like stars suddenly arranging themselves into constellations, or disparate shapes of fabric sewn into the folds and pleats of a gown. Lucette could hardly breathe for surprise and pleasure as the wide range of her parents' conversation rearranged itself into a coherent whole.

Mary Stuart was the easiest piece, for she was Queen of Scotland (or had been) but had recently fled into England from her rebellious subjects. Don Carlos, though, was King Philip's son and heir to the Spanish throne, as Princess Anne was Philip's daughter and Elizabeth's heir. Don Carlos was dead. King Philip needed another heir. Either he would try to take Anabel to Spain, or he would need a new wife, for surely Queen Elizabeth would not have any more babies now?

Spain and England might become enemies. If they did, it wouldn't be long before France was pulled into the fight.

And at this very moment a French family was resident at Wynfield Mote.

At last Lucette had something important to say to Nicolas LeClerc. News that would make the tall and handsome eighteen-year-old look at her with something other than indulgence in his expression.

Unfortunately for her, when she finally located Nicolas, he was in the stables with his brother Julien. Lucette was suspicious of Julien LeClerc. He laughed too much and smiled too often, and she'd heard one of the serving girls giggle, "His charm will be the death of him, like as not, as soon as he meets a father he can't talk his way round."

Besides, he teased her as though she were still a child, no older than Kit and Pippa. So when she heard the brothers talking, Lucette darted into the nearest stall while she figured out how to detach Nicolas from Julien.

And thus, once again, found herself eavesdropping. They spoke in French, which Lucette could follow almost as easily as English.

"So we'll be off home sooner than later?" Nicolas mused. "Father won't want to risk being caught between England and Spain if Philip moves against his wife."

"Seems a pity to run when there's trouble. Father might just as well decide to offer support to Lord Exeter."

"You know better than that, Julien. Father and Exeter are two of a kind—men who know when to sit out trouble rather than rush to meet it. And I daresay Lord Exeter will be relieved to see the last of us—or at least of you."

"What does that mean?"

"His wife. You've been panting after her all summer like a dog in heat. There's a limit to the man's forbearance—"

The sound of quick steps, and sudden violence. Lucette covered her mouth to stifle a gasp, but the brothers' scuffle pushed them down the center aisle and directly into her line of sight. Julien's wheat-coloured hair hung in his eyes as he shoved his brother. Nicolas, his hair several shades darker, was the first to see her.

"Hello," he said in English, and the change of tone was enough to alert Julien, who dropped his hands and whirled round.

Lucette would not be cowed by Julien's grim face, nor—more disquieting—the sudden smile like the sun blazing through a summer storm. "In faith you do get around, child. Everywhere I turn, you seem to be at my feet."

"Not your feet," she said, then stopped as her face flamed.

She wished she knew some bad words to hurl at Julien as his smile broadened. "No, of course not. Why would you haunt me when my brother is at hand? Nicolas is all that is good and pure. But sweet as you are, I don't think Nicolas is quite so pure as to wait the necessary years for you to grow up."

"Julien." Nicolas, usually so mild, could make his voice whip like an adult's when he wished it.

With a shrug, Julien lost interest. "Were you looking for me?" Nicolas asked her kindly.

As it was clear they already knew about the death of the Spanish prince, Lucette scrambled for something interesting to say. But her mind, usually so quick, supplied nothing. "I came," she finally said loftily, "to look at the kittens."

As long as she lived, she would never forgive Julien LeClerc for the slow, cynical smile that said, *I see right through you, child.*

SIX

"Thus far," Elizabeth announced, "I have not found this June especially to my liking."

The court was still at Greenwich, from whence it would soon set out on its way to Portsmouth to welcome the Spanish. Elizabeth paced the eastern gallery, resplendent in gold velvet and damask, the bodice and skirt encrusted with crystals. Her open ruff of lace rose stiffly to frame the coiled plaits and curls of one of her many wigs, and ropes of pearls swung to the pointed V of her waistline. Burghley and Walsingham were alone with her as she preferred when she was out of sorts.

Gravely, Walsingham said, "There is no doubt that the Jesuit mission has begun. Even now there are priests slipping into England with the pope's blessing to stir up rebellion."

Burghley played devil's advocate. "According to their own statements, they are come only to teach, not to meddle with affairs of state or politics."

"There is no difference." Walsingham would not raise his voice in her presence, but Elizabeth could hear his fury. Because she knew it was prompted by concern for her, she let it pass.

"Is it true," she asked, "that Edmund Campion is leading the Jesuit mission?"

Burghley, who had been Campion's patron when the man was a scholar at Oxford, nodded. "With Father Robert Persons. He's a gentler man than Campion, no doubt meant to rein him in. I doubt he'll be successful."

If there was one thing Elizabeth detested, it was ingratitude. "No Anglican cleric benefited more from the crown's favour than did Campion. I was seen to publicly praise him, he was allowed to offer the Latin oration when the founder of his college died! How dare he throw such gifts back in my face?"

"He says it is for conscience's sake," Burghley said mildly.

"I take no issue with his conscience. If he feels he must follow Catholic doctrine, let him. I did not pursue Campion when he left our kingdom. But now he dares return to publicly oppose the religious settlement that has kept England at peace for twenty years."

"Your Majesty," Walsingham said, "we must consider on the wisdom of allowing King Philip to land so many Spanish with him when he arrives. How do we know he is not importing members of this mission to stir up violence against you?"

Burghley bore the first argument on her behalf. "It is a diplomatic entourage of the queen's husband. We can hardly ask King Philip to reduce his party while coming to visit his wife."

"Coming to divorce his wife," Walsingham said bluntly. "If we're lucky."

"Oh, come now," Elizabeth said with a casualness that was partly feigned. "Do you really expect Philip to import an assassin to do away with me when all of Europe knows our marriage is but a sheet of paper that will be ripped in half this summer? There is no need for Philip to have me killed. If nothing else, the man I married is not stupid. He would not risk such a step while he himself is on English soil to be made suspect."

"But not all of his men are so prudent. Philip may not be fanatic enough for Rome, but many of his subjects would gladly give their lives to end yours."

"Perhaps," Elizabeth said sharply. "But then, that is why I employ you, to prevent fanatics from carrying out their schemes."

"Like the Ridolfi plot or the gunman along the banks of the Thames? I need not remind you that those might as easily have ended badly. So much depends on luck."

Elizabeth gave a bark of laughter. "Luck? And here I thought I employed you for your skills. You are not usually so modest, Walsingham."

"I am not usually so frightened, Your Majesty. With the dissolution of your marriage to Philip, the last protection you have from Catholics will be withdrawn. Pope Gregory will undoubtedly restate the terms of your excommunication of ten years ago. Your Catholic subjects will once more be absolved by the pope of any allegiance to you; indeed, he will declare not only your reign but your life forfeit in Catholic hands. That is what the conspirators in France are waiting for. To be given absolution for murder, so they might remove you from England's throne."

"And do what?" Elizabeth flung it at him like a challenge. "The Catholics are divided on who should succeed me. Mary Stuart might have the purest Catholic pedigree, but her only heir has been raised by violent Protestants."

It was Burghley who stated the other choice. "Or Princess Anne, daughter of the King of Spain and who, should she prove willing to return to Catholicism and marry appropriately, might be mooted as Philip's heir as well as yours."

"Which means France and Spain will never come to agreement," Elizabeth finished. "France will not allow Spain to take charge of England, and Spain will not permit France the same. They are united only in despising me—kill me, and their unity dissolves."

"Small comfort to England if you are dead."

"You underestimate my daughter. Anne will never allow herself to be used by our enemies. Which is why there will be several eligible young men of England in the court party to meet Philip. Scotland may or may not be the right match for my daughter, but I will not overlook the uses of English nobles."

"Francis Hastings, son of the Earl of Huntingdon, and Robert Devereux, the Earl of Essex." Burghley supplied the names thoughtfully.

"Of course."

"Have you considered bringing the Earl of Somerset to court as well for the duration of the Spanish visit? He is heir to the wealthiest duke in the kingdom."

She shook her head at once. "Stephen Courtenay is needed at Tutbury." And also, she thought, it is a bad idea to pair Minuette's son with a Tudor royal, even in play. There is far too much of pain and history there.

Burghley understood what she did not say and accepted her refusal. Then Elizabeth added one name to his list, knowing it would raise eyebrows not only among her advisors but in England at large. "And Brandon Dudley."

After a delicate pause, Burghley said, "Your Majesty, he holds no title, and his unfortunate relationship to the late Duke of Norfolk—"

"Norfolk was his stepfather in name only. Brandon was raised by his uncle, the Earl of Warwick, and all his allegiance by birth and blood is to the Protestants. As for titles, I intend to invest him before we leave for Portsmouth, and so you may let leak to the Spanish ambassador."

"What title will you give him?"

"The Earl of Leicester." Elizabeth stared down her chief advisor, daring him to say what he thought, that this was nothing more than a sentimental gesture on the queen's part to a young man who reminded her of the only man she'd ever loved. Robert Dudley had been dead for twenty-two years, executed for nothing more than serving Elizabeth.

She would not be scolded for making his nephew an earl. Small enough repayment for the loss of Robert.

They were three days on the road to Blanclair. The second night was spent at an inn in Pithiviers, the LeClerc men once again sharing a chamber. Julien stumbled up late, but Nicolas wagered he'd been doing nothing more than drink to try and take his mind off Lucette Courtenay. Nevertheless, they were all up just after dawn, eager to finish their journey.

The Englishwoman traveled well, Nicolas admitted. He'd been prepared for a pampered girl, as she should be in her position, but she seemed unspoiled and refreshingly direct compared to the French. And she had wide-ranging interests. As he'd listened to her talk with knowledgeable enthusiasm on such disparate topics as the plague treatments of Nostradamus and the heliocentric model of the universe, Nicolas recalled a report from a recent German visitor to England: after praising their beauty, he had noted that "the womenfolk in England wish to be in at everything."

Julien had been in something of a daze since the night he'd laid eyes on her at the Pearces' reception. Nicolas found it amusing how hard his brother worked to turn his usual charm on Lucette, hampered as he clearly was by actual feelings. Amusing . . . and something else. Something darker.

Why should Julien have everything his own way?

Nicolas might have wanted Lucette in France for a very specific purpose, but that didn't mean he couldn't appreciate her virtues. Clever but innocent, highborn but generous, wary but willing to be won . . . he should have guessed that the honourable, romantic Julien would be smitten. Well, he didn't mind opposing his brother for principle's sake. Charlotte thought she had lured her friend here to capture a LeClerc son; for all anyone knew, it could just as easily be Nicolas.

So Nicolas didn't mind when Julien maneuvered his horse to ride next to Lucette shortly after leaving Pithiviers. Letting him have his pleasure while he could would make it all the more sweet when it ended.

Renaud took the opportunity to ride by Nicolas. Through the turmoil of the last years—especially Nicole's death—Renaud and Nicolas had maintained the relationship they had settled into early in Nicolas's adolescence: his father rarely correcting him, Nicolas keeping up appearances as a respectful eldest son. Julien and Renaud had often argued long and loudly, but Nicolas knew what was expected of him, and was careful to keep up the image of those expectations. He knew people said he and Renaud were alike, but that only proved how good he was at manipulating responses.

The one thing he had never been able to completely hide from his father was his bitterness.

"She is a very lovely girl," Renaud said in an offhand manner that didn't deceive Nicolas. "Of course she would be, being who she is. But I confess I did not expect both my sons to be intrigued by her. You and Julien are usually so different."

"Meaning I married dutifully at twenty-two and produced a son? Or that only Julien could be expected to still find a lovely girl . . . desirable?"

Renaud was not a man to be ruffled. "Meaning that I wonder at my wisdom in allowing her to visit. It is one thing to welcome a girl born in our house—it is another to set my sons at odds."

"How can we be at odds? I will never marry again, and Julien knows it."

He let the bitterness leak into his words, for it would help blind his father to his true interest in Lucette. That she was lovely was a pleasant surprise—but what he wanted from her, he would take if she were covered in pockmarks or had lost all her teeth.

And if his interest tormented Julien, so much the better.

It was just as well, Julien decided, that he had Lucette Courtenay's presence to distract him on the road to Blanclair, or he might have been driven mad by memories and bolted back to Paris. He had not been south since his mother's death, keeping his clandestine activities confined to areas well away from Orléans and St. Benoit sur Loire. During the last hour of their ride, it was as though every tree, every bend of the road, every vista called to him body and soul. *Welcome home,* they said—and, beneath that, the accusatory hint of: *You should not have stayed away so long.*

But Julien was adept at suppressing accusatory voices, so he shoved these reactions below the more immediate tension of keeping an eye on Lucette and wondering how the hell he was supposed to pull information from her. In just the relatively short time of travel, it was abundantly clear that she was no simpering girl to prattle away English royal secrets to the first man who paid her any attention. Julien knew how to work with those girls. He also knew how to work with women as suspicious as he was, who would trade information for information and whose morals stretched only as far as their self-interest. But Lucette was not that sort of creature, either.

Indeed, he thought there would be only one way to approach Lucette: honestly. Or at least as honestly as possible. Which meant letting his initial immediate attraction guide him, to approach her as, in another world, he might have: as a woman who intrigued and attracted him in equal measures. And that would be no easy task, particularly when she still seemed as smitten by Nicolas as when she was ten years old.

Julien at first did not recognize the grip of displeasure that took hold when Nicolas rode beside her to her obvious pleasure. When he did recognize it as jealousy, he had to repress a groan at the predicament. What a mess! His Catholic contacts wanted information from a woman his sister had enticed to France to marry either her dissolute, wanton brother, or her damaged and solitary brother. And now it seemed both brothers were actually amenable to her charms.

So really, by the time they all clattered into the courtyard of Blanclair, Julien was in such a welter of emotions that he nearly turned his horse around and made straight back for Paris. But there was one person at Blanclair Julien would never ride away from, and that person stood waiting on the steps.

"Uncle Julien!" Felix cried, and launched himself down the steps so quickly that Julien barely managed to dismount before the boy was upon him. He was absurdly pleased at being greeted before anyone else and swept the boy off the ground and into an embrace that turned into a spin.

"How tall you've grown, *mon petit!*" Julien exclaimed when the seven-year-old was once more on firm ground. "Soon you will have to be the one to lift me."

Felix turned pink with pride and stood straighter in an attempt to come near his uncle's height. He was tall for his age, with hints of the gangly years to come when a boy was all arms and legs and had no idea how to coordinate them. He had his dead mother's brown hair and eyes, but his smile was all Charlotte's sweetness untinged by either his uncle's mockery or his father's resignation.

"Felix," said Renaud, and the boy instantly turned to his grandfather. "It is polite to greet a guest first."

"Of course, *Grandpère.*" Felix made a charming bow to Lucette. "*Pardon, mademoiselle.* I hope your journey was without trouble. Welcome to Blanclair."

"Thank you." In just those two words, Lucette met Felix on the ground he was so eager to establish—that of a contemporary. From her tone, one would never know she spoke to a child and Julien unwillingly added that to the things he liked about her. "I hope, *monsieur,* that you will show me your home."

"You do not remember it?" Felix asked unguardedly.

"No, for I was not even a year old when I returned to England. Perhaps you will help me remember."

"*Certainement, mademoiselle.*" Felix glowed with her approval, and Julien thought resignedly that one more LeClerc male seemed all too eager to fall for Lucette Courtenay. The thought made him snort and sent him moving toward the house, the horses relinquished into the effacing but well-trained hands of Blanclair's grooms.

He felt his father's disapproving eyes at his ungracious retreat, but so be it. He needed to be alone to settle his head. And heart.

But Blanclair had too many memories for Julien to find a clear head. Everywhere, he felt his mother, as though Nicole would step around a corner or appear on a landing at any moment. *This is why I haven't come home,* Julien thought with gritted teeth. *I don't like ghosts.*

There were only two ways he knew to keep ghosts at bay—well, all right, three ways, but he wasn't about to take any of his father's maids to bed. So it was either drink heavily or work.

He supposed there wasn't really a choice. Renaud did not tolerate drunkenness in his home, and his Paris masters had demanded information. Time to get to work on Lucette Courtenay.

Though Lucette had no memories of Blanclair, only stories told by her mother and Carrie of their time here, she found herself unexpectedly moved as she settled into the beautiful chateau. Compared to Tiverton and Wynfield Mote, both medieval—in design if not actual age—Blanclair was distinctly modern and French. Built by Renaud's father in a horseshoe pattern, the three symmetrical wings of white stone rose to steeply sloping slate roofs. There were arcades and mullioned windows, the family coat-of-arms in plaster surrounds, and gardens that Lucette found frankly astonishing in their elegance and design.

The engaging young Felix, taking his task seriously, appointed himself her guide and was solicitous that she see every corner of the house and every vista in the gardens and courtyards. The afternoon after her arrival, they spent several hours together. Though the chateau itself was pleasingly lovely, it was the gardens that were the real star.

Linden trees formed the avenues separating four terraced gardens. They began at the bottom, with two acres of decorative vegetable gardens, plants carefully arranged in geometric shapes. Then came the Garden of Love (instructed Felix), its box hedges and yew trees the structure within which colours ran riot in embroidery-like symbols. Then the water garden and, at the top, the Sun Garden. From there one could look down on each of the terraces below, giving a spectacular overview of the symmetry and geometry that contained without stifling the boisterous abundance of plant life.

Once released by Felix, it was a relief to escape to the guest chamber set aside for her use. She was glad she had not brought a maid with her from England, for it gave her more solitude. Renaud had provided an attendant from his household, but with no woman currently residing at Blanclair, the girl was unused to tending a lady and unlikely to press her way into Lucette's business without direct orders. So Lucette was able to tidy her face and hair, breathe deeply, and focus.

First things first. Whenever she was about to embark on a new course of study, Dr. Dee had taught her how to make a space for the information in her mind so that it was readily accessible whenever she might need it. *Books are not always available,* he'd lectured, *nor other tangible sources of information. You must learn to store it all in your memory.*

The first step was to conjure up the image of the library at Wynfield Mote. It was a small chamber—as everything at Wynfield was on a smaller scale than, say, Tiverton Castle—but beautiful with its coffered ceiling and ebony wood floor. The library was her Memory Chamber. The shelves in her imagination were not filled with her family's books, but with tall quarto-size ledgers, spines neatly aligned along each shelf. Each ledger—or sometimes shelf of ledgers, if the subject matter was complex—represented a single subject.

Eyes closed, Lucette conjured up the image of herself walking to a previously unused shelf and taking down the first ledger. Then to the circular table in the center of the library, where quill and ink awaited her. She opened the cover and on the first page imagined herself writing THE NIGHTINGALE PLOT.

She did not have to imagine the actual writing—sometimes she did it merely for effect, occasionally to underscore the importance of how she felt about a piece of information. Now, eyes still closed, she poured out on the first pages of the ledger the information gleaned from Walsingham and Burghley and Queen Elizabeth back in February. The names of those she'd met in Paris; the impressions of the Catholic priests she'd seen along the way, friendly or not; and finally she headed a page simply CHATEAU BLANCLAIR.

Opening her eyes, Lucette stretched as though she had actually been sitting hunched over a table writing. Time to start snooping, so she might begin to fill in the next pages. Felix had given her a good foundation, with his thorough tour of Blanclair, but the kinds of information she needed would not come from a child. She would need to be visible, need to chatter to as many of the household staff as possible, and most of all be present with family members every hour she could manage.

She summoned the maid to help her dress for dinner and began with gentle questions about the family. But the girl—Anise—had only been here for a year, after Nicole LeClerc's death, and had never even met Julien until now.

Not that it kept her from talking about him. "Felix is very taken with his uncle," she confided as though it were a great secret, rather than something that radiated from the boy's very being. "I hope for his sake Monsieur Julien behaves himself properly. Apparently he can be quite wicked in Paris."

Lucette was torn between the impropriety of gossip and the necessity of investigation. "I imagine Julien can behave properly when he wishes. And there is much less scope for wickedness at Blanclair than in Paris."

"Oh, yes," Anise—who had surely never been farther than ten miles from Blanclair—agreed. "Though there is the Nightingale Inn in the village. Cook says it's the first place Master Julien goes when he's home. Hours he spends there, but he must hold his drink well for she says like as not he comes back no more addled than when he went."

"Indeed?" Lucette said no more while the girl finished attaching her starched ruff of finest lawn. She was thoughtful as she descended to dinner. On the surface, Julien passing time at a tavern seemed perfectly natural. But a tavern called Nightingale? That detail, combined with the cook's commentary that Julien did not seem to be especially drunk, had Lucette tucking that piece into the landscape of the puzzle she was attempting to put together. Taverns, she imagined, were a good place for clandestine business.

That night she set about being, if not quite charming, then something more than just polite toward Julien. And, to her surprise, he seemed prepared to match her attempts. She was seated next to Nicolas, facing Julien across the table. He had Felix on his left, with Renaud at the end of the table. It was she and Julien who carried the bulk of the conversation.

He seemed especially interested in talking about Wynfield Mote and the LeClercs' long ago visit to England. He didn't quite have the nerve to frame it as "do you remember how nice I was to you when you were little," but Lucette was forced to admit he was ruefully charming in talking about her younger siblings and the constant crowd he and Nicolas had drawn whenever they had sparred at Wynfield.

"What I recall," Lucette said, "is your father chastising you for depending on luck when you fought."

"True," Julien laughed. "I did have a rather careless attitude when young, but time has taught me that fortune may not always be wholeheartedly on my side."

"And did you learn that lesson before your carelessness caused much damage?"

It was astonishing the swiftness with which his features changed. All at once Julien was as forbidding as he had been open before. But only for a moment. Then his expression cleared, if not quite regaining its former openness. "I am still here, at least," he said. "And with a lifetime to atone for my former errors."

No one else spoke or even, it seemed to Lucette, breathed. Through the thickening tension, she managed a noncommittal smile and then asked Felix about his Latin studies.

When they broke for the evening, Lucette was wondering how to ask what the men were doing the next day when Julien said abruptly, "Would you care for a tour of the valley, Lucette? I'd be happy to ride with you tomorrow around St. Benoit."

"I should like that."

Lucette glanced at Nicolas, wondering if she could invite him as well, but Julien said roughly, "If you'd rather go with my brother, of course . . ."

Nicolas rescued her. "I have estate business to do with Father tomorrow. Enjoy yourself, Lucette."

She looked back to Julien, the same grey eyes as his brother, but inspiring quite different feelings. "I don't know if I'm brave enough for all your attention." She meant it to tease, but there was a catch in her voice that left her a little breathless.

Julien seemed to feel it as well, for his voice dropped to something confidential. "Then I shall have to be brave for the both of us."

The tension was broken by Felix, who asked hopefully, "May I come, Uncle?"

"You, young sir, have lessons to do. If you work hard with your tutor tomorrow, I will spar with you in the afternoon. And perhaps Mademoiselle Lucette will favour us with her presence—she quite liked watching LeClerc boys spar when she was younger."

Julien winked at her, and Lucette knew that the two of them were now engaged in sparring of quite another nature.

Before she slept that night, Lucette wrote to Dr. Dee. She could have encoded it to an algebraic equation, but chose the faster method of their key phrases. She told herself it was because she was tired, not because her mind kept stealing away to images of Julien—the grey eyes that seemed meant for seduction, the way his blond hair fell about his face until her fingers itched to push it away. Whatever the reason, she had a hard time keeping to mathematics.

Dear Dr. Dee,

The journey was uneventful. I have found Blanclair to be more moving than I expected, and the family has been nothing but welcoming.

You may report to my family that I am taking it all in to remember later. And yes, I am keeping up with my reading in German.

Lucette Courtenay

SEVEN

Julien whistled his way down the stairs next morning, jubilant at the thought of several hours alone with Lucette. Not even his brother's troubled expression as they passed on the steps bothered him.

"Don't worry, Nic, it's just an hour or two of riding. Even I can manage to be polite for that length of time."

"Rather more than polite," Nicolas said slowly. "Julien, this is not one of your Paris society ladies. Don't insult her—and don't get either of your hopes up."

That sobered Julien, for he knew Nicolas was right. Whatever Charlotte's plans (and his own rebellious emotions), there were no marital options for Lucette, he thought as he strode out to the courtyard. Not here. How disappointed Charlotte would be when Lucette returned to England without a husband, leaving him to his dissolution and Nicolas to his solitude.

Lucette was already mounted in the Blanclair courtyard, atop a fine-boned chestnut mare that might have been chosen to highlight her appearance. She could not have looked more lovely if she were deliberately trying to snare him. Though they had shared the road for three days from Paris, today she wore a riding dress he hadn't seen before. Rather than a ruff, an organza partlet rose from the square neckline to her throat in a maddening tease of sheerness; the dress itself was black embroidery on a white background. She might have been one of the ancient Greek deities condescending to visit mortals for her own pleasure: Aphrodite, perhaps, or the more elusive Athena.

Julien felt the hard truths of his life slip away and, with reckless abandon for either of their hearts, decided to revel in the pleasures of the moment.

As he took his reins from a groom and swung into his own saddle, he said lightly, "Good morning, Lucie. May I call you Lucie?"

At his request to address her so familiarly, she blushed but her voice was steady in reply. "I suppose since you've actually known me longer than my own siblings, you may as well."

The two of them rode out of the courtyard unaccompanied. He carried two long daggers about him, and they would not go farther than the village. St. Benoit sur Loire was not Paris; there was little need to suspect violence at every moment. When they were well down the long, tree-lined road that led away from the chateau, Julien picked up the previous conversational thread. "What I recall of you as a baby is precious little, I'm afraid. I hardly paid any attention to my own little sister in those days."

"And my mother? Did you pay her as much attention at Blanclair as you did when you came to Wynfield Mote?"

"Ah." Julien fumbled for a moment, then remembered that honesty was his only hope. "Lady Exeter was an uncommonly kind woman to a small boy, though I do remember that she rarely smiled. Only at you, in point of fact."

"You were . . . seven years old then?"

"Yes. I knew that your mother had lost her husband in England—at least, we all thought so at the time—and that the king was angry with her. Nicolas had a memory of Dominic visiting Blanclair years before that. I was too young to remember him, but Nic told me he was that rarest of creatures—an honest Englishman." Julien paused. "Do you know, the first time I ever saw my father cry was the day he got the news that Dominic Courtenay was still alive."

Lucette drew a breath that might have had a slight hitch to it. He had not thought to wonder what reactions might be called forth by her return to the place of her birth. But she did not linger on that point. "Then you all came to Wynfield that long ago summer. Where you were old enough to realize how very beautiful my mother is."

Julien spoke carefully, knowing he had to get past this particular issue, upon which she seemed so fixed. "I hope . . . I have always remembered what you overheard between Nic and me that day at Wynfield. I do hope you have never allowed it to trouble you. I thought myself very adult at sixteen, but of course I was barely more than a boy with a silly infatuation. I never meant disrespect to your mother."

What he left unsaid was an apology for his first words to her the other night: *You're not very like your mother, are you?* Why had he even said that? Shock, he supposed. For all that he proclaimed it now an infatuation, he had indeed been dreadfully in love with Minuette Courtenay. That summer at Wynfield had been passed in a state of heightened sensitivity, an alertness to her presence, the painful hope that she would speak to him, dreams of her looking at him warmly and letting him touch her . . .

What a fool he'd been—but no more a fool than most boys that age. If nothing else, that hopeless calf-love had kept him away from any enticements the local girls might have offered. Nicolas had not been so circumspect. Julien wondered what Lucette would say if he told her how his brother had graced the bed of more than one young woman in the Wynfield household and its surrounding neighbors. He had covered for his brother against Renaud's suspicion, and he remembered how little Nicolas had cared for the feelings of the girls he so casually used. Julien may have been two years younger and desperately in love with a married woman twice his age, but even he had noted his brother's callousness.

Of course he said nothing about that now. Because for all Nicolas's faults when young, the price his brother had since paid for Julien's own faults had been grievously high. And if heaven had disapproved of Nicolas's past lechery, then it had found the most cruelly ironic punishment possible.

"You've no need to apologize." Lucette's voice dragged him back to the present moment and the more than pretty woman riding beside him. "Any man who doesn't appreciate my mother's beauty does not have eyes. And of course I never suspected you of anything . . . base."

The number of base things he'd done in the last eight years was too high to count. But he appreciated the effort and, with that reckless abandonment she called forth so easily, let himself flirt with danger. "I promise you one thing, Lucie—I have never in my life kissed a woman who has not asked it of me."

He captured and held those blue eyes with his long enough that he was dimly grateful both their horses knew their way along the road. A spark had kindled in Lucette's that he wanted to believe meant she took his words as a challenge rather than an apology.

A swift smile, like spring sun, crossed her face and she turned her attention back to the road. "Where are you taking me today?" she asked.

He easily tipped into one of his more seductive smiles. "I want to show you off around the village. Most of them have never seen an Englishwoman, so don't be surprised if there's staring. They'll be wondering where you hide your Protestant horns."

Her eyebrows shot up, but she smiled in response. "I suppose the same place all of you hide your Catholic cloven hooves."

Julien laughed in true delight. "I begin to believe I was a fool not to appreciate you properly when you were young, Lucie. Your tongue and your wits have not faltered."

But beneath his genuine appreciation, Julien could only hope those wits of hers would not delve too deeply into his own secrets.

In just a few days at Blanclair, Lucette had already begun to amass a tidy collection of intelligence. She stored it all carefully away, bit by bit, in her Memory Chamber ledger and didn't try yet to force a pattern. She knew from experience that the pattern would come when it was ready. One trifle, one fact, one overheard remark, would be the tipping point when the chaos became a design centered on a true north point and there could only be one answer to the variable she sought.

The household of Chateau Blanclair was serene on the surface but swirling with unnamed tensions just below. It was as though there were strings run between people, and some of them were pulled so taut as to practically vibrate. Lucette categorized them by colours, the deeper the colour, the more tense the connection: every string running to and from Julien was red, but even Nicolas had a good many blue threads between him and his family members. Renaud watched both his sons with a concealed caution that spoke of concern. The only truly open person in the household was Felix (his threads were all a sunny yellow).

As for the household and outdoor servants, Anise was Lucette's entry point. She could hardly pop into the kitchens or the stables for a friendly conversation (though her Englishness was a convenient mask behind which to hide impertinent questions), but Anise liked to talk and soon Lucette had odd and intriguing bits to store in her ledgers: there was a groom who rode out a great deal more than the others and often spent days away from Blanclair; half the staff had Huguenot relatives who'd fled to England; the steward knew to the penny the state of the Blanclair accounts at any given hour; in the last five years, four maids had quit the household with no notice.

Felix's tutor was someone Lucette could speak to without comment, and she did. With difficulty. Richard Laurent did not like her;

whether because he disliked females on principle or just Protestant Englishwomen, she wasn't clear. Laurent was obviously a committed Catholic and had even studied in a Jesuit seminary. He spent most of his hours with Felix, and though Lucette believed in keeping an open mind, she refused to believe that a seven-year-old was the Nightingale connection Walsingham was searching for. But Laurent himself might be a possibility.

On the fifth day—Sunday—Lucette claimed a headache when it came time for church, and the LeClercs accepted the polite fiction that would keep a Protestant away from a Roman mass. Lucette had little moral issue in attending a Catholic service, in truth she was rather curious, but it was her first time in the house without family and the bulk of the staff. Only a skeleton few were left in the chateau and Lucette drew a deep breath to suppress her ethics and set about searching her hosts' bedchambers.

She began with Renaud, because she might as well do the most uncomfortable first. Logically, she supposed there was no reason her host could not be the Catholic mastermind: he was intelligent, he was dedicated to his kingdom, as a soldier he was accustomed to following orders, and no doubt he could be ruthless. Against the logic was only this: that she could not bear that it be Renaud. He was as honourable a man as Dominic, and she did not want to believe that, having met Elizabeth in person, as Renaud had when visiting England, he would countenance a plan to kill her.

She was not here for emotional reasons, however, but logical ones, so she shoved aside her distaste and searched Renaud's bedchamber and adjoining small study. His were the surroundings of a soldier, such as she was accustomed to from Dominic. Spare without quite being impersonal, nothing cluttered, paperwork neatly ordered and put away. Although Lucette made a quick search of his clothing and bed itself, it was the paperwork she concentrated on. It was mostly personal—no doubt the account books and ledgers would be kept by the steward—but she plowed on through the neat journal that mostly recorded the weather and harvests and cloaked

emotional subjects in the sparest prose. There was a gap of six
months that she calculated was at the time of Nicole LeClerc's
death.

The only thing she would not search was the collection of letters
from Nicole to her husband, kept in their own coffer and tied with
a length of black silk ribbon. Lucette returned everything to its
proper place—that useful visual memory of hers—and tackled Nicolas's chambers next.

For all that he looked like Renaud, Nicolas's surroundings were
much different. Both more luxurious and more careless, as probably
befit one who had not followed his father into the military but spent
his days as a gentleman widower, looking after his son and running
the estate under his father's eye. Anise had elaborated on the image
of Nicolas as entirely broken by the death of his wife and his with-
drawal from Parisian society. He must have loved his young bride
very much to mourn in such determined fashion for such a length of
time. Lucette could not fathom why he had not remarried. But that
thought took her to her unstated reason for being at Blanclair and
she shied away. She did not want to think of Nicolas as a potential
husband. For one thing, she was not Catholic. For another, she
would never settle out of England.

From the carpets on the floors to the tapestries on the walls, from
the brocaded silk of the bed hangings to the whisper soft linen in the
chests, everything about Nicolas proclaimed quality. But his clothes
were folded a degree less precise than Renaud's, the down pillows
were askew on the bed, and the inlaid desk in his personal alcove was
awash in letters and books.

He apparently had a fondness for Italian poetry, judging by the
number of volumes she counted. Catholic writers like Thomas More
jostled for space with Machiavelli's *The Prince* and Dante's *Divine
Comedy*. He, too, had a journal, but it was written in even sparer form
than his father's—often no more than a series of initials and dates
and cryptic notes that Lucette stared at, imprinting in her ledger,
before finally laying the journal aside.

His books were stamped with his personal badge, a silver cinque-foil that Lucette remembered from childhood. Nicole had decreed that each of her sons bear a cinquefoil for a badge—Nicolas in silver for peace and sincerity. He certainly appeared to live a peaceful life.

Unlike Renaud, Nicolas had kept nothing from his wife, unless the St. Catharine's medal she found mixed in with several heavy rings had belonged to her.

She had left Julien for last and wondered if that was because she hoped to be interrupted by the family's return from church. Not the mark of a very good intelligencer, she supposed, and with com-pressed lips and thudding heart hurried about her task.

Of course Julien had spent very little time at Blanclair for years—and not at all since Nicole's death. Anise had overflowed with stories of that scandal: that Julien was summoned from Paris when his mother's condition worsened, but delayed his coming until it was too late. He had arrived in time for the funeral mass, where he sat apart from his family and left abruptly after an hour closeted alone with his father. This was his first visit home since then.

He was messy, no surprise. A jerkin and shirt tossed across the top of a chest, the bedclothes rumpled and untouched by maids. In-teresting. She would have to ask Anise if Julien forbid servants in his chamber, which might argue a desire to avoid prying eyes. Or maybe he just couldn't be bothered. There were books—more lib-eral and humanist than those of Nicolas—that she guessed had been there since he was young. Aside from clothing, the personal effects he'd brought with him from Paris consisted of a string of silverwork beads, a carved wooden soldier that matched the set Lucette had seen in Felix's care, and two exquisite miniatures: his mother and his sister.

No journal. No letters. Not even a sign of his own cinquefoil badge except on the frontspiece of dusty books: his badge blue, for truth and loyalty. There was nothing in the chamber except cryptic clues as to his character and no evidence of deeper conspiracy. If Julien were the Nightingale mastermind, he'd either left any evi-dence in Paris or else he carried it all in his head.

Either way, she wouldn't be able to lay her hands on anything in the way of physical evidence.

She returned to her chamber and, before the family returned from church, wrote a brief note to Paris. This time she created an equation that, when solved for x, gave the number seven. Creating the resultant code in an apparently innocent letter kept her ruthlessly focused on the business at hand, leaving no time for qualms of conscience.

When deciphered, Dr. Dee would read the following message: *The house is full of secrets, none of which may be relevant. I shall look to the village for more information.*

Elizabeth received her daughter in royal state at Hampton Court Palace on the first stage of the court's progress to Portsmouth. Anne arrived by barge to all the fanfare and pomp accorded the Princess of Wales, and as she watched her daughter approach, Elizabeth felt for a moment that if she blinked, she would be the princess presenting herself to the king, her brother . . .

But Elizabeth was a master of time and memory, and she knew perfectly well who she was. Anne made a gracious obeisance and, at her mother's command, drew ahead of her attendants to walk alone with her mother toward the palace.

"You look well," Elizabeth said, and heard an echo of her own youthful impatience at her mother's formality thirty years ago. *Why can we never talk about any but trivialities?* she'd wondered then—and wondered now. And it wasn't simply the conversation. Sometimes she wished that she had not given her mother's name to her heir, for Anne Tudor occasionally manifested the brilliant, biting wit of her grandmother. Not to mention her stubbornness, although that could also be easily explained by either of her parents.

"I am delighted to return to court, my lady mother." Anne always knew to the precise word and shade of tone how to judge her conversations. Today she meant to come near to intimacy.

"I should think so," Elizabeth replied tartly. "Seeing as how you have been hounding me and my ministers for months."

Anne slid her gaze sideways. "It was you who taught me the virtues of judicious pressure applied with a modicum of charm." Her grin, which flashed and vanished, was so redolent of William that Elizabeth nearly faltered.

"Very well," Elizabeth conceded. "We two are here and as alone as we are likely to be anytime soon. Let us speak plainly. You are at court to ensure your father's welcome and ease the discomfort of our divorce. Philip will want to assure himself of your health and education and, no doubt, the firmness of your religious sentiments. You know as well as I do that your father's first order of business upon leaving England will be to remarry. He has no heir for Spain as long as you remain firmly Protestant and firmly in England. Encourage him, Anne, to marry quickly. It will be to your advantage."

"To have a royal stepmother?" she asked lightly. "Perhaps. And you, Mother? Shall I soon be required to endure a royal stepfather?"

"Don't be impertinent. I am wed to England, and always have been. That is why my marriage to Philip has faltered—no man can endure a rival."

"And what of my marriage, Your Majesty?" Nicely judged use of her title, for Anne knew that her marriage would be decided by the monarch and not the mother.

"I am pleased with how you have begun your correspondence with James. I will be pleased if it continues in the same vein. Equally, there will be more than one English noble in our entourage to meet Philip who might be seen as a possible domestic match for you."

"Francis Huntingdon and Robert Devereux."

"Naturally. As well as the soon-to-be-invested Earl of Leicester, Brandon Dudley."

Anne stopped walking abruptly. Elizabeth did not. The Queen of England did not alter her stride or her destinations for anyone. She counted to twelve before Anne caught up with her once more, this time with an attitude edging toward insubordination.

"I am not going to marry Brandon Dudley, Mother."

Or perhaps throwing herself right off the edge into absolute in-subordination. "You will do as you are told," Elizabeth said coldly.

"I apologize, Your Majesty." Anne knew how to pull herself back. "I meant to say that I cannot envision the political advantage of matching the Princess of Wales with a newly made noble. Particularly one born in the Tower, and whose father and grandfather both met their ends at the hands of a royal executioner."

"You must learn to see the wider view, daughter, and not simply details. Brandon Dudley will make people nervous, particularly your father. That makes him useful in this context without any commitment to a final outcome."

"Are you trying to make people nervous," Anne asked with low intensity, "or are you trying to re-create your own past? You know people say that Brandon only flourishes because of his resemblance to his uncle Robert. Is it wise to give further ammunition to such rumours?"

No one spoke to Elizabeth of Robert Dudley—absolutely no one. "That is enough. You will behave with impeccable courtesy to every member of my court and will not presume to tell me what is wise."

She knew that particularly intent look on her daughter's face meant she was thinking furiously. Philip looked the same when he was about to propose something unexpected.

With perfect humility, Anne curtsied. "I am, as always, yours to command. My lady mother, I would never presume to know more than you, but may I make a request?"

"You may ask."

"If your intent is to unsettle the king, my father, and give room for all manner of speculation throughout Europe as to my future marriage, then I would suggest one more addition to the royal party."

"And that would be?"

Anne met her gaze steadily. "I want Kit."

"Christopher Courtenay?" Elizabeth barked a laugh. "I hardly think a second son would be considered a serious contender for your hand."

"The second son of England's wealthiest duke, and with the closest of personal ties to the throne. Besides, I rather thought you were fond of Kit."

Elizabeth was very fond of Kit Courtenay. Precisely because he was so little like his father. Stephen Courtenay was exactly what one would wish for in an eldest son and future duke—steady, serious, and contemplative—in other words, a perfect mirror of Dominic. But Kit . . . ah, Kit Courtenay was Minuette reborn. Tumbled blond hair, laughing hazel eyes, and charm enough to spare.

It was precisely for those reasons that Elizabeth did not want Kit Courtenay tied, even obliquely, to her daughter as a possible mate. That would never do.

But beneath her discomfort and dislike of being manipulated, Elizabeth grudgingly conceded Anne's point. Also, it would keep her daughter amenable, which was not a gift to be overlooked.

"I suppose, as Philippa Courtenay is wherever you are, that we might as well include her twin."

Anne smiled, and it was so like her grandmother that Elizabeth nearly shuddered. Anne Boleyn had looked just as unnerving when she'd got her way. "Thank you, Your Majesty. I promise to give you no cause to regret that decision this summer."

Only later did Elizabeth remember the subtle emphasis on the last two words.

EIGHT

Nicolas's customary life at Blanclair since 1572 had been one of solitude and contemplation. Not a natural state, and one to which he had only disciplined himself from sheer necessity. He had become a reader these last years, though he knew himself for only a dilettante scholar. Though he could still ride and hunt and hawk, he'd found less pleasure in physical activities after St. Bartholomew's Day. Each one served in some way as a reminder of what he'd lost.

With Julien in residence this summer, at least Felix stopped pressing him to come to the practice yard. With Julien in residence, the child paid not the least attention to his father.

That was hardly a new experience. Julien had always been the more engaging of the two, the more openhearted, the more likely to make friends. It hadn't bothered Nicolas when they were younger because he had plenty of companions of his own and ways to pass the time. After Paris, there had been several very bad years, but then Nicolas woke up to his new life and found new means of entertaining himself.

And now here was Lucette, going out of her way, it seemed, to entertain him.

In her second week at Blanclair, Nicolas spent part of each day with her. What might have been merely a chore was actually something close to a pleasure. If only this were before Paris, he might have seriously considered proposing to her. He could never entirely predict what she would say or how she would respond, and after eight years spent with so few people, Nicolas took great delight in the unexpected.

On Thursday the sixteenth of June, Nicolas invited his son to ride with him and Lucette on an afternoon excursion. The boy could hardly contain his excitement, only slightly dampened when informed that his uncle Julien had work to do and would not be accompanying them. (Nicolas knew that work of his brother's would involve being shut up in his chamber writing mysterious letters to mysterious people for a mysterious purpose. Though not so mysterious to Nicolas.)

"Very well," Lucette said with spirit as they rode out of Blanclair, "where is this surprise tour taking us today?"

Felix looked to his father to confirm, and Nicolas nodded once. With a near-shout of joy, Felix burst out, "We're taking you to Fleury Abbey!"

Nicolas didn't know why he was so excited. Though, with Lucette to ride next to, Felix would probably have taken similar joy in simply circling the stables for several hours.

The purpose of the afternoon wasn't really the abbey, though Nicolas was never less than perfectly prepared and had a host of stories with which to entertain her. The purpose was to insinuate himself further into Lucette's graces, and to glean as much about her family and England as she could be manipulated into sharing.

It was only four miles to the abbey—a distance they could easily have walked—but the brief ride was enlivened by Lucette's intelligent questions and seemingly genuine interest in their destination. Nicolas told their guest of the founding of the Benedictine abbey, and of how the bones of St. Benedict himself had been brought there in the seventh century from Monte Cassino.

"That's how the abbey and the town got its name," Nicolas pointed out. "St. Benedict on the Loire," he pronounced in careful English. Then again in French, "Much of the building is Romanesque, but there was a good deal of damage inflicted by the Huguenots in 1562. Still, it is true that England's abbeys suffered destruction on a far greater scale," he ventured, willing to prick her Protestant heart a bit.

"So they did," she agreed. "It is a pity that beauty cannot be considered safe from sectarian violence. Still, better to lose art and architecture than lives. England at least has not had religious massacres."

And clearly she was willing to prick right back. Nicolas inclined his head in acknowledgment of the hit and changed the subject. "I understand your parents are at court just now. An unusual event, as I recall."

"Yes."

"And your siblings?" Though he knew perfectly well where all three of them were.

"Stephen is at Tutbury, with Queen Mary Stuart. Kit and Pippa are also at court with my parents."

"But principally in attendance on the Princess of Wales, no? I remember how close the three of them were, even as little children. I could never be certain who was the most mischievous—your brother Kit, or Princess Anne."

That wrung a smile from her. "They incite each other in the worst way. At least Pippa is levelheaded enough to keep them from the worst excesses."

"And do you think it a good idea that the princess is kept so separated from her own father?" Nicolas didn't really know where he was going with this line of questioning. He trusted that anything Lucette said of importance would make itself known.

For some reason, this last question displeased her. With a slight

stiffening, Lucette replied, "Fathers and daughters are always complicated. Who can say if their relationship might not be the better
for the distance?"

He lapsed into silence after that, allowing Lucette to draw Felix
into delighted conversation. He could not care less about Anne Tudor's relationship to her father, except insofar as her birth made her
valuable. And because of that value, the princess would always be
closely guarded. The man who could manipulate the nature of that
guard . . . that man would hold a critical piece of European power in
the balance.

They made a quick tour of Fleury's highlights: the eleventh-
century Tour de Gauzlin, the square tower built by the abbot who
was also a bastard son of King Hugh Capet; the Gothic north portal
with its black pointed arch and stunning reliefs; the spacious sanctu-
ary with its Roman mosaic floor in polychromatic marble; and the
tomb of King Philip I and the shrine of St. Benedict himself.

On the return ride, Nicolas dropped all politics and history and
simply made himself agreeable to Lucette. He might not have used
those skills on a lady like herself for many years, but he had not forgotten. His charm was not as natural as Julien's, but it sufficed to
bring colour to her cheeks and no doubt remind her that she had
once thought him the very pinnacle of male perfection.

That she had been ten years old then hardly mattered—he knew
how to play on a woman's emotions.

But all that playing left him in an uncomfortably aroused state.
When they returned to the chateau, he ate alone at a small round
table in his bedchamber, then wrote two letters for his personal
groom to hand deliver to Paris. After midnight, when he was sure
the household was mostly sleeping, he sent for Anise.

The girl was country-pretty with her fresh skin and natural figure. Nicolas had anticipated her assignment to attend Lucette and
begun cultivating her several weeks in advance. Now the maid was
all too ready to gossip between kisses. About Lucette's curiosity.
About her questions concerning the family . . . but mostly Julien.

And most intriguingly, about the casket Lucette kept in the bottom of her trunk. Anise had been frankly shocked to discover it contained a dagger. Nicolas had been less shocked.

The maid would be useful for a time. And when she wasn't? Nicolas had ways of ridding himself of women who got too near.

19 June 1580
Hampton Court

We leave the day after tomorrow for Portsmouth to await the Spanish. I would prefer not to make the trip, since all will return here soon enough, but Elizabeth has asked me to come. For her sake. "I had to go to Philip without you when I married him," she said plaintively. "Because Stephen was an infant at the time," I retorted, but she had wrung my heart and so I agreed.

Just as well to keep an eye on the twins—or really, to keep an eye on Kit. Pippa was born wise, a trait she surely did not inherit from me. And also I will go for Anabel's sake, though she has not asked me. She is high-strung, like her mother, and vulnerable, like her uncle. I have loved her dearly from her birth, and if my presence in the background is a comfort, I am happy to provide it.

Besides, it will keep me from fretting about my older children. Lucie has written only twice since leaving Dover, dutiful letters that break my heart with their courtesy. I have written to her, of course, but I have also written to Renaud, asking him to use his judgment and perhaps speak to my daughter of the pain she has carried since Elizabeth gave her that damned necklace of Tudor roses.

Stephen writes more often and warmly, but no less evasively than Lucie. Whatever he is truly doing at Tutbury, I do not think it confined to playing gracious attendant to Mary Stuart. Whenever I see Walsingham at court, I eye him balefully and wonder what games he is up to with my son.

Life was much simpler when I was the one conspiring with

powerful men and women. But then, I knew everything when I was twenty. Don't we all?

Julien was finding it seductively easy to enjoy himself at Blanclair and forget about the many balls he traditionally juggled in Paris. Another reason not to come home, his professional mind scolded. But since he was here—and, as far as the Catholics were concerned, on legitimate business—he let himself be lulled into the pleasures of a simple life. Family, home, gardens and horses, swordplay and swimming with Felix. They were headed to the river for the last when Renaud delayed his second son.

"A word, Julien?"

His hesitation was, he hoped, unnoticed. "Of course. Felix, I'll meet you in the Sun Garden in a quarter hour." He was relieved when his father did not correct the timing; he could endure anything for a quarter hour.

When had his father's company become something to be endured?

Renaud seemed to be asking himself the same question, for once they were in his study, he began, "You should come home more often. Blanclair has been a livelier place this summer."

"I'm flattered that you think me the reason, but surely all the credit goes to Lucette."

And just like that, his father had gotten him to speak of her. Julien could see from Renaud's expression that he was satisfied, and perhaps also wary. "I know you agreed to come for Charlotte's sake, but to all appearances you are glad enough to stay for Lucette's sake."

This could get dangerous very quickly. Julien picked his way with care. "She is engaging in her English way."

"Since when do we speak to each other in such formal terms, Julien? I have never seen you look at a woman the way you look at her. I would like very much to be glad of it, if only I am assured your interest is serious."

"Isn't that a question *her* father should be posing?"

"I stand here in his place, as you perfectly well know. I don't know entirely why Lucette agreed to come here—nor do her parents. But we all suspect it was not her sole purpose to snare a husband. Still, if you are serious about her, then I would caution you to be certain of her feelings before proceeding further. She most definitely has a mind of her own."

"Why, Father, are you worried about a mere girl hurting my pride? How very strange. I can take care of myself, thank you. But your concern is noted."

"Is it? Then add to my concerns the fact that Nicolas is also eyeing her with more interest than is wise. If you're only trying to torment him, using Lucette, then don't. I do not want her caught between the two of you trying to best the other. Is that clear?"

"I promise not to mix up Nicolas and Lucette. I think I can keep my intentions toward each straight in my mind."

Unfortunately for Felix, Julien's mood had been spoiled by his father's warnings. The poor boy kept trying to engage his uncle in his water horseplay, but Julien could not stop thinking of Nicolas and his interest in Lucette. That could not come to a good end, for anyone. And was it fair for Julien to take advantage of his brother's misfortune, when that misfortune lay at his very own feet?

After a half hour in the river Felix gave up and the two of them threw on shirts and breeches soon made damp, hair tousled dry by rough linen. Julien repented his abstracted mood and, in a sudden fit of playfulness, tackled the boy into the high grass. "You're it," he called, then took off running.

Felix bolted after him like a colt, and Julien took care to be caught now and again. Thus laughing and damp, they ran into the low-bordered rose garden and straight into Lucette.

She was reading a letter, and shot to her feet, dropping the pages. Julien stopped dead, staring like an idiot. Only Felix kept his composure, gathering the pages and returning them with a bow.

"*Pardon, mademoiselle*," he said. "You will forgive our appearance, but we have been swimming."

"Yes, I see," she said, that telltale flush colouring her cheeks.

Julien swallowed. How could he not think of anything to say? Being quick with his tongue was his stock-in-trade. Finally, he managed to stammer out, "News from home?"

"Mmmm."

He knew that noncommittal sound—he'd made use of it plenty. It meant one did not want to answer the question.

Once again Felix was quicker than his uncle. With a worried tilt of his head, he said, "Are you quite well? You look . . ." He trailed off politely. Even at seven years old, a Frenchman knew better than to utter anything but compliments about a lady's appearance.

Lucette did look distracted. Flushed, as he'd already noted. And as though she could not look him in the eye.

"I am not feeling well," she said. "I believe I have a sick headache coming on. Perhaps I'll retire now and miss dinner. I'm sure a good rest will see me better tomorrow."

She threw a general, determined smile in their direction before retreating rapidly. Julien's wits began working in direct proportion to her increasing distance, and so did his cynicism.

You're lying, Lucie, he thought. Whatever the reason for locking yourself in your chamber tonight, it is not because of a headache.

The Spanish ships anchored in Portsmouth on June twenty-fourth, a day of near-Mediterranean sunshine and a freshening breeze that blew the sea-salt scent to where Anabel stood on an open balcony of her grandfather's Southsea Castle. In a few minutes she would be expected to appear at her mother's side to welcome King Philip, but for now she let her heart be tugged toward the impressive ships and bright Spanish colours. It was the nearest to sentiment she could allow herself, for it would not do to show weakness in the coming days.

She could feel Pippa two steps behind her, Kit silently at his twin's side. Kit wasn't often silent, but he knew how to choose his moments, and more than anyone on this earth her two dearest friends knew how Anabel had longed as a child for her father's presence.

In her eighteen years, she had passed less than a thousand days total with Philip, some of that when she'd been just an infant. Since then the King of Spain had made only two protracted visits to his English wife and daughter—in 1570 and 1575. Looking back, Anabel could recognize that both those visits had less to do with her and more to do with attempts to breed another child, but she'd been too delighted when young not to believe Philip's sole interest in England was his daughter.

Usually it was Pippa who said the instinctively right thing, but today Kit approached her and said softly from just over her shoulder, "I feel sorry for him, Anabel. His Majesty of Spain is about to be confronted with the most beautiful princess in Europe. The shock of what he cannot regain will be, I imagine, very painful."

Anabel reached back with her left hand and Kit grasped it, quick and reassuring. "Time to go, Your Highness," he murmured, and Anabel turned away from the ships and braced herself for the game that was about to begin.

For once, her mother had waited for her before entering the hall. She flicked a glance over Anabel—from hair dressed intricately at the crown, then falling loosely down her back to the blue and silver gown edged with pearls—and nodded once.

"Adequate," Elizabeth pronounced, then nodded to the steward that they were ready.

Elizabeth herself wore a cloth-of-gold gown studded with gems, a cartridge-pleated ruff so stiff and wide her head seemed entirely separate from her body. It was a dress meant both to proclaim her position and reinforce her solitude. It was the dress of a queen meeting the king of a not-entirely friendly nation, not that of a wife reuniting with her husband.

Kit and Pippa had already joined the crowd, and Anabel felt a moment's piercing solitude as she followed her mother to the two thrones side by side—one beneath the colours of England, the other beneath the arms of Spain—and the slightly plainer chair with curved arms set defiantly at the queen's side.

They did not sit, yet, for it would be another quarter hour before the Spanish arrived, and Elizabeth kept her close as she conversed with the Earl of Shrewsbury and Sir William Paulet. Anabel would have preferred her own circle, but was this not what she had been pressing for—to be at the center of court life? She could hardly complain about getting what she wanted.

At a signal from the attendants, Elizabeth proceeded to her throne, where she stood for a moment—not so much studying the crowd as allowing herself to be studied. With a graceful movement, she sat, and Anabel gratefully took her own seat. She was cross to discover that she was trembling.

Not exactly a private family reunion, though those invited to witness it were few, only three dozen of the court's most important. (Besides Kit and Pippa, whom even Elizabeth rarely tried to exclude, as though she also thought of the three of them as a single unit.)

And then the doors at the far end were opened and Lord Burghley preceded the Spanish entourage.

Anabel's first impression was that Philip had aged more rapidly than Elizabeth, though logically she knew it was only that she had seen him so infrequently. Considered objectively, Philip was an upright figure, unmistakably royal in bearing apart from the understated luxury of his deep black clothing. His light brown hair, once noticeably tinged with red, was now sprinkled liberally with white, but not to his detriment. He had the same mustache and pointed beard she had always known, and she had to bite down hard to keep tears from forming.

She did not, of course, come first. Where another father might impulsively swing into his arms a daughter he hadn't seen in five years, this was a family of royals. Her father did fix his eyes on her as he came up the hall, and she flashed him the briefest of smiles.

Then Elizabeth stood, in a nicely judged piece of theater, and took the last two steps to greet her husband. "You are most welcome, Your Majesty."

Philip gave a low bow and his English was perfectly serviceable. "It is my great pleasure to return to England, Your Majesty."

As her parents faced off, both clever and calculating and forever wary of each other, Anabel knew that she would do everything in her power to keep from being married to a king. She did not want a marriage of balanced equals, always pushing against each other for the advantage. Better to marry a man who would owe everything to her, for then at least there would be a chance of personal affection—or at least a good imitation of it.

Then it was her turn. She had stood, naturally, when her mother did. Now her father stepped to her and gently lifted her hand to his lips. "*Cielita,*" he said, "I have counted the hours until this day for many years. My heart could not be happier."

As a royal princess born, Anabel knew how to accommodate two states of being at once. Just now there was an undeniable burst of little girl pleasure that her father loved her. But that did not discount the calculation that was as much a part of her parents' legacy as her hair or eye colour.

Philip felt guilty at his years of absence. And a father who felt guilty might be manipulated into giving more than he meant to.

NINE

Even a husband and wife on the brink of divorce, and who had spent many more years apart than together, could be expected to withdraw into privacy. Elizabeth kept Philip waiting until evening, when the reception festivities and feasting were finished, when Anne had bid her father goodnight with a mix of little-girl longing and womanly wariness. She had her ladies remove the elaborate court gown and dress her in something simpler, a loose Spanish gown of navy silk left open to show the blue and white kirtle beneath. Then she made herself comfortable in the privy chamber decorated for her use, sent her ladies away, and waited for her husband.

Philip had also changed, she noted when he bowed to her on the threshold of the open door. His attire was as nicely judged as her own, between casual and familiar, which did not surprise her. She could never have married, let alone remain married this long, to a man who she did not respect.

When he stepped into the chamber, the door was politely

closed from outside and the two of them faced each other alone for the first time in five years.

"You are truly looking well, Elizabeth," Philip said. "It was not simply courtesy when I said it before."

"Would it be rude if I mentioned that you look a little tired?"

The ghost of a smile that came and went so fast as to be almost missed. "I am the one who has had the burden of travel. As I always have through the years of our marriage."

And that slight sting was perhaps the most attractive feature of her husband—for not many men in this world could speak to her like that. She arched an eyebrow with feigned disapproval. "I was not aware that you ever wished me to visit Spain. It's one thing to have married a heretic bastard queen—quite another to force your people to accept me in person. I thought you liked me at one remove."

"We are both easier, perhaps, with a silent partner rather than the complications of a daily partnership."

Except it wasn't a partnership, and never truly had been. In Spain, Elizabeth would be nothing more than the barely tolerated Protestant wife of their Catholic monarch, as likely to be assassinated as welcomed. And in England, Philip fared little better. No one had tried to kill him, but he'd only ever received grudging acceptance. England had a long history of disliking foreign royal spouses. There had never been a question of Philip receiving the crown matrimonial, such as the wives of kings did, and Elizabeth admitted there was little to tempt her husband in this country. Save herself, and their daughter.

And now, after twenty years, those temptations were no longer enough.

She waved her courteous spouse to a chair. "Do we begin the end of marriage wrangling tonight?" she asked. "The discussions of Anne's future husband?"

"That is not why I came. There will be time enough for necessities in the days ahead. Tonight, I thought, we might simply talk to each other. As we used to do, in the first weeks of our marriage."

Damn the man. Philip was not a charmer, not careless in bestowing affection—in short, nothing in the least like Robert Dudley had
been—but there was no denying that their marriage had been more
than business. Never easy, never simple, never uncomplicated . . . but
none the less vital for all that.

"And what," Elizabeth said with a tartness that Philip would be
able to read as affection, "shall we talk about if not business?"

Philip had several different smiles. The one he gave her now she
wagered only a handful of women in his lifetime had been privy to.
Elizabeth felt a flash of jealousy as she wondered what woman would
have the benefit of that smile in the coming months and years, then
quashed it. "You are my wife," Philip said softly, "and the mother of
my only living child. You might try simply sharing your burdens with
me. Not your royal burdens, but your personal ones."

I am tired, she considered saying. *I worry about Anabel all the time—is she
safe, is she happy, will she ever understand why I do what I do in her interests? How
can I make her strong enough to bear the burden she will one day have as queen?
There is nothing I will not do for my daughter . . . or for England.*

And that was why she said nothing. Because there was nothing in
her life that was not political.

As if he could read the reasons for her reluctance—as perhaps he
could after so many years—Philip took her hands in his and said
softly, "Or we need not speak at all. Some of the finest moments of
our marriage have been entirely wordless."

With his fingertips, he caressed her skin from palm to wrist, teasing touches that were both familiar and arousing. Philip had always
known what to do with his hands, she remembered. Not every moment of their marriage, as he'd said, had been political. For a heart-
beat of piercing pain, Elizabeth felt the loss of never again being
touched by a man.

But one could not go back. Withdrawing her hands from his,
Elizabeth said cautiously, "It is not unpleasant to have your company
one last time. You have been a friend to England when most we
needed it. I hope that friendship will continue."

His expression darkened briefly, for no man and for certain no monarch liked rejection. "My daughter shall always have my friendship. But you must know that Spain's interests continue to diverge from England's with each passing year in which you keep your people from the comfort of the Church."

Five minutes—that's all it took for personal concerns to become political. "I think," Elizabeth said, "that this is enough for now. No doubt we have plenty to say to each other in council with others. If it were likely that we should agree on these points, then I don't suppose this visit would end with a divorce."

Philip stood, a righteous sorrow evident on his still handsome face. "I am sorry for it," he said simply. "I hope you will not object to my spending time with my daughter, at least?"

Her own smile was a thing of frosty power. "No objection at all. You will find Anne quite capable of defending her own positions without my aid. Goodnight, Philip."

Not a bow this time, but an incline of the head and the familiar calculation had returned to his expression. "Goodnight, Elizabeth. Tomorrow, the end begins."

And not a moment too soon, she finished for him.

Julien's worry about Lucette's lies vanished the moment he reached his chamber still damp from the river. A courier had brought him a letter from Paris, anonymous in the address, but in a handwriting he knew instantly.

In a code that Julien could decipher almost by instinct, Cardinal Ribault had written: *There will be a man at the tavern of the Nightingale Inn tonight to receive your report. Be there by midnight.*

"Damn it," he said under his breath, and crumpled the message in one hand.

He had no idea what he would report. The truth? *My conversations with Lucette Courtenay have been challenging and engaging and about every subject under the sun except her connection to the English royal family.* Hardly. He would have to lie, which was no great issue. He had done little but lie to the cardinal for seven years now.

He might have encountered difficulty in getting out of the chateau unseen, but Lucette's retreat to her chambers made things easy. Without a guest to entertain, the men of the LeClerc family reverted to type: the meal was mostly silent and they all scattered as soon as they decently could. Julien waited until well after dark and set off on foot to the village tavern. No need to alert anyone to his absence by rousing a groom or taking a horse. Dressed in subdued fashion, a cloak despite the June weather, in order to offer some concealment to his sword, he trudged to the village and thought about Lucette.

All he'd done for days now was think about Lucette—no, Lucie. Lucette was suspicious and restrained and did not like him at all. Lucie, on the other hand . . . Lucie laughed. Lucie teased. Lucie was no less intelligent than Lucette, but she wasn't defined solely by her mind, and inhabited her body in an entirely different way.

Not that he should be paying attention to her body.

When Julien reached the Nightingale Inn, he still didn't have the slightest idea what he intended to tell the cardinal's emissary. Good thing he was used to thinking on his feet.

He couldn't be anonymous here the way he could in Paris, but the people of the village knew enough about him to read his moods— either entertain me or, as today, leave me be. Aside from a nod from the tavern keeper, Julien made his way to a corner table and waited for the emissary to come to him. It was easy enough to pick him out—he might have been in exile in France but Englishmen moved differently than Frenchmen. The man was bearded and fiercely mustached, with a scar running across the back of his right hand.

The emissary turned a chair around and straddled it, arms resting on the chair back. *"Monsieur,"* he said in a hoarse voice that made Julien wonder in which gutter the cardinal had picked him up.

"Orders?" Julien asked softly.

"To tell me what you've learned of the girl."

Julien leaned back and stretched, hands clasped behind his head, his pose of ease covering a mind working furiously.

"She's unlikely to be of any real use," he said negligently. "Queen's niece or not, the girl is not a royal intimate. I'd say it's by her own choice," and as he spoke, Julien felt it to be true. As though putting Lucette into words helped him understand her. "She" (for he could not bring himself to use her name to such a slimy man) "is unwilling to be used by anyone, friend or family, and surely the English queen is too intelligent to think otherwise."

"That is not what you were asked to discover," the man said. "Surely she communicates with her sister, who is such an intimate of the young princess."

"I have no news on that score," Julien said bluntly. "Whatever the princess's plans this summer, they have not, to my knowledge, been communicated to my guest."

"How hard have you tried to learn?" The man's very tone was a leer, and Julien wanted to smash his face.

Instead, he leaned across the table and said, "I don't know how it's done in your world, but gentlemen do not take advantage of young women of good family."

"But by all accounts, *monsieur,* you are by no means a gentleman."

Julien swung his gaze away, furious, and made himself survey the tavern simply to give his mind something to do. No, he wasn't a gentleman and hadn't been for years. A gentleman would not be having this conversation. A gentleman would not have quite so thorough knowledge of the intimate habits of every maid in this tavern. There was Madeleine with her tumble of red hair, and Sophie who giggled when kissed, and Blanche with her exceptionally skilled hands.

There had been a time when Nicolas would have been the one to know (in every sense) these women, but Julien had picked up his brother's habits in an effort at staving off guilt. As though by following in Nicolas's footsteps he could undo what had been done to his brother.

And then his uncomfortable thoughts stuttered and stopped as his eyes skimmed over something that caught his attention. He slowly moved his gaze back, tracking, and stopped dumbfounded at a table in the corner farthest from him. It was occupied by two men and a woman. A woman in plain skirts and low-cut linen, dark hair braided tightly to her head beneath a cap, eyes modestly lowered while no doubt her brain ran along five times faster than the idiots she was listening to.

Lucette.

Pride might be a sin, but Lucette was undoubtedly proud of how she'd managed tonight. Anise had been heaven-sent as her maid, for the girl was all too easy to persuade to lend her clothing, and vowed to maintain the fiction that the Englishwoman was confined to her chambers with illness. Lucette also knew (thanks to Felix) the less traveled corridors of the chateau and the side gate through which she could pass at a distance from Renaud's men at arms and not be spotted.

It was only two miles to the inn, and Lucette passed the time not, as she should, in preparing for what lay ahead, but in uncomfortable dwelling on this afternoon. Uncomfortable because she had completely lost her head and her ready tongue the moment she'd seen Julien with a damp shirt clinging to his chest, hair tousled as though he'd just risen from his bed.

We have been swimming, Felix had announced, as though she could not see that perfectly well for herself. She had brothers—she knew men swam without any clothes—but having Julien stand so near her without the armor of doublet and stockings, brocade and silk, had given her far too vivid an impression of the body beneath the linen shirt and low-slung breeches. So she had flushed to her hairline, stuttered like a girl, and run away as soon as Felix unwittingly gave her a way out.

But once fled to her chamber, easy enough to put in motion the plan that had been swirling in her head for several days.

Before she knew it, the village appeared and the very first inn tavern that Lucette had ever entered alone. That did require a few deep breaths and a stern reminder that she knew what she was doing. (That latter phrase mostly thrown defiantly at Dominic's imagined disapproval. Somehow, she thought her mother might understand and, if not approve, at least find it amusing.) The carved sign in the shape of a nightingale steadied her nerves, reminding her as it did of the seriousness of her purpose. As well as the likelihood of finding something provocative in a place that might well be the namesake of Walsingham's suspected plot.

The difficulty in blending into the tavern crowd, Lucette quickly found, would be her voice. And her posture. And her white hands. She was a quick study, though, and after a half hour spent lurking in the shadowy corner, felt safe enough to drift around the room, ears open.

But it wasn't her ears men were interested in. Lucette had thought herself prepared to be leered at, but she quickly learned that these sorts of men did not confine themselves to leering. They were free with both their hands and their comments, and she had to keep re- minding herself that here she was neither the acknowledged daugh- ter of the Duke of Exeter nor the unacknowledged niece of the Queen of England, and thus could not afford to be outraged at the liberties.

She had decided she didn't dare pass as French, so Lucette made herself into Ellen, a half-English orphan trying to get back to her mother's Catholic family in Provence. As long as she allowed a hand to wander every now and then, she found men willing to talk about the LeClerc family.

The general tenor of the community was respect for Renaud and a deep and genuine liking of his late wife. Lucette heard more than one reference to Nicole's kindness, her care for individuals regard- less of position or—interesting in this valley—religion. There had been violence in the area (Lucette had seen that for herself at Fleury) and death, but not the wholesale slaughter seen in other communities. "Blanclair wouldn't stand for it," was a phrase she heard more than once.

As for the younger members of the family, Julien was spoken of fondly as a youth, more outgoing and easy in his camaraderie than his older brother. Nicolas, for all that he'd spent the last eight years at the chateau, was spoken of more warily. Respect, she supposed, but not as instinctive as that given Renaud. There was a general sense that he'd shut himself up since his wife's death, and the same wondering Lucette had: why had he not remarried?

One of the traveling men pronounced, half-drunkenly, "Could be taking a single wife for honour's sake was enough. Mayhap he prefers boys."

There was a burst of laughter at that. "No, no." One of the villagers slapped him on the back. "Nicolas LeClerc was wild for the girls since he was a lad. In and out of more beds in the area than any six men combined. No, if he's not married again, it's for a damn good reason. Maybe there's a fortune says he has to remain widowed to lay his hands on it."

"Maybe he loved his wife," Lucette ventured. This did not draw the same outburst of loud laughter, but she had the definite sense of amusement at her naïveté.

As the night tipped toward the witching hours, Lucette began to grow dizzy. No doubt a result of the fug of smoke and the ale and no food and trying to keep her head and speak like someone who didn't personally know the Queen of England. She had just decided to escape back to the chateau and hopefully clear her head on the way when Julien walked in.

Lucette froze. Had he learned of her absence, tracked her down? But she realized almost at once that Julien had no idea she was here. She assumed he must have looked the room over, but she had her head tucked down so far her chin was on her chest. When she dared peek, she saw that he had settled himself at a private table that no one interrupted until a most disreputable man confidently sat down across from him.

She was torn between sneaking out and watching the encounter. Surely this was evidence—for what legitimate purpose could Julien LeClerc be meeting with a man like that in a tavern? Finally she decided to wait for Julien to leave and then tackle the unsavory man herself.

She never got the chance. On her next quick peek to the corner, Julien was looking straight at her, horror writ large on his face.

She stepped away from the table so hurriedly that she upset her chair. Julien reached her in five strides and gripped her arm above the elbow.

"Hey, now!" One of the merchants she'd been talking to protested. "Hands off, she was ours first."

Julien glared down at him, eyes blazing, and, through the haze of drink, the man recognized the lord of the manor. Julien's cultured voice didn't hurt, either. "I think I'll exercise my *droit de seigneur*," he said cuttingly, and pulled Lucette after him out the tavern door into the inn yard.

"What do you think you're doing?" She jerked her arm away and turned on him, half furious and half humiliated.

"You're welcome," Julien retorted with elaborate insult. "Those men do not care who your father is. All they saw was a likely wench who was in way over her head."

With her arm free, Lucette reached behind her back and had her bodice dagger out of its concealment beneath her waistband and in Julien's face before he could insult her further. "I know what I'm doing," she said, hating that she felt so fuzzy. "I was not over my head."

He eyed the tip of the dagger, eyes nearly crossed, then smiled that seductive, mocking grin of his youth that she'd hated. "Where, Lucie mine, did you learn to wield a dagger so handily?"

Lucie mine. He had spoken the endearment in English.

Without moving it away, she said, "My father does not trust men with his daughters. He required us to be able to defend ourselves."

From somewhere below the fuzziness of her brain and the sinking hollow of her stomach, she realized she'd used the word *father*.

"A wise man," Julien said.

"A dangerous man." Finally she let the dagger drop, her hand feeling suddenly too heavy to hold up. "And don't worry about the tavern, those men didn't know me, they thought I was . . ." She hesitated over the description.

He smiled grimly. "You think you can disguise your nature with a little paint and none-too-clean skirts? Not in a thousand lifetimes could you ever pass for a . . ." It was his turn to hesitate, unsure how to proceed, which Lucette found amusing considering his Paris reputation.

"A whore." She said it for him. "Men will say things around a whore that they won't around a lady."

"Damn right they will, and not a word of it do you want to hear. If my father finds out where you were—"

"He'd be angry."

"He'd be furious! But if *your* father knew? Your extremely dangerous father who makes his daughters carry daggers? If Dominic Courtenay hears of this, he will hunt me the length and breadth of Europe and string me up like a dog!"

"This is nothing to do with you." *But isn't it?* For the most useful thing she'd learned all night was that Julien was meeting unlikely men in out-of-the-way places. Suggestive, at the least.

"Fine. If you're so determined to play the whore, then allow me to give you some advice."

Julien stepped into her space and Lucette refused to back away, though she was very conscious of his nearness. And even more conscious of the bristle of beard on his chin, the sharp plane of his collarbone, the solidity of his arms and chest. He extended a hand and laid it on her cheek. It took all her control not to flinch.

"Whores are cold creatures, Lucette. They're in business, and though they may play the wanton, the only emotion that is ever truly roused is greed. You have no pretense in you. You are too warm and too honest and too . . ."

Her cheeks burned with the words and with the way he looked at her. He leaned in to whisper in her ear. "Whores do not blush." His hand stroked down her cheek to her throat, which fluttered with each catch of her breath. "Their breathing is always even . . ." His hand dipped farther, resting on the swell of her breast above her neckline. ". . . and their hearts do not beat faster with desire."

Why was she so dizzy? Certainly not because of Julien. Not at all. She stepped away from his hand, so much more intimate than the strangers who had touched her tonight, and tried to think of something dignified to say. But the dizziness was growing worse, her ears were ringing and her head would not stay up and . . .

Down she went.

There followed a terribly long time of alternating dizziness and blackness and, most humiliating of all, vomiting. Or she would have been humiliated if she hadn't been consumed by how awful she felt. She didn't really become aware of her surroundings until she felt Julien going up steps, with her in his arms, and realized they were back at Blanclair.

Instinctively she squirmed to break free, but Julien said, "Don't be stupid, Lucie. I'm taking you to bed."

"But I'm too sick for that." Only dimly did she realize what she'd said when she heard Julien choke back a laugh.

"I may not be gentleman enough not to take advantage of a beautiful woman, but I do like my women to be conscious. You're safe with me."

Yes, she thought, as the blackness slithered back for her, Julien will keep me safe.

TEN

"So, Philip and the Spanish are in Portsmouth," Mary Stuart mused to her confessor, who had brought the news from the south. "And by the time they sail away, my dear cousin will no longer have a husband."

She felt an exultation she worked hard to conceal. It would not do to let slip her excitement at what the coming weeks would bring. By summer's end, there would be more changes in Europe's royal landscape than simply the Queen of England's divorce. As long as everyone kept their word and their heads, the game would be shaken into a completely new form. Mary could hardly wait.

Her confessor said, "It will be useful to hear other perspectives on the Spanish visit than our own. No doubt the young Lord Somerset will receive letters from his family. His younger siblings are exceptionally close to Princess Anne, and his parents have a long history with Elizabeth."

Mary gave a small, secret smile. "I am perfectly aware of Stephen Courtenay's connections. And I shall be spending plenty of time with him in the weeks to come." And not simply because he could provide useful information. No, Mary had to admit that Stephen was extremely engaging for a young man so thoughtful and reserved. When younger, she had preferred more outgoing, almost flamboyant men. But she was forced to admit there was something attractive about a man—even one so very young—who did not make himself the center of attention.

"I also have a letter for you, Your Majesty," her confessor said, handing her a letter whose seal had undoubtedly been lifted so Walsingham and his ilk could read it first. It was addressed to her in her son's not quite wholly formed hand.

"Thank you," she said, dismissing her confessor. "Send my women to me. And tell Lord Somerset that I should like his company this afternoon."

When she was alone, Mary opened the letter and read.

> 15 June 1580
> Edinburgh Castle

My Lady Mother,

I am quite well and pray you are the same. The winter was exceptionally cold, but the summer bids fair to be pleasant. I travel north next week, to Stirling.

I have lately begun a correspondence with Her Royal Highness, Princess Anne. Her first letter was all that could be gracious and kind. Morton warns me against setting too much store by her words, for no doubt she is directed by her mother the queen, and matchmaking is a business for councils. He need hardly have issued such a warning, for I have learned from my earliest hours the danger of love matches. That is one lesson you imparted extremely well, Mother.

With the Spanish in England this summer, I hope that due thought is given to your comfort and care. I have never wished you other than well.

HRH James VI

Hardly the stuff of filial affection, Mary thought. If there was real pain, long acceptance of their positions moderated it. What could she expect when her son had been taken from her when he was an infant and into the care of the most radical Protestants? Her half brother, Moray, had had the earliest raising of James, followed by the Earl of Mar when Moray was assassinated. Mar had formed James into a child king willing to do whatever his council directed. Her son had never expressed anything less than dutiful respect for her, but also nothing more. There had been no demands for her release, and Mary could not ignore the fact that James did not want her out of England. What king, though only thirteen, would wish to hand over his own crown?

She creased the letter and laid it aside, wondering what her son would do when Mary took matters into her own hands.

If anyone had ever told Julien he would one day cherish an experience that involved him being thrown up on more than once without himself being very drunk, he would have thought them mad.

Getting Lucette home from the village had taken three times as long as walking there had. He carried her much of the way, but had to keep putting her down to vomit, and then she would insist on trying to walk, stubborn even through her undeniable distress. Getting her into the chateau itself posed little problem, for Julien had plenty of experience getting in and out without being seen. But then there was the problem of getting her out of her peasant clothes and into a nightgown before calling her maid. He didn't want there to be questions about her attire.

Julien stripped her to her shift, careful with his hands and keeping his eyes averted as much as possible. She curled up on the bed and he pulled the linen sheet over her and smoothed her tangled hair away from her face. She was clammy and her skin had a greenish tint to it in the candlelight. On second thought, he got her the basin from her washing stand to keep near.

"I'll send your maid," he whispered, not sure what story he would tell the girl.

"Don't," she said, weak but plain. "She's the one who lent me the clothes. I told her to check on me every hour until I was back. Just in case."

"You thought of everything."

"I didn't think of this."

The blue of her eyes gleamed with flame and fever, and something Julien was afraid to name in case he was wrong. Impulsively, he dropped a kiss to her forehead. "Sleep well, Lucie mine."

He sat up, his door cracked open, until he heard footsteps and checked that the maid had indeed gone to Lucette's chamber. Then he lay down and tried to sleep. He wasn't successful until the first streaks of daylight appeared to the east.

When he rose just a few hours later, it didn't take long for reports of Lucette's illness to be provided. The first came from Felix, who shot out of the schoolroom when he heard his uncle pass.

"She is sick, Uncle," he announced, sure that Julien would rightly read the pronoun. And why shouldn't he? Lucette was the only female in residence other than servants. "We are all to keep away from her! I wanted to see her but they won't let me."

"Good," Julien said. "You must let the lady rest, Felix. Write her a note, perhaps? I'm sure that would cheer her." Catching sight of the tutor Laurent's sour disapproval, Julien added, "Write to her in English. It will be good practice. And surely your tutor cannot mind that."

Laurent looked as though he minded every suggestion not made by himself, but Felix could be stubborn, and Julien left certain that the boy would write the most beautifully awkward English note ever.

If only he could do the same without risking comment.

The next one to waylay him was Nicolas—though *waylay* was a strong term. His brother was in the library when Julien went restlessly looking for a book to complete his pose of nonchalance. Charlotte was expected the next day, and once she descended with Andry and their girls, the chateau would be a noisier, busier place, easier for Julien to go unremarked.

Nicolas remarked him quick enough. "When you didn't appear for breakfast, we thought maybe you'd been stricken with the same illness as Lucette."

"Not at all. I merely stayed up late reading. I suppose it was the maid who reported?"

"Yes," Nicolas said slowly. "She woke Father at first light—Lucette wouldn't let her bother anyone else or any earlier. She's sleeping now."

"Best thing for her," Julien replied. Why did he feel like his brother was searching him for signs of lying? Surely if he knew Julien had been up to something last night, he'd have tasked him with it straight off.

And for certain he could not suspect Lucette of having sneaked out. Nicolas might once have played fast and loose with many different women, but a woman like Lucette was different, and he would never suspect a lady like her of anything underhanded.

"Charlotte will be disappointed," Nicolas observed. "To find her friend confined to her chamber with illness, locked away from both of us? How is she supposed to effect a match under those conditions?"

When Nicolas teased, there was always an underlying sting to it. "I imagine Charlotte will subsume her disappointment in caring for Lucette," Julien said. "You know how our sister likes to mother everyone. A girl who cannot leave her bed is a perfect target."

"True. But Charlotte needs her on her feet again as quick as possible. Her masked ball is just two weeks away." Nicolas cast a look around the library, unchanged in their lifetime, solitary and proud. "I think Father's already regretting giving permission, but you know how hard it is to say no to Charlotte."

"I think she's incapable of actually hearing that word."

Locking his eyes on Julien, Nicolas said slowly, "All the more reason to act with care toward Lucette. Charlotte might read more into your behavior than you mean—and so might Lucette. You wouldn't want to actually break her heart, would you?"

"I have no reason to suppose her heart is in any danger at all. Have you?"

Nicolas merely considered him, then picked up a sealed letter from the table. "This was left with one of the grooms this morning."

Retreating as rapidly as possible, for more reasons than one, Julien didn't open the slightly grimy letter until he was alone in the gardens. It was from Ribault's emissary. *You left in a hurry last night,* it ran. *Why was the English girl there? Were you followed? This raises concerns. Will stay in village until reassured.*

Julien swore long and inventively. Why couldn't he have a simple life, one that involved nothing more than fretting about Lucette's illness and wishing that her heart was as much in danger from him as his was already lost to her?

Let the man rot at the Nightingale Inn. He had no intention of going there or even writing. He'd send straight to Ribault instead, with as careful a lie as he could construct.

Lucette felt desperately ill for two days. After a solid eighteen hours of vomiting and other stomach distress, she was so weak and dizzy that she was fairly certain she would never be able to leave her bed again, let alone go outside Blanclair's walls or return to England. She had been remarkably healthy in her life, suffering only a handful of fevers in twenty-two years and the time she'd injured her ankle out hawking with her brothers. So when she woke late in the morning of the third day, Lucette was somewhat astonished at how clearheaded she felt, if rather limp.

Charlotte was there, regarding her with high good humour along with a touch of concern. "Trust a household of men to not even be able to keep you well! I should not have left you alone with them all so long."

"Hello, Charlotte," she said. "How was your journey?"

She pushed herself up, but Charlotte was having none of it. "You stay right where you are," she commanded. "You may be looking better than when I got here yesterday, but you are still weak and I will not risk a relapse. Not with the *bal masqué* less than two weeks off."

There was a thought—if she stayed ill, they would have to cancel Charlotte's elaborately festive plans. But Lucette knew she wouldn't do that to her friend.

"All you need is rest and soft foods," Charlotte pronounced. "I'll have you on your feet in no time. My girls very much want to meet you, and Felix has taken to hovering in the corridor outside your chamber like a frightened lover. If only he were ten years older, I wouldn't have to try at all to get you matched to a LeClerc!"

"You shouldn't be trying to match me with anyone, Charlotte," Lucette retorted. "How can you possibly know what kind of wife I would make?"

"No one knows before you're actually married what kind of partner one will make. We learn by doing, Lucette. What I do know is that I would very much like to make you my sister. I have no wish to leave the matter in my brothers' hands, for who knows what sort of woman they might bring home?"

"They haven't pressed the issue thus far."

"Not since Célie, no. She was well enough, quiet and submissive."

"If that's what Nicolas prefers, then he's hardly likely to want me." Lucette didn't know why she was speaking so openly. It must be the lingering weakness of her illness; she must take care not to reveal too much. Embarrassing herself was one thing—jeopardizing Walsingham's investigation was something else.

"Well, Julien likes you very well. He's haunted this sickroom corridor nearly as much as Felix. And that has not gone unnoticed by

Nic. Whatever catches Julien's attention so firmly will make Nicolas think it's something worth investigating."

Lucette laughed a little. "I've seen that in my brothers," she admitted. "Why are men so competitive?"

"You think it is only men? Women are every bit as competitive—we just have different methods. And we don't always show that we're competing, or what it is we're working toward."

That was coming uncomfortably close to Lucette's secret, so she closed her eyes and let a grimace of exhaustion twist her mouth. There was no immediate reaction from Charlotte. After a minute she opened her eyes.

Her friend was studying her with an intensity that tightened lines around her brown eyes. "You're keeping secrets, Lucette," she said finally. "You and Julien between you. I know when my brother is lying, and he's definitely lying about what happened the night you fell ill."

So Julien had lied for her. Lucette supposed she'd have wondered that before but illness had clouded her usually quick mind. Since she didn't know what particulars his lie had involved, she simply made a noncommittal sound and kept looking at Charlotte. She would not give her further reason to suspect evasion by looking away.

Charlotte's sudden smile was all mischief and hope. "I've never known Julien to lie over a woman before. I think Nicolas had better move quickly if he doesn't want to be outmaneuvered by his own brother."

If Charlotte was determined to plot and plan, then Lucette could give her a convenient—and less dangerous—outlet. "Charlotte," she said winsomely, "can you help me with my costume for the masked ball? I've spent much too long wavering about what to wear and I shall need help with the sewing."

She almost felt guilty at how her friend's face lit up with pleasure. "I know the most wonderful seamstress in St. Benoit! I'll have her here tomorrow. Have you decided, or shall I have to make that choice for you as well as find you a husband?"

Lucette smiled, determined to cause mischief if nothing else. "I shall need feathers on the gown," she announced. "Lots and lots of feathers."

Nicolas rarely acted in haste. He waited, pondering on the perfect course of action, until Lucette had emerged from the worst of her sickness, until Charlotte and her quiet husband and boisterous daughters arrived. Then he went to the kitchens and sent a maid up to Lucette's chamber to relieve Anise and send her to him in the small study closet off his bedchamber.

The maid curtsied, but her smile was much more familiar than that of maid and master. Seated behind his desk, Nicolas jerked his chin at her. "How sick was she truly?"

"You think she was pretending?" Anise shook her head. "You can make yourself retch, but you cannot make yourself that clammy and green. She was right ill enough. But she'll do now."

"Where did she go that night?"

Anise fidgeted, hands twined in her skirt front. Nicolas already knew where Lucette had been—and Julien also—and he wondered if the maid would bother lying for her.

In the end, Anise knew whose side she needed to be on. "She wanted to visit the Nightingale. See how people live, she said. Harmless enough, surely."

Nicolas simply kept watching her, waiting for her to say more. Which she did. "You didn't tell me I had to report everything on her. What's it to you if she wants to go slumming a bit?"

"If a guest of my father, a lady well-connected to the highest of English nobility, who counts royalty among her friends . . . if such a lady wishes to leave my father's house at night, alone and without anyone to aid her should something go wrong . . . you did not think I would want to know that?"

Anise bit her lower lip, clearly struggling between appeal and dumb resentment. Appeal won. "My lord, you know I would do whatever you ask. She is still weak, and in her illness will be easier to press. Shall I ask her what she was doing?"

"Let her be. We'll speak again later."

But not to your advantage, he thought as she curtsied and left. Any dalliance of his had an end date from the very first—if Anise had reached hers a bit earlier than he'd planned, no matter. Better to get her out of the way before things got messy. With Charlotte and her family in noisy residence, the maid's departure would hardly excite much comment.

But first, best to deal with the scruffy courier from Paris, who was no doubt increasingly impatient as he waited at the Nightingale Inn for a report Julien didn't seem likely to provide.

Nicolas had plans for that courier.

It was another three days before Lucette emerged from her bedchamber. She had considered claiming a relapse out of pure cowardice, but as her body healed, her mind reawakened, and she knew why Julien had been haunting the corridors. As soon as he could, he meant to question her closely about what she had seen and guessed about his contact that night at the inn. He could only be highly suspicious, and she decided she might as well confront him on her own terms.

Though Charlotte spent several hours each day with her, Lucette had most of her time free to close her eyes and work inside her Memory Chamber. She had quite a bit of new information to add to the ledger—not least of which was Anise's sudden departure from Blanclair. She'd simply been there one evening and gone the next morning, leaving Lucette in the hands of a younger—and much more nervous—girl from the kitchens. Charlotte had assured Lucette she'd share her own maid with her for dressing and hair, but that was the least of her worries. In her mind, Lucette turned the ledger page to a previous entry and added Anise to the list of Blanclair maids who had left in the last five years without giving more than cursory notice.

The personal information gathered at the tavern about the family was written on a separate ledger page. Then there was the item she had avoided thinking about too closely since coming back to herself: the man with the mustache and long scar to whom Julien had been talking with such fierce concentration that night that he had not seen her straightaway.

Julien . . . a stranger . . . a meeting at the Nightingale Inn . . . this was the kind of information Walsingham wanted. He would want a description of the man, the details of the time and place, and then probably he would have other agents who could track down his identity. *You are not the only asset,* Dr. Dee had consoled her. *It is not on your word alone that any man will be condemned.*

She didn't find that so reassuring now. For Julien LeClerc, despite her efforts at disinterest, was not just any man. And in the end she trusted herself before she trusted Walsingham.

It had been the twenty-fourth of June when she fell ill—it was the twenty-eighth, a Tuesday of fitful sunshine that peeked in and out from behind high, fast-moving wisps of cloud, that Lucette finally dressed in a lightweight gown of green and white stripes and warily left her chamber.

It was Felix, as Charlotte had predicted, who met her first. The boy had apparently set up camp in a small antechamber at the end of her corridor, with books and papers, where he'd been studying. He had the company of his two little cousins, Charlotte's daughters, who had all their mother's confidence and greeted Lucette as though they had always known her. Indeed, the younger, just two years old, came straight to Lucette demanding to be picked up. Somewhat awkwardly, Lucette complied. The weight of such a small girl was a little surprising, and she didn't know what to do with her once she was up.

Which was how Julien found her, perplexed and overwhelmed by three young voices all speaking rapid-fire and colloquial French, overlapping one another on apparently three completely different subjects.

"Like casting a Christian to the lions, isn't it?" he observed, plucking the child out of Lucette's arms and tossing her once in the air. He caught her, to a delighted shriek, then set her down. "Leave the English lady be," he commanded. "You don't want her to sicken again and retreat behind closed doors."

Felix instantly obeyed, shushing the girls and corralling them back to a game. "Thank you, Felix," Lucette said, and was rewarded with a blinding smile.

Since it was either remain awkwardly with the children or walk downstairs with Julien, she chose the latter. It was Julien who spoke first, while she was still wondering how to broach the subject of their uncomfortable encounter at the inn. "You have smitten that poor boy until he can't see straight. I'm afraid you've ruined him for life. He'll never find another woman as entrancing as you."

"Like you've never found a woman more entrancing than my mother?"

He barked a laugh. "You're never going to forgive me that, are you? I promise, Lucie, I have not remained unattached simply because Lady Exeter is unavailable."

"Why *have* you remained unattached?" This was not at all the conversation they should be having.

"I've been busy."

That was as good an opening as any. "Busy with what? Meeting questionable men in questionable places for a no doubt questionable purpose?"

"A lot less questionable than your own presence in such a place," Julien retorted, and there was a grimness to his tone that reminded Lucette of his size. Somehow, he had directed her to a part of the chateau from which nothing could be heard, and she wondered fleetingly if she should have secreted the dagger about her before leaving her chamber.

"If I said I was following you, would you believe me?" She didn't think there was much point pretending any longer. At least not about the undeniable things. Her purpose could always be obscured, if not her actions.

"I might, but you weren't. I saw the look in your eyes when you realized I was there. The look of a hart about to be slaughtered. Not only did you not follow me, you had no plans to be discovered. I've had a lot of time to wonder why."

"And your conclusions?"

"First option, that you are a libertine in search of experiences—and men—you cannot hope to meet under the watchful eyes of your parents and the English queen. I do think there is a stubbornly adventurous streak to you."

Damn it, why could he make her blush so easily? "And another option?"

"That you're not in France for the scenery—or the company. At least, not in the way you want us to think. How close am I to the truth?"

"As close as I am to guessing that your purpose in meeting with that shady man in the inn had to do with clandestine activities of your own."

He stilled, watching her beneath hooded eyes, and in that stillness was a promise of crushing strength and violence when necessary. "*Merde.* Ribault was right. You're working for Walsingham."

She kept her countenance blank. "Why would you think that? I am a woman."

"All the better for deception, Lucie—and very adept you are. The question is, why didn't I know this before?"

"I may not know much about intelligencers, but surely the first requirement is secrecy. The enemy is hardly likely to let you know you're under suspicion."

A blank pause, then, to her astonishment, Julien threw his head back and laughed. "*You're* letting me know," he pointed out, amusement colouring his voice. "As no doubt Walsingham knew you would eventually. Lucie mine, you really aren't a natural to the shadow world of spies if you just believed everything Francis Walsingham told you without question."

"What do you mean?"

"Did he set you on me in particular?"

She picked her way through what she could say without revealing too much. "No. It was Blanclair in general he was concerned with."

"A fishing expedition, damn the man."

"What are you talking about?"

Julien sobered, and put his hands on her shoulders. She nearly trembled under the weight of them, the width and warmth of his palms, the steadiness that promised here was a man who could keep you grounded.

But his words pulled the ground right out from beneath her. "I have been Walsingham's man for eight years, Lucie. I work for the English."

INTERLUDE

August 1572

P aris in August was a mess of muggy skies and tempers that
flared in direct proportion to the temperatures. But the
weather notwithstanding, everyone who mattered in French society and government was in Paris this August for the wedding of
the king's sister, Margaret, to Henry of Navarre. The Huguenots
had come to support their champion, Henry, and the Catholics
had come to register their dissent to the Catholic princess lower-
ing herself to this marriage.

The LeClerc family had come because Renaud was still a member of the royal military, though much less used since the death of
the previous king, and had distant ties to the throne. Their home
was Catholic, but not doctrinaire, and Nicole LeClerc in particular had become something of a well-known friend to the Huguenots.

At twenty-one, Julien LeClerc cared nothing for religious di-
vides, except for the fact that he'd fallen in love with a very pretty
Parisian Huguenot, Léonore Martin, who served as a companion
in Francis Walsingham's house. As the English queen's ambassa-

dor to France, Walsingham was naturally a lightning rod for both Huguenot and Catholic—the former in approval, the latter in hostility.

The sense of real trouble began the day Renaud was dispatched out of Paris by the king to settle a report of unrest near the Italian border. Coming just a few hours after the attempted assassination of the well-known Huguenot, Admiral de Coligny, the order made Renaud jumpy.

"I'd tell you to leave for Blanclair," he told his sons, "but I'm not sure that the roads will be the safest place just now for your mother and sister. Probably better to stay in Paris for a few weeks until things quiet down. Use your best judgment," he instructed Nicolas, "and Julien, don't do anything rash. Nothing comes before the safety of your mother and Charlotte."

Two days later all hell broke loose. Julien had felt it coming for hours, the heat of the day containing violence in its oppression. He'd insisted his mother and Charlotte remain in the house, but Nicolas had left hours earlier for who knew what tavern or woman. Julien kept pacing the house, from top to bottom, until his mother said sharply that he was frightening the servants.

Shortly after the bells rang for Matins, the first sounds of open fighting began to filter through the streets, seeping in through the upper windows opened for a breath of air. That was it; he couldn't just sit here. If there were clashes between Catholic and Huguenot, then the English ambassador would be a target, and so might those French Protestants who worked in his home.

He explained himself tersely to his mother. Nicole LeClerc might not approve, but she was a naturally kind woman and she loved her children. She must have read his aching need to do something, for she reluctantly agreed that he should try to make his way to Léonore's home and see if he could get her and her family back to greater safety in the well-defended, royally connected LeClerc house.

Leaving the house and its armed guards under his mother's command, Julien slipped through back streets in the dark, plain clothing he'd borrowed from one of the men-at-arms.

Léonore's family lived just a mile away, but it took him nearly an hour to detour around shops being pillaged and burned, homes invaded and destroyed. He heard screams and smelled blood, so thick in the air one could almost taste it. Julien carried both sword and dagger, but he had no wish to add to tonight's bloodshed if he could help it. Sickened by what he'd already seen, he knew they should have gotten out of Paris when they still could. He would never be able to forget the things he'd seen tonight. Or forgive the fact that it was Frenchman against Frenchman.

Which again led him to wonder uneasily where the hell Nicolas was. His brother should have stayed at Blanclair with his wife, heavily pregnant with their first child, but Nicolas spent as little time as possible with Célie. He preferred the readily available women of Paris.

Julien knew the moment he saw the front of Léonore's house that he was too late. The door hung off its hinges, splinters around the frame where it had been battered down. There didn't appear to be any great mob still inside, but there were several men stationed near the front door. Catholics—wearing white crosses on their hats for quick identification.

One of them knew Julien by sight. "LeClerc, isn't it? Renaud's son?"

He nodded warily. "What happened here?"

"All dead." The man jerked his head inside. "Except your brother. You'll find him in the chamber up the stairs, first on the right. We found a surgeon for him."

Julien moved without thinking. What the hell was Nicolas doing here? And were they really all dead? Sweet-faced and sweet-tempered Léonore, her grandmother, her two brothers?

There was certainly enough blood for death. And when Julien reached the top of the stairs, there was Léonore, wearing only a torn shift, throat cut and body sprawled like an abandoned doll. Clutched in her right hand was the string of silverwork beads Julien had given her a week ago. He crouched and, swallowing against nausea and sorrow, took back the gift. Something to always remember her by. When he straightened, he caught sight of her two brothers farther down the corridor, so covered in blood that he could not distinguish individual wounds.

In the chamber on the right, Nicolas lay on a bed, white-faced and covered in sweat, eyes wild. A surgeon stood over him.

"Nic?" Julien shoved the surgeon aside. "What the hell is going on?"

It took Nicolas a minute to focus. "Julien," he gasped. "I'm sorry, I didn't think this would happen—"

"What happened?"

"I was a block away when I heard the mobs. I remembered the street, because of the girl. Because you were so besotted with her. I tried to warn them, to get them to come away, but the mob was here too fast. I wanted to help her, for your sake—" Nicolas groaned.

Julien grasped his brother's hand. "Are you all right?" he demanded.

Nicholas closed his eyes. "I hope to God I'm dying," he said bitterly.

Julien looked at the surgeon, who, rather than answer, removed the linen that was soaking up blood by the moment. When Julien saw his brother's injury, he knew that, until the day he died, he would never be able to repay Nicolas for what he'd lost in trying to help Julien.

He would simply have to find a way to pay back all that the Catholic fanatics had taken from them today.

ELEVEN

Julien watched Lucette's expression, judging the moment she went from open disbelief to suspicion to cautious understanding. She opened her mouth and he anticipated the question. "Why?" he asked. "Which I suppose covers all possible avenues. Why do I work for Walsingham? Why am I telling you? And why didn't Walsingham let you know?"

She coloured, which she always did so appealingly at any emotional moment. What emotion was she feeling just now? Her tone, at least, was caustic. "I imagine he did not let me know because either he does not trust me . . . or he does not trust you."

"He has no reason not to trust me," Julien said.

"Which is precisely what you would say if he had reason. If, for example, you were only pretending to work for Walsingham and instead were using your knowledge to undermine England and help the Catholics."

Julien couldn't help himself; he laughed out loud. "That is the problem with conspiracy. It so easily twists back on itself. No, I don't suppose I can make you believe me. But it is nonetheless the truth. Since September 'seventy-two I have been in the employ of Francis Walsingham. Well, employ is not quite accurate—I will not take English money."

"Is it any less treachery if it's done for free?" she shot back. "So why, then, merely as a game? To spite your father and brother?"

He'd have expected her to be happier to hear that he was, in some sense, on England's side. Instead she seemed truly upset at the thought of him betraying his country.

Fine, she wanted the truth, he'd give it to her. At least to a point. "Tell me, Lucette, what happened in August 1572?"

Whatever her temper or mixed emotions, Lucette could always be counted on to use her mind. He saw the beginning of understanding as she answered him grudgingly. "St. Bartholomew's Day."

"And what happened on the eve of St. Bartholomew's Day?"

"Admiral de Coligny was assassinated."

"Correct. Two days after the first attempt on his life, de Coligny was pulled from his bed and slaughtered. And he was not the only victim. When the bells for Matins were rung at St. Germain l'Auxerrois, the Swiss Guard spread throughout Paris. They murdered the Protestant leaders that were in the city for the marriage of Princess Margaret and the Prince of Navarre."

"I know all this!"

"You may *know* it, but you didn't *live* it. What were you ... fourteen at the time? I was twenty-one and in Paris myself. Have you ever seen streets actually running with blood, Lucette? I have."

"What has this to do with Walsingham?"

"Walsingham was resident in Paris at the time as Elizabeth's ambassador. It was something of a miracle that he and his family escaped death. But not everyone in their household was so lucky. They had a handful of French attendants, one of them a young woman of good family. Only sixteen. Her name was Léonore."

"And you were in love with her?"

Julien didn't bother to confirm the obvious. Or was it so obvious? He had certainly thought himself in love with the girl, and perhaps that was all that mattered. "Léonore was a Huguenot, which is why she served in that household. She was not actually at Walsingham's house itself at the time, though, which might have saved her life. It was the middle of the night, remember? She was at home. Her house, known to be Huguenot, was attacked and Léonore had her throat cut after being raped by the Catholic mob."

"Where were you?"

How the devil did she know precisely the most painful question to ask? "I was not in her bed, if that's what you mean. More's the pity for her. Losing her virtue would certainly have been preferable to losing her life. But she was blamelessly sleeping alone, with only women in the household. Her brothers had been summoned to the fighting. They returned in time to be slaughtered as well."

He expected another piercing question, another flaying of the sensibilities he kept carefully guarded, used only as motivation. Instead she said simply, "I am sorry for you both."

That naked compassion shook him; it had been so long since he had traded in any relationship other than those based on mutual lies.

Roughly, he said, "You know, of course, that the massacres did not stop that night, and were not confined to Paris. For weeks whole Huguenot communities were wiped out—men, women, children. All in the name of a vengeful God I found I could not satisfy my conscience with. It was then I offered my aid to Walsingham."

"What sort of aid?"

"Exactly the sort you would imagine. For eight years I have been embedded in a Catholic network in France that wants to see Queen Elizabeth assassinated and Mary Stuart on England's throne. Them, I do allow to pay me. I give them just enough fact not to make them suspicious, but most of what I learn goes to Walsingham."

Lucette was studying him intensely. After what looked like an internal struggle of some kind, she asked abruptly, "Have you heard of Nightingale?"

"The bird or the inn?" he joked. "No. Some sort of plot, I imagine. What is it?"

Another, much longer pause. "I think that if Walsingham wanted you to know, he'd have told you. Or instructed me to tell you. As he did not, I can only assume that he is perhaps suspicious of you. Or of those you are in contact with. I think I shall keep the details to myself."

"I suppose that is why you were at the inn the night you ... fell ill?"

"Perhaps I was merely looking for adventure."

Her lips curved and the atmosphere turned from tense and suspicious to tense and ... playful? Flirtatious? It lightened his heart, though perhaps that was only the relief of sharing a secret that not a soul other than Walsingham had known. "Poor Charlotte. She thought she was bringing you here for romance. How disappointed she will be when you leave Blanclair with your heart intact."

"Who says my heart is intact?" Those uncanny eyes of hers did not waver, fixing him with a gleam he had last seen faintly when he'd laid her down on her sickbed.

His own eyes narrowed, though his heart stuttered. "There are some things about which a Frenchman never teases. Hearts are one."

"Julien," she said softly, so that he had to tip his head closer to hear her. "Do you remember what you said to me the first day you took me riding?"

I have never in my life kissed a woman who has not asked it of me. He remembered. He remembered the gloss of her dark hair, the gleam of her pale skin in sunlight, the organza partlet that covered her throat and shoulders, almost but not quite see-through ...

She took a step, and then another, until he could feel it when she breathed out. "I'm asking," she whispered. "Will you kiss me, Julien?"

He had not kissed a woman like her since Léonore. He'd had a lot of practice since then and thought himself hardened to feminine charms, using them to his advantage and enjoying the process without ever being swept away, but he was lost the moment she touched his cheek with her hand.

With all the skill he could remember to muster, Julien kissed her. And then he completely forgot every skill he possessed and simply let instinct guide him. Instinct—and Lucette's innocent warmth. If he hadn't already been certain she was a virgin, he'd have known it from the way she kissed. There was little experience there, and even less deception.

At some point Lucette drew back enough to whisper, "I don't know if I'm brave enough for this—"

"Then I shall be brave for the both of us." He cupped her face in his hands, smoothing the skin across her cheeks with his thumbs, and studied those bright blue eyes for a sign to stop.

But then, belying her words, Lucette kissed him once more and Julien's last clear thought for some time was, Perhaps Charlotte will get her way after all.

After two nights at Portsmouth, the royal procession to Hampton Court was stately but not especially leisured. There was no reason to linger along the route, seeing as Philip and the Spanish had never been all that loved in England, and now that he was about to divorce their queen, why would people turn out to cheer? They did come out for Elizabeth, of course, and Anabel was warmed by the response she herself received. She had traveled so rarely in her mother's company that she never failed to be thrilled by the love that poured out of the English people to their monarch and her daughter.

A good lesson, she marked, that however calculating her mother might be in person, she had the gift of inspiring her people and holding their love.

They rode into Hampton Court on June 28, where Lord Burghley and Walsingham waited with Elizabeth's council to greet them. Though Anabel found this particular palace a little old-fashioned, it certainly showed its best with the red brick warmed by neat turf and a riot of wildflowers and more exotic blooms. They dismounted outside and walked across the moat bridge in procession. Anabel looked up with fondness at the King's Beasts that lined the bridge. As a child she had loved the whimsy that peeked out from behind their sometimes grotesque features—even when Kit claimed that the stone beasts came to life at night and gobbled up unfortunate children.

After a brief welcome, the English and Spanish parties went their separate ways into different wings of the palace to rest and prepare for the night's public festivities. Tomorrow would begin the tedious and delicate diplomatic dance of ending one generation's marriage and preparing for the next.

Pippa accompanied her to the chambers that had once been Elizabeth's, and Anabel impatiently dismissed the other ladies. She admitted only Pippa into her bedchamber, where her friend helped her out of the tight overgown for riding. Perhaps not quite fair, for Pippa could not change or wash until Anabel dismissed her, but who ever said that being friends with royalty was fair? And just now Anabel needed her friend's particularly intuitive brand of advice.

"So," she said, throwing herself inelegantly into a chair and impatiently motioning Pippa to do the same, "who am I going to be betrothed to by the time my father leaves England for good?"

"You're certain you'll be betrothed?"

"As good as." Anabel shifted impatiently and stretched. She looked up at the corniced ceiling, pretending an indifference she didn't feel. "What are the odds my father will agree to James of Scotland?"

Pippa was silent, and Anabel took heart. Sometimes Pippa was quick and charming, but whenever she took her time it meant whatever she said would be truthful. Not just honest, but truth of the kind that John Dee offered.

Finally Pippa spoke. "In the end, Your Highness, it will only be your father's decision if you choose to let it be. Possession, as they say, is nine-tenths of the law, and King Philip does not possess you."

"So it is my mother who will get her way on my marriage in the end. I suppose I knew that all along."

A long pause, the kind that made Anabel's skin prick and kept her eyes turned away so as not to spook her friend. Then Pippa said slowly, "I did not say that. I rather think it will be you who gets your way. If only you can decide what that is."

Anabel caught her breath, and swung her gaze to Pippa. "Are you saying that my husband will be whomever I choose?" She chewed on her lip for a moment. "I don't suppose you want to tell me who it is I'm going to choose?"

Just like that, Pippa lost her air of otherworldliness and her impish grin made her once more a girl. "Where would be the fun in that?"

Anabel studied her friend, the dark blonde hair with that single streak of black framing her face, the green eyes deep and knowing, dressed in a riding gown the colour of the midnight sky. Pretty, polished, self-sufficient . . . outwardly unremarkable in a court teeming with pretty and polished women.

But inwardly? Anabel could never quite make up her mind. Was Pippa truly visionary, or just very skilled at reading people and guessing their hopes and dreams?

Anabel supposed there was wisdom in people being left guessing. It was one thing for a scientific, respected man like John Dee to speak guardedly of what his star charts told him, but for a woman—especially a young and pretty woman like Pippa—the word *visionary* could all too quickly turn to the much more dangerous *witch*. No child of Minuette Courtenay would ever be so careless as to hand an enemy a weapon against herself.

"All right." Anabel stood and straightened herself. "Go rest and make yourself beautiful for tonight. I shall need you to keep Brandon Dudley occupied later so my mother doesn't grow too complacent in her plans for mischief."

"Does that mean you have your own plan for mischief?" Pippa teased.

"I rather think Kit will be all too happy to aid me in mischief-making. You shall see."

After all, what was the use in having friends like Kit and Pippa if you couldn't count on them to fall in with all your plans? Anabel wouldn't mind discomfiting her mother and making her father pause. If Pippa was right, then she would end by choosing her own husband. And she could not envision a future in which that choice would be James VI of Scotland.

"Stephen," Mary Stuart asked, "tell me, are you very close to your mother?"

The young man had a way of slipping out of direct answers. "What do you consider 'very close'?"

She pouted prettily over her embroidery of a ginger cat wearing a crown, her teasing jab at her cousin. Stephen was the only man she allowed into this chamber of feminine pursuits. Unlike most men, he did not seem uneasy or out of place, merely as though he were content wherever he was.

Considering his own question, she finally answered, "I mean a son who makes his mother his confidante. Who permits her access to his worries as well as triumphs. Who trusts her entirely, as the woman who gave him life and must surely be his fondest advocate."

"I think, Your Grace, that such a paragon of a son can hardly exist. We are all human, after all, and thus flawed."

No one could ever accuse Stephen Courtenay of stupidity. With a huff, Mary complained, "But the bond between mother and son is sacred and should not be lightly tampered with."

There was a thoughtful pause, then Stephen ventured to address her real unease. "I am sorry that His Majesty displeases you when he writes."

It was no great conjecture, for all Mary's legitimate post came through the hands of the Earl of Shrewsbury and his men. And yes, her temper was being increasingly tried by James's lukewarm attempts at affection. But this last letter had struck a blow that outdid in bitterness almost every other blow of her life.

"Do you know what my most unfilial son has written to me?" She asked it rhetorically; if Shrewsbury and his men were reading her letters, they were too polite to openly admit it. "He says that as I am kept captive, he has no choice but to disassociate his sovereignty with mine and must decline to treat me as other than Queen Mother."

Stephen held his silence long enough for Mary to feel the prick of a single tear in one eye. She swallowed it down sternly. Self-pity would get her nowhere.

"That is unkind, Your Majesty. I should be sorry to cause such pain to my mother. But you must consider his youth, and that his companions since infancy have been those most opposed to you."

It was more generous than she'd expected, and she extended her hand for Stephen to take. "Thank you," she said. "Trust me, I know who my real enemies are and I shall not forget to add to their sins the charge of subverting my son's love for me."

She had already done so, writing a furious letter to Elizabeth against the boy who had transferred his traitorous affections to that bastard queen. *Without him, I am and shall be of right, as long as I live, his Queen and Sovereign . . . but without me, he is too insignificant to think of soaring. I refuse the claim of Queen Mother, for I do not acknowledge one; failing our association, there is no King of Scotland, nor any Queen but me.*

She had once thought to include James in the Nightingale plans, but now her wisdom in not doing so had been borne out. Soon she would have all the power she desired to take back Scotland and punish the son who had so traitorously abandoned her.

"No fresh concerns?" Elizabeth asked Walsingham. The two of them were closeted alone in her study early the morning after her return to Hampton Court. Last night's reception had gone late, but Elizabeth had withdrawn after only two hours and left the younger members of court to entertain themselves. Might as well allow Anne a modicum of freedom.

"About Mary Stuart and Nightingale?" Walsingham responded to her question. "No, nothing new. That doesn't mean I am not still sufficiently worried to press you to restrict her liberties further."

"How much further do you suggest? Shall I bring her to London and confine her to the Tower? That is certain to send every Catholic in my realm into open revolt. And the last thing I need these next weeks is a further weapon for Philip to use against me."

"It would not be provocative to increase the security around Tutbury. And keep her from riding out for the duration of the Spanish visit."

Elizabeth sighed. "Honestly, Walsingham, do you expect my cousin to once again make a dash for freedom on the back of a horse? She may be a fine rider but she is no longer an especially young woman"—Elizabeth ignored the twinge that reminded her Mary was nine years younger than herself—"and she is always accompanied by at least a dozen armed men. Including Stephen Courtenay. You sent him there; do you believe he is at all likely to turn traitor now? Surely Mary's charms are not still so great that she could twist that particular young man to treason."

"It is the things we have not considered that worry me, Your Majesty. One cannot protect against a blow one has not anticipated."

"Well, then, set your imagination loose and bring me your possible anticipations and I shall consider them. For now, our first concern is Spain and getting out of this marriage with as much advantage to England as possible."

"Do you think you can persuade Philip to intervene with the pope against the Jesuit mission to England?"

"I mean to try. But I was thinking more of Anne's future. Philip can cause trouble while he is in England. I do not want to be maneuvered into concessions that he can use against me or her later."

"How serious are you about matching Her Royal Highness to James of Scotland?"

Elizabeth waved a hand, as though that thorny issue could be solved simply. "I am very serious about making Philip nervous. We shall see which worries him more—a Protestant king or a Protestant English noble. I suppose Anne gave a good performance last night after I left?"

She was certain of it, for Anne had done very well in the earlier hours while her mother was in attendance. She had been seated with Brandon Dudley at dinner, and despite her protests behind closed doors, had acquitted herself with dazzling charm and smiles to turn any man's head. It had unaccountably pleased Elizabeth that Brandon had remained steady and, perhaps, even cynical about the entire affair. Very much as his uncle Robert would have.

"If her performance was intended to flit from eligible noble to eligible noble, then she did well enough. Until she landed on Christopher Courtenay shortly after your departure. They did not separate for the remainder of the evening."

Elizabeth laughed. "That is Anne being mischievous. And no doubt young Kit was all too ready to play the game with her. The two of them have always been irrepressible."

"Yes, Your Majesty. But there were definite concerns paid last night. I would say King Philip did not look particularly pleased at his daughter's rather . . . affectionate behavior."

"If King Philip knew his daughter better, he would not be concerned. Kit is merely a convenient piece for Anne to use. If it unsettles her father, all the better for England."

Elizabeth could not deny, however, that Walsingham's report left her slightly unsettled as well. Surely Anne was only playing. But when royals played with hearts—particularly Tudor royals—disaster tended to follow.

TWELVE

When Lucette woke the morning following Julien's surprising revelation, her body luxuriated in remembered pleasure. Desire danced along her skin as she remembered the softness of his lips mixed with the roughness of his not-quite-shaven cheeks and chin. His hands were every bit as strong and steady as she'd guessed, and her own had gone from the solidity of his shoulders to where his hair curled slightly against his neck.

But marching along with those memories, her mind demanded that she pay attention to what he'd told her before those kisses. She was inclined to believe Julien about his working for Walsingham, but that didn't mean she thought he'd told her anything approaching all of it. And nor had she in return.

And then there was the a priori puzzle: why had Walsingham sent her to Blanclair without all the necessary information? As she'd said to Julien, that might imply that Walsingham had cause to doubt Julien's current loyalty. Or it might simply mean that he'd told her only what he thought she should know.

But of one thing she was certain: Nightingale was a true Catholic

plot, with ties between Spain and France, aimed at depriving Elizabeth of her throne and setting Mary Stuart free. And she was also
certain that Blanclair was part of that plot. Not because Walsingham
had sent her here, but because of what she'd felt since her arrival.
Things were not entirely as they seemed at the chateau, and she had
that sense she got when she was on the verge of solving a puzzle: that
all or nearly all the pieces were in her hand, and waited only for the
last bit of information to tilt everything into its proper place.

Lucette spent the morning alone in her chamber, telling Charlotte she wanted to make sure she was strong enough for the upcom-
ing ball but instead reviewing everything she'd gathered into the
ledgers of her Memory Chamber. The time had come to sift out the
important from the trivial, a process that she could not have explained if she tried. It was simply instinct, honed by Dr. Dee's training in puzzles and logic and mathematics and even history. With
little effort, the essential information appeared to her from among
the rest.

She began with the servants.

The maids—five of them now, including Anise—who'd left Blanclair with little or no notice paid, were particularly troubling. Why
would a young woman with few options for work leave a situation as
stable as Blanclair? There could be a man involved, of course, a sudden elopement without wanting family to know, or a determination
to seek out opportunities in a larger city. Orléans was only twelve
miles off, or even Paris, which must exert the same kind of pull on
French country girls as London did on English ones.

Lucette might more easily have believed any or all of those reasons if there had only been two or three maids vanishing—five was
somewhat alarming. Had they come too close to a knowledge they
should not have? But Nightingale was a relatively recent plot, according to Walsingham. What other secrets might be harbored
here? Whatever they were, she was certain a connection to Nightingale existed.

Then there was the surly groom who apparently answered only to

Nicolas and who was noted for coming and going at odd times and with no one else the wiser. What did Nicolas use him for? And last (or first) among the servants: Felix's tutor, Richard Laurent. He of the impeccable Catholic credentials and thinly veiled contempt for everything English. Including her. On her second Sunday at Blanclair, she had thoroughly searched Laurent's belongings while everyone was once again at Mass and found only what would be expected of a man both religious and scholarly.

The only item that had given her pause was a religious tract written in Spanish. The contents were no different from those in Latin or French or even the English ones scattered through London, but written in Spanish? Lucette remembered that narrow, nebulous thread she'd seen in Walsingham's notes connecting France and Spain. Other than that, she admitted that she simply did not like Laurent and the open hostility with which he treated her.

Thus far, everything mysterious at Blanclair tied itself more to Nicolas than Julien. The tutor, the groom . . . and even the maids. Julien might have dallied with several of them, but the last three had gone away after Nicole LeClerc's death, and he had not been anywhere near Blanclair in that time.

Turning the mental page of her ledger, Lucette confronted the family members. Felix was out, and so was Charlotte. (Charlotte not so much for lack of opportunities at Blanclair as because her entire being was open and outward. She would make the worst spy in the world.) Neither Andry, Charlotte's husband, nor Renaud had been absolutely ruled out of Lucette's calculations, but she considered them highly unlikely. She did not know Andry well, but nothing about him suggested duplicity or fanaticism. Besides, would he have the power at Blanclair to make housemaids disappear? As for Renaud—well, she could as easily believe that Renaud would resort to secrecy and plots as she could believe it of Dominic. Both men were painfully honest. Whatever they did, they would do openly.

And that left, as always, Julien. Either he was part of Nightingale,

or he wasn't. If he wasn't, then there were further options—that
Walsingham was being paranoid and checking on him without reason, or someone had been making it look to the English as though
Julien were involved. Lucette knew it was impossible to prove a negative. Thus, it would be a waste of time trying to prove that Julien
hadn't done something. The only way was the most straightforward
(that being a relative concept in espionage): to uncover evidence of
actual guilt in whomever it attached to.

And do it before she went home in two weeks.

She emerged from her chamber to the chateau's public rooms in
the early afternoon, wearing a gown of lightweight silk embroidered
with flowers and vines in a riot of bright colours, deliberately chosen
to catch a man's eye and attention. If her body hoped it would be
Julien thus drawn to her, her practical mind was pleased enough that
it was Nicolas. His face lit up with a genuine smile of warmth and
pleasure when he saw her.

"*Ma chère mademoiselle,*" he said, getting to his feet and coming to
greet her. "How very well you are looking! We were all so sorry for
your illness. Are you sure you are quite recovered?"

"All I need to complete my cure is fresh summer air. Would you
care to join me?" She knew how to pose the question flirtatiously—if
she wasn't quite as naturally charming as Pippa, she could imitate it
quite well.

In his gentle way, Nicolas replied, "Nothing would be a greater
honour."

They went around the water garden, enjoying the splash and play
of the fountains, then descended to the Garden of Love, where
Nicolas pointed out the roses, which he said her mother had loved.
"She brought you here nearly every sunny day," Nicolas remembered. "I think the roses reminded her of England, if not our French
sunshine. I am so glad to be able to show it to you."

"You have all been so kind. Much more than mere family sentiment demands."

"I confess," he said hesitantly, "that I did not expect to be more than polite to you this summer. When you were merely theoretical, with my last memories of you as only a child, I could not envision how very much I would . . . well . . ."

"How very much you would . . . ?" she prompted.

"How very much I would like you."

His simplicity was such a contrast to Julien's demanding convoluted teasing. Lucette felt a stab of shame at her duplicity, but only for a moment. Nicolas might present a more straightforward face than Julien, but she wagered he, too, had his secrets. The maids, the groom, Richard Laurent and his inflammatory religious tracts . . . many threads traced back to Nicolas. The task was to tease out which had specific bearing on her quest.

Her next question, broached delicately, was the first salvo. "Thank you, Nicolas. It is very kind of you to say. I, too, have been unexpectedly caught by liking here."

"Julien can be very engaging when he wishes."

She was quite sure she did not imagine the dark undertone to his words. Did it mean he was jealous? "I was thinking of Felix, actually. I don't know when a boy has so stolen my heart."

That pleased Nicolas. "It is mutual, Lucette. I do not know how Felix will be content to let you go. My son has had so little of a woman's love in his life. Charlotte is busy with her own family, and since my mother's death, I fear the boy is often lonely."

He was practically leading her to where she wanted to go. "How sad that his mother could not live to take joy in her son. You both must miss her very much."

Nicolas was silent, and seemed to be studying the gravel at his feet as they paced sedately through the summer flowers. "It is a great loss to a child not to know his mother, but I confess that, for myself, the loss was . . . less."

He met her eyes then, and said almost urgently, as though desperate to make her understand, "Célie was very young, you see, and the match was made by our parents. Pretty and pleasant, but we had little time together to approach anything like my parents' love for each other. I think I bewildered her, and I confess I was not the wisest of husbands. I should have made more of an effort. But I thought we would have many years to get to know and appreciate each other. And then she was gone."

"I do wonder why you have not given Felix a mother since," Lucette ventured, knowing she was on delicate ground. There could be no excuse for this impertinence.

But rather than take offense, Nicolas answered thoughtfully, "Do you? It was not for any great loss of love for Célie. Guilt, perhaps, as much as anything. And also . . ."

"Also?"

"I was in Paris during the St. Bartholomew's Day Massacre."

It was so unexpected, especially coming on the heels of Julien's revelation, that Lucette could think of nothing to say. She tried to look encouraging, and it must have sufficed, for Nicolas continued. "It was a horrific experience. I was somewhat—"

He broke off. Lucette bit her tongue, sensing that he would stop if she gave him any reason to.

Finally he continued, almost angrily, "I was injured, rather severely, in the violence. A difficult recovery, compounded by Célie's death and the shock of becoming a father to a motherless son, meant that I had little reason to leave Blanclair at first. And then it became a habit.

"But habits can become crippling." He stopped walking next to a rosebush that was nearly as tall as she was, starred with creamy buds of ivory and yellow. Lucette was only slightly surprised when he took both her hands in his and fixed her intently with his eyes. "More than anything, Lucette, your presence here has shown me that life goes on. And perhaps even joy."

For several breaths she thought he was going to kiss her. She did not pull away, but nor did she move closer. She left it to him, and in the end he dropped her hands with a wry smile. Lucette could not ignore her relief; Nicolas was handsome enough, but he wasn't Julien. His hands were softer, his body thicker, and though she knew it for shallowness, Lucette felt not the slightest physical attraction.

"We shall see," he said cryptically. "But I hope that coming here will end in bringing you joy as well."

As she worked out what best to answer, the sound of booted feet on gravel came from behind. They both turned, and there was the groom that ran so many private errands for Nicolas, looking straight at his master.

"What is it?" Nicolas said with a touch of impatience at being interrupted.

"Apologies, sir," the groom said in a manner not at all apologetic. "I was down the river's edge just now and found something."

"Found what?"

With a glance at Lucette and then away, as though dismissing her presence, the groom said bluntly. "I found a body. A man. Stabbed through the heart, looks like."

Nicolas attempted to send Lucette back to the chateau, but not very hard. So she was on his heels, as he was on the groom's, as they approached the river's edge. The corpse lay tipped on its back, looking like nothing so much as a loosely jointed doll cast to the ground by a careless child. But it had been no child who had thrust a blade into his chest, leaving a mass of bloodstains hardening around the edges of the torn cloth of his doublet.

But it was his face that struck Lucette, and she inhaled a little sharper than intended. Nicolas said, "You should not be seeing this. My father would be furious. Come away now."

As he took her by the arm, issuing low orders to the groom to have the body removed to the stable block and to alert Renaud and Julien, it was not horror or disgust that occupied Lucette's mind. It was confusion.

She knew the man. Bearded and mustached, looking subtly out of place in the countryside, with a scar down the back of his right hand.

The man Julien had been meeting at the Nightingale Inn the night she fell ill.

Julien had spent the morning in a state of uncertainty. When Lucette did not appear, he quizzed a maid who told him she was studying in her chamber. He could hardly knock on her door and ask if she was avoiding him, so instead he wrote several letters to Paris and then took Felix for a ride after the noon meal.

They were just returning up the lane—Felix's horse only a little smaller than Julien's, for he was a fierce rider for his age—and bickering about the relative merits of swords on horseback when Julien caught sight of Lucette's unmistakable dark hair and figure in a dress that looked as though she had plucked flowers from the garden with which to adorn herself. She strolled next to Nicolas, and the two of them looked deep in conversation as they passed beyond sight into the terraced gardens.

For a seven-year-old, Felix was unusually observant. Or perhaps it was that he was nearly as besotted with Lucette as his uncle was. "I don't suppose my father would like it if we joined them," Felix said half hopefully, as though wanting Julien to disagree.

"No, I don't suppose he would."

Still, Julien helped brush down the horses, lingering in the stables as long as he could without arousing too much speculation, hoping to encounter them returning. When they did, it was with a haste he had not anticipated.

Julien stepped out of the stables into their path, bringing Nicolas to a sudden halt. Lucette's eyes looked as though she were contemplating something far away.

"Julien!" Nicolas grasped his shoulder. "I'm glad to find you. I've sent the groom for Father. We need to make arrangements to bring the body up here."

"Body? What do you mean?"

Nicolas drew a ragged breath and shook his head once, as though to clear it. "Sorry, I'm still a bit shocked. There's a man on the river-bank, with a dagger wound in his chest. Dead as can be, and most violently. I do not like the thought of it on Blanclair's grounds."

"Surely not one of ours?"

Nicolas shook his head, but it was Lucette who spoke up. "He looked like a city man. Down from Paris to meet someone, perhaps. He had the look of a man who frequents taverns."

Her blue eyes locked on his, Julien felt the tingle in his spine. She was telling him who it was—though even she didn't know his full identity. The emissary from Cardinal Ribault. A man who'd assumed Julien served the same master. And now he was dead, just when Lucette was trying to decide if Julien was a French traitor or an English one.

He wished Nicolas wasn't here, but there was no help for that now. "Take her to the house," he told his brother. "I'll take some men and bring the body in."

Several grooms followed him down to the river, bringing a wide plank on which to lay the body. What a disaster! Charlotte had the entire neighborhood and half of Paris coming to the chateau in less than two weeks; she was going to be very cross at this dead man disturbing her party atmosphere.

She might be less cross if Lucette agreed to marry one of her brothers. Marry me, Julien thought, even as half his mind scolded him for not focusing on the chaos of the moment. *If it's anyone here, it will be me.* Nicolas might enjoy her company, but he could not marry her.

Sure enough, it was Ribault's emissary lying dead on the river-bank. Julien swore vividly, and knelt by the corpse to make a hasty search. The last thing he needed was something incriminating turning up now.

But the man was clean. Only a handful of francs, no paper, no letters, nothing even to identify him. Could Julien get away with denying any acquaintance? Lucette could hardly claim differently without revealing that she had been in that inn as well. There had been others in the tavern who must have seen them speaking, but Julien knew he could probably get away with insisting the man had been a stranger striking up conversation about nothing at all.

It was, as always, Lucette who was the open question.

With a resigned sigh, Julien shuffled the coins in his hand before dropping them back in the man's pockets. No need to be a petty thief as well as a traitor.

But his eye was caught by one of the coins. No, not a coin at all. It was lighter, more oval than circular, and imprinted with something other than a king's image. He plucked it up and held it to the sunlight, squinting to see details. It was reminiscent of a pilgrim badge, but he couldn't immediately identify from where. Was that a bird? With a single word above it . . .

NIGHTINGALE.

The first official meeting of the English and Spanish took place in Elizabeth's council chamber at Hampton Court. She and Philip sat next to each other in separate gilded chairs, with canopies of estate over king and queen. Where usually Elizabeth's privy council would fill all the seats that radiated out in a circular fashion, she had hand-picked the men to attend her in these matters, and they filled only half the circle, to her right. The other half was given over to Philip's men. It was very much like the councils that had ended, twenty years ago, in their betrothal and marriage. For a moment she thought of herself as she had been then: twenty-seven, not two years on her throne, but firm in her positions and well-backed by her men.

But she had been young. And, as much as she could have expected, in love. Or at least, in desire. She had noted her attraction to Philip the first time she met him, when he came to England to meet with her brother, the king. The desire was not necessary for the bargain of marriage, but it was a pleasant enough addition. If her heart had been buried with Robert Dudley, her body had been willing enough to accept a distant second best.

But now she was forty-six and Philip over fifty, and neither hearts nor bodies would have any say in the matters of state.

Husband and wife sat rigidly royal five feet apart and never once looked at the other. The Spanish party, like their king, favoured black and their half of the council chamber resembled nothing so much as a flock of crows flown into the low-ceilinged chamber through the single window that overlooked the privy garden.

The Englishmen had more variety of colour to them, and more ostentation. Burghley and Walsingham might always wear black, but many of her hereditary nobles liked to adorn themselves in damask and velvet, slashed sleeves and jeweled robes.

But none in that chamber could match Elizabeth. She had always cared about her appearance, and as queen her appearance was as much a part of ruling as her edicts. The nobility wanted a woman they could admire and pretend to understand, and the people needed a figure of myth so that they might not remember that she was only a woman. She had chosen an overgown of royal purple today, edged in ermine and buttoned tightly to her stomacher with pearls.

If she had inherited anything from her father—besides his red hair—it was his sense of occasion and drama.

Lord Burghley, always at her right hand whatever his particular role might be, addressed the gathering. "We are here, Your Majesties, and lords all, to consider on the necessary business of dissolving the marital union between our two countries. With, of course, the desire to continue our union in friendship and mutual support."

Elizabeth noted Dominic Courtenay, in the second row of seats. His expression didn't change, but somehow he managed to convey the impression of rolling his eyes. She bit back a smile and was fiercely glad he had agreed to be part of this particular council. Dominic had consistently refused all other offers of leadership—a refusal she would not have brooked from any other man in her kingdom—but every now and then he would accept a brief assignment. Elizabeth thought his presence during these meetings probably had more to do with his fondness for her daughter than for his queen.

That might hurt, but she could use it.

Philip's chief advisor, Cardinal Granvelle, expressed in English the Spanish party's polite gladness to be present, and then, continuing to address Lord Burghley in Latin, said, "The first concern of our king—and each of us—is to protect the future of the Infanta, Princess Anne."

Infanta was a loaded word, implying that Spain saw Anne as a legitimate choice to be Philip's heir. In truth, it was a very tricky situation. Philip had had a son, Don Carlos, from his first wife, but that young man had died twelve years ago. Under admittedly mysterious circumstances. There had been no shortage of English gossip about Don Carlos's vicious nature, how the prince physically attacked attendants even as a small child, and set fire to a stable full of his father's horses. He had starved to death while being held in close confinement—whether on Philip's orders or by his own perverted choice—but Elizabeth knew that Philip, whatever his sense of personal loss, had never once regretted the loss to the Spanish throne. Don Carlos would have been an absolute disaster as king.

But it did mean that Spain was in a delicate position at the moment. As Anne was Elizabeth's only child, so was she Philip's. In another place and time, she might thus have risen to join two kingdoms, as her own great-grandmother, Isabella of Castile, had when wedding Ferdinand of Aragon. But in the modern world there was no chance of Spain and England combining into a single empire. Not only was there the impediment of religion, but Europe itself would never permit that degree of unity between two powers. There needed to be balance.

Which, after all, was the point of this divorce. If they'd had another child, then perhaps she and Philip could have split them to rule in different countries. But there was only Anne, and Philip needed to look to his own succession. Elizabeth knew there were wagers flying around court as to how quickly he would remarry. She herself was certain it would be before year's end. To a young and fertile lady, no doubt.

But that didn't mean he would cut all ties with England. Philip was, if nothing else, a loving father. He would want his daughter well cared for. He might have lost the bid to make Anne Catholic, but he could press for her marriage to someone Spain approved of.

The question was, how far would that pressure go?

This first encounter was conducted almost entirely between Lord Burghley and Cardinal Granvelle. The two men were nearly of an age, both in their early sixties, and practiced similar wily approaches to state business. Elizabeth and Philip themselves sat silently watchful, and she could almost feel her husband's amusement and intensity of purpose. It was possible to feel both at once. She often did.

Burghley pointed out that Anne, by English law, was Princess of Wales and her mother's direct heir. The Spanish advisor pointed out that laws can be changed. Burghley replied that English laws were not susceptible to change merely for Spanish benefit.

At which point Granvelle changed tactics. "We do not dispute Princess Anne's right to the English throne. However, it is a source of great pain to her father, the king, that she has never seen his country. May we not negotiate a visit from the serene princess?"

Absolutely not, Elizabeth thought loudly, but she kept her expression neutral. Burghley handled it smoothly. "Our first and most pressing need is to discuss the possible marriage settlement of the princess. We have several possibilities in mind. No doubt His Majesty"—Burghley nodded to Philip—"has his choices as well."

"He has."

"I propose we each submit to the other a list in writing, with the possible suitors and their advantages to Princess Anne. We can reconvene in a day or two, while King Philip enjoys his daughter's company."

All very scripted and deliberate. Elizabeth wagered she could write the Spanish list as well as they could write the English one. But formalities were what made it possible to rule. As both a lady and queen in her own country, she rose first.

"Thank you, gentlemen. Please enjoy our English hospitality until we convene once more."

Once, Philip might have followed her out, but today he merely rose and bowed to her as she left the council chamber. She imagined he would be on his way to Anne, presumably to present a personal plea to his daughter to consider his choice in matches. Or to raise a fuss and press her for a visit to Spain.

Good luck to him, Elizabeth thought. Anne would be polite and friendly, and only afterward would Philip realize she had given away nothing. It cheered her to think her daughter had gotten that impenetrable facade from her.

As for Anne leaving England . . . never in her lifetime would it be considered.

THIRTEEN

19 June 1580
Hampton Court

Lucie,

We leave tomorrow for Portsmouth to receive the Spanish. Anabel is nervous but will not admit it, even to herself. Is it condescending to admit that there are times I feel sorry for her? Well, I do. At least we have been allowed to grow up together as a family, difficult as that may sometimes be. I wonder if King Philip has any idea of the daughter he and the queen have created.

Kit is furious that Brandon Dudley has been invested with the earldom of Leicester. But like Anabel, he is not fully aware of how he feels . . . or why. I shall have quite the task keeping the two of them in line this summer.

And how are your Frenchmen, Lucie? Do you know, even when I was six years old, I did not think Nicolas LeClerc was all that attractive. Handsome, perhaps, but attraction has more to it than looks. Not that my opinion matters. But I offer it, because I am your sister and irritating you with unwanted opinions is part of my raison dêtre!

Keep your eyes open, sister, as well as your heart.

Love,
Pippa

19 June 1580
Hampton Court

Pippa says I must write. How are you? Everyone here is as normal— Pippa is bossy, Stephen is absent and important, Mother and Father are watchful. And Anabel is uncertain, but covering her uncertainty with imperiousness. All we need is you to look at us disdainfully as a reminder that you are so much more adult than we are.

Kit

21 June 1580
Tutbury

Lucie,

I find when perusing your latest letter that I cannot decide if you are enjoying yourself highly or simply enduring a trial you would rather have finished. I need to be able to read your eyes rather than your words to gain a true perspective. You do know that you are not as hard to read as you think yourself. Your eyes always give you away.

As for myself, I am well enough. It is hardly a taxing assignment, at least not physically. Queen Mary is bright and restless and seems to enjoy having someone to match wits with. She is more playful than our queen, and enjoys recounting ancient myths to me. Her latest story is the Greek legend of Philomela. Do you know it? Philomela is violated and mutilated by her sister's husband (he cut out her tongue, presumably so she could not

witness against him), but the gods intervened and turned her into a
nightingale.

   Queen Mary seems to identify with Philomela, particularly the
sorrowful lament of the nightingales' song. She was not best pleased when
I pointed out that the female nightingale is mute; it is only the male who
sings.

   Be happy, Lucie. And come home to us soon.

                              Your loving brother,
                              Stephen

Her siblings' letters arrived in a bundle from Dr. Dee in Paris. Reading them was almost like having her brothers and sister with her, for each had a distinctive voice. Pippa serious beneath her teasing, Kit in a scrawl of impatience, and Stephen . . .

Stephen wrote to her of nightingales. Her brother was not given to digressions. He wrote as he spoke, thoughtfully and meaning every word.

And in that moment Lucette realized how very blind she had been. Stephen was at Tutbury *because* Walsingham wanted him there. How could she have missed it? That master intelligencer would not overlook multiple avenues of aid from the single family considered the most personally loyal to Elizabeth's crown!

Still chastising herself for overlooking such an obvious piece of the puzzle, Lucette read quickly through the other letters. Dr. Dee was curious how her German studies were progressing. There was a dutiful letter from her mother. Nothing from Dominic.

Turning from thoughts of home to the immediate situation at Blanclair, Lucette considered that it had been three days since the discovery of the body—the man had been quietly interred in an unnamed grave at the local church—and there did not appear to be any sort of official investigation into his death. Naturally, the neighborhood deferred to Renaud. So when he summoned her to his study a short time later that day, she thought uneasily that he might have uncomfortable questions for her in that matter. But instead, after seeing her settled in a comfortable cushioned chair next to him, Renaud asked, "You had no news from Dominic?"

Instantly, she was on alert. For the first time since she'd handed it over weeks ago, she wondered what was in the letter Dominic had sent to Renaud. She answered with wary care. "No. My mother wrote briefly, but they are attending the queen at Hampton Court during the Spanish visit. No doubt they are both far too busy to write when they know I am in such good hands."

"Do you think so?" Renaud leaned back in his chair, fingers steepled. "Dominic has written to me, as has your mother. They both seek to know how you are enjoying your stay. Which leads me to wonder why they do not simply ask you yourself."

"I wouldn't know."

"Ah, *mademoiselle,* that I do not believe for a moment. Our daughters always know far more than we would like them to. But, though you may not believe me, that runs both ways. Parents, too, tend to know their children far better than would make those children comfortable."

"Such as?" She would not be cowed, or tricked into speaking of her family.

"Such as, I am perfectly well aware that, second only to matching one of her brothers in marriage, Charlotte is concerned with providing me with a second wife. I believe there will be several women of a more mature age invited to Blanclair for her festivities. She seems to think I need the companionship."

The conversation was growing more awkward by the moment. Just as she could not imagine her parents matched with anyone else (which was why the thought of the late king was so painful), she also could not envision Renaud with any woman but Nicole LeClerc. Lucette had only the memories of their few months' stay in England, but their devotion had been absolute, if understated.

Should not love between spouses be absolute? How could one ever love a second person as much as the first?

How could my mother have given in to William for pity's sake, and even love, when she had been so fiercely in love with Dominic?

Renaud had a cynical half smile when he added, "I fear if you do not take Julien, there are tongues that will begin to match you with me."

She didn't know which horrified her more: the speculation about Julien, or the thought of being matched to Renaud instead. Renaud laughed, in that inimitable French way that meant no offense had been taken. "Do not fear, I speak only of what a stranger might suppose. I know your father well enough to be certain he would never allow his daughter to be wasted on an old man like me, no matter how much we are friends."

Well, if Renaud was going to be blunt, she might as well do the same. "But he is not my father, is he? So how much say in my future does he have?"

"And so we come at last to the thorn in the paw. I know what gossip says, child. And yes, your blue eyes are very like the late William of England."

"You knew him?" How could she not have known that?

"I met him, yes. Once upon the battlefield, where our encounter was not especially close. But after the battle I was the crown's hostage for some weeks and had the chance to speak to him before I was released."

Lucette's heart was in her throat. She had never met anyone not William's subject who had known the king. *What was he like?* she wanted to beg. *Was there any more to him than his position and his rages?* Questions she could not ask her mother, and certainly not Elizabeth. Either one would hint too much at Lucette caring, and she would not give them that power over her.

Renaud tipped his head and considered her quizzically. "May I speak personally, Lucette, as though you were my own daughter? For certain, I was the first man to lay eyes on you, and you were under my care for nearly a year of your life."

She nodded, unable to speak even if she'd wished to.

"I think you are far more like Dominic than you know. Blood or not—and that is something neither of you will ever know for certain—you have his iron sense of right and wrong. But this is not a black-and-white world, *ma petite*, something Dominic learned at great cost. You are so afraid of not being wanted, you will not put it to the test. Thus you create the very distance you fear."

She blinked and stared over his head. More gently, as though she were still a child, he offered, "If it is information about William that you crave, I suggest you ask Dominic. No man living knew him better."

With a little gasp half sob, half shock, she protested, "I could not possibly do that."

"Because it would hurt him? I assure you, you are hurting him far more with your politeness."

"What could he possibly tell me of the king that I would want to know? The king died his bitter enemy."

"Anger there was between them, yes, and betrayal on both sides. But do you think Dominic Courtenay a man to report only one side of any issue? Whatever you ask him, he will answer honestly and fairly, probably with as much emphasis on his own sins as those of the king."

He leaned forward and plucked up a square, sealed letter. "This," he said, handing it to her, "you yourself brought me when you came. It is for you, sent with a covering letter to me, asking me to use my best judgment on when it might be most wanted."

The handwriting was Dominic's. She managed to escape the study without humiliating herself with full-blown sobs, and escaped into the first empty chamber she found.

Like Dominic himself, the letter was bracingly straightforward, written to her as though they happened to be in conversation.

I'm not a complicated man, Lucie. I don't like plots or secrets or political manipulation. William Tudor was adept at all those things, and I definitely don't like a dead man wrecking my family from beyond the grave.

Worse when that dead man is the closest friend I have ever had.

I don't know how to play games, Lucie. And I don't know how to fix this.

Whatever you need of me, you have only to ask. I will do whatever is in my power to make you happy.

That is what fathers do.

Anabel had not enjoyed herself more in her life. Perhaps when she'd been a child, left to run free at Wynfield Mote with Kit and Pippa, almost able to forget for a few weeks who she was and the weight of expectations upon her. There was no forgetting this summer who she was, and in its way it was far more satisfying. The Princess of Wales reveled in being at court—and not just being there, but central to all that was happening. Outside the council room, at least.

Naturally, Philip wished to spend as much of his free time as possible with his daughter. Naturally, Anabel concurred, though she kept her inner coterie tightly around her. For this particular summer, that meant not only Pippa and Kit, but Brandon Dudley and Francis Huntingdon and Robert Devereux and others of lesser rank but equal ambition. There was also the shy Nora Percy, twenty-five and recently brought to court as one of Elizabeth's ladies. She was an acknowledged daughter of the late king, which made her Anabel's cousin, but they had rarely ever met. Nora had been raised by her maternal uncle and his wife in Yorkshire and seemed to prefer that retired life, but she had a fiercely ambitious mother who was only too glad to use her daughter as an entrée to inner circles.

"Watch out for Nora," Elizabeth had instructed Anabel when lending the girl to her service for these weeks. "And even more, watch out for Eleanor. She will seek to use you for her own benefit."

"And how is that different from everyone else at court?" Anabel had shot back.

Her mother's expression had been grimly amused. "You've never spent time with Eleanor Percy. Trust me, you have not met her like before."

But Nora was quite agreeable, musically talented as suited her upbringing and well-read, her only real flaw a lack of easy humour that left her always guarded and uncertain if she were being teased. Kit, of course, took advantage of that, and Anabel had heard Pippa scolding her twin about it.

The other men were unfailingly polite to Nora, considering her relationship to the throne, and rather more attentive to both Anabel and Pippa. They seemed happy to divide their smiles and attention, simply glad to be where they were, almost as glad as Anabel to be of serious importance at last.

A week after their arrival at Hampton Court, Anabel and her bevy of young nobles were gathered along the Thames, shooting arrows in King Henry VIII's tiltyard, built west of the palace. The fickle sun of English summer shone in full force this afternoon so that their movements were deliberate and conserved in the heat. Anabel wore the lightest layers she could manage—embroidered linen and silk so fine it was nearly sheer. She was an accomplished shot and nearly every arrow she loosed hit the white circle in the target's center.

The men took care not to outshoot their future queen . . . all except Kit.

"Ha!" he crowed, as his arrow sung straight into the clout, the pin at the very heart of the white circle. "Told you I'm better."

He looked unbearably smug. Of his siblings, he looked the most like his mother, all honey-gold hair and hazel eyes. Despite the heat, he wore a leather jerkin casually laced and his grin was pure taunting.

"I beat everyone else," she retorted.

"Because they let you."

Brandon Dudley took up another arrow. "Doesn't mean I'll let *you* beat me, Courtenay." He sighted and loosed his arrow only slightly off Kit's.

Light applause came from behind, and there was Philip, with that cynical smile that was so unreadable. "Bravo to the sportsmen . . .

and women," he added in heavily accented English, bowing to his daughter.

"Finished already?" Anabel replied in Spanish, which she spoke rapidly and colloquially. "The council meetings continue to grow shorter. Is that because all the decisions have been made?"

"The council meetings, as you well know, continue long after Her Majesty and I depart. There are details that our advisors will wrangle about without us."

"And in all that wrangling, have you expressed your opinions on my future husband?"

Philip eyed her keenly, and Anabel wished she had spent more time with him, that she might more easily know what his expressions meant. Then, with a considered acknowledgment of those around her, he said, "Perhaps that is a subject for private discussion. Would you care to walk with me, daughter?"

She forced a smile. "Gladly." Surrendering her bow to Kit (who, despite opinions to the contrary, knew when to keep his mouth shut), Anabel left her friends and fell sedately into step beside the King of Spain.

It struck her suddenly at times, like now, that the mother and father she knew were also reigning monarchs. Easier to adjust herself to Elizabeth, but here was the most powerful king in the Western world, with the wealthiest kingdom, and nothing he'd rather do at this moment than walk with an eighteen-year-old girl.

Except she wasn't just a girl. No matter that she could nearly forget herself in the company of friends—mostly the Courtenays—Anabel knew perfectly well who she was and what it meant. And just now she was determined to discover what her father had in mind for her future.

First, it seemed he wished to discover what she knew of Elizabeth's intentions. "Is it true," he asked, "that you are writing to the King of Scotland?"

"At my mother's request, yes."

"Not at your own desire?"

"He is a thirteen-year-old boy. My desires do not enter into it."

He cast her a sideways glance. "As your father, of course, I would rather your desires never enter into your thoughts of boys or men."

That was not a comfortable topic, so Anabel continued on the theme of James. "It is hardly surprising that England should consider pairing me to Scotland. And surely James must be in favour. The island would be united and one day, God willing, there would be a half-Scottish monarch on England's throne. How could even Mary Stuart disapprove of that?"

"But she does disapprove. So I hear."

Anabel shrugged. She had little time to waste thinking of a woman who had been imprisoned for the last twelve years. Mary might occupy her mother's conscience, but not hers. "Her opinion does not enter into the matter."

"And does mine?"

"If you care to express it, of course I shall always consider your opinion, Father."

"There are many on the Continent who would feel compelled to resist the combining of England and Scotland, particularly with your religious inclinations."

"You mean the Catholics fear a stronger Protestant state."

"Yes."

"And what do you fear, Father?"

The expression of melancholy was one she recognized. Philip was in many ways more thoughtful than her mother, or at least more likely to show it. "I know religion is not a comfortable topic between us, *cielita,* but you must know it is not merely a political topic for me. I truly fear for the state of your soul. England has wandered far from God's path thanks to both heretics and ambitious men. Your late grandfather laid a heavy price on his country and his descendants when he broke with Rome."

"Rather good that he did, or neither my mother nor I should ever have been born, or at least not born to rule."

"I could never wish you unborn, Anne. But I could, and do, wish you willing to consider the truth from which your mother has turned away."

She held her tongue, then said finally, "You are right. I dislike the topic of religion. If that is your main objection to James, then I can assume none of the English candidates have your blessing, either?"

"The candidates are all devout Protestants. I might like an Englishman in the manner of, say, Henry Howard or Thomas Arundell. Men closer to the Catholic cause. Of course, I should very much prefer it if you would consider a Spanish husband. The women in your family have not found us entirely lacking."

She stooped to snap a blossom between her fingers. "Replace one Spanish lord with another? I do not think there's any chance the council would approve. And would it not lend weight to any faction wishing to be named your possible heir in Spain? Unless you have given up all hope of more children, I would not think you ready for such a step."

"You are as quick as your mother, and nearly as outspoken. If not England or Spain or Scotland . . ."

"France," she said, with pardonable skepticism. "The King of Spain is urging me to consider a French marriage?"

"At least the Duc d'Anjou is a Catholic, and only twenty-five. I believe your mother's council would be willing to consider him. It has been a generation since the last proposed French match ended so tragically."

One could say that—with the King of England blithely overthrowing the Duc d'Anjou's older sister for an English commoner who had in turn spurned him. One could trace the late king's fall to that remarkably bad choice.

Anabel considered what she knew of Anjou. The youngest of Catherine de Medici's numerous brood, he had been born Hercule but changed his name to Francis when his oldest brother died. Now his brother Charles was King of France, and with no children yet, Anjou was his heir. He had reportedly been scarred heavily by smallpox as a child, but that was neither here nor there in terms of politics. And indeed, England might well consider him as a possible match. For one thing, he had taken sides with the Protestants during this last decade of religious warfare.

But she was suspicious. If the Spanish did not want England and Scotland matched, even less would they want England and France united.

"I suspect," she said lightly to her father, "that you are only offering names in the belief that I will instinctively choose in opposition to your wishes. You should know better. I am the daughter of the two cleverest, wariest monarchs of the last hundred years, and though I may have instincts, I will always consider carefully before making my choice."

"And if it were truly your choice, *cielita*? If you were not who you were and married solely for your own pleasure?"

"My pleasure is England's pleasure, as well you know. Do not worry for me, Father. I shall be the princess I have been bred to be."

And that, she thought, is what worries you. Because that might well end in my personal opposition to Spain. And that would be a conundrum indeed. Which did Philip honour more—his religion or his daughter?

Mary perused the latest missive from France with a thrill of satisfaction. She never felt more alive than when engaged in conspiracy, and she had not had such an endeavour to occupy her since the Throckmorton plot. That, granted, had ended badly, but she had learned from her mistakes and did not mean to repeat them. And how could she fail with such an ally as Spain on her side?

Nightingales are everywhere, the letter ran. *Europe has not seen so many in years. Soon, very soon indeed, we expect to hear the same of England.*

Under cover as coming from a de Guise cousin whom she had not seen since her early years in France, the letter was signed once in the copperplate handwriting carefully copied from said cousin. And then, more subtly and more truly signed in the upper right corner of the top page. A tiny but perfect ink miniature of a nightingale in outline.

Mary did not actually know the identity of the Nightingale mastermind. Plots were always best when kept discrete, its separate parts unable to betray any but themselves. She trusted the clerics through whom Nightingale had come to her attention and looked forward to the day when she could meet—and thank in person—the man behind the plot that would finally see her free of English captivity.

It was never supposed to be this way. When Mary had made her daring escape from Loch Leven in 1568 and the Protestant lords who had imprisoned her—including her half brother, Moray—there had been those who urged her to ship immediately for France and her de Guise relatives. But Mary, knowing how little the Queen Mother of France liked her, and trusting a fellow Queen Regnant—not to mention cousin—could better serve her, had instead impulsively crossed into England and remained there.

She had thought to be taken direct to London to speak with Elizabeth face-to-face and begin the process of returning to her proper place. But Elizabeth had failed her. Surrounded by men as rigid and distrustful as those in Scotland, the English queen had dithered and delayed and allowed Mary's flight to England for aid to become, instead, a prison.

Mary was a woman of strong passions. She once had thought to be Elizabeth's greatest friend. Now she was prepared for implacable enmity.

Even alone with her confessor, she spoke guardedly and in coded terms. Gracious or not, Tutbury remained a prison. One that she intended to leave very soon.

"There has been concern expressed for my plight by the Spanish?"

"We understand that you have, indeed, been discussed in council. Of course, one would not expect much from that particular kind of talk."

Mary didn't expect anything at all from talk. But Spanish talk meant Spanish thoughts, and that was all she needed to know.

"And the talks will dissolve . . . when?"

"Philip and his entourage intend to sail from Portsmouth the first week of August. Matters should be resolved before summer's end."

They would not, of course, move while Philip himself was in England. Too risky. He needed to be well out of reach of Elizabeth's anger. When she learned that Spain had conspired to free the Scots queen . . . well, everyone knew what terrible rages Elizabeth's father had been prone to. Not to mention Anne Boleyn's colder wrath. Still, if all went as planned, Mary thought, she could be standing directly in front of Elizabeth and not fear so much as a slap.

It was a perfect plan. All that waited was the passage of time.

FOURTEEN

In the days running up to Charlotte's *bal masqué,* Lucette divided her time between dressmaking sessions with Charlotte, being entertained by Felix and his two little cousins, and avoiding Julien. When she realized the last, she argued to herself that it was because she needed distance to consider what she'd learned thus far, and time to properly place the puzzle of the murdered man on Blanclair's grounds.

She had written to Dr. Dee, describing the man and his death and his appearance at the Nightingale Inn, in a painstakingly ciphered letter. She had not revealed that it was Julien he'd been meeting. That could wait until Dr. Dee himself arrived at Blanclair. As for herself, she found it difficult to imagine why Julien would have killed the man. More than that, why had Julien turned English spy in the first place? All for the pretty face of one Huguenot girl? Although she wanted to believe him (more than she found comfortable), she maintained a healthy skepticism.

At least, she remained skeptical whenever she was away from

him. Near him, even with half a dozen others present for meals, say, Lucette found herself dwelling far too deeply on how he'd kissed her. Admittedly, she did not have a wide range of experience, but there had been a handful of others besides Brandon Dudley, though none else had gone so far. Was her response to Julien simply because he was very, very skilled? Which he must be if the Paris reports passed through Walsingham and Dr. Dee and the Blanclair household were true. Was it that he was dangerous? She knew herself well enough to recognize that she might like the element of uncertainty in both his character and in predicting his behavior. She spent so much of her life surrounded by the predictable.

But he wasn't the only unpredictability at Blanclair. Nicolas had become incredibly attentive since her illness, and part of escaping Julien meant turning to the older brother. Nicolas appeared perfectly willing to spend hours with her, riding or walking or simply allowing her to read in his study while he worked on account books. She'd caught him staring at her in contemplation, as though she were a thorny puzzle of logic he was trying to put right, and it made her uneasy. Renaud seemed uneasy about his elder son's interest as well, which Lucette found puzzling. Did he not think her good enough for Nicolas? *What if I said you ended with a French husband after all?* Pippa had been teasing. Hadn't she?

Felix, at least, glowed with pleasure whenever he saw his father and Lucette together, and Charlotte radiated approval. One evening before bed, she sailed into Lucette's chamber ostensibly to discuss the progress of her feather gown for the masquerade, but mostly to launch prying questions that were parried only with difficulty.

Charlotte was determined to be smug. "I thought this was how it would be. Nicolas has been so determinedly solitary for so long that when he asked me about you at Christmas, I knew he must be serious."

"Nicolas asked about me?" Surely not because of his fond memories of a clingy ten-year-old, she thought. Why, then? The puzzle pieces in her head began to vibrate.

"Asked about your letters, and your studies, and if you ever wrote about any man in particular. He didn't exactly order me to invite you to France, but he hinted rather strongly."

Lucette smiled instinctively. "I'm flattered."

But it wasn't flattery that sent her mind spinning, but possibilities. It sharpened her observations, and made her wary of his attentions.

She could not deny that there was something restful about Nicolas. He was not challenging, like Julien, she didn't have to think quickly or guard herself from unwariness. Perhaps restful was not to be underestimated in this world.

But it was not of calm, restful Nicolas she dreamed at night.

The day before the first of Charlotte's guests arrived, Felix finally begged his way into arranging a training bout between his father and uncle. It had been Julien who spent time with his nephew these last weeks in the practice yard, supervising the child's training in blades. Cannons might be the backbone of today's warfare, but there was still a need for men skilled in individual combat.

There was an unusual three-way tension at lunch that day, lines of deepest burgundy running between Renaud and both his sons. Even Charlotte seemed to feel it, for her usual chatter was conducted at a slightly lower level of brightness than normal. Felix, however, could hardly contain himself in his seat. His tutor spoke to him once or twice rather sharply, but Felix could apologize so winningly he managed to make even Laurent sniff and smile.

Julien did not even look at Lucette once, and she was cross to feel guilty. Someone who spent so much time in Paris climbing in and out of women's beds had no business sulking because she hadn't followed up their kiss with more liberties. So why, then, did she feel responsible for hurting his feelings?

Julien did, however, address her as they left the table to reconvene at the practice yard. "Do you think my brother and I shall put on as good a show today as we used to do at Wynfield Mote?"

"I think you are both less likely to show off in quite the same way," she replied. "At least I hope so, or what is the point of getting older?"

"But showing off is an end in itself, is it not? And not confined to men."

"Just don't let showing off get in the way of your fight. I would imagine distraction is a problem when fighting."

He looked at her with eyes that made her feel liquid and wonder why she had taken such care to stay away from him. "Unfortunately, we cannot always choose our distractions. And if I'm tempted to show off today, you have only yourself to blame." His smile was one she had never seen from him before—an almost heartbreaking mix of wistfulness and hope.

Words trembled on her lips, pushing her to say things she'd never thought she'd be brave enough to say. "Julien," she managed to begin . . . and was interrupted by Felix practically bouncing from excitement.

"May I escort you to the practice yard, *mademoiselle?*" he asked with endearing charm.

Instantly, Julien's smile twisted into rueful mocking. "Enjoy yourselves," he told them. "Felix, I expect you to help the lady understand the finer points of what she's seeing."

If only there were someone to help her understand the finer points of Julien's behavior.

The practice yard at Blanclair was surrounded by trees, not dissimilar to the one at Wynfield Mote. Both those houses were manor houses, meant for family living and not defense. The practice yard at Tiverton Castle, by contrast, was far more serious in purpose, meant for exacting military training for the Duke of Exeter's retainers and liege men. Renaud LeClerc had done most of that sort of training in Paris or at court, so Blanclair retained the homey sense of familiarity.

Lucette had spent many hours watching her brothers and other young men of their household train, and so she expected a certain degree of teasing. Stephen and Kit always threw taunts at one another—Kit more than Stephen—and did not give quarter in their fights. She was accustomed to Dominic's eagle eye on his two sons, and could remember occasions when he took the yard himself against them. Having only one hand might change his balance and necessitate a lighter sword, but it had not materially affected Dominic's skills, and her brothers had always paid the closest attention.

Renaud was present today, but he kept well back and did not shout either encouragement or directions, as she remembered him doing when his adolescent sons fought at Wynfield. Of course, they weren't adolescents anymore. As Lucette watched Nicolas and Julien finish lacing their padded jerkins, thickly quilted for protection, she was struck anew by the fact that both were far removed from being boys. And how, she wondered, was the unacknowledged tension between these men going to manifest in physical form?

Charlotte seemed to wonder the same. She leaned against the fence, with Felix bouncing on the balls of his feet on Lucette's other side, and said pensively, "It has been a long time since I have seen my brothers spar openly. I think perhaps they have much between them that will arise when fighting."

"Did they disagree often when they were young?"

"No more than most brothers, I should think. But these last years . . . I wish I knew what was keeping Julien from home. And not just since Mother died. He has kept himself in Paris since . . ." She hesitated.

"Since when?" Lucette expected to hear about St. Bartholomew's Day, wondering if Charlotte had guessed about Julien's love for a Huguenot girl.

But though Charlotte's timing was right, her conclusion was wildly different. "Since Nicolas was injured in Paris and then lost his wife. Julien seemed so stricken with guilt. I have never dared ask, and I can't say that I saw any signs during her life, but I have since wondered if Julien was in love with Nicolas's wife."

Oh, dear. Another possible woman in the mix! Why did Julien attract troublesome women like flies? Although she supposed grudg-

ingly that it wasn't fair of her to assume they were troublesome simply because they were dead.

And yet, wasn't guilt something she could well understand? Although how guilt over loving his brother's wife might have prompted
Julien to work for Walsingham . . . no, she couldn't quite make that
piece fit. She could, however, turn it around. If Julien had been in
love with Célie—and Nicolas had known it—then the older brother
might well be targeting Lucette simply to upset Julien. Though that
did not answer why Nicolas had apparently been interested in her
months before her arrival.

Did that make it more or less likely that Nicolas was involved in
Nightingale? That was the piece she was still missing—his motivation.
Whatever injury had been done to him in Paris had been committed
by the Catholics. Wouldn't that make Nicolas unlikely to aid their
cause?

She shook her head, forcing the tumble of overlapping thoughts
into the background. Puzzles were solved out of the corner of the
eye, when the mind was focused elsewhere. So she focused on Nicolas and Julien and their fight.

Lucette supposed that training bouts had not changed substan-
tively in several hundred years. Using either wooden replicas or ra-
piers with their deadly edges blunted, men had a way to practice the
skills that might mean the difference between life and death. The
LeClerc brothers used rebated steel today, and the flash of sunlight
on swords looked deadly enough.

"I'm only allowed to use wood," Felix informed her regretfully.
"Uncle Julien says if I work very hard, I can try rebated steel when
I'm ten. That's how old he was."

"And your father?"

"Father doesn't often like to fight. Not with me. The master tells
me he and Uncle Julien were well matched when younger, but they
have not fought against each other since I was born."

Another link to the year of 1572. The threads surrounding that date in Lucette's ledgers were beginning to vibrate with suppressed meaning.

The match was little different from the ones Lucette had seen, not only between her brothers, but at court. She was accustomed to the dance of men and weapons, but she quickly realized that there was more behind this bout. Nicolas might be out of practice—she could see that his early movements were half a beat slower than Julien's—but his instincts had been so well honed that it didn't take long for his body to remember what it had once done without thought. As Lucette remembered from watching them when she was a child, Julien was the gambler and Nicolas the thinker. But they had both grown, and not just physically, since those days. She had no doubt that Julien had killed men with the moves he used now, and it sent shivers down her back.

Nicolas, more precise than Julien, had once been more focused as well. But Julien had a ferocious concentration today that fixed itself on his older brother as though he were fighting his own demons incarnate. It was Charlotte who murmured in her ear, "There is always ferocity when a woman is involved."

Plainly, Charlotte thought she was that woman. It was an ... intriguing thought. Lucette had never imagined herself a femme fatale, leading brothers to duel one another for her favour. Not that she intended to bestow her favour on either of them—at least, not as a result of a practice yard fight.

True to his uncle's command, Felix kept up a running commentary on the match. "See how Uncle Julien moves his feet? If it were an opponent who did not know him, the surprise would be very useful. But father knows him too well. He can always anticipate where Uncle Julien will be."

Indeed, after a bit it did seem as though Nicolas were fighting with all the foreknowledge of a seer. Julien seemed to realize it as well, if the narrowness of his eyes and tightness of his jaw were any indication. His wheat-coloured hair tumbled about his face as he whirled suddenly away and back, out of his brother's reach, and they stood facing each other with an intensity that suggested they had momentarily forgotten there were spectators.

"Quitting?" Nicolas asked, with an ugly edge to his voice that seemed to hint at an unknown number of grudges. So might a man sound who hated his brother, perhaps for loving his wife or perhaps for something else. Even if Nicolas had not greatly loved Célie for herself, the possessiveness of a husband could easily make a man territorial and unwilling to share.

Like Dominic and William.

Julien just laughed. "When, dear brother, have I ever walked away from a fight?"

"No, you don't walk away so much as send someone else to finish the fight for you. Who will it be today, Julien? Going to send Felix in your place next time?"

All the irritation previously alive in Julien's expression flattened into blankness. "That is unfair."

"So's war. And also, I believe, love."

Julien dropped his sword. "Well, then, in the interests of brotherly love, let us call it a draw."

There seemed to be a wealth of unspoken communication between them, and Lucette chanced a sideways glance at Renaud. His hands were knotted together until his knuckles were white. Suddenly she knew that something terrible stood between these brothers. Something only they and their father knew.

Something—she was sure of it—that had happened in 1572.

Nicolas held his position as though contemplating striking the unprepared Julien, but at last he shrugged and dropped his own sword point. "We shall call it a draw for now. But brothers cannot ever leave matters entirely alone. We shall finish the fight one day."

Julien jerked his head in acknowledgment and strode out of the yard without a glance for Felix or Lucette or anyone else watching. After only a moment's hesitation, Lucette followed him.

As she went, she heard Felix say, "*Mademoiselle . . .*" and then Nicolas reprove his son.

"Let her go, Felix." Lucette fancied she could feel the force of Nicolas's gaze at her retreat. "There's no need to chase the lady down. She'll come back of her own accord quick enough."

He sounded absolutely sure of himself.

When Julien heard Lucette following him (who else would be foolish enough to come after him when he was clearly in a temper?), he wanted to turn his eyes to heaven and ask piteously, *Why now?* She had asked him to kiss her, appeared to enjoy the experience, and then taken every effort to keep out of his way since.

Not, he admitted to himself, that he had made any great efforts otherwise. He hadn't been lying—he did only kiss women who asked it of him—but the asking had always been a game, the words a mere formality considering that those women had given every indication of wanting far more than just a kiss. There had been times when he wished he hadn't told Lucette that, having been so sure that she would never ask. Whether from pride or disinterest . . .

But then she did. In the most honest, winsome manner that had the effect of a spear blow to his chest. No woman had ever looked at him like that—except Léonore. And see how badly that turned out, he reminded himself blackly.

He was not used to jealousy, at least not on his own account. But as Lucette had taken to spending much of her time with Nicolas this last week, he'd at times been so jealous he couldn't see straight. He'd rather have the Paris strumpets, he told himself. At least the whores never pretended.

All in all, he'd been glad enough to fight Nicolas today. Until his brother took the single worst moment of Julien's life and openly threw it in his face.

This was why he never came home. Forget pleasing Charlotte—he would leave tonight. He did not want to be here while Paris descended and Lucette paired herself with Nicolas.

Except she can't, his selfish side whispered. *No matter how much Nic may want her, he can never give her what I can.*

So he wasn't pleased when she caught him up. "I thought you said you didn't run away," she noted shrewdly.

"I would think you'd be pleased with my restraint," he said, halting because he could not go on without rudeness and because, finally, she was speaking to him, and damn it all if it didn't make him dizzy. "I assure you, I could have finished my brother with a few carefully chosen strokes. I have always been the more violent one."

"Julien, what happened in Paris in 1572?"

He shook his head, startled by her change of topic—and unnerved by her insight. How did she know that all of this traced back to Paris? Only a guess, of course, for she couldn't know the truth. And she would never hear it from him. As furious as Nicolas made him, he owed his brother that and much, much more.

"St. Bartholomew's Day happened. I told you this. A girl I cared for was butchered, not to mention tens of thousands of others in the weeks that followed. Whatever the Catholics say, it was no carefully targeted assassination of political rebels. It was a massacre of innocents. And whatever you may think of me and my working for Walsingham, I do not care to see my countrymen wallow in the blood of their neighbors."

"I meant . . ." She bit her bottom lip and her eyebrows drew together in concentration. "I meant more specifically—what happened to the girl? And to Nicolas?"

"What do you mean about Nicolas?"

"He told me he was severely injured during the riots. Did that have anything to do with you?"

No, and no again. He didn't care how appealing Lucette Courtenay was, how she made his knees want to buckle into her and hold himself up on her soft shoulders, how the sight of her furrowed brow made him want to smooth it away with kisses . . . It didn't matter. No one was going to get him to talk about Nicolas and Léonore

and Paris. Not even his brother or Renaud—the only two living be-
ings besides him who knew the truth—ever spoke of it. Only occasionally, and pardonably, did Nicolas allude to it. And if that cut Julien to the heart, so be it. He knew he deserved much more.

But he suspected he wasn't going to be very good at lying to Lucette.

So he did what he always did when cornered. He attacked. "If
you're so interested in my brother, why did you ask me to kiss you?
The sake of curiosity? Or perhaps for comparison. Tell me, do I kiss
as expertly as Nicolas?"

She never could control her colour. A flush swept her cheeks and
neck and she willingly attacked right back. "I wouldn't know. Ask
him yourself if you don't believe me. Although I cannot imagine why
you care."

"Surely you are not that innocent, Lucie. You know perfectly well
why I care. Do you think I kiss every woman like that?"

"Only the ones who ask you." But her voice was not as confident
as her words, and suddenly Julien wondered if she'd wanted him to
come after her. "Which must be a great many, considering the stories
I've heard about you and women's beds."

He laughed aloud. "Since when does a hardheaded thinker like
yourself accept stories at face value? I assure you, Lucette, if I spent
half as much time in women's beds as I'm credited with, I would not
be able to walk straight."

Flustered, as he'd intended, she dropped her gaze to the ground.
What a mess! Walsingham and England and France and dead men
and apparently plots even he knew nothing about . . .

And all he wanted was to be the sort of man who could tell her
how he felt and see what happened next.

But even in honesty, Lucette was quicker than he was. "The
Nightingale Plot might seem like a game to you, but Walsingham is
not a man to jump at mere shadows. If he is worried for my queen's
life, then so am I. I don't know exactly what your politics are—and

frankly, I don't care. As long as those politics don't include an attempt to destroy my own government."

"I can't prove a negative, Lucie. I have nothing to do with any
Nightingale Plot, and that includes hearing about it from the Catholics who think I work for them. Either it's been kept deliberately
close to avoid leaks, or possibly I am suspect among the Catholics
I've been lying to. Either way, I'm afraid I'm of little use to you in
political matters. Though I am very interested in why Walsingham
did not tell you about me when he sent you. Perhaps the English no
longer trust me, either, which rather leaves me out of a job."

"Are you sure there is nothing you have heard?"

He had been carrying it around with him for days. Now he drew
out the flimsy metal badge he'd found in the dead man's pocket. He
handed her the rough image of a nightingale and said, "This was on
the body. It argues that he, at least, knew of the plot. But if so, he said
not a word to me. I would like to know why. If the Catholics have
discovered I'm a traitor . . . well, their reach is much closer than
Walsingham's just now."

She'd drawn in her breath in almost a hiss, and he could practically see the wheels in her mind turning. What he wouldn't give to
turn that mind off for a few moments. But then, he suspected, she
would not be herself.

"I don't suppose it's any use telling you to quit prying," he said
resignedly.

"If you know nothing of Nightingale, then there's no danger in
my prying."

He threw up his hands in frustration. "Fine. Ask your questions.
Turn over your conclusions. Follow your suspicions to your heart's
content. Soon you'll be on your way back to England and can tell
Walsingham whatever you wish."

And then, no matter how rude it was, he turned his back and
walked away. If he didn't, he might very well find himself spilling out
words he couldn't afford to say. She had come to Blanclair as a spy,

not a woman. If she left here with his heart, it was certainly far more than she'd intended. No need to burden her with it.

Lucette retired early that night, unwilling to sit through a family meal with all that turmoil of emotions beneath the surface. Her previous illness was a convenient excuse to retreat whenever she wished, and even Charlotte tactfully left her alone. If her friend was curious about what had occurred between Lucette and Julien after the training bout, for once she did not press.

Unable to sleep and unwilling to think deeply, Lucette spent an hour creating algebra equations. Not for ciphering purposes, since Dr. Dee would be with her very soon, but simply to give her overwrought mind something straightforward to think about. It worked, too—when a knock sounded on her door, Lucette jerked as though she'd been dozing.

It was a maid she'd never seen before, dressed for the kitchens or perhaps scullery. She looked highly nervous, as though afraid to be caught in the more elegant areas of the chateau, but also determined.

"Forgive me, *mademoiselle*. I am sorry to disturb."

"It's no disturbance. What can I do for you?"

The girl thrust something at Lucette, which turned out to be a tightly folded paper with an unmarked seal of wax keeping it closed. There was no covering address.

Perplexed, Lucette asked, "For me?"

"A boy brought it today, all the way from Orléans. Said it was for the English lady Courtenay." She slightly mangled the name, but went stubbornly on. "He said I were to give it to you direct and no one should know."

How very odd. "Thank you," Lucette managed, and the maid scurried away as though she couldn't get back to the kitchens fast enough.

The intricate folds, when undone, disclosed a fragment of a second page. Lucette looked at the covering letter first, written in a careful but inexperienced hand.

> I beg you to remember me, mademoiselle, as Anise who served you as
> best I knew. But my soul will not let me rest now I am gone from
> Blanclair and so I write to confess I sometimes reported on you to
> Monsieur Julien. There seemed no harm in his questions, but now I think
> I may have been wrong.
> When he sent me away, in my anger I returned to his chamber when it
> was empty and pulled this out of the fire. It had fallen to the hearth, and
> though I cannot read it, I saw your name.
> You were never anything but kind to me, and I am sorry for any harm
> I did. I am well enough now, serving in a fine house in Orléans, and there's
> a gardener's boy who will deliver this for me. Take care, mademoiselle.

Shivering with anticipation and that singing sense beneath her skin that the puzzle was nearly shaken into a whole, Lucette studied the enclosed half page. It was written in Spanish.

> . . . must be certain you can get into England without undue notice.
> Lucette, as you say, is the safest way. To travel as her intended would be
> for the best as it would attract the least notice. The window for action is
> narrow and the nightingale grows impatient.

Spanish correspondents. Anise and at least one other reporting her movements. A fragment fished out of a fire. If this were a mathematical equation, all logic would point to one simple answer: Julien LeClerc was running Nightingale.

And he planned to use her to get himself to England.

Against the logic was only this—that the answer felt wrong. In her bones, Lucette could not make Julien fit into that answer. *Trust your instincts,* she'd been counseled. Well, her instincts told her that the answer was too convenient. Too perfect. She distrusted it.

And yet, she also distrusted herself. How could she, who had never made anything but a mess of her relationships, believe that Julien was innocent simply because she wanted him to be innocent?

On the other hand, the convenient, perfect answer might have been deliberately constructed to appear so. If, say, Julien were being framed. By a brother who hated him.

Nicolas and Julien. Everything came back to the brothers—and not just as individuals, but because they were brothers. She needed them both to unravel the truth. The fragment of the Spanish letter seemed real enough. Which meant that, in the few days left her at Blanclair, one of the brothers would move to persuade her to invite him to England.

And she would allow herself to be persuaded.

FIFTEEN

J ust thirteen days into the Spanish visit, London erupted in violence. Burghley and Walsingham brought Elizabeth the news after she rose that morning. There was rioting in the city, apparently indiscriminate violence that upon closer examination had a pattern.

"Attacks on foreigners," Burghley said as his fingers worried at a ring on his left hand. When the imperturbable Burghley fidgeted, it meant his nerves were pitched to an extreme. "Shops were looted and burned, apprentices beaten, women pelted with rotten vegetables and even some stones. The French Huguenots in particular were harried by both English and Spanish."

"Do we have it in hand?" She hated sending troops into such volatile situations, but she could hardly afford to let London burn.

"I'd call it an uneasy truce at the moment," Walsingham answered. "It needs but a spark to flame into greater violence. Such as the Spanish making statements about their wish to have Princess Anne matched to the Duc d'Anjou."

"That's been spoken of in London?" Elizabeth asked sharply.

"Not by us. I think you should ask His Majesty about the loose-ness of his men's tongues."

"Why would the Spanish leak gossip?"

"Perhaps merely for the pleasure of watching your kingdom turn upon itself."

Elizabeth snapped her fingers at a lady hovering at the door. "Send word to Philip that I will see him in my privy chamber in one hour."

No one played games with her people's lives.

Having spent the hour being dressed and coiffed for battle, Elizabeth swept into her privy chamber, where Philip met her on his feet. They neither of them wasted time in pleasantries.

"Do you really think stirring unrest in London will gain you points with your daughter?" Elizabeth demanded of the Spanish king.

"One would say that your people live on the edge of unrest, and it hardly needs stirring for it to erupt."

"What do you want, Philip?"

He hovered on the edge of an offhand retort, then his face darkened and she knew she was going to hear the truth. "What I want is a wife and daughter who are not determined to throw away their souls for the sake of pride. I loved you, Elizabeth, for yourself and not just your position, and well you know it. And Anne is my own flesh and blood. But you will not see reason. And thus I must tear out my affections to do what is right. England cannot hold out against the Church forever. Truth always wins, Elizabeth. I would not like to see you crushed in the coming fight, but that does not mean I will not wage it."

"You are finished here." Her voice was like a lash. "There is no point in further discussion. We both knew when we started how it would end: you will divorce me with the blessing of the pope and wed a faithful Catholic girl who will give you sons. And Anabel will follow me on the throne of England and hold firm against the threats of petty religious demagogues. England is not to be bartered over. It is mine and my daughter's after me, and there is no place for you here."

"I am sorry for it. I indulged myself in a dream these twenty years because I loved you and because I hoped persuasion would be of greater influence than force. I should have known you better."

"If it is force you want, Philip, do your worst. England will never bend to Spain."

With his dark eyes full of memories and melancholy, Philip bowed to her one last time. "Farewell, *mi corazón*."

My heart. He had called her that on their wedding night, and on the day of Anabel's birth. Elizabeth allowed herself one moment of private regret before resuming her mask as queen.

With very little fanfare, the Spanish left Hampton Court. They rode to Portsmouth under the courtesy guards of Elizabeth's personal household, but there were almost no nobles to bid them farewell this time. Save the Princess of Wales, who'd had a flaming row with her mother and was finally permitted to spend the last days with her father before he sailed away for good.

With Anabel was Dominic Courtenay, who rode with Kit and had personal command of a dozen men of his own to keep her safe. The only other court official was Walsingham, who always made Anabel wary. She thought sometimes that the old man didn't like her very much, but perhaps that was only because his devotion to Elizabeth was so absolute there was no room left for anyone else. Did his wife and daughter feel the same? she wondered.

Kit kept her entertained along the way, but it was to Dominic she turned for advice as Portsmouth came into view and the hour of her parting from her father was imminent.

Settling her horse into a walk next to Dominic's, Anabel asked, "Have you any words of wisdom for this parting?"

She often thought Dominic the most restful person she knew, but that was mostly when she wasn't in his presence. He was quiet, true, and still—but whenever she was near him, she realized just how much intensity he radiated. Not like Kit, whose emotions and energy were thrown widely into the world like a gift. And not precisely like her own father, who seemed to hold his peace out of dozens of mixed motives.

She could feel that intensity turned toward her, though he kept his eyes on the road. "Why do you ask?" The unspoken word was clear—why do you ask *me*?

Anabel had known him long and well enough to know she could risk impertinence. "You have had experience with farewells you thought would last a lifetime."

"But I didn't expect to survive long enough to have to live with them."

"If you were Philip, about to say goodbye to your only living child without expectation of meeting again, what would you like to hear from that child?"

"What would I want to hear, Your Highness? The truth of your own heart. What we think and feel, for good or bad, is all we can honestly offer another human being. Tell your father what you are feeling."

Easier said than done. For one thing, that meant she would have to quickly sort through a wealth of emotions to decipher what she was feeling. It would be so much easier to simply play her royal part, to mimic her mother's velvet-and-steel touch. But she had asked— the least she could do was take Dominic's advice.

The party stopped at Portsmouth Castle, where Philip and his closest advisors would take refreshment and rest for an hour before following the servants and horses aboard ship. By sunset the Spanish fleet would be out of sight of the English coast.

Dominic made it easy for Anabel and Philip to leave the larger chamber gracefully and withdraw into a stone-floored chamber that was obviously rarely used. The walls were bare and there was no furniture to speak of, certainly nothing on which to sit, so the two of them stood at the window, which gave a lofty view of the harbor.

"Have you ever been to sea, *cielita*?"

"You know I haven't."

"Pity. There is nothing like the sea to teach man his proper place in the world."

"What about woman's proper place?"

He smiled, a little sadly but genuine. "So like your mother."

"As I will be queen after her, I devoutly hope so."

"My only regret in leaving England is you."

"We are neither of us dying, Father. As most of our relationship has been conducted by letter, surely not that much will change?" This was not at all what Dominic had counseled, but brought to the point, she was horrified at the thought of crying. Queens did not cry.

"I hope you will remember, my child, that you have two parents in this world. If ever you need my aid or counsel, I shall swiftly supply it."

"Even if my choices are not what you would approve?"

"Even then." He touched her cheek, so lightly she almost could not feel it, and Anabel felt the tears hover at the edge of her eyes.

"I do love you," she said, and impulsively grasped his hand with hers. "And I will miss you more than I can say."

"Remember, *cielita*," he whispered into her hair as he hugged her close, "the best way to honour me is to honour God. Think very carefully about the nature of truth, child, and don't be blinded by Satan's silken lies."

And that, she realized, is at the very essence of our relationship. That my father will always care more about my soul than anything else about me.

That dried the tears trembling on her eyelashes, and she was perfectly composed—not to say hardhearted—when the two of them exited into the more populated chamber. There, the Spanish bid their formal farewells to the party, and Walsingham joined them for the short journey to the harbor.

As Anabel watched her father's elegantly attired and always royal figure depart, Dominic moved noiselessly beside her. "Did you tell him how you felt?" he asked her.

"It seemed kinder to not," she said. "Not all fathers care for emotions of a personal nature."

She turned and gestured to Kit to join her. His sunny smile and genuine pleasure at being with her went a long way to easing the sting of an absent and emotionally distant father. Anabel caught Pippa's eye as her twin moved forward, an unusual expression of concern on her friend's face. But it quickly turned into a reassuring smile.

Best to look on the bright side. Philip had come and gone and she was no nearer a binding betrothal than before. And now she had only one parent to deal with. Anabel laughed at Kit's impression of Cardinal Granvelle and linked her arm in his.

Time to enjoy herself.

The day after the disastrous fight between brothers, Charlotte's Paris guests began to arrive. They came two or four or six at a time, a mix of old and threadbare aristocracy, newer merchant money, and scholars. Lucette noted with amusement that, as Renaud had prophesied, there were several unattached older women, lovely and warm, but none so engaging as Nicole LeClerc had been. Lucette didn't think Charlotte would succeed in marrying her father off just yet.

Dr. Dee arrived in company with his Paris hosts, Edmund and Marguerite Pearce. Lucette declined to meet the group upon arrival in the courtyard, afraid that she would make a fool of herself before everyone present. She'd left Dr. Dee a message in his bedchamber instead, and shortly he was knocking on her door.

She flung open the door and nearly into his arms. He patted her back a little awkwardly, no doubt bemused by her behavior. She didn't cry—just—but drew a steadying breath as she pulled away.

"Welcome to Blanclair," she said wryly.

He laughed. "It would seem your time here has been rather more intense than your letters indicated."

Closing the door, Lucette waited until they were both seated on chairs with matching cushions embroidered by Nicole LeClerc before she spoke again.

Her summary was in the manner Dr. Dee himself had taught her: succinct, information laid out without undue emphasis on any one point, leaving room for interpretation and new connections to be made. She drew no conclusions and thought she spoke with absolute neutrality.

And then she asked her single, accusatory question. "Did you know that Julien LeClerc was in Walsingham's employ when he sent me here?"

"I did not know. I wondered—that is, I always accept as axiom that Francis Walsingham's success in protecting Her Majesty is that he never tells all of what he knows. I am not surprised by this omission. He would not want you prejudiced beforehand."

"You might have warned me!"

"That you were going to a place where all was not what it seemed? I thought you'd had sufficient warning for that. You know how to read a puzzle truly."

Not when that puzzle is a man like Julien, she thought.

"And so?" prompted Dr. Dee.

"And so nothing. I have provided the information. Nightingale most definitely has some connection to Blanclair. As to the who . . . that is for a wiser head than mine to sort. Have you identified the murdered man I wrote you of?"

She asked the last question to deflect him from pressing her. She had said nothing, still, of Julien meeting the dead man in the tavern. And she had not turned over the fragment of the Spanish letter or Anise's explanation for it. There were any number of arguments she could have used to defend her omissions, but in the end she knew it for simple arrogance.

This is my puzzle to solve, and my heart that is at risk in the solving of it.

He answered her readily enough. "The dead man appears to have been a certain English Catholic, exiled these ten years to France. No one of consequence, made his living doing the nastier sorts of work for various cardinals and conspirators."

She stood up, suddenly as anxious to get away from Dr. Dee as she had before been eager to see him. He rose more slowly, watching her keenly. His eyes, which always looked into a distance Lucette could not fathom, were troubled—by her lies?—and she suddenly couldn't bear the familiarity of his sober black attire and precisely pointed beard.

"I shall let you be, Lucette," he said. "I am afraid this has been more difficult on you than you anticipated."

"Did *you* anticipate it?" *Did you see how my heart would be conflicted?* she meant. *How I cannot trust my mind when my feelings are so wrapped up in my conclusions?*

But, like Pippa, John Dee never told her what she wanted to hear. "Don't mistrust yourself," was all he said. "Your instincts are as sound as your logic."

When he left her, Lucette fled her chamber. She would have gone to the gardens, but they were filled with visitors in loud ecstasies of praise at their beauty. Instead she took the river path down to the point where that mysterious body had lain.

She was not the only one who'd fled the house and gardens. Sitting on a flat-topped rock overlooking the river was Nicolas.

Hesitating, unsure whether to disturb him or if she felt up to conversation, Lucette had the decision made for her when he half turned and smiled.

"Looking for a hiding place?" he asked drily.

"Clearly I'm not the only one."

"I confess, I find the crowds ... wearying," he said. "Strange to think how I once thrived in large circles. Now I prefer my own company and that of one or two special people."

"Like Felix?"

"Felix is growing up into a very interesting character. I look forward to seeing him develop. Of course, it would be so much better for him to have a woman in the household."

"You're starting to sound like your sister," Lucette warned, but with a hint of unease beneath her teasing.

Nicolas had a very engaging way of half smiling, his eyes never flickering from her face. "It never seemed quite so important when my mother was alive, for who could be more loving and gentle than she? But having you here these weeks . . . yes, it has made me consider how much I would like to give Felix a mother."

"You are interested only for Felix's sake?" Beneath her dry tone, Lucette's mind sharpened. If Nicolas was prepared to offer for her, it was not for his son's sake. And surely not for her own. Beneath all his charm and careful words, she would have bet everything she owned that Nicolas was no more in love with her than she was with him.

His smile vanished, and he looked at her with an appeal that was strangely vulnerable. "Lucette, I think you will not be entirely surprised if I say that I have grown quite fond of you." He made an impatient gesture with his hands, as though angry with himself, and said, "No, that is too weak. You know that I did not love my wife, beyond a surface affection. I thought it was simply because we did not have the time to develop that sort of love. But since I have met you, I have discovered that it is not time alone that determines love."

"Nicolas . . ."

She was glad when he spoke over her, for she did not know what to follow that with. If it were Julien offering up his love . . .

She still wouldn't know what to say.

"Before I speak of my feelings too closely, Lucette, there is something I must tell you. Something that no woman living knows. It's about my injuries in Paris eight years ago."

"I'm listening."

"The mobs—I don't know if you've ever seen a mob. I pray not. They are vicious and mindless. They strike without thought and move on, leaving destruction in their wake. On the eve of St. Bartholomew's Day, when the assassinations began, they quickly spilled into explosive rage against anyone and anything in their way. I got caught in the middle between Huguenot and Catholic and I suppose I am lucky not to have been killed. Not that I didn't wish it for years afterward."

"What did they do to you?" She catalogued what she knew of him: his face was untouched, and his limbs—although he did have a slight hesitation to his gait. He must have been beaten, but so badly that he'd wanted to die?

"My father would be very angry at my telling you this." He gave a harsh bark of laughter. "And I don't suppose your father or brothers would be any too pleased, either. It's not a fit subject for a lady. But there is more I would say to you that I cannot say if you do not know the whole of what I could offer."

"Are you asking me to marry you?" It seemed that one of them would have to get to the point sooner or later.

"I would very much like to ask you that, but I cannot until you know how I was crippled."

"Crippled?"

He grimaced, then looked at her straight on and said, "Unmanned, more like. When the Catholics got hold of me trying to save a Huguenot girl, they thought I had dishonoured myself with a heretic whore. So they killed the girl—and castrated me."

SIXTEEN

Nicolas held his breath. It was a very calculated risk he was taking—but he did not believe Lucette was the kind of woman to recoil in horror or faint in shock. He rather thought she was a woman who liked being treated as though her mind mattered as much as her body, and so he had at last decided to risk that particular truth.

But for all his calculated risk, he did find himself curiously light-headed. It was the first time he'd ever said the words aloud. Not that words could convey the full damage that had been done to him.

Lucette went perhaps a shade paler. "I am sorry—" She broke off, forehead creased, and said impatiently, "What a ridiculous thing to say! Of course I am sorry and of course those are mostly empty words."

"Not coming from you." He paused, and added, "I do apologize. This is not a proper topic for any woman, and I don't doubt that you will be eager to escape my company now."

"Why? We cannot choose our injuries."

"It would be different if you were a married woman, for then you would begin to realize what I lost. But then, if you were married, we would not be having this conversation."

"Why *are* we having this conversation?"

"Because for the first time I have met a woman whom I very much want to be my wife. And that is the most selfish desire I have ever had in my life. Which is saying something," he added wryly.

"Selfish?"

"You realize that the Church would never sanction a new marriage for me. I am not fit for such a state in their eyes."

"Does the Church know of your state?"

"No. Only Julien, who found me, and my father. My mother knew, of course, for it was she who nursed me personally. Even my wife was kept in the dark, seeing as she was so near her time. Felix was born just weeks later and Célie died without ever knowing how her husband had been ruined."

Nicolas could hardly bear to recall the months that had followed Paris. The pain had been as nothing to his interior torment. He had screamed at his mother, told her to let him die, refused to listen to her gentle counsel or his father's more measured practicalities. "You are not the only man to be so injured," he'd told his son. "Battlefields are messy and not a few have had to live on without all they once had."

But it was Julien who had, unwittingly, shown his brother how to survive. He had hovered around Nicolas in both Paris and, after he could travel safely, at Blanclair. Nicolas had refused to see him. But at last, three weeks after Felix's birth, he admitted Julien to his chamber.

And Julien had vowed vengeance on his behalf. He had gone on and on about the viciousness of the Catholics, the wholesale slaughter of Huguenots that seemed to disturb him, the stupidity of France tearing itself to pieces over religion. But Nicolas had focused on one word: *vengeance*.

He had decided at that moment to live, and seek his own vengeance against the man whose doing this had been. It had been a long time coming, but now he was so very close.

Lucette had been sitting throughout his reverie with a thoughtful expression. Now she said, "So if I were to marry you . . ." She looked at him quizzically and he almost laughed. He had definitely calculated right. Lucette would be intrigued by the thought of doing something forbidden.

"As I said, the most selfish desire of my life. For it would mean, of course, that you would never have children."

She nodded, but seemed more thoughtful than repulsed. "Except for Felix."

"Except for Felix. But it is not just children, Lucette. I could never be what a husband should be for his wife. Of course there would be affection and even—how do I say this delicately?—pleasure. There is more than one way for men and women to experience pleasure. I would like nothing more than to make you happy in every way."

"I assume your father has no idea of what you're proposing."

"No. If it were I alone, he would laugh me to scorn. But if you wanted me, Lucette, if you stood your ground beside me, then who could oppose us?"

Many people, he answered himself. All his father would have to do was tell a priest and then no church official would agree to perform such a marriage. But that was supposing the marriage took place in France. If it were England . . . surely Lucette would have to go home first.

Taking her betrothed with her. To England.

Exactly where Nicolas needed to be.

She bit her lip in concentration and he didn't move, afraid to let her see how desperately he needed her to say yes.

"I think . . ." she ventured, then cleared her throat before continuing in a firmer voice. "I think that, once Charlotte's party is over, we should speak to your father."

———

At last Charlotte's carefully thought-out night was upon them and all Julien could think was thank goodness it would be over by morning. And the day after that, Renaud would set out to escort Dr. Dee and Lucette to Le Havre, and Julien could return to Paris and a normal life.

Except that normal didn't seem so appealing anymore. There were one or two women from Paris at Blanclair whom he had known rather well, but he felt very little except resignation when encountering them. They were so mannered and brittle and casual—when all he could think of now was Lucette's stubbornness and passion and clarity of thought. There was nothing studied about her, no matter how sophisticated the quality of her mind.

Only once in his life had Julien come close to speaking truly to a woman—or a girl, for Léonore had been very young. He had not quite dared to say he loved her, but he'd come near it with small gifts and giddy notes and a handful of kisses. It all seemed so far removed from now. He'd been very young himself, too young to recognize the dangers inherent in sharing his heart with anyone.

What if, his heart whispered to him now, he dared just once to speak aloud what he never had? What if he stopped making gestures, stopped hoping that Lucette could read his mind from the way he behaved, and spoke openly? What if he told her that *Lucie mine* was not simply a flirtatious phrase, but a wish he hadn't known he possessed until she appeared?

I love you, Lucette, he imagined saying, without equivocation or charm. A simple statement of fact. *I love you.*

If he'd been drinking, he would assume it was the alcohol speaking. But he was as clearheaded as he'd ever been and she was the reason.

By the time Julien left his chamber, attired in the masquerade apparel chosen by Charlotte, he had just about decided to take the risk.

Attending formal events was a learned skill, and fortunately one that stuck with you. Julien allowed himself to be attired in clothing borrowed from Nicolas and made over to suit Charlotte's exacting standards. It was easy to forget how confining formal dress could feel, with its tight seams and heavy satins and brocades. Mostly he hated not having a weapon close to hand. Would Lucette have managed to conceal her bodice dagger about her no doubt elaborate gown? It would be a fine thing to declare his love only to have her pull a weapon on him. Still, he grudgingly supposed the only thing he was in danger from tonight was boredom.

Julien had been to numerous *bal masqués* in Paris. Society appreciated the opportunity to pretend not to know one another and thus behave with a greater degree of licentiousness. In Julien's opinion, it was a thin disguise at best. There were plenty of people he did not recognize tonight, but that was because he didn't know them well in the first place or simply didn't care. But Charlotte, for instance, was unmistakable in her diaphanous white and silver finery meant to resemble that of Aphrodite (though anyone less like the remote and capricious Grecian goddess of love he could hardly imagine).

She fluttered over and immediately began scolding him for things he hadn't done yet. "You are not to scowl tonight," she lectured. "Don't scare anyone away. And don't hide in corners."

"My dearest sister, have you never seen me in Paris? I assure you, I am not accustomed to hiding in corners."

"No, just women's bedchambers. Flirt all you like, Julien, but don't do anything stupid."

"Such as?"

"Such as behaving badly so as to drive Lucette away from you. I know you, Julien. You are head over heels for her, and you hate it because you can't control it."

He looked at his little sister, who so resembled their mother, and felt a moment's pang for Nicole's loss. And another pang that he was so easily read by the women in his family. "Charlotte, my love, I promise to behave impeccably tonight. If you will promise not to tell me how I'm feeling."

Her smile was all indulgent triumph. "Just don't hide away, from either her or yourself."

He kissed her on the forehead to shut her up, then took her by the shoulders and steered her in the direction of her husband. Andry, as usual, wore a look of benevolent forbearance despite the fact that Charlotte had dressed him as Zeus. "Go and harass your husband as you're supposed to."

If Charlotte's intent had been to transform Blanclair into Paris for one evening, she had only partially succeeded. The décor was stunning, all silver and black as a backdrop to the costumes. And Charlotte's guests did not disappoint in richness and imagination of their attire: Julien saw men and women in all manner of costumes, from the crusading St. Louis and Jeanne d'Arc and even (either compliment or insult to the English guest) a very large Henry VIII. There were any number of soldiers and Queens of Heaven.

Blanclair, however, could never achieve the delightful decadence of Paris, not while Renaud LeClerc called the chateau his home. There was wine in abundance, and food of delicacy and beauty: asparagus and roast quails, capons and tiny sausages, quinces and a range of candied spices. But it lacked the garishness of society banquets, for Renaud was not interested in display for display's sake, and Charlotte, for all her enthusiasm, cared more about actual hospitality than merely impressing others.

Julien managed to get through the hours by turning off his mind and behaving by instinct. He knew how to give the appearance of drinking enough to be friendly, how to smile without meaning and flatter without commitment, how to dance with a woman daringly dressed as a satyr whose name slipped straight through his memory before the music ended.

And through it all, he was aware every moment of Lucette. When he first saw her, he was unable to compose a coherent thought. It was his body that answered her appearance, so that it was a good ten minutes before he was able to assemble the clues as to her masked identity. The underskirt of her kirtle was entirely covered with beautiful buff-coloured feathers, weightless in appearance if not fact. The overgown had a bodice and sleeves of iridescent taffeta in copper and bronze, and the sheerest organza partlet encircled her in a collar of lace and left bare a triangle of skin from the base of her throat to the edges of her square-cut neckline. From her waist, the overgown flowed into a cutaway skirt of more feathers—in shades from ochre to chestnut to mahogany—so cunningly wrought that she looked almost to be flying as the gown moved with her.

Her mask was not of feathers, as might have been expected, but delicate gold and copper filigree that swirled and swooped across her cheeks, rising to a winged peak at her right eye.

Most of the women here had dressed in either white or rich, deep colours that paired well with jewels. Why the cream and brown combination?

Feathers. Lucette was not some historical maiden fair or literary allusion: she was a bird. A bird with a buff chest and wings and back of soft browns.

A nightingale.

He actually laughed aloud when he realized, and murmured, "Clever girl." The woman he was dancing with at the time seemed to think the compliment meant for her.

Lucette danced with at least half of the men in attendance and Julien heard her praises sung everywhere he turned. By the men, at least. The women mostly watched her through narrowed eyes, no doubt giving thanks she would not be a permanent fixture in their society.

Renaud danced with her (they seemed to be having a private discussion despite their surroundings), and then Nicolas followed their father. They looked good together, Julien grudgingly conceded. Why shouldn't they? He and Nicolas had similar hair colour, the same eyes, only the differences in height and build to differentiate. Either of them would set off Lucette's beauty nicely.

When the musicians finished the pavane, Nicolas spoke to Lucette, heads close together as though confiding secrets. Or intimacies. As Julien headed toward them, he told himself he was interrupting because if he delayed dancing with Lucette for any longer, Charlotte would ascribe it to rudeness.

"May I?" he asked to the air between them. He expected Nicolas to look annoyed, but his brother smiled faintly.

"As the lady wishes," Nicolas said.

As the opening strains of a galliard sounded, Lucette answered, much too quickly, as though covering her nerves, "Yes, of course."

Julien chose the safest topic of conversation he could think of. "I believe my nephew will never get over the fact that he is not old enough to dance with you tonight."

"Perhaps Felix will have another chance when he is older."

"Do you plan to return to France someday, then?"

"Or Felix could come to England."

Julien quirked a skeptical eyebrow. "The French are generally not welcome in England."

"Some French are. We have lots of Huguenots," she said softly.

"So says the woman dressed as a nightingale. Trying to get yourself killed, or simply noticed?" he asked.

"If I wanted to be noticed, I'd have chosen a more striking masquerade than a nondescript bird. A swan, perhaps?"

"Lucie mine," and as he said it, he could almost see the shiver of her response, "you could never, in your life, be nondescript. And I don't want to talk politics or religion tonight."

They moved apart to the music, and came back together. "What do you want to talk about?"

"Maybe I don't want to talk at all."

He did, though. His hands tightened against her waist and he knew he was venturing onto thin ice. He could not afford to lose his head, no matter if his heart was already in her keeping. No matter if he spent his nights wishing he could turn back the clock and undo everything that kept him from speaking up. Not with this woman who solved puzzles and spied for Walsingham and didn't trust him. Lucette had come to France for a purpose, and falling in love with him was not that purpose.

He didn't care. Whatever she felt or didn't, whatever her purpose, Julien must speak or forever hate himself for his cowardice.

"I wondered," he began, and had to clear his throat in order to continue. "Might we go riding tomorrow? One last time before you leave. There is something I would like to say to you."

He would never get over the effect of those blue eyes fixed on him as though daring to read all his secrets. "I don't know if—"

"Please."

He added the plea in English and thought her lips trembled. But she managed to smile. "Yes, let's talk. There is something I'd like to tell you myself, before . . ."

He did not like that hesitation. "Before what?" he prodded.

"Before someone else can."

What could she possibly fear him hearing?

That she'd cracked the Nightingale Plot and knew him to be innocent? That she'd had orders from Walsingham to arrest him? (He'd like to see her try.) Maybe she had decided to extend her stay in France.

As the galliard drew to an end, there was the usual chatter of the crowds, and then, unusually, a brief flourish from the musicians that drew everyone's eyes to the top of the steps.

It was not Charlotte who stood there, nor even Renaud, to thank their guests for coming to Blanclair. It was Nicolas, taking his place as the eldest son, heir to the estate, something Renaud had long wanted Nicolas to do. It should have made Julien happy, to see his brother more engaged in the world. But guilt was a habit with him, and he distrusted happiness.

"Thank you," Nicolas said. "It has been a great pleasure to have you in our home. But it has been an even greater pleasure to have had for some weeks the company of our guest, Lady Lucette Courtenay. Though, of course, she has always been more than a guest to our family. She has belonged to Blanclair since the day of her birth, and so I have at last moved to make that permanent by asking her to be my wife."

Julien froze, certain that he'd heard wrong. Nicolas couldn't get married. And even if he'd asked her, Lucette would not have said yes. She wasn't here to fall in love, with either of them.

But then he looked down at her, as frozen as Julien was, and he knew it for truth. *There is something I'd like to tell you myself, before someone else can.*

He came back to himself suddenly and shoved himself through the crowds, knowing only that he had to get as far away from her as possible.

For one terrible moment, when Nicolas spoke so easily of their being betrothed, Lucette thought she might faint. What the hell is he doing? she thought profanely. But even through her shock, she recognized that he had chosen his words with care. He'd said he had *asked* her to be his wife; he did not claim that she had accepted. From Julien's reaction, Lucette knew that few would have parsed his words that carefully. And from the almost instant swell of cheerful voices surrounding her, everyone took it for granted that she and Nicolas were officially betrothed.

She found she was still clinging to Julien's arm only when he pulled away violently. She wanted to stop him. She wanted to follow him and explain . . . what? That she had trapped his brother into coming to England in order to deliver him to Walsingham? That, if she was right, Nicolas had done all in his power to implicate Julien in the plots? That she had no intention of marrying Nicolas, or anyone else, for that matter. That there was only one man she could now imagine marrying—

And he had just looked at her as though she were less than the dust beneath his feet.

She could not remain frozen or give way to fury or despair, for almost at once she was surrounded by well-wishers.

Charlotte gave her an enormous hug. "Oh, Lucette," she said. "You know this is what I'd hoped for! Although I do wonder . . ."

"Wonder what?" Perhaps Charlotte could sense her shock.

But her friend simply shook her head. "I wonder how fast the news will fly upstairs to Felix, and how quickly he will fly down the stairs to welcome you."

Oh, no. She did not want Felix to be part of the joyous aftermath of Nicolas's announcement. This wasn't about Felix. This was about Nightingale and her suspicions, and she hadn't actually said yes, but how could she tell that to a boy who would rejoice at the thought of her staying at Blanclair with his father?

But better to face Felix than the other LeClerc men. Even without being able to see Renaud through the throngs that pressed around to congratulate her, she imagined she could feel his disapproval beating at her and knew a difficult interview lay in her immediate future.

But Renaud's disapproval would be nothing in the face of Julien's outrage. He had vanished from her side before she had even been able to draw breath, and somehow she thought he would keep out of the way until he could confront her on his terms.

She would have given a great deal to know precisely the nature of Julien's outrage. And what it was he'd wanted to say to her tomorrow.

Knowing herself for a coward, Lucette stayed glued to Charlotte's side in order to protect herself. She let the wash of French voices flow over her, smiling and confining herself to a murmured "*Merci*" whenever there was a pause. Though Charlotte looked at her curiously once or twice, she did not press.

Although Lucette was not generally the last reveler at a party, tonight she wished desperately that things would continue until morning. But long before she was prepared (though when might that have been?), the last guests drifted away to the guest chambers and local inns and she was left with only the fragile guard of Charlotte and a quizzical Andry against the combined might of the LeClerc men.

Renaud had never seemed more the commander of men he was, anger beating beneath his calm exterior.

He kissed his daughter on the forehead. "Thank you, *ma chère*. You must be tired. I'll see you in the morning." It was clearly a dismissal.

Andry shot a look at his father-in-law, and with a quick read of the situation, tucked his wife's hand through his elbow and led her out before she could protest.

"I think my study would be the best place for this," Renaud said, and Lucette could not decipher the neutrality of his voice. "Julien, go to bed."

Only when he addressed his second son did Lucette realize that Julien was present. She could not help but look. He stood in a far corner, half the chamber away, with face locked down. She wondered if he would protest being sent away—did she want him sent away?—but Nicolas intervened.

"I'd like Julien to be there, if you don't mind. He has always been intimately involved with my . . . affairs." The look between brothers was of a nature that Lucette thought might lead to drawn weapons.

Renaud drew breath, surely to refuse, then shot a keen glance at Lucette. "What do you say, *mademoiselle*?"

That I want this to be over as quickly as possible. Without looking at Julien, she said formally, "I have no objections."

Nicolas put a possessive hand at the small of her back as they followed Renaud and Julien to the comfortable study. Fortunately, she'd had a lot of practice feigning disinterest and the illusion of perfect control. She'd been able for years to hold off the penetrating interest of both her mother and Queen Elizabeth as to her emotional state—Renaud LeClerc should pose little problem.

Nicolas sat next to her and held her hand, facing Renaud behind his desk. Julien lounged behind them, leaning against the wall, but Lucette fancied she could see tension radiating off him in streaks of black.

"I wish," Renaud said softly, "that you had spoken to me first, Nicolas. Now you have put the lady in an extraordinarily awkward position when she is forced to decline. As she must."

"Why must I?" Lucette asked.

"Nicolas knows why. I don't know what he was thinking—"

"He told me," Lucette interrupted bluntly. Might as well get that awkwardness over with at once.

She heard Julien's breath hiss between his teeth. Renaud's expression flickered, and she knew he was shocked. "Told you what?"

"What happened to him in Paris. I know the nature of his injuries. And why you believe him unsuited for another marriage."

"It is not a matter of belief," Julien said through tight throat. "He *cannot* marry again. The Church would never allow it."

"I am not Catholic, and who says your Church has to know about it?" Lucette shot back without looking at Julien. It was Renaud she needed to have on her side. "I believe the matter of marriage lies primarily between the man and woman concerned."

Renaud lifted his eyebrows in mock surprise. "Surely the daughter of Minuette Courtenay knows better than to believe that."

She flushed, but did not waver. "As her daughter, I also know that she will be well persuaded by my own wishes in the matter."

"But Nicolas is my son, and I am not persuaded by the wishes of a girl too young to know what she would be giving up. Surely you must want children."

"Father," Nicolas broke in. "I have discussed the implications with her."

Julien let out a choked laugh and shoved himself off the wall behind them and into Lucette's sight. "That must have been an interesting conversation. How detailed did you get, brother?"

"That's enough." Renaud's tone was familiar—that of a man used to command.

Julien choked back whatever else he'd wanted to say. Renaud kept his eyes fixed on Lucette. She stared back, willing him to be reasonable, knowing that if he did not make some concession, she would have ruined things with Julien for no reason at all.

Finally, Renaud sighed. "As I stand in France in lieu of your parents, *mademoiselle,* then I cannot give consent. I should send you back to England, away from my sons, and give thanks to see the last of you."

"But . . ." Lucette prompted into the space he left at the end of that speech.

"But frankly, I fear the impulsive lengths to which you might go if I issued a flat refusal. Only one man can give consent to this marriage, and that is Dominic Courtenay. Nicolas, if you are convinced of the merits of your argument, then you may make them yourself to Lord Exeter. I will send you to England with Lucette and Dr. Dee. Whatever Dominic decides I will abide by."

Because you know there's no chance Dominic will agree, Lucette thought cynically. Fine. All she needed was to get Nicolas to England and see what followed. There was only one more piece to the Nightingale puzzle, and she would bet her soul that Nicolas would solve it for her.

She had memorized the words of the Spanish letter sent to her by Anise: *To travel as her intended would be for the best as it would attract the least notice. The window for action is narrow and the nightingale grows impatient.*

Nicolas had made his play for her, and she must see it through to the end. Julien might hate her now, but how much more would he hate her if he knew she intended to deliver his brother to Walsingham? No, best to let him despise her for a foolish girl who had finally landed the brother she'd wanted since she was ten years old.

"I'll go with them as well," Julien said abruptly. "If Nicolas does not object?"

"I insist upon it," Nicolas replied. "Who else would I rather have by my side in this than my brother?"

Renaud shook his head, as though recognizing the disaster that could only ensue. But he did not object.

She escaped to her chamber, glad to get away from all of them, and Charlotte's efficient Parisian maid had her out of her ballgown and into her nightdress and robe in short order. She took the pins out of Lucette's hair, but then Lucette dismissed her. Unplaiting and brushing her hair would give her something to focus on. Something she could cope with.

Two hours later she still sat before the table. She had tried working in her Memory Chamber, but the ledgers in her mind kept dissolving into images of Julien; laughing at her at Wynfield when she was little, insulting her in Paris, surprise writ all over his expression when she'd asked him to kiss her. *I shall be brave for the both of us.*

She could have used some of his bravery now.

There came a single knock on her door, then it was pushed open even as she got to her feet. The moment she saw Julien, Lucette knew that he was very, very drunk. It must have been instinct, or something in his eyes, because he moved into her chamber with the same arrogant grace, and when he spoke, his words were perfectly distinct.

"Why so shocked, Lucie?" he asked with that mocking tone that had made her hate him when she was ten years old. "Never had a man in your bedchamber before?"

Though she knew she coloured, she would not cower. "I do have brothers."

He laughed, and that did sound a bit slurred. "And that statement proves your entire innocence. But of course you are innocent, or you would not possibly be entertaining my brother's insane proposal."

"It is none of your affair."

"The hell it isn't." He strode closer and looked her up and down so that she was very conscious of how little fabric clothed her. Only her linen nightdress and a thin silk robe. Compared to the yards of fabric she was usually draped in, she might as well have been naked. Her hair hung loose as well; she had brushed it but never replaited it.

Julien let his breath out, and that, too, was shaky. "Do you think," he whispered, "that Nicolas doesn't know exactly how I feel about you?"

"Then he knows more than I do," she snapped.

"Oh, Lucie, how can you be so smart and so damned stupid at the same time?" He took another step closer and she knew she should back away, put distance between them, but she didn't think she could make herself move. Julien continued to speak in that low, seductive voice. "You do not even know what you will be giving up. I've no doubt Nicolas can please you. He had a lot of practice when young—far more than I ever did at his age—and he's not so cruel as to not want to give you what pleasure he can."

Julien's right hand touched her shoulder, so light but with that ever-present promise of strength that made her swallow hard. "He will touch you," he said, suiting his actions to his words, "run his hand across the soft skin beneath your throat, then trace your curves—you have such curves, Lucie—to your hips."

Both his hands were on her now, but he touched her nowhere else, though his lips were so near her cheek she could smell the wine that had made him so reckless.

"He may even," Julien continued, and suddenly scooped her up and strode to the bed, "lay you gently down so that your hair spills across the linens."

She must stop him, they could not do this, but her body rebelled against her scruples and wanted nothing more than to be laid on her bed by Julien. And more—she wanted him with her.

Julien complied, at least partially. He stretched over her, palms flat on the bed above her shoulders so that he hovered just inches over her without touching. "And what then, Lucie?" he whispered. "What is it that you will want then?"

Without thought, she raised her head and kissed him. Her hands went to his shoulders, tugging at him, but he would not move even when she—to her great shame—found herself arching up to try and feel him against her. She had never guessed that the promise of touch could be as unbearably arousing as touch itself.

And then, with a shudder, he gave in, and she could feel the whole long length of him against her and she would have gasped if her mouth wasn't so thoroughly absorbed. She ran her hands across his chest, trying to find the laces of his doublet and shirt.

But Julien pulled back sharply, his eyes no longer seductive, but harsh. "This is what you will want," he ground out. "Two bodies moving entirely as one. And that is what my brother can never give you. Because it is not just your pleasure that matters. As much as I want to undo you, Lucie mine, to make you tremble until you have forgotten yourself entirely, there is one thing I want even more than that."

"Julien—"

He shoved himself off the bed, backing away from her as he spoke. "I want to be undone by you. I want to be the one to come to pieces in your arms, to forget there is anything in this world but the two of us. That is what should be between a man and woman, between a husband and wife. Nicolas can never give you that. He will always be in control. Is that really the man you want in your marriage bed, Lucie?"

She scrambled to her feet, the colour in her face blanching to white as desire turned to fury. "What I want is none of your business, Julien. Except to respect my choices and leave me alone."

He turned his back on her, but moved no further for what seemed to be hours but was probably no more than a minute or two. When he faced her again, incredibly, he had himself under control. His voice was brusque. "I apologize. I am, as you no doubt noticed, extraordinarily drunk. It will not happen again. I shall accompany you and Nicolas to England. And I shall come no nearer to you the entire time than the most correct gentleman ever would."

When he'd left, Lucette huddled on her bed, arms wrapped around her knees, and wept until her head ached. She felt as desolate as she had at fifteen, when she'd learned that Dominic might not be her father. She should have known better than to fall in love with Julien—every relationship in her life Lucette had managed to destroy.

Perhaps that was the legacy left her by the king.

INTERLUDE

September 1574

"Her Majesty, Elizabeth!"

At the herald's cry, every man bowed and every woman curtsied, all eyes modestly lowered as the Queen of England, Ireland, and France entered the Great Hall and processed slowly to her throne. Lucette Courtenay was accustomed to the formality of Queen Elizabeth's birthday celebrations, for she had attended with her family since she was twelve years old.

Today was different. She was sixteen now, and she stood alone, on the opposite side of the hall from her siblings and parents. *Parent, singular,* she corrected herself fiercely, and kept her eyes averted from where the Duke and Duchess of Exeter stood with their three children. Like her, they ignored the curious glances of the crowd.

One could always count on the Courtenay family to scorn public opinion with dignity.

Lucette did the dance of appearing carefully attentive while assessing which of the young men present would be the best partner in her planned act of defiance. She had considered logically beforehand, but now let her own interest guide her. Henry Howard looked as though he'd spent the previous night doing something other than sleeping blamelessly alone; Matthew Arundell looked puffy and yellow. Not that she needed to be attracted to her partner in crime, but it wouldn't hurt.

Finally, she admitted that there was only one real option: Brandon Dudley. He had just turned nineteen, and those who'd known Robert Dudley swore Brandon was the very image of his Gypsy-dark uncle. After an unpropitious infancy—born in the Tower to Margaret Clifford, a royal cousin of Elizabeth; his father, Guildford Dudley, executed immediately after the boy's birth—Brandon's fortunes had improved when Elizabeth took the throne. Margaret Clifford had been married off at the queen's command to the onetime rebel Thomas Howard, fourth Duke of Norfolk. And though Norfolk had condemned himself to death this very year in another rebellion, Brandon Dudley had not suffered for it. He had been raised by John Dudley, the Earl of Warwick, older brother to both Robert and Guildford Dudley, and was thus protected both by his Protestant upbringing and by Queen Elizabeth's personal favour.

Perfect, Lucette thought grimly. Two personal favorites of the queen will make a very good pair.

She set about her seduction at once. When the formal reception dissolved, Lucette snaked her way to Brandon's side and greeted him with a flattering smile. "Might I beg the favour of your company?" she asked. "A certain persistent gentleman is determined to talk at me until, presumably, I am so bored I would agree to anything simply to have done listening to him."

Brandon's lips quirked to quite charming effect. "I should never abandon a lady to such a fate," he said gallantly, offering her his arm. "Would you care to walk in the gardens?"

It was a very pleasant hour. Brandon was as good a conversationalist as he was handsome, and his sense of humour aligned nicely with Lucette's—a certain cynical point of view that led more to amusement than disdain. By the time they separated, Lucette had promised to dance with Brandon that evening and she thought matters were progressing nicely.

As Lucette finished dressing for the evening, Pippa, only twelve, watched her fuss with the enameled necklace of Tudor roses around her neck, and there was a crease of concern between her green eyes. Pippa herself was elaborately gowned in dark pink, for she would spend the evening in attendance upon Princess Anne. Only when she opened the chamber door to leave did Pippa say, "Do you know what you're doing, Lucie?"

"Feasting and dancing?" Lucette answered lightly. "I've known how to do that since I was eight."

Pippa sighed and Lucette walked away before her disconcerting little sister could say anything else. I do know what I'm doing, she thought crossly, and set off with firm steps to do it.

Apparently she had hit the right note in both dress and manner, for Brandon's eyes lit up when he saw her. As they danced, Lucette put into practice all her theoretical flirting skills and was very pleased with his response. More than once throughout the evening she caught her father—*no,* she corrected, *Dominic*—watching them with an impassive expression that pleased her even more.

It was ridiculously easy to maneuver Brandon into a secluded corner of the lantern-lit garden and get him to kiss her. She had nothing to compare it to, but he clearly knew what he was doing, and despite the careful calculation that had led her here, Lucette found herself dizzy.

From there matters progressed as she had planned. Brandon followed her from the gardens to the orchards and pressed her against a tree. He was an enthusiastic partner as long as she kept her hands in his hair. But when she began to unlace his doublet, Brandon hesitated.

"I don't think—" he began.

"Good," she whispered. "Don't think." She kissed the base of his throat and felt him swallow.

"Lucette . . ."

She moved one of his hands to the neckline of her bodice and for a few minutes he ceased to protest.

His doublet was unlaced, her hands on the fine linen of his shirt and marveling at the hard lines of his chest. If this was what men felt like, why had she waited so long? Brandon's hands roamed across her stiff bodice and tightly cinched waist, and she whispered, "We don't have to stay outdoors."

He groaned. "This is not a good idea. You are so young—"

"Old enough to know what I want."

"Your father will kill me."

Lucette felt herself flush and snapped, "Do you not want me?" Wouldn't that be the greatest irony—to set about a seduction that she could not fulfill for lack of compelling male interest.

Further proof that she was nothing like her mother.

She was torn between retreating and launching herself at him to force the issue. And then, like so many other things in her life, the issue was decided for her.

"Walk away, Dudley." Dominic stepped into view, looking as disinterested as ever but no doubt taking in every detail of Brandon's open doublet, his hands cupping Lucette's curves, her mouth red and full from wanton kissing.

Brandon dropped his hands as though burned, stepping away so hastily that Lucette could not but be insulted. "Lord Exeter," he stammered, looking suddenly very young himself. "My lord, my deepest apologies, I would never—"

"Did you not hear me? I will not say it again."

Lucette had never heard Dominic sound like that before, and ice swept through her veins.

At least Brandon had the courtesy to shoot her a look of apology, but he disappeared without another word.

Dominic didn't speak, either, but took Lucette by the arm. She let him lead her back to the palace, head high and fury bright as he towed her to the family apartment. Minuette was there, and seemed to take in the situation in a single glance. Lucette waited for her mother's reproaches, but this time she kept her mouth closed and allowed her husband to lead.

"What," Dominic said, his tone all clipped fury, the more dangerous for his habitual control, "in the name of God were you doing?"

"I should think it was fairly obvious."

His eyes narrowed. "What are you playing at, Lucette? Do you want to destroy your reputation and dishonour your family with so little thought? And don't tell me you have conceived some grand passion for the Dudley boy. You were simply using him."

"Perhaps I was," she shot back. "Like mother like daughter, after all."

Dominic raised his hand and Lucette took a step back. Was he really going to strike her?

"Dominic!" Minuette commanded, and Dominic dropped his hand at once.

"Apologize to your mother," he ground out through a tight jaw.

Lucette stood tall and met Dominic's eyes without faltering. "You cannot command me," she said clearly. And then, the five words that had been aching inside her for months, the words that would put an end to years of lies. "You are not my father."

SEVENTEEN

After riding to Portsmouth to bid Philip goodbye, Anne returned to court, which had moved the short distance from Hampton Court to Richmond Palace. Elizabeth had fretted uncharacteristically while her daughter was gone, and for once she did not make haste to remove the princess elsewhere. After the trauma with Philip and the end of their marriage, it was affirming to look at her daughter each day—and to know that she had won.

Not that she let Anne know how pleased she was. Being allowed to remain at court was reward enough, was it not? Besides, there was other news aplenty to keep Elizabeth occupied.

The anger in and against London's foreign population continued to erupt in intermittent violence. Amidst the usual xenophobic graffiti and smashing of doors and furniture were disturbing undertones of religious dissension. Slurs and taunts against Protestants in general and the queen in particular kept having to be scrubbed off walls. But once seen, such venom could not be unseen.

Walsingham reported on the latest beatings and burnings of

property one hot Thursday in July. "It was the Flemish weavers who bore the brunt this time," he said.

"Is it time to send in troops?" Elizabeth asked, already knowing the answer.

"Not wise, Your Majesty. At least not yet. The last thing we want is to inflame the situation. Better to support the City and London's mayor for now." He paused, then added, "More disturbingly, we've found Jesuit literature in the houses of some of those arrested. It appears at least some of the instigators have Continental backing."

"We've always known that."

"Suspected it, yes. But now we have proof."

"Proof for what purpose—to drag Philip back to England and try him in court? And what would be the charge? Hardly treason, as he is himself head of a separate kingdom. One that is politically and religiously opposed to ours."

"The danger, as Your Majesty well knows, is that Continental backing means Continental funding. Money talks, and dirty money talks loudest of all."

"What do you want from me, Walsingham? To let events play out in order to trace the money trail? I have little patience for allowing violence to flourish in my kingdom simply to aid your investigations."

"What if I told Your Majesty that, among the Jesuit literature, we found several crude badges in the shape of nightingales?"

"I would ask how you can possibly be certain that a crudely shaped bird is a nightingale? Perhaps it is a swan, and is meant to represent my throne."

Beneath her surface dismissal, Elizabeth was deeply uneasy. She was starting to dream about nightingales, great flocks of them descending from a clear sky to peck at her hair and face. It was irritating. She could not fight dreams; she needed hard information.

"You've heard from Dr. Dee?" she asked abruptly. "He and Lucette are set to arrive in Portsmouth in three days."

"Yes, Your Majesty. Dee tells me that there will be two additions to their party: both Nicolas and Julien LeClerc."

"Indeed?" Elizabeth pondered that somewhat surprising news. "Could it be that Lucette is actually coming back to England with a proposed husband in mind?"

"Or she intends to deliver the Nightingale mastermind into my hands."

Elizabeth gave a pointed smile. "Or perhaps she intends to do both. She is a remarkably resourceful girl. Does Dee think she has found the mastermind?"

It was never easy to decipher Francis Walsingham. In sober black, only his white ruff relieving the effect of a man dressed for death, he had a face made for secrets. The deep-set eyes beneath the dramatic widow's peak of his hair gave nothing away. Not even to her.

"Dee has committed little to writing, which could be for safety's sake so as not to alert the opposition that we are aware of their plot, or because Lucette herself has not confided much."

"If it's a choice between the two," Elizabeth noted drily, "I tend to favour the latter explanation."

"You know her better than I do, Your Majesty. It will be interesting to see what occurs when they land in England. I think I shall take my cues from Lady Lucette for the present. Is her father riding to Portsmouth to meet her?"

"No. He is sending his second son to fetch her. Would you like to ride along?"

Walsingham sat pensive, then said carefully, "I think I will let her have her head for now. If she is bringing us the Nightingale mastermind, then she has earned the right to set the immediate direction of events."

Elizabeth pondered that unusual trust of Walsingham's. He was addicted to control—whatever he himself did not personally handle, he did not trust. So his wariness with Lucette, she decided, was more likely to do with a wish not to spook a high-tempered noble girl into opposing him rather than because he trusted her intelligence instincts.

She spent the afternoon being entertained by Anne and her coterie of youngsters. It was flattering to have men twenty years younger than herself paying court, even if she was far too intelligent not to be cynical about such attention. But cynical or not, what woman wouldn't enjoy having her beauty praised and her wit honoured? Though the clumsier of the young men were not so smooth, and thus made it plain they were aiming merely to please their queen.

Of them all, only Brandon Dudley and Kit Courtenay managed to be truly engaging. Brandon, as the gossips had long noted, was very like his late uncle Robert. Of course he did not have the easy familiarity with her that Robert had enjoyed, but he had the same Gypsy-dark good looks, and a dry wit that stung those it targeted without drawing blood—quite.

Kit, on the other hand, was as innately charming as his mother, with a ready smile and sense of mischief that encroached on without quite violating propriety. Of all the young men in her court, Kit was the most familiar with her, a privilege he was quick to exploit.

"You will let Anabel come to Wynfield, won't you?" he said. "It wouldn't be summer without her visit."

"Her Royal Highness has been so eager to come to court," Elizabeth replied. "Why should I let her retreat from responsibility merely for her own pleasure?"

"But it not just her pleasure," Kit said. "It is mine . . . and all my family's. Besides, if Lucie has finally chosen a husband, you'll want Anabel's firsthand account of the excitement."

"If your sister thinks she has chosen a husband, she may find herself brought up sharply against your parents' wishes. And mine. Surely she does not think she is entirely at her own liberty in the matter?"

"No," Kit said ruefully. "But that only adds to the excitement. Lucie can be very stubborn when she's made up her mind."

Like Will, Elizabeth thought wistfully. Not that William's stubbornness in getting his own way had worked to his benefit. All the more reason for her to ensure her own daughter knew perfectly well how to subdue her desires to the greater good of England's people.

But Elizabeth could never bear to shoot Kit down entirely. Besides, he had a point. She herself meant to travel on progress from the last week of July through August, to escape London's heat and odors and illness, and she had not anticipated taking Anne with her.

"I will discuss matters with my council," she told Kit repressively, extending her hand, glittering with jewels, to allow him to kiss it. "And if their approval is acquired, I shall consider allowing the princess to visit Wynfield."

He kissed her hand with the kind of graceful flourish that had always eluded his father, and said, "You are truly our most gracious and wise queen."

Even if she knew it for flattery, she was willing to accept the triumph such praises brought.

Mary was quite pleased with the progress she'd made with Stephen Courtenay. Knowing something of his family, she did not expect open admiration from him, but he had taken to spending significant parts of each day in her company. He always rode with her, and she made a point of seeking his company and attention while she worked with her ladies at more feminine pursuits.

"Do you not weary of a being in a household of females, Lord Somerset?" she asked archly as she drew her needle through her current tapestry-in-progress, a depiction of Penelope at her own loom, spinning and unspinning day and night until her husband's return. "I imagine your upbringing was much more masculine."

"I do have two sisters, Your Majesty, and a mother. I think our household was well balanced between physical and intellectual pursuits. And if I am not myself handy with a needle, I admire those who are."

"I am, of course, no stranger to physical pursuits," Mary mused. "I was an excellent huntress, and loved both the pursuit with hounds and falconry. I miss the wider options of my former life greatly."

"Then you must at least appreciate being allowed to ride. You have not always enjoyed such freedom."

She shot a suspicious glance at him, but even when bordering on an indelicate subject, Stephen Courtenay managed to look innocent. She decided not to take offense. "It is true that my cousin has occasionally exercised her will against me most unjustly."

"Unjustly?"

"I am as much a queen regnant as my cousin, and so it is unjust by any law of men to keep me confined. And even more unjust according to God's laws. You must agree."

His eyes were opaque, in a way that piqued Mary's interest. He really was a most handsome young man. "I agree," he said thoughtfully, "that God's laws are always just. The difficulty is in how men and women interpret God's laws. I am inclined to think we see the world as we ourselves are, and not always with the clarity of God's vision."

She sighed, and shook her head. "Dear Stephen—may I call you Stephen?" It was a courtesy easily offered, and if he did not look appropriately abashed by her kindness, he did nod at the honour she was bestowing on him by using his given name. "Stephen, do you not know that difficulty is at the very heart of Church doctrine? We must have priests, anointed by God and his earthly representative, the pope. Without that authority, who can we trust? Any man can claim to speak for God. We must listen to those who are rightly ordained."

"My lady Mary." It was said so earnestly that Mary forgave the familiarity of the address. In truth, it touched her and reminded her that, despite being thirty-seven, she was still a woman young enough to fall in love. "I have no quarrel with the honest faith of any man or woman. I am quite certain that I do not speak for God, and so my concern will ever be with upholding the life of my queen and the security of this realm of England. Elizabeth would be your friend if you would let her. Why oppose her?"

Because I can, Mary nearly retorted, but that was not entirely true. Because she must, or else be resigned to offending God by relinquishing a position He himself had given her at birth.

And because this time Mary was going to win. One did not give up the game when one was on the brink of triumph.

But she merely smiled that lovely, heartbreaking smile of her youth, and rested her long white fingers on the back of Stephen's hand. "It is kind of you to trouble yourself about me. I shall remember that always."

When I am free, she meant. *And have it in my power to reward those who were kind.*

The day after Kit rode out to Dover to bring back Lucette, Anabel talked Pippa into a quiet cruise along the Thames in a pleasure barge. She invited no one else.

There were plenty of guards, of course, and sometimes Anabel felt sorry for them. Caught between her own wish for independence and her mother's commands to keep her close, she imagined the men had often had cause to curse the two high-spirited women who were the center of England's political life. A pity for them, she thought, and kept Pippa close enough to her that they could speak without too much being overheard and reported back to Elizabeth. Or Walsingham.

"What do you think of Lucette's Frenchmen?" Anabel demanded. "Is she going to marry one of them? I cannot imagine why else they would return to England with her."

Pippa was unusually pensive. "I think the situation is complicated," she finally ventured.

"Well, she cannot marry them both, so perhaps I'll enjoy myself flirting with the spare one when I come to Wynfield."

"You don't think that might reflect poorly on you?"

"What do you mean?" Anabel asked sharply. There were some privileges even the closest of friends should not take, and scolding her was one of them. "My mother practically demands that men flirt with her. No one thinks less of her for it."

"*You* do."

Anabel's temper, which slumbered deeply but roused like a dragon—or like a proud Spaniard—announced itself in the tightness of her lips and the narrowing of her eyes. She could feel it pounding in her temples as she said, "Do not presume to tell me how I feel. Ever."

But Pippa was her dearest friend partly because she could not be cowed by the most royal of furies. "Of course not. You are well able to know your own mind and feelings."

They remained in huffy silence for a bit, but Anabel could never stay angry with Pippa. "So, my reader of the heavens, is Lucette going to marry one of those handsome Frenchmen or not?"

"If she asks me, I will tell her. Otherwise, it is no one's business but her own."

"And presumably one of the LeClerc brothers."

"Or both of them," Pippa said softly.

Anabel looked at her sharply, but she didn't press. Even a royal recognized when Pippa's limits had been reached. If she tried to press her now, her friend would simply slip through her fingers, all graciousness and laughter but without revealing anything of substance at all.

Time to turn to something less fraught. Like politics. "The queen has asked me to write to Mary Stuart. I do not think her council is in agreement with that request."

"As James's mother, I suppose," Pippa said thoughtfully. "It's a clever move on the queen's part—show due deference to Mary's birth. She's prickly about her status and always complaining about your mother. I imagine inserting you into the middle is by way of defusing the situation."

"Do you think so?" Anabel mused. "I rather think I'm more likely to inflame Mary's pride. Whatever fawning letters I may write, she can never overlook the fact that she is as surely imprisoned as if she were in the Tower. What use will she have for contact with a girl whose only interest is in the son who, in Mary's mind, should not be King of Scotland? At least not yet."

"Then you will just have to employ every single bit of your royal charm so that Mary feels she is doing you a favour by allowing you to correspond with her son."

Anabel raised a skeptical eyebrow. "The son she has not seen since he was a year old?"

"I rather think Mary Stuart is prone to the romantic vision of life, as opposed to the practical. Make it easy for her, Anabel. It costs you nothing and might ease tensions with the Scots queen. And that can only be to England's benefit."

They returned to Richmond in a sedate fashion, only to be met at the Richmond Castle pier by a phalanx of grim-faced guards who would not answer questions and practically swept the girls off their feet until they were safely behind several pairs of locked doors. Even then there were no answers forthcoming, and Anabel paced until her feet hurt while Pippa sat silent, turned inward.

At last Lord Burghley entered. He looked tired and every year of his age, lines etched deeply around his mouth. "I apologize, Your Highness," he said, raising a hand to stop her flow of complaints and worries. "We did not mean to leave you in suspense, but there were measures that needed to be put into place immediately."

"What measures? What is going on?" Anabel heard her sharpness and knew it for fear.

"An hour ago, there was an assassination attempt on Her Majesty. A pistol at close range, that mercifully misfired. The man has been taken to the Tower for closer questioning, and a search made of the grounds and chambers to ensure there are no others lying in wait."

Anabel drew a steadying breath. This was not the first attempt on her mother's life. It was, however, the first time she herself had been in close proximity and part of the immediate aftereffects. She felt almost light-headed with relief and was glad when Pippa put an arm around her shoulder.

"Thank you for your care, Lord Burghley," Anabel said. "I imagine my mother is even now arguing with Walsingham about whether she is permitted to leave her chambers in the immediate future."

The Lord Treasurer said wryly, "I wager that is an argument the queen will win. Her Majesty will never allow her movements to be dictated by fear or threats. Tomorrow she will be about England's business once more. No doubt she will summon you shortly to reassure you herself."

When Burghley had gone, Anabel looked at Pippa. "Do you still think a few letters to Mary Stuart will ease tensions? As long as there are two queens on English soil, my mother's life will never be safe."

Elizabeth refused to settle, forcing Walsingham to pace with her as she restlessly circled her privy chamber. She had sent her ladies away after the immediate furor, not wanting to be surrounded by shocked females, and she gave full vent to her displeasure.

"In my own palace, Walsingham!" she raged. "The temerity of the man! To threaten the Queen of England in her own home."

"Would it have been less offensive if he had shot at you in the street, Your Majesty?" She always knew when Walsingham was annoyed with her; he clipped off the ends of his words and let sarcasm colour his tone.

"Who is he?" she demanded.

"We'll know more tomorrow. I'll go to the Tower myself tonight and question him."

"I want answers," she ordered. "Answers that can be trusted. How am I to rule if I do not know precisely what my enemies are about?"

"As I've long said, information is our most precious asset. If this man is part of the Nightingale Plot, then our need for information grows more acute. May I suggest that when Lucette Courtenay lands in Dover, she be brought to court with the LeClerc brothers? I feel certain that one or both of them has information pertinent to Nightingale. Let us deal with them up front."

Elizabeth stopped moving and closed her eyes. The bands of a sick headache were making themselves felt around her head, and she had to will herself not to show it. For one brief moment she wished that she didn't have to deal with this, that she was nothing more than a king's sister placidly wed and valued mostly for her appearance and wit.

She opened her eyes and looked out at the privy garden, sedate and controlled in its beauty. As she must be controlled. "Very well," she answered. "Bring Lucette and her trailing Frenchmen to court. Phrase it as a generous offer on our part, to welcome them. Might as well remind everyone that Lucette's future is very much of interest to me, and you can do whatever it is you do to uncover their secrets. In ten days I leave on progress."

"What of Princess Anne?"

"I want her out of London," Elizabeth said flatly. "I will not risk her being confronted by an assassin. She can go to Wynfield Mote. There is no one I trust more than Dominic Courtenay, and Wynfield is easily isolated from outsiders."

"If one of the LeClerc brothers is involved with Nightingale—"

"Then you must make certain you uncover the danger before Lucette takes either one of them home with her."

"Yes, Your Majesty."

Now to deal with the emotional reactions from her daughter and Lucette. All told, Elizabeth would prefer to deal with assassins.

EIGHTEEN

Lucette presented herself to her queen within two hours of her arrival at Richmond Palace. Her journey from Blanclair weighed heavily on her. Nicolas had been impeccably polite and appropriately affectionate; Dr. Dee had been puzzled both by the unexpected announcement of her betrothal and her refusal to discuss it with him; and Julien . . .

She could not allow herself to think about Julien. The terrible starkness with which he had made his last farewell in her bedchamber haunted her. But she would not break. She had set herself a task and she would finish it. No matter the cost.

Although she had hoped to find Pippa in residence with Anabel at court, she was resigned when told the two of them had gone ahead to Wynfield Mote. Her little sister's wisdom would have to wait. For now, Lucette appropriated a maid and had herself dressed in the same plum-coloured gown she had worn the night she met Julien in Paris.

Then she drew a deep breath and presented herself to the queen.

Elizabeth met her in her presence chamber, though the elegant space might have seemed too large for simply herself, Walsingham, and Lucette. But no chamber that Elizabeth inhabited could be too large, for she fit herself to every surrounding. As Lucette executed a heartfelt curtsey, she was swept by a genuine feeling of humility and thankfulness for England's ruler, a reminder that the Nightingale Plot was not an intellectual puzzle but a matter of life and death. It sobered her, and tempered her previous irritation with Walsingham's lies.

After a frank appraisal, Elizabeth said, "You do not seem to have materially suffered on your journey. It might even be thought that France agreed with you. France ... or at least a Frenchman or two. Dr. Dee tells us Nicolas LeClerc has all but claimed you for himself. What have you to say to that?"

Perhaps it was possible to be appreciative and irritated at the same time. Lucette said carefully, "Surely the more pressing question is what I have learned of the Nightingale Plot."

"And does not that have something to do with a specific Frenchman?"

"It does."

"Care to tell us which one?" Elizabeth probed. At her side, Walsingham had not moved his fixed gaze from Lucette, as though reading her every expression for truth.

Lucette turned her own gaze to his. "First, I should like the Lord Secretary to explain why he lied to me by omission. Why did you not tell me that Julien LeClerc is in your employ?"

"Because I was—and am—not certain that he is only in my employ. Indeed, technically he is not in my employ at all, as he has never accepted a single pence from England. In the last eight years, he has provided good intelligence and helped save the lives of many Huguenots by diverting them here. He has done so by maintaining contacts within various Catholic conspiracies in France, and thus can never be wholly trusted. How do I know he is not playing me for the benefit of his French friends?"

"It was critical information. By omitting it, you made my job harder."

"By omitting it, I left you able to observe what was actually happening rather than what your prejudices might make you believe was happening. I have kept Her Majesty alive for more than twenty years now—I know what I am doing."

Since a fit of pique would get her nothing but a reputation for stamping her feet like a spoiled child, Lucette acknowledged his explanation with a curt nod.

"Now," Walsingham leaned forward, "what did you learn of Nightingale and the connection to Blanclair?"

"How much detail would you like?"

Elizabeth spoke sharply. "We would hear it all."

And so Lucette talked, much as she had at Blanclair to Dr. Dee. The queen kept her standing the entire time. She began with the cardinal with whom she'd seen Julien speaking that first night at the Paris reception, through her initial days at Blanclair and her impressions of the key players in the household—from Felix's hostile tutor to the slightly too familiar groom who spent long periods away from the chateau—her search of the family's personal spaces, up until the night she went to the inn and found Julien with the English Catholic courier.

Only then did she pause, not so much for effect as to make sure she didn't get lost in her own flow of words and spill out everything personal that had followed between her and Julien.

"After he discovered me in the inn that night," she said carefully, "I fell ill and spent the next few days confined to my chamber. On the day after I emerged, the body of that same messenger was discovered on Blanclair's grounds. Just one day earlier, Julien had informed me that he himself had been working with England since 1572. In light of those two events, I began to reconsider the information I had gathered thus far."

"And would you care to share your conclusions?" Walsingham drawled.

"The dead courier had a badge carved with a nightingale on his person. Julien gave it to me."

"You think that clears him?" Walsingham asked.

"Why would he give it to me, when he knew I was looking for connections to Nightingale?"

"Precisely because he knew you were looking. Sometimes it's wise to preempt any discoveries that an enemy might make. That does not prove innocence."

"It doesn't prove guilt, either," she shot back.

"Do I detect a wish to prove Julien's innocence?"

"You told me when you asked me to do this that you would be just as glad for Blanclair to be cleared of involvement as to discover their guilt. Did you speak truly?"

"Why do I think you are uncomfortable with your own defense?"

For the first time, not caring what weakness she revealed, Lucette looked away from both queen and intelligencer. Beating in her head was that damning message from Anise and the fragment of the Spanish letter with it. She had told not a soul of either. At this point, it was more than instinct guiding her. It was fear. She did not trust anyone to understand the whole of the puzzle as she did. Walsingham and the queen had not been at Blanclair. They had not felt the pressure of secrets and hatred beneath the surface. They would have no reason not to believe the maid's evidence against Julien.

So Lucette equivocated.

"You were right—someone at Blanclair is running the Nightingale Plot. And so I have brought you both brothers, that one wiser than I might turn his mind to the conundrum of guilt or innocence."

"What evidence do you have pointing at Nicolas LeClerc?"

"Nothing significantly more nor less than that pointing at Julien. It's simply . . ." She trailed off.

Elizabeth, silent through their exchange, leaned forward in her seat. "Simply what?"

"I have no firm evidence, but I am certain that it is one of the brothers. It is the elegant answer. It is the piece that makes the pattern whole."

Walsingham studied her for a long minute, expression inscrutable. At last he nodded once. "I have a plan to flush out the mastermind. We shall welcome your guests with courtesy tonight, and set things in motion tomorrow. I expect we will not need to keep you at court longer than a week at most."

Lucette curtsied, and wondered bleakly what her life would be like a week from now. If it were Nicolas, as she believed, Julien would, first, refuse to believe it, and second, never forgive her for setting his brother up. And if it were Julien . . .

Either way, she'd lost Julien. Elizabeth's life and England's security would have to compensate for that loss.

Nicolas positively relished every moment of the journey to England and the heretic's court. Though Lucette was not as easily pinned down as he'd expected, she accepted his affection with good grace, considering how her heart must be breaking for Julien. In fact, Nicolas took far more satisfaction from Julien's grief and fury than he did in Lucette's company. His brother had had things his own way for so long, why should not Nicolas enjoy discomfiting him?

You want her, Julien? Welcome to my circumscribed world, in which wanting must remain forever unfulfilled.

Once they reached court, there was business to attend to. Nicolas's English contacts were waiting for him, eager to be of use to bring down the Protestant queen. It was simply a matter of manipulating their expectations. A matter at which he was highly skilled. What had his life ever been but a manipulation of expectations? He'd spent his youth running rings around women and their expectation of love, while simultaneously presenting his family with the face they'd expected to see—that of a dutiful eldest son. Intelligence work was no different. These days people saw in him what he'd conditioned them to see: a studious, introverted widower who preferred to keep his distance from politics and violence.

Only with Julien did his well of anger and ambition and envy occasionally spill out—but Julien was too damaged by his own guilt to read rightly his brother's emotions.

On the very first night at Richmond, Nicolas made contact with a French official of the ambassador's party who knew of the Nightingale Plot. Only a piece of it, which was all most people knew. Nicolas alone held the whole in his hands. The man received his brief orders and slipped away, unaware that his part in the whole was about to come to an end. Across the crowded hall—to which the English queen had not appeared, though both Lord Burghley and her Lord Secretary, Walsingham, were in attendance—Nicolas watched Julien watching Lucette.

For all the times Nicolas had burned with envy of Julien's whole and perfect body, the life open to his brother that had been so violently shut to him, he was repaid a thousandfold now. Perhaps a casual observer would mark nothing in Julien's controlled expression. But Nicolas could read every shade of his brother's torment and reveled in it. His eyes tracked Lucette almost against his will, as she moved through the crowd with ease in a yellow dress that set off her dark hair to perfection. Around her neck she wore a circlet of Tudor roses. She avoided both brothers in equal measure and Nicolas didn't mind giving her space tonight. Let her maintain the illusion of control while she could.

Shortly afterward the leading men withdrew, and not ten minutes later so did Julien. *Sloppy, brother,* Nicolas criticized silently. *Anyone might guess you're up to something secret.*

Julien always played his part to perfection, even when he had no idea he was but a player in Nicolas's drama. Let him talk things over with Walsingham—soon, Julien would be in a trouble he could not talk his way out of.

Leaving Nicolas free to act.

Julien had once learned to cope with misery by throwing himself into a chaotic mix of intelligence work, drinking, womanizing, and avoiding his family. Now he'd had to adapt his methods for a misery he'd never anticipated. He had never thought to fall in love—not like this, a love that made him want to shout to the heavens and dance through the fields, a love that had humbled him to the dust and shaken everything he thought he'd known about himself and his ambitions. But in the end, Lucette had been no different from any of a dozen women he'd known. She did not love him. Desired him, yes. But desire was easy. Desire had been all he'd wanted for eight years. Now he wanted more. And the woman he wanted it from could not give it to him. All he had left was to cope with bitter disappointment and do what he could to ensure Nicolas wasn't destroyed when Dominic Courtenay forbade their marriage.

Even now, with no hope for himself, Julien could not bear the thought that the marriage might be blessed. He was mean enough to hope that if he could not have her, neither could Nicolas.

So all-encompassing was this misery and its effects that Julien had barely spared a thought for the fact that he would be facing Walsingham for the first time in eight years. Only when he reached Windsor did the reality of his professional situation sink in. He'd been an enemy spy in his own country so long that he hardly knew how to act in the company of his spymaster.

Especially one who clearly harbored doubts about his trustworthiness.

It all combined to leave him spoiling for a fight, heightened by Lucette's cool beauty and avoidance of him. True, he was avoiding her as well, but she didn't have to look so unaffected by his ignoring her. So when Walsingham invited him to step out of the hall and meet him in a private chamber, Julien set out in an explosive mood.

His explosive moods mostly manifested in a darkly sarcastic cheer, so as he passed into the chamber to which an indifferent guard motioned him, Julien said, "From ambassador to Lord Secretary—you've done well for yourself, Walsingham. How many have you killed to get here?"

"No more than you've killed to keep your secrets."

Julien grunted, remembering anew that Walsingham was unflappable. He declined the proffered seat and lounged insolently against the linenfold paneling, arms folded as if he hadn't a care in the world. "And which secrets would those be? The ones I keep for you—or the ones I keep from you?"

"That is the question," Walsingham agreed. "Where exactly do your loyalties lie at this moment?"

"Where they have always lain. With myself."

"Don't try that on me," Walsingham said sharply. "A man devoted only to his own interests would not have thrown my money back in my face so long and with such venom. Only a man touchy about his honour would be so insulted by reward."

"What do you want?"

"Have you turned against me and England?"

"*Turned* against you—or always been against you?"

Walsingham shook his head. "No. I know how to read men, and when you offered yourself into my hands, it was done from principle and honestly. I am simply not certain if that principle has continued to sustain you this long."

"I have done nothing against the interests of your queen, nor will I," Julien said wearily. "I still believe what I did before—that Europe needs a balance, and places where those whose beliefs are unpopular in their home countries can go for safety. I would prefer that the Huguenots be able to remain in France. But as long as they are despised and hunted, I will continue to do what I can to keep them safe from the fanatics in my own country."

"How I want to believe you, LeClerc. But there have been troubling signs pointing in your direction for several months now."

"I don't suppose you want to tell me what those signs are?"

Walsingham simply gave him a look and Julien sighed. "Right. Well, as I pointed out to your latest intelligencer, I cannot prove a negative. And I certainly cannot prove it when I don't know precisely what pieces of evidence are causing you to suspect me."

"Do I detect sarcasm in your assessment of Lady Lucette?"

"Oh, come now, Walsingham—engaging a woman? I don't suppose her father would be too happy about that."

"Don't change the subject, LeClerc. Although speaking of that, I don't suppose Lord Exeter would be any too pleased to know how desperately you are pining after his eldest daughter."

Julien shoved himself away from the wall. "Tell me what you want me to do, and I'll do it. But I will not discuss Lucette Courtenay with you—or anyone. Am I clear?"

Walsingham's rare smile was laden with meaning. "More clear than I think you care to be. You are right, proving a negative is troublesome. But not impossible. All you need do for the next week is enjoy yourself at my illustrious queen's court. At the end of that week, I shall decide what to do with you."

"I can't wait." Julien's head was near to splitting. He threw open the door to the chamber and stalked past the single guard. Surely there was wine to be had in England.

Maybe if he got drunk enough he would forget the feel of Lucie beneath him on her bed. The last night he would ever touch her.

NINETEEN

E lizabeth was snappish and irritable as July progressed under serenely sunny skies. The weather was oppressively hot and she could hardly wait to leave Richmond for the cooler North. By the time she left, Walsingham assured her, the Nightingale mastermind would be in the Tower—she assumed, if he could not positively identify either of the LeClerc brothers he would simply throw them both into prison and sort it out in the aftermath—and upon her return to London Elizabeth could begin to contemplate her future without even an absent husband to consider.

Against Walsingham's advice, Elizabeth granted a brief audience to Nicolas and Julien LeClerc the day after their arrival at court. "If one of them is bent on killing me, I should like to look him in the eye," she snapped at her Lord Secretary, and so he stood behind her throne today, no doubt glaring balefully at the Frenchmen.

Dr. Dee and Lucette attended them, and Elizabeth greeted the doctor warmly. "I trust you have brought back many fine books for my libraries," she teased. "I shall look forward to examining them in future."

To Lucette, she merely nodded in acknowledgment of the girl's curtsey. She had noted yesterday this new composure of Lucette's—disconcertingly like her mother's when Minuette had been keeping secrets from Elizabeth. The queen was in no doubt that Lucette's emotions had been engaged by the brothers, though she showed no obvious signs of affection toward her supposed-intended.

Nicolas and Julien LeClerc were clearly brothers, with a marked similarity of colouring and features, but also undoubtedly individual. Nicolas a shade darker of hair and carrying more weight, Julien taller and grimmer. She suspected Julien would have a dashing smile, but it showed no evidence today.

The men bowed and rose at her gesture. "So," she said sternly, "what is this about wishing to remove one of my favorite subjects from England?"

"Your Majesty," replied Nicolas in accented English, "I doubt any force short of heaven could persuade Mademoiselle Courtenay to abandon her allegiance to Your Grace."

Elizabeth sniffed, not displeased. "Still, as you have not yet obtained the Duke of Exeter's permission, I suppose I need not worry overmuch. I am not certain there is a man on earth to whom Dominic Courtenay would willingly entrust Lucette."

Through the banter, neither Julien nor Lucette moved, hardly even blinked. Without showing the least outward sign, somehow Elizabeth knew that they two were powerfully, almost painfully, aware of the other.

Interesting, she mused afterward. Lucette fell in love in France, all right—but not with the man she's linked to now.

She found the problem mildly diverting until, with a suddenness that shocked her, there was another assassination attempt.

In her oft-threatened years as queen, there had never been two so close together. The second attempt was not a direct physical threat such as the man with the misfiring pistol had been, but the more subtle and disconcerting use of poison.

It had been planted in her drink—a cup of sack, the dry Spanish wine sweetened with sugar—brought to the tennis courts where Elizabeth was the center of a crowd watching Brandon Dudley and Kit Courtenay play. The queen had a small round table next to her canopied seat on which sat a variety of treats. Of course, like all royals, Elizabeth had a taster. Nothing came within her reach that had not been tested on someone less exalted. Nothing had ever happened, as usually nothing ever did. This was England, after all, not Italy.

But this time the drink had not been set down for five minutes when there were shouts from the kitchen buildings and then the running feet of guards, with Walsingham in black swooping among them like a crow of foreboding. Elizabeth rose, expecting violence, but the guards surrounded not her, but her refreshments. Bewildered, she met Walsingham's eyes as he reached her and, forgetful for once of status, ran frantic hands down her arms.

"Are you well?" he demanded urgently.

"Yes, of course, what has—"

In the rarest form of discourtesy, he turned away while she was still speaking and seized the goblet. "You did not touch this?" he asked her brusquely. His face was pale.

Understanding began to dawn. "No," she said softly, "I have not. Who has?"

But with the knowledge that his queen was not about to fall dead at his feet, Walsingham gained control of himself and the situation. "Let us walk," he urged her.

She allowed herself to be led away, the two of them flanked by armed guards. "Poison?" she asked, voice carefully pitched so as not to carry beyond the knot of guards.

He nodded grimly. "Your taster collapsed within minutes of the drink leaving the kitchens. She was dead when she fell."

"Nightingale?" Elizabeth asked.

"It must be."

"Nicolas LeClerc was at the tennis match, sitting not ten feet away from me for the last hour."

"Whoever did this will have taken care to be blamelessly elsewhere. They pay men to do their dirty work."

"But?"

"I already have men turning out the chambers of the LeClerc brothers. If they are lucky, evidence will be forthcoming."

"How would that be lucky for them?"

"For one of them, at least—the innocent one. If I do not find evidence, then both of them will be locked up by nightfall."

Elizabeth shivered once, seized by that feeling of someone walking on her grave. *Not yet,* she told the shadows firmly. *Death cannot have me yet. Not for many long years, and not by violence.*

Julien did not attend the tennis match. He was moodily alone in his chamber—a tiny rectangle that at least he did not have to share with Nicolas, and certainly cleaner than his rented space in Paris—when the door was flung wide and a man in clerkly black flanked by two guards rasped, "On your feet. Don't touch anything."

Slowly, Julien rose to his feet from where he'd lain stretched full-length on the bed, jerkin unlaced over his shirt, boots tossed carelessly on the floor.

"What do you want?" he asked.

"For you to stand still in the corridor and go nowhere." The man stepped aside for Julien to exit the chamber, but the guards remained in place. No doubt to keep him from fleeing. Every inner alarm that had kept him alive so long in a dangerous profession was ringing, but he knew how to feign ease.

Even the most thorough search couldn't last long, for there was nothing in the chamber except the bed, a chair, and Julien's trunk. The clerk (or whatever he was) removed everything from the trunk, shaking out the clothes, running his hands along the interior looking for secret hiding places, then swiftly dismantled the bed and mattress. He was too well-trained to express frustration, but there did seem to be a remoteness to his face when he finally conceded there was nothing to find.

He faced Julien, speculation writ large in his eyes, and said, "Walsingham wants to see you. The guards will take you."

"I suppose you wouldn't care to tell me why?"

"You suppose correctly."

Julien whistled tunelessly, more to settle his nerves than annoy the guards. They marched him through the Richmond corridors to another in what he assumed would be a series of rather anonymous meeting places for Walsingham.

Instead he ended up being directed into what could only be the primary office of England's Lord Secretary, an imposing chamber decorated to awe. Even Walsingham looked more substantial, the intelligencer in him subsumed by England's premier politician and one of the two most powerful men in England.

"Wait outside," he told the guards. When they closed the door behind them, he turned curtly to Julien. "Sit."

Julien took a seat across the desk from Walsingham, wary at the anger in his voice. Walsingham rarely let any emotion show. Something was very wrong.

"What has happened?"

"A woman is dead, here in the palace precincts."

"Who?" Despite himself, Julien couldn't help the spurt of fear. There were lots of women at Richmond, there was no reason to think anything had happened to Lucie . . .

"The queen's taster."

Relief meant it took him a few seconds to put it all together. "The taster . . . Poison?"

"The queen," Walsingham said repressively, "is perfectly safe. Clearly God is watching over her life."

"That man you sent to search my belongings—you believe I did this?"

"I did not want to believe it. I have never wanted to believe you have betrayed me."

"He found nothing, you must know that. Though I grant that doesn't prove much. Surely you don't think me stupid enough to keep incriminating evidence in my own chamber."

"I had to look."

"Fine," Julien said. "You looked. You found nothing. So why are you speaking to me like you think me guilty?"

"We found the poisoner, with his throat cut, in one of Windsor's less traveled wings. He still had the vial of poison with him, along with a single seal of command."

Walsingham produced it from nowhere, like a court entertainer, and held it in his palm for Julien to see.

It was a scrap of paper, two inches square, with a coloured picture of a seal. Julien expected to see a nightingale.

But it was not a bird. It was a cinquefoil—shaded blue. Truth and loyalty.

Julien just stared, shocked beyond measure. His personal badge planted on the poisoner could mean only one thing: he was being deliberately set up.

"Julien LeClerc." Walsingham rose, his black robes and chain of office settling around him like judgment incarnate. "I hereby arrest you on the charge of murder of an innocent and the attempted assassination of Queen Elizabeth. You will be taken to the Tower to answer for this and any other charges that may follow."

Before Julien could think of a single thing to say—or how to make his mouth work even if he could think of something—the guards opened the door behind him. They were apologizing to Walsingham, but Julien understood only one voice—Lucette's.

"What have you done to him?" she was demanding as she swept into the room, and then he was on his feet and turned toward her.

She was white-faced, but with fury rather than fear. Or maybe it was both. After one look at Julien, she turned her formidable focus on Walsingham. "What are you doing?"

"Arresting him for trying to kill Queen Elizabeth," Walsingham responded flatly. "You should not be here, my lady."

Julien waited for her to defend him, or to question him. To do anything except stand there and stare at Julien as though she were trying to read the secrets of his very soul.

But all she did was, at last, ask him softly, "Did you do this?"

He'd never thought he could be so hurt by a question.

But why wouldn't she believe Walsingham? She had little reason to trust him.

And yet it was suddenly the most important thing in the world that she should trust him. The Tower, interrogation, the threat of torture, the knowledge that someone had set him up . . . all of that faded. Only one thing in the world mattered—that this woman believe him.

"I did not," he told her firmly, even while the guards gripped him by the arms and prepared to lead him away. "Please, Lucie, you must trust me. I have never threatened the life of your queen. I would not do that to you."

They pulled him out of the chamber, leaving him with the image of Lucie's face, blue eyes wide and unreadable. He had no idea if she believed him or not.

Lucette had known instantly that something was dreadfully wrong. When guards draw away the queen and sequester her food and drink, one does not have to look far for the cause. She shook off Nicolas as soon as she could possibly manage, because from the moment she'd seen the guards surround the queen, her heart had been pounding out a single question: *Where is Julien?*

After a frantic search and the heart-droppingly bad moment when she'd found Julien in the midst of being arrested in Walsingham's office, she made her way blindly back to her chamber. Ignoring her expensive skirts, she sat on the bed with arms wrapped around her legs. She knew she should be thinking fast and hard—

indeed, one level of her mind already was whirring away at important threads—but all she could focus on was Julien's plea: *I would not
do that to you.*

To you: why did it matter so much more that his care was for her
opinion? That even if he'd been so inclined, he would not have
moved to assassinate Queen Elizabeth because of what hurt that
might cause Lucette?

But she did not have time for self-indulgence. Beneath her terror
for Julien, her mind had been nagging at her, wanting her to focus.
So she did what she always did: closed her eyes, entered the library
in her mind, and opened the ledger relating to Nightingale.

She turned to a blank page and waited, fingertips resting on the
paper so that she could almost fancy she felt its smoothness. Her
mind was like a separate entity, whirring away below her focus. Don't
force it, don't coax it, don't pay it the slightest attention and then,
like magic, it resolved.

From the beginning this case had vibrated with much more than
simple conspiracy or fanaticism. There had been a venom to it, a
corrosive hatred that had contaminated nearly every piece of cir-
cumstantial evidence. If Walsingham had arrested Julien, she believed it was because of evidence, hard evidence. The kind of
evidence manufactured and planted. And there was only one person
in all of this who hated Julien.

Nicolas was the Nightingale mastermind. She had believed it
before—now she knew it for fact. She might not have every piece—
motive, beyond that of screwing his brother, was still out of her
grasp—but it didn't matter. Like mathematics, it was the only answer. The elegant answer.

And no one but her would believe it.

She'd been half expecting Walsingham to drag her back to his office for close questioning, but when the summons came, Lucette instead followed the guards directly to the queen's privy chamber.

"You may go." When the queen dismissed the guards, it was only
Elizabeth and Lucette, facing each other across five feet of polished

marble floor that might as well have a been a fathomless chasm for how far apart they were.

At last, after a deliberately uncomfortable minute of waiting, Lucette curtsied to her queen.

Elizabeth tipped her head in challenge. Her eyes glittered. "Do you have nothing to say about this attack?"

"You are clearly unharmed." Where was she getting the nerve to be rude? Perhaps, she thought, I am finally reacting to Elizabeth's forced intimacy. If she wants me to be family, then she'll have to deal with all my flaws.

"My taster is not unharmed. She is dead."

Lucette blinked away her instinctive sympathy for the unknown woman. "And what do you want with me?"

"An apology perhaps. You have delivered a killer straight into the heart of my court."

Lucette knew she had to walk a very careful path. "Nicolas was with me, as you well know."

"Julien was not."

"Is that the only reason for Julien's arrest—because he wasn't fortunate enough to have someone vouch for his whereabouts?"

"Walsingham has evidence. And no doubt more will be forthcoming once Julien is properly questioned in the Tower."

Lucette shoved away her too-vivid imagination of what such questioning might entail, for she could not help Julien if she collapsed into a puddle of tears.

"Has Nicolas been told of his brother's arrest?"

"His chamber was searched along with Julien's. I imagine he is well aware of what has happened."

"And will you—or Walsingham—require Nicolas's continuing presence at court for now?"

"You would send him away?"

Lucette raised a cool, interrogatory eyebrow, hoping she did it as well as Elizabeth. "We are expected at Wynfield Mote in four days."

She managed to surprise Elizabeth to the extent that the queen laughed in astonishment. "What a cool head you have! One brother arrested, and you seek to introduce the other to your family? Not to mention my daughter, who is currently at Wynfield."

"Do you have any reason to suspect Nicolas? No doubt Walsingham would have thrown him in the Tower if he had the slightest misgivings."

Elizabeth narrowed her eyes. "How hardhearted you are, Lucette. I will take it under advisement. You may go for now. No doubt Walsingham will wish to speak with you at further length."

She didn't say no. Lucette clung to that, instinctively knowing that the only way to get to the end of this muddle was to convince Nicolas he was safe. Best to get him away from Elizabeth, too—but Lucette admitted that her primary motive was to do whatever she had to do to discover the truth of Nicolas's treachery. Lie to her queen, lie to her family, seduce Nicolas (or allow him to seduce her in whatever manner he had perfected since his injuries)—she would do whatever was necessary.

She would bring Nicolas down to set Julien free.

3 August 1580

To Her Royal Highness Mary Stuart, Queen of Scotland and France:

The nightingale's song will soon wake you from your long slumber. Be prepared to fly free.

The rush of being so near to freedom drove Mary to restless action and imprudent conversation. She knew she was dancing on the edge of disaster, but then she had always felt most alive at such moments. Stephen Courtenay was a willing partner to her reckless mood, indulging her without open encouragement. But she could see that her rising passion sparked something in him in return.

Summoned to her presence chamber on a rainy afternoon that closed in around Tutbury as though enforcing her hated imprisonment, Stephen joined her in circling the large room. As always she chose the subject of conversation. "So your sister is to bring one of her Frenchmen home. How lovely for your family to host such an illustrious guest at the same time as the Princess of Wales. Do you not regret not being with them all?" Did he know how lucky he was to be teased by Mary Stuart? Few men had had the privilege.

He answered equably enough, rather maddening for a woman not averse to being flirted with, "I am content to do my duty."

"Am I merely a duty?" she asked archly. "Or dare I hope you take some pleasure in my company?"

Stephen slid her a sideways glance, those eyes of his so hard to read. Sometimes Mary thought that alone was reason enough to find him attractive. "I serve at the pleasure of my queen."

There was an undertone to his voice, a hint of ambiguity in those last two words. Mary had always been a gambler. Now she threw the dice as though she could see which way they would fall. "I hope your queen appreciates your service."

"How is one to recognize a queen's appreciation?" Now, that was more like it—subtle, but undeniable. He was letting her know she need only sanction it.

She paused, instinctively choosing the best position for the weak light to gleam on her hair and skin. She might not be the sylph she was as a newlywed in France, or even when she'd married Darnley, but Mary knew how to highlight her beauty and shadow her flaws.

With a smile that just hinted at seduction, Mary said, "Stephen, Stephen . . ." She rested one of her lovely hands on his sleeve. "The chance that has so cruelly kept me locked away might just as easily swing to my side and restore my fortunes. I shall be most generous with those who have been my friends."

Rumour was that Dominic Courtenay was a silent, disapproving sort of man who disliked games of sex or politics. It seemed that his eldest son was more pliable. With admiration and familiarity playing across his handsome face, Stephen made his own gamble. "Lady, what are you up to?"

"Perhaps," she whispered, "we shall talk about nightingales."

Without another word, he bent his dark head to her—not in acknowledgment, but to brush his lips across her knuckles. Mary caught her breath. Straightening, he looked at her, as though waiting an unspoken permission. He must have seen it in her eyes, for his next kiss was pressed gently to her lips.

He tasted young . . . like new grass and spring rain. He knew how to judge his moments; the kiss was not too bold or too long and he did not touch her other than where he still held her hand in his.

A pity, Mary thought, that I cannot take him with me. But she rather doubted she could have both husband and lover. Ah well, she knew how to take the sweet while she could. Another week or two, then she would lay Stephen aside and embrace her future.

TWENTY

It wasn't the isolation of the Tower of London that bothered Julien. Or its grimness. He was accustomed to having only himself for company, and though his cell was bare and damply chill even at summer's height, it was actually bigger than his Paris chambers and only slightly less clean.

No, the problem with being a prisoner was the pesky lack of freedom. The awareness that you were utterly at another's mercy—hauled out of sleep in the middle of the night to be interrogated, no choice of when or what to eat, always with the threat of sudden, sanctioned, violence hanging over you—those were the things likely to drive prisoners mad. Julien would have dealt with it as he'd always dealt with uncomfortable difficulties in his life (burning inwardly, profanely cheerful outwardly) if he hadn't carried with him like a talisman the memory of Lucette's unreadable face upon his arrest.

He had to get out of the Tower and prove his innocence, if only so he could see relief in her eyes. Or at least an acknowledgment of his honesty with her. She might never love him, but he would make her believe him.

So he bit his tongue and forced himself to answer civilly the barrage of questions he was asked. Unfortunately, civil denials were not what his questioners were looking for. They wanted a detailed confession. Julien was almost sorry to disoblige them.

Until Walsingham himself came to question him.

He was familiar with the intelligencer's hooded eyes and detached demeanor. Walsingham had looked at him no differently the night Julien had so passionately offered himself as an agent to Protestant England. The memory of that did burn, and made Julien more flippant than was wise.

"Come to beg my forgiveness?" Julien asked. "I'll think about it."

"Why would I forgive a man who tried to kill my queen?"

"Because you know I didn't do it. You *know* me, Walsingham. I have done nothing these last eight years to give you cause to doubt my word."

"For eight years you have done little but lie to men of your own faith and country. Why should I expect honesty from a man like that?"

"I lied as necessary to save lives, as you no doubt have done a thousand times for your queen's sake. This is the easy answer, Walsingham, and when have you ever trusted the easy answer? I have been set up. While you keep me here and bend all your time and attention to wresting knowledge out of me that I do not have, the very men you seek are free to wreak havoc on your precious England."

"That may be true, and certainly I have no wish to waste time. There are ways to question a man that can hasten his answers. We will see how long your outraged innocence lasts on the rack."

Julien blanched, for he truly had no desire to be set to the rack. "I am a gentleman," he said, knowing it didn't matter.

"In France, perhaps. But you are in England now and there is nothing—*nothing*—I will not do to protect my queen and her good government. I will use the methods at my disposal, and that includes distasteful ones. You would do the same."

"If I did," Julien bit off, "at least I would have the decency to do it myself. I don't suppose you will be dirtying your hands with my torture."

Was that genuine regret that passed across Walsingham's face? "Do you think I enjoy living in a world where I can trust no one? But I must live in the world that is, not the one I wish it to be. Answer truthfully, son, and it will go all the better for you."

"Not when the truth is one you don't want to hear. Would you rather I lie to you?"

"You know something, Julien, and if you will not share it, I will press until you do."

Julien closed his eyes and leaned against the wall with feigned indifference. "I shall endeavour to make it worth the interrogator's time. But I will not lie, not even for my own convenience."

He kept his eyes closed and heard Walsingham's soft sigh, as if truly sorrowful, then his footsteps and the heavy door scraping open and closing. Julien shook his head. It seemed his only chance was to figure out whatever useful information Walsingham thought he had and share it before his joints were permanently pulled out of place and he was left crippled.

Though if Julien were crippled, perhaps Nicolas would accept it as proper atonement for his sins and stop torturing them both for what had happened in Paris.

They were four days on the road from London, Lucette growing more tense the farther they got from the Tower and Julien. Nicolas's attention kept her aware of how carefully she had to play her part, not to mention the fact that Richard Laurent hardly left his master's side. For a man supposed to be a tutor, Laurent seemed comfortable taking menial orders from Nicolas. "He's a good clerk," Nicolas told her casually, "and efficient in whatever he's asked."

What precisely had he been asked? she wondered. To hire a man to poison the queen? To kill the hired man after and plant evidence against Julien? She wouldn't put any manner of violence and deceit past Laurent. And the way he watched her on the road to Wynfield Mote warned her that he was not as taken by her charms as Nicolas. She would have to be careful not to spook Laurent. She must have been adequate at impersonating a lovestruck girl, enough that Kit's frown grew more pronounced as the days passed. He took to separating his sister from Nicolas while they rode, which was a great relief.

When they were still two miles away from Wynfield, she saw the riders approaching and knew them at once: Dominic in the lead, with several men riding behind in the Exeter colours. But it wasn't all men—there was her mother, riding next to Dominic, and for one moment Lucette was glad that Julien was not there to see how beautiful Minuette still was in her forties. But a moment later she thought passionately that she would gladly suffer the pangs of ridiculous jealousy if only it were Julien riding at her side rather than Nicolas.

But she would not live any longer wishing that things could be different. How many years had she wasted wishing there had never been a king to interfere in her parents' lives, wishing that she could be certain of her birthright? No more. She had only one life, and she meant to live it as it presented itself. So she smiled at Nicolas and said, "We've quite a welcome party."

"I'm flattered," he said, his tone carefully balanced between pleasure at being with her and grief at his brother's betrayal of his English guests. He was very good at hitting the perfect note. If only she wasn't so cynically certain of his own guilt, she might be deceived. It made her wonder what her family would make of him.

Kit spurred ahead and met the party first. By the time Lucette and Nicolas approached, all the attention was on the two of them: Minuette warm as always, Dominic even more wary than usual.

Being on horseback provided a measure of courteous distance, for which Lucette was grateful. She had been surprised by the swell

of tears in her throat and the sudden, intense urge to throw herself
into Dominic's arms and then demand that her wise mother tell her
what to do.

But she did infuse her words with genuine gladness as she said, "I
am so glad to see you both."

She saw the quick startled glance of her mother, and the twitch of
a muscle in Dominic's cheek. "We missed you," he said. And then, as
welcome as a streak of sunlight during a spring shower, he smiled at
her as he had not since she was sixteen.

Minuette, ever gracious, welcomed Nicolas with a tact that was
unparalleled even by the queen. "We welcome your return to Wynfield Mote, Nicolas. We'd rather your brother was with you."

"That is very kind of you, Lady Exeter." Nicolas's English was so
charmingly accented that Lucette could not but suspect guile. She
pretty much suspected everything he did these days was guile. Certainly he had motivations she had not yet guessed. That was what
the next week or two was about: motivations, evidence, and freeing
Julien.

With unsurpassed skill, Minuette managed to match her horse
with Nicolas's, leaving Lucette to ride next to Dominic. He shot her
a sideways glance and said with remarkable restraint, "Rumour
reaches even here, Lucette. From those rumours, I expected today to
meet the man you have set your heart on. But you do not quite have
the look of a woman lost to love."

"Have you generally found rumours to be trustworthy?"

"I have generally found them to possess at least a core of truth."

She chose her words carefully, not wishing to be a liar directly to
his face. "I have brought to Wynfield the man upon whom all my
thoughts are focused at present."

"Your thoughts . . . not your heart?"

She bit her lip and risked a glance at him. He rode effortlessly, in
her lifetime always favouring a string of very large horses. His current mount gleamed a rich brown, and Dominic held the reins in the
manner he had fashioned when she was a baby: right hand holding

both, after a loop was passed around the wrist above his missing left hand.

Then she raised her eyes and found him watching her steadily, with those jewel-deep green eyes she had spent years regretting because they were not hers.

"I'm not ready to talk about my heart," she answered. "Not yet. When I am, I promise you and mother will know it all. Will you trust me until then, Father?"

She thought she would hesitate or stutter over the title she had refused to give him for six years. But it came out so easily, she wondered why she had been so stubbornly resisting for so long.

Dominic blinked, and his body seemed to relax before her eyes. But, true to himself, he did not make a fuss. "I trust you, Lucette."

For all the beauty of Wynfield Mote in high summer, Lucette could not but feel it contaminated by the man who entered alongside her. Her father steadied her as she dismounted before the gracious house, square-fronted behind its shallow moat, but almost at once Nicolas was next to her and she smiled up at him and he let her tuck her hand in his arm.

The reception was a curious mix of formal and familiar. Nicolas, as an adult heir to a significant French estate paying court to the eldest daughter of the house, was accorded ritual politeness. But as one who had also previously lived in the household for some weeks as little more than a boy, he behaved with a courtesy and grace extended equally to family and servants.

Asherton, who had been Wynfield Mote's steward for forty years, was asked several intelligent questions about the crops and weather; Harrington, who came out to take her father's horse as he always did, managed a few words in reply to Nicolas's warm greeting; and Carrie Harrington had her hand kissed.

She did not look impressed.

Pippa and Anabel met them in the hall, the high-beamed lofty chamber with a stone fireplace large enough for a woman to stand inside and the long, polished oak table and sideboard set with silver.

There were times, coming upon the two side by side, that Lucette thought it might be hard to tell which was the princess and which not. Anabel was regal, but Pippa had a presence hard to match for self-possession. From their childhood they had tended to dress in similar fashion—today they both wore cream silk, Anabel's embroidered in jewel-bright blues and reds, Pippa's a more muted palette of green and silver. The princess had the same vibrant red hair of her mother, and Pippa's was warm gold with that attractive streak of black, but their faces had a similarity that reminded people they shared a degree of both Boleyn and Plantagenet blood.

Nicolas made no difference between them in his greeting, dividing his charm equally in a manner that made Lucette's skin crawl. Anabel, though polite, seemed only amused. She had men falling over themselves to be charming to her—what need had she for the attentions of one good-looking Frenchman?

It was a relief when the two swept Lucette away with them, leaving Nicolas to be tactfully housed as far from the girls as possible. Lucette wouldn't put it past her father to set a discreet guard on Nicolas simply to ensure he didn't take liberties with his daughter.

Which would her father rather know—that Lucette would cheerfully offer her virtue if it would save Julien, or that even if she did, Nicolas was in no condition to take advantage of it?

Despite her royal upbringing, Anabel could be tactful when she chose. After a significant glance between herself and Pippa—in which Lucette recognized the same sort of silent exchange the sisters could share—the princess said, "I want to hear all about France," hugging Lucette lightly. "But for now Pippa is dying to press you with questions herself. I shall see you at dinner."

When the sisters were alone in Lucette's bedchamber, Pippa did not immediately launch into questions. Instead she studied her sister with an expression somewhere between fondness and worry.

Lucette expected to be asked about Nicolas's amorous intentions or her own, to have Pippa press or even just tease about the likelihood of having a French brother-in-law after all.

She did not expect Pippa to ask with real worry, "Do you know what you're about, Lucie?"

There were times when her little sister seemed much, much older. Not just older than her eighteen years, or older than Lucette—but the kind of old woman that had lived a long and eventful life and stored away vast wisdom in all that time.

It was actually quite irritating at the moment.

"What do you suspect I'm about that makes you fear I am in over my head?" she replied caustically.

"Nicolas is not your Frenchman, Lucie. Why have you brought him here?"

Is Julien my Frenchman? she nearly asked. But she wasn't prepared to hear a no, so she refrained from asking. "I have brought him to Wynfield because I need him at Wynfield. Is that enough for you?"

Pippa sighed deeply, and her troubled look did not ease. "No. But it is all you are going to tell me, so I'll desist. For now."

When younger, Nicolas had never been bothered by what people thought of him. Save for his father, whose good opinion he needed, and his mother, whose good opinion he had actually cared for, he had never extended himself overmuch. That had changed on the bitter night of blood and agony in Paris. When they cut away the core of what made him a man, they'd left him with the need to cloak himself in the opinions of others. Give them what they want or expect to see, and few people will bother to look deeper.

He didn't expect serious difficulty at Wynfield Mote. Lucette's brother, Kit, clearly didn't like him at all, but he thought that had more to do with either a general dislike of the French or a specific dislike of any man interested in Kit's sister. Possibly both. But Kit was merely a boy—what could a spoiled eighteen-year-old guess about his own motivations? Dominic Courtenay was another matter. The Duke of Exeter had learned suspicion from the harsh master of his own betrayal and a king's fury, and Nicolas could feel the man's judgment from the moment they met on the road. Even were Nicolas a whole man, he'd be unlikely to get Exeter's permission to marry Lucette.

The women were simpler. Although Nicolas had not been as struck by Minuette's beauty as Julien, she at least would be sympathetic to a tale of desperate true love. Pippa was little more than a girl, and he'd heard stories of her fey disposition. She did not worry him.

And then there was the Princess of Wales. To Anabel, as the Courtenays called her, Nicolas was absolutely pitch-perfect in his manners. She was the same age as Pippa, but he guessed she had never been precisely a girl. She might not have a wide experience of the world yet, but she was royal born and raised by a canny queen who knew how to manipulate the world around her. Nicolas studied Anabel's proud face and guessed she was well advanced in manipulation herself.

But not as advanced as he was.

He was housed as far from Lucette as they could decently put him without quartering him in the stables. No matter. Lucette would come to him, for she was practically bursting out of her skin with the need to help Julien. Nicolas had amused himself on the journey from London debating how far she would go to seduce him of his secrets. Far enough, he guessed, that she would not be able to look at Julien ever again without guilt.

If there was one thing at which Nicolas was a master, it was inducing guilt.

Sure enough, they had not been at Wynfield for an hour before Lucette appeared at his chamber door, asking if he would like a tour of the grounds.

She had changed into a gown that made her look younger, the bright blue of the kirtle echoing and sharpening her remarkable eyes. Her expression was carefully calculated innocence, such a good simulation that for a moment Nicolas could see his late wife standing before him. Célie had often looked at him with that same sort of appeal—though her innocence had been purely instinctive—and it had never moved him to anything but contempt.

If only Lucette knew that it was her deception and calculation that truly roused him.

The grounds, like the house, had not changed overmuch in twelve years. Pleasantly English with wildflowers a riotous carpet of colour among the low walls of stone. As English as the house that had been burnt to the ground by the late English king as punishment to the faithless Minuette, who had married against his will. What would it be like, Nicolas wondered, to so desperately love a woman that one would destroy everything in his path to have her? He'd found women to be mostly interchangeable, at least in intimate respects. The only ones that mattered were the ones that could get him something he wanted.

And Lucette had delivered him exactly the thing Nicolas had most wanted for months. As reward, and because it pleased him to think of Julien wanting what he had, he touched her lightly at the waist, and she turned willingly toward him as though she, too, knew the steps of this dance.

He kissed her—not too deeply nor too long, for they were in her very house and he did not especially want Dominic threatening him just yet. There was a moment's instinctive resistance, then she folded herself into his embrace. It pleased him, how hard she worked to accommodate his supposed expectations. The next few days could be very interesting.

He remembered the rose garden—the Courtenay women seemed to have an unaccountable fondness for roses—and teased her as they passed the stables in the distance.

"Do you remember the day we found you eavesdropping? You claimed you had come to see kittens. But that wasn't really so, was it?"

He had seen her blush for Julien, but the most he drew from her even now was a slight quirk of her lips. "I was looking for you," she answered freely enough. "And I was furious to be treated like the child I was."

They both danced around the subject of Julien, and Nicolas thought that discretion had gone far enough. "My brother was never very good at giving people what they wanted. It would have cost him little to speak kindly, but instead he riled you into almost spitting at him. It would have served him right if you had."

"What are you going to do about Julien?" she asked bluntly.

"What do you mean?"

"Are you content to leave him in the Tower? When you leave Wynfield, will you simply sail home and forget about him? Or do you mean to find a way to help?"

He spoke the simple truth, if not quite with all the details. "When I sail for France, Lucette, my brother will be at my side. I promise you that."

Then he drew her to him again, made more reckless so near to his desired end. "And I expect," he whispered to her, "that you will be by my side as well, Lucie mine."

He felt her stiffen at his appropriation of Julien's term for her, but also her determination not to show it. The triumph of subduing her pride was almost as intoxicating as her promise of abundant warmth.

Just because he couldn't finish the job didn't mean he couldn't enjoy every step along the way.

TWENTY-ONE

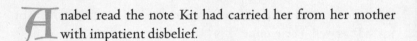

Anabel read the note Kit had carried her from her mother with impatient disbelief.

> You will leave Wynfield Mote tomorrow and journey to Ashridge. I have sent instructions to Lord Exeter to make it so. I will send for you from Ashridge when I have need of you.
>
> HRH Elizabeth R

She had hardly time for the outrage to sink in before Pippa burst into her chamber and announced, "We are leaving Wynfield."

Sometimes Pippa was positively eerie. Anabel looked from her mother's note, still in her hand, to her friend and said, "How did you know that?"

But almost at once, reason asserted itself and Anabel sighed. "Of course, Kit told you. Or perhaps your father. I don't know what my mother's about—"

"This is nothing to do with your mother," Pippa broke in, with a bluntness that made Anabel blink twice. "It is yourself. We must get you away from Wynfield."

Unsettled, Anabel tried to make light of it as she tossed her mother's note on the bed. "Why, what is wrong? Are they afraid I'm going to steal Nicolas LeClerc away from Lucette?"

"I don't know what's wrong, not precisely."

"Don't the stars tell you?" Anabel teased. "Or no, not stars. Is it other symbols for you, Pippa? Do you read the flowers? The pattern of silver set for a meal?"

Pippa had gone very still and very white. "Is that what you think of me—a fool who jests for your amusement? Do you think it is a play, the things I know? It is a terrible gift, Your Highness, and one I think you could not bear without running mad."

"Philippa, I am—"

"I do not know the details of what will come, but I know its shadow in my bones. There is danger here, Anabel. We must get you away."

Her faith in Pippa was greater than her irritation with her mother at being moved about like an inconvenient parcel. "Ask Kit to come with us. I'll speak to your father." She looked outside, where the sun was setting low and gold across the fields. "Must we go in the dark?" It was only half a jest.

Pippa was not as comforting as Anabel would have liked her to be. "I suppose it will have to be morning. But I do not like it."

"If I promise to keep to the chamber tonight and let no one but you in, will that make you easier?"

After a hesitation, Pippa managed to smile. "I suppose I'm unlikely to hurt you now if I haven't in the last eighteen years."

"Pippa, is it Nicolas LeClerc?" It seemed the only likely answer. The Frenchman was the anomaly at Wynfield. But what interest would he have in her? "And if so, are you certain it is not Lucette that is shadowed by whatever you see?"

Pippa's expression both sharpened and faded, as though her focus were on something not in this chamber, nor perhaps even in this world. "I think," she whispered, "that Lucie knows exactly what she's doing."

It gave Anabel chills. Suddenly she was almost glad at the thought of leaving Wynfield if it would shake Pippa free of whatever haunted her mind.

When Pippa serenely announced at dinner that Anabel had retired early preparatory to the two of them leaving for Ashridge the next day, Lucette blinked away surprise. That had not been part of any plan she'd known about. Though to be fair, the only plan she was interested in was her own just now. It was a pity to lose her sister, but probably safer for everyone to stay away while she brought down Nicolas.

After dinner she and Nicolas played chess in the hall. She didn't go so far as to let him win, but did dampen her normal play—chess was just puzzles and patterns and she'd been beating her mother since she was six—and Nicolas's flirtation just approached the edge of propriety. Words only, for Dominic and Kit both sat in the hall as well and would have marked any caresses between them.

But words could be just as laden, and Lucette had to bend all her wits to parrying Nicolas's strokes and casting her own back.

"I am surprised," he admitted as he moved a bishop. "I did not think you would be able to dismiss Julien's fate so easily from your mind. You have a tender heart, and I know how charming my brother can be when he wants something."

"As he wanted to find a way to get to England through me?" She shrugged. "Julien knew what he was about playing games with Walsingham. He should have known better than to put himself within reach of the man."

"Perhaps the mission was more important to him than the risk."

"Do you think so?" Lucette's tone was polite disbelief, her skin crawling with the duplicity of this conversation. She felt like offering a silent apology to the maligned Julien, though surely he had larger worries at the moment in the Tower.

Nicolas lifted a shoulder. "Or perhaps he merely thought he could never be caught. Arrogance rather runs in my family."

"Felix is not arrogant."

"Felix is a child still. He will learn it as he grows."

I hope not, Lucette thought fervently. But then she had to stop thinking, because Felix was a real worry to her, intending as she did to destroy his father.

After three matches that Nicolas conceded gracefully to her superior skill, they bid each other goodnight, Dominic carefully positioned so no liberties would be taken. He had requested a private conversation with Nicolas the next day, and Lucette wondered just how far she would have to go in deceiving her family. She did not especially look forward to explaining Nicolas's condition to her parents. Some things were simply too awkward to be borne.

But Nicolas managed to kiss her hand in a lingering and intimate manner that made her want to snatch it away. Instead she met his eyes and said softly, "I suppose you must be very tired. Sleep well."

"I never sleep easily away from Blanclair. I will be awake for some time, I imagine."

Lucette took it for the invitation it was. Pippa attended Anabel whenever she was in residence and so she was alone. She waited two hours, changing into a slightly less confining dress but not so casually as she would dress for bed. She tried to read but her mind kept jumping. At last she simply sat and pondered. Men talked in bed, didn't they? Whispered secrets to their paramours? All she needed was a hint, the barest suggestion of what was in Nicolas's mind. If she could only make an intelligent guess as to his next move, she could warn Walsingham and catch him in the act.

Hopefully.

She tried not to ponder Julien's fate if she could not deliver, but her imagination was vivid and all the darkness and shadows of her fears wrought too clear a picture of torture and ignominious death.

When she was as sure as she could be that the household was settled, Lucette left her chamber and crossed the hall to the far wing, where Nicolas and Laurent were quartered. Dominic had wanted to keep Nicolas away from his daughter—he hadn't anticipated that isolating him would make it easier for her to visit.

She knocked once, barely rapping with her knuckles, and Nicolas called with the same restraint, "Come in."

The moon was high and shed a watery light on the small but comfortable chamber. Nicolas sat at the desk, a handful of papers before him. He half turned to where she stood in the doorway.

"Lucie mine," he said. "I knew you'd come."

"And do you know why?" She meant it to be seductive, but it came out warier than she'd meant.

"Oh, I think so." Nicolas continued to sit, his body angled away from her. "You want to save my brother. And you will do whatever you think necessary to that end."

She opened her mouth and stopped, frozen without an idea of what to say next. The impasse lasted only a moment, for Nicolas shoved the chair back and rose. It took him three strides to reach her, just enough time to realize he'd been turned away from her for a reason.

In his right hand, he held a dagger, long and wicked-looking, stamped on the hilt with a blue cinquefoil. By the time she'd taken it in, the dagger point was at her breast. Julien's dagger.

Sickeningly, she thought she read lust in his eyes. Without moving the dagger, Nicolas stroked her cheek with his free hand. "So certain that you had me at your mercy," he purred. "But you have been playing my game for me. And quite appealingly, I might add."

She would not let the fear rule her. "What do you want?"

"The one thing you could not figure, the motive that has eluded you from the first. All this time spent protecting your queen . . . and in the end, you have delivered my quarry straight into my hands."

It took only two heartbeats for comprehension—and horror—to dawn. "Anabel," she breathed out. "You are here to kill Anabel."

He smiled broadly and shook his head. "Not at all. Princess Anne is my greatest asset. With her daughter in my hands, your heretic queen will fall over herself to give me what I want."

"And what is that?"

"Mary Stuart's freedom."

Lucette refused to cooperate. In the end, Nicolas had Laurent tie her hands behind her back and gag her, then the two men, armed with both daggers and swords, marched her across the hall to the family wing. Even subdued, Lucette was troublesome. He could have knocked her out, but absolute silence wasn't necessary. Laurent carried her, though she managed to kick at the walls a few times.

But the family wing remained dark and still when they arrived outside the chamber where Pippa Courtenay and Anne Tudor slept. Nicolas tried the door and found it barred.

He would have preferred to have the princess in his hands before everyone knew, but as long as he had Lucette, he was confident of success. So he pounded on the door with the dagger's hilt and waited for an audience.

The royal girl and her friend were no fools—the door remained barred. He heard Pippa's suspicious voice ask, "Who is it?"

"I have your sister," he announced. "With a dagger at her throat. Untie the gag, Laurent, and let them hear her."

Laurent complied, though Lucette was pulling furiously away. Nicolas rolled his eyes and slapped her twice, hard. "Do that again," he warned, "and it will be the butt of my sword next time."

That was the moment Dominic Courtenay flung open his door, sword in hand and his wife just behind him with a dagger. Kit Courtenay was just a moment later.

Nicolas smiled coldly. "There will be no blood shed tonight," he promised. "As long as Her Royal Highness opens this door and surrenders herself to me."

"Don't do it, Anabel!" Lucette shouted.

Everyone else stayed still, though Dominic Courtenay's eyes glittered dangerously in the hints of moonlight that played through the corridor window. "You'll never get out of this alive, Nicolas. Give me my daughter, and perhaps I'll see to it that your father deals with you instead of my queen."

"You can't threaten a man who's willing to lose everything," Nicolas said. "I have uses for Lucette that require her to be alive, but I will kill her if I must. And you will have no one to blame but yourself and your stubborn princess."

He pounded on the door once more. "What do you say, Your Highness? What price your life and honour? Willing to get your friends killed for you? I hear that's a particularly Tudor trait."

There were harsh whispers behind the door, and what sounded like a scuffle. Then the door was flung wide. Anne Tudor faced him, clad in a lavish taffeta nightrobe trimmed with silver lace. Her hair lay across her shoulders in two long plaits but she stared him down with a blazing scorn that didn't entirely hide her fear. "Here I am," she announced with that arrogance that was purely royal. "Do what you will."

"Good girl," he said, and in two steps had the dagger at her throat, matching Laurent's pose with Lucette. "What I will is for everyone to leave this house now. No getting dressed, no snatching valuables. I have no interest in the contents of your home and promise to leave them unharmed. But within five minutes I need this house cleared. I believe you will find armed men just outside the grounds waiting for my signal. When you have gone, my men will take position to ensure no one comes back in. Again, I have no interest in bloodshed. Laurent and I will remain here with the two women."

"Until when?" Surprisingly, it was Minuette who asked, looking nearly as fierce as her husband, but practical with it.

"I have a message for your queen. Tell her that her daughter will be freed when I have received assurances that Queen Mary has left England in safety. There is a ship prepared to reach her at King's

Lynn. Perhaps your menfolk would care to take that message. The sooner it's done, the sooner you may have your house—and women—back."

Dominic Courtenay did not move and his face was unreadable. Kit, on the other hand, had the fine tremble beneath his skin of a thoroughbred aching to run. There was a boy who would gladly kill him without thought.

But Dominic controlled both his house and his family.

"Very well," Dominic said, still holding his sword in the left hand and looking as though he would very much like to run it through Nicolas's chest.

"Father, no—" Kit began.

"Take your mother and Pippa and go," Dominic ordered.

Pippa looked as murderous as her father, but she only glanced once between her sister and her friend before stepping into the corridor and following her family.

Dominic left last. "Don't do anything reckless," he said to Lucette, "and trust me." Then, to the princess, "That goes for you, too, Anabel."

"Father," Lucette said, "tell Walsingham to get Julien out of the Tower."

Nicolas laughed. "Single-minded in your devotion, aren't you? But why not? Julien has his part to play in this as well."

And then it was just the four of them. Nicolas nodded to Laurent and they switched in one smooth movement, the tutor to drive Anne back into her chamber and Nicolas to confront Lucette.

"Don't even think about it," he told her softly.

"Think about what?" she shot back. "Killing you?"

"Among other things. Lucie mine, you are truly the best thing that's happened to me in years. I never lied about that. I will not hurt your princess and I will not hurt you—as long as I am not given cause. I am doing this for Queen Mary, and then . . . then I will be free and maybe we can begin again."

"You set up Julien, you bastard! You set the Catholics on his trail and delivered him into Walsingham's hands. Now he's in the Tower being tortured while you blithely go your own way."

He slapped her once, more lightly than before. "Not everything in this world is about Julien," he snapped. "For eight years he's had it all his way. It won't hurt him to learn a little humility. And don't worry—I'm sure they'll turn him loose when they hear what I've done. Walsingham will think my brother might get through to me. Or perhaps knows the best way to kill me. Either way, I'm confident that the three of us will soon enough be alone in a place where the truth can finally be told."

For a moment, Nicolas thought he'd finally cowed her. He should have known better.

"That's Julien's dagger you have," she pointed out, with a control that barely wavered. "If you were planning to use it as evidence against him, you should have taken care to act before he was locked in the Tower. Not to mention that you've showed your face to my family."

Stroking her cheek with the flat of the stolen blade, Nicolas said, "Julien's dagger, and Julien's lover. It's time I took back all that my brother stole from me."

He seized her arm and wrenched her into the bedchamber with the princess.

Nicolas would not touch either of them, not seriously. But that didn't mean he couldn't enjoy himself. Being castrated had taught him to take his pleasures in many ways, and he planned to exercise them all in the immediate future.

Elizabeth had just reached Cambridge on the first leg of her summer progress when Dominic and Kit Courtenay pounded into the university town with demons at their heels and blew apart what she only recognized in the aftermath as her relatively ordered world.

Of course she and her council had imagined threats to Anne over the years. Why else keep her sequestered away from court? But the moment Dominic told her that her daughter was in an enemy's hands, Elizabeth felt time suspend, and when the clock began to move again, fear had entered her heart in an icy wave she had never imagined.

There were only five of them in her privy chamber: Elizabeth, Dominic, Kit, Walsingham, and Burghley. Other than Kit—and that reservation solely because of his youth—there were no men Elizabeth trusted more in her kingdom.

"No one else must know," she said first, and was pleased and a touch surprised at the firmness of her voice. But then, she had always coped well in extremis.

"Agreed," Burghley said. "And we must move quickly."

"Will you let her go?" It was Walsingham who asked, and in his roughness Elizabeth heard all the arguments he'd made over the years for the necessity of Mary's death. God help him, if he so much as hinted that this was her fault . . .

He wouldn't. He didn't have to. Elizabeth knew it all too keenly herself.

For twelve years she had ignored Walsingham's advice, and that of her council, to bring Mary up on charges that would end in her execution. How could she have done otherwise? Mary, for her faults and silliness, was her cousin. And a queen crowned and anointed. But once violate that holy gift, and how quickly the future blood of royals might be spent. Including Elizabeth's own.

Mary had not been so circumspect, more than once lending her approval to plots to assassinate her cousin. Elizabeth had not minded those. But now Mary had brought Anabel into play . . . and at the moment Elizabeth would cheerfully have swung the sword of execution herself.

Now that it was too late. Because there could be no other answer. "Mary goes free," Elizabeth announced grimly. "Walsingham, ride in all haste to Tutbury. Take Christopher with you." She nodded at Kit. "Stephen Courtenay might be harder to persuade of this step than even Shrewsbury, but he will take his brother's word where he might not take my Lord Secretary's. I will meet you all at King's Lynn."

Burghley intervened. "Do you think that wise?"

"From the first, Mary has pressed to meet me face-to-face. It would be rude of me to let her go without granting her that request. You ride to London, Burghley. Take Dominic with you."

"I must return to Wynfield," Dominic insisted flatly.

"And you will soon enough. With Julien LeClerc. If Lucette wants him there, that is good enough for me."

They broke up with only a few more words. There was little to say and plenty to do. Elizabeth ached to be in motion like the men around her. Burghley would see to it that the government and London were held stable and in ignorance of what was happening. Time enough to announce the peril once it passed. When Anabel was safely in her power once more, and Mary set loose to wreak what havoc she could outside of England.

The men did not even wait until morning. Walsingham and Kit rode northwest for Tutbury, Burghley and Dominic south to London. Elizabeth spent a restless night in Cambridge, and when the sun had risen, rode for King's Lynn on the Norfolk coast. Her brother had fought and won a notable battle there in his last years, sending the Duke of Norfolk fleeing across the waters as Mary now meant to flee. Elizabeth took grim satisfaction from the fact that Norfolk had eventually lost his head in another rebellion, attempting to bring her down and wed Mary Stuart himself. Justice might be delayed, but it always came in the end.

Julien waited every day in expectation of the rack, but it never came. The closest he got was being shown the device—along with the other instruments of torture, some of which he could guess at, others too horrifying to contemplate when one might be on the receiving end—as a sort of prod to giving the answers they wanted. But he couldn't, because what they wanted was not the truth.

He might be a liar, but he had a strange devotion to the truth. Also a perverse wish to do the opposite of what anyone wanted of him.

Walsingham did not return, which Julien found increasingly ominous. Mostly because no one else would even hint at what was going on outside the Tower walls. Where was everyone? What were they doing? Mostly, though, *everyone* simply meant Lucette.

After eight days (the stone of the walls was soft, and though he was no artist he could at least mark the passage of time), Julien lay on his hard bed, arms behind his head, wondering why he'd never had the nerve to tell Lucie how he loved her, when the cell door opened. He didn't bother getting to his feet; it would simply be a guard checking on him or taunting him, or the lieutenant to ask him more meaningless questions.

Dominic Courtenay walked in.

Julien had never shot to his feet so fast in his life. For one thing, the Duke of Exeter was that sort of man—and would have been even without his exalted title. It had been twelve years since Julien had met him, but Lord Exeter looked less changed than Renaud. Of course, his wife still lived. The thought of Minuette made Julien flush with embarrassment at how he'd fawned over this man's wife, then deepened to regret at how Lucette still held it against him. Heaven forbid Dominic Courtenay had any idea how he had tormented himself with boyish dreams all those years ago.

It was a remarkable amount of humiliation and hope to swing through in three seconds. Frankly, Julien was surprised he managed to make it to his feet and stay there steadily. Lord Exeter had the kind of black stare that made one certain the worst was about to happen to you and he was completely uninterested in your fate.

But fear for Lucette conquered even fear of her father. "Is your daughter well, my lord?" he asked.

That provoked a crack in the facade, a querying expression that quickly resumed forbidding. "I suspect you and I are going to have a long talk about Lucette in the near future," he said grimly. "But not today. I have horses below, and we must set out at once."

"Set out where?" This was slightly dizzying. Where was Walsingham in all this? Was Exeter so powerful that he could release Tower prisoners on his own demand? Hadn't he been a Tower prisoner himself years ago?

The tumble of thoughts came to a halt at the man's next words. "Your brother has taken my daughter hostage at Wynfield Mote, along with the Princess of Wales. They are leverage for the release of Mary Stuart. You and I are riding back to Wynfield to try and bring this to a peaceful end."

"Nic?" Julien asked numbly. "I don't understand . . ."

But he found he did understand, all too well. Julien felt as though he were spinning, but recognized that it was not his body but his world spinning off center. If Walsingham had suspected Blanclair, he'd had good reason. Julien had been so caught up in Lucette that he hadn't troubled to decipher the obvious—there were men at Blanclair besides himself. And his badge maliciously planted on the body of the man who'd tried to poison Queen Elizabeth? Who could—would—have done that but Nicolas? For eight years he had existed in a world of guilt—for Léonore's death, Nicolas's castration—guilt that had sent him to Walsingham, guilt that drove him through violence and occasional mercy, guilt that had kept him away from home. Guilt that had kept him from telling Lucette how he loved her until it was too late.

And at the thought of Lucette, his world stopped spinning and settled on a new axis. For she remained unchanged. *Lucie mine*, he thought grimly, *I'm sorry. And I'm coming for you.*

Julien started for the open door. "What are we waiting for?"

Dominic stopped him with his single, powerful right hand square on his chest. "One thing you should know, son. The government's concern is the princess. Mine is my daughter. Whatever else happens, Lucette comes out of this unharmed. Is that clear?"

"I assure you, Lord Exeter, I have no greater interest than in seeing Lucie safe."

If Dominic narrowed his eyes at Julien's familiar use of her name, the duke seemed to accept it for the promise it was. "Even at your brother's expense?"

"Nicolas and I have a debt to settle, I believe. But he can go to hell before I'll see Lucie hurt."

Dominic dropped his hand and his expression lightened just a shade. "Oh yes," he murmured as if to himself, "you and I are going to have a very long talk when this is over."

TWENTY-TWO

It was with the greatest triumph that Mary received Francis Walsingham at Tutbury. She met him seated in the nearest thing to a throne her prison could provide, a pretty enough chair of gilded wood and ornamental cushions beneath the arms of Scotland and France. She wore a black velvet gown over sleeves and kirtle of striped grey silk and a black velvet cap.

"Master Secretary," she said coolly. "Am I to take it you will ride with me to the coast?"

The Earl of Shrewsbury was not present, presumably having been told by Walsingham to keep away. But Stephen Courtenay was at her side, and a young man next to Walsingham who was apparently Stephen's younger brother, Christopher.

"Yes." He bit the word off, clearly furious at having been outmaneuvered at last.

"Why so dark, Master Secretary?" she asked blithely. "Your queen is unharmed. And soon you will be free of a troublesome guest. I thought you would be pleased."

Stephen had been watching them both, clearly bewildered. "She is to be released?" he asked Walsingham.

"We'll ride with her to King's Lynn, where Her Majesty awaits. It is necessary to move swiftly, so I hope, madam, that you are prepared for hard riding."

"I have been prepared these twelve years."

"Why?" Stephen demanded to know. He did not sound as pleased as Mary would have thought, given all the care he had taken for her.

"Nicolas LeClerc has taken Anabel and Lucie hostage at Wynfield," Christopher Courtenay burst out, obviously smoldering. "The French bastards have stooped to threatening an innocent to free *her*." He jerked his head at Mary with disdain. She would have liked very much to slap him.

"I did not know what means would be used, and in any case the girl will not be harmed. If my cousin had only listened to reason—"

"Enough." Walsingham's tone brooked no dissension, and Mary shut her mouth sourly. "We leave in an hour. You may bring one lady with you, and your confessor. The others will be allowed to leave Tutbury on their own when the princess is safely in our hands once more."

Mary turned to Stephen. "You will ride with me to King's Lynn, will you not?"

She meant it as a mark of favour, a reminder that she would remember his kindness and service to her when she was free.

His face had never been so difficult to read, which was perhaps just as well with the disapproving Walsingham standing by, not to mention the fuming younger brother.

His words, like everything he did, were spoken with care. "I will ride to King's Lynn for my sister's sake, not yours."

The venom in his tone was all the worse for its control. Mary flinched. "I thought we understood each other, Stephen."

He was no longer the silent English nobleman, nor the handsome young man who had flattered her. He sounded at once older and harder. "I understand you very well. You are the center of every story you weave, and no one's life matters as much as your own. You use people, Your Majesty, and you should have taken care to be certain of my allegiance before giving me access to your secrets."

She drew back, stung and furious. "You insinuated your way into my good graces to spy my secrets? How dare you!"

"I dared very easily, though not successfully enough, it seems."

She slapped him. The younger brother took a step forward, but Walsingham restrained him. Stephen merely stared her down, every bit as cool as she was incensed.

"You have made an enemy today, Lord Somerset," Mary told him.

"I was always your enemy, lady. You just didn't have the wit to see it until today."

Anabel had heard stories of her mother's captivity at the hands of the Duke of Northumberland when Elizabeth had been Princess of Wales. She had thought it mostly a romantic tale, for it was long past and the outcome certain. Actually being held, she discovered, was an entirely different matter.

Also, the Duke of Northumberland had not been a fanatic or a madman, just an ambitious lord who overreached and was eager to save his family from falling. It was unlikely he would have actually harmed Elizabeth. But Nicolas LeClerc was a different matter entirely. Anabel didn't trust him an inch, and she didn't like the way he looked at Lucette.

The women were kept confined to Anabel's bedchamber. They were allowed a screen in the corner behind which to change and use a chamber pot that Nicolas made his man empty. They were brought the simplest of foods twice a day: porridge, apples, cheese, and beer. Nicolas stayed with them eighteen hours a day, only locking them in at midnight while he slept on a pallet outside the locked door. They had briefly considered trying to escape through the window, but it was a forty-foot sheer drop, and Nicolas had a dozen armed men inside the moat, scruffy and ill-dressed but handling weapons knowledgeably enough.

"He won't hurt you," Lucette had told Anabel the first day, and continued to repeat as something of an incantation as the days wound endlessly on. They did the calculations on how long it would take riders to go their various directions and figured it would be at least ten days before they would know if Mary had been freed.

Of course Mary would be freed, Anabel thought firmly. Her mother might find Anabel troublesome at times, but Elizabeth would never risk her daughter's life. If for no other reason than that England's throne must have an heir.

But mostly, Anabel didn't talk. Except for her title, Nicolas was uninterested in her. It was Lucette who consumed him.

Nicolas liked to talk, and Lucette had to spend hours each day parrying his conversation. It was exhausting merely to watch. But Anabel learned plenty through his endless discourses. Such as the fact that his younger brother, Julien, was head over heels in love with Lucie. That Nicolas might have set his sights on her merely to upset his brother, if he hadn't had a use for her already. That he'd maneuvered his sister into asking Lucette to France precisely in order to gain a reciprocal invitation to England, thus giving him his chance to seize Anabel herself. "And how fortunate for me that you were beautiful and spirited," Nicolas said, "for thus I gained pleasure along with necessity."

But it was the fact that Lucette had apparently fallen in love with Julien that upset Nicolas beyond measure. It made him try all the harder to break her.

Eight days into their confinement, Anabel kept her usual silent perch on the deep windowsill, the diamond-paned glass offering an alluring view of hills and freedom beyond the immediate ring of armored men inside Wynfield's perimeters. It was possible from here to see the camp put up by the Courtenays and faithfully attended by Minuette, in command while her husband was absent. It made Anabel feel better simply to have someone faithful in sight, no matter how far it might be from practical help.

Lucette sat in the chair Nicolas liked her in, hands folded in her lap and her face as inscrutably unreadable as her father's at its most forbidding. Anabel knew the technique—refuse to give a bully the reaction he was hoping for and eventually he will tire of provocation.

Nicolas never tired of provocation.

"You should write to Felix," he told Lucette today. "I know how much he is longing to welcome you officially as his mother."

"I will be truly sorry to disappoint Felix."

"But not to disappoint me? See, there's your trouble in miniature—you worry about hurting a seven-year-old boy thousands of miles away, but not the grown man with a dagger in his hand and a dislike of your tongue."

"If you dislike my tongue, why not cut it out?"

"I have no wish to damage you, Lucie mine. At least not permanently."

"Don't call me that," she said softly, almost under her breath, and Anabel had the impression the protest was wrung from her against her better judgment.

"Because it's what Julien calls you? Ah, but Julien is not here." Nicolas walked around her and with one hand stroked her dark hair. Both girls were, by necessity, dressed simply and with their hair done in plaits. Nicolas lifted the end of one of Lucette's braids and said in a tone clearly meant to be seductive, though it mostly made Anabel's skin crawl, "You are mine for now. And if Julien should reappear? Then may the best man claim you."

"I am no slave to be claimed," she blazed. "And there is no question which of you is the better man."

"If only he could hear your valiant defense of his character . . . but I rather think the only thing on Julien's mind will be that you lied to him. You suspected I was the one behind Nightingale, and you didn't tell him. For all his easy lies, my brother is quite stupidly devoted to honesty. He will not take your betrayal lightly."

"Nor yours."

"Good!" Nicolas jerked his hand away and circled restlessly, hand tightening on the dagger hilt at his belt. "I never meant him to take it lightly. I meant it to dig his heart out, squeeze the guilt he deserves into every part of his soul and then squeeze harder."

Anabel swallowed, and though he gave no sign of noticing her, it seemed to break Nicolas's dangerous train of thought. He squatted easily before Lucette and studied her with a light smile before cupping one hand against the back of her neck. "So lovely and so wicked, like every woman ever."

When he kissed Lucette, Anabel shut her eyes. But then she opened them, refusing to retreat when Lucette could not.

It had not gone further than kisses, and Lucette did not seem concerned that it would. But Anabel did not like the alarming light in Nicolas's eyes, and she prayed for all she was worth. *Lord, let them ride fast. Get us both out of here before something is done that cannot be undone.*

Elizabeth reached the environs of King's Lynn a day and a half before the Tutbury party. She had never been very good at waiting, and never more so than when waiting for something distasteful. But as they did not want word slipping out of their careful net of secrecy until Anabel had been safely retrieved, she kept her demeanor as steady as possible and used fatigue and a sick headache as an excuse to take refuge in the somewhat derelict Castle Rising five miles outside the town. Bequeathed to the Howard family by her father, she had repossessed the castle shortly after her brother's death, and though much of the medieval castle had been overrun by rabbit warrens, the guest lodgings built in the 1540s were acceptable. Burghley's report from London arrived the morning after Elizabeth's arrival and confirmed that Dominic and Julien were setting off immediately for Wynfield Mote.

An outrider appeared at Castle Rising an hour before noon to announce the imminent arrival of Mary's party. Elizabeth sent him back with orders for Walsingham to conduct her cousin anonymously around the outlying areas of the town and meet her at the French ship that had waited prudently offshore for the last week.

Elizabeth dressed with care. Though not as glamorous as she would have been in her own court, her brocaded crimson damask and high ruff were impeccably royal. She wore a wig closely curled and set with pearls. Though she had been dressing the monarch's part for almost half her life, she admitted one moment's weakness to have Minuette tell her how well she looked, or Kat Ashley to sniff and pronounce her appearance "adequate."

When reunited with Anabel, she would take care to be freer with her compliments.

She took only two guards to escort her and rode in a carriage, not wishing to be on display. The ship stood a polite distance off, with a skiff waiting to board its royal passenger. Elizabeth ignored them.

She could hardly admit, even to herself, that mixed with fury was a hint of—nerves? anticipation?—at finally coming face-to-face once more with the woman who had been her greatest rival. They had met once, many years ago in France. Elizabeth had been attending the French court as her brother's representative to his betrothed French bride, and Mary had been still a girl. Thirteen at the time, but Elizabeth remembered her as tall and breathtakingly beautiful. They had similar colouring, from their shared Tudor blood, but Elizabeth knew herself to be the better ruler. Mary might style herself Queen of France and Scotland, but her French reign had been astonishingly brief and the dislike of Catherine de Medici—Mary's French mother-in-law—had driven her back to her rightful island crown. But she had barely managed six years in Scotland, running through two husbands and multiple scandals, and alienating her firmly Protestant people so thoroughly that they had not wanted her returned these dozen years.

All the while, Elizabeth had held England together, sometimes by the mere force of her will. And if it galled her to let Mary slip through her fingers today, there was consolation that at last the hated queen would be off English soil. For good.

Mary still managed an upright figure on horseback, though even from that vantage one could see the extra weight she'd put on in captivity. Elizabeth took petty pleasure in noting that—she herself was nearly as slender as she'd been as a girl. Of her famous beauty, Mary had retained the outlines, but eroded by time. She might be years younger than me, Elizabeth thought, but not so very much more desirable.

And that was only counting the physical. What price would Mary command on the open market, a woman so smeared by sexual and violent scandal? It almost cheered Elizabeth, so that she was able to greet her cousin with a modicum of politeness.

"So eager to leave our hospitality?" she asked as the Scots queen faced her down. It was slightly disconcerting not to be curtsied or bowed to, but it wasn't worth fighting over at the moment.

Not that she wouldn't mark every charge against Mary, that she might pay her back in kind one day.

"I would have thought you eager to rid yourself of me all these years, and yet you delayed. Perhaps you merely found my presence convenient." Mary had been helped down from her mount by Stephen Courtenay, with a particular blankness of expression with which Elizabeth was long familiar on his father's face. Mary ignored the men standing behind Elizabeth—Stephen, Kit, and Walsingham—as well as those who would be allowed to sail away with her. There might have been no one on earth at the moment save these two queens.

"You have never in your life been convenient," Elizabeth said. "Only necessary."

Mary's smile was frost and glass. "And now it is necessary to let me go."

Elizabeth's smile was ice and daggers. "You set violent men on my daughter. I will not forget."

"I did not know what means would be used. Your daughter will be unharmed, and after all, if only you had been reasonable, it would never have come to this."

"If you found me unreasonable before, you will not like what follows today. It is as well that you are leaving England, for I could sign your death warrant this instant without regret."

"If you had it in you, you would have seen me dead years ago. For all your vaunted hardness, you avoid the difficult choices, cousin. And that is why I win—because I made them."

Surprisingly, it was not Walsingham who interrupted, but Stephen Courtenay. "What is the phrase we take back to your men?" he demanded of Mary. Elizabeth noted the fierceness in his voice and the lack of title he gave her. Interesting—she would not have taken Stephen for a man of any kind of passion.

But then, he was Dominic Courtenay's son. And though it might be strictly controlled, Dominic was a man of deep and dangerous passions.

Mary eyed him slantwise. "When I am in the skiff and sure of not being seized, I will tell you."

"Then what are we waiting for?" Stephen demanded. "Although if my queen asked it of me, I'm quite certain I could get the phrase from you here and now."

Elizabeth sketched a dismissal at Stephen. "I will not take that risk. Go, then," she told Mary. "If ever we cross paths again, your life will be forfeit for your treachery."

"Ah, cousin, how I once longed to be friends. It is you who has made us enemies. Remember that."

Mary and her woman and confessor were helped into the skiff, the ladies' voluminous skirts crushed against each other. From her seat, Mary looked at Stephen with a certain resentment that spoke more of the woman's feelings than the queen's. "The phrase you need to set your princess free is this: 'The nightingale sings her freedom.'"

"My queen and her council value Anne's life sufficiently," retorted

Stephen. "But as for myself, it is my sister's life I hold against you. I will see you paid for it one day."

Mary set her chin and looked away. Elizabeth watched motionless from shore until the skiff had crossed the choppy waves and the occupants brought on board the waiting French ship. She stayed until it had passed from sight over the eastern horizon.

Long before that, Stephen and Kit Courtenay had ridden west for Wynfield Mote. They carried with them the Great Seal of England with Walsingham's affidavit of their authority, and the phrase from Mary Stuart that would see Anabel freed.

Elizabeth would not draw a deep breath until her daughter was in her hands once more.

TWENTY-THREE

Julien had been camped outside Wynfield Mote for four days before anything of import happened. He had thought himself a patient person—or at least one able to entertain himself while waiting—but he truly thought he might run mad within sight of Wynfield Mote and unable to do a thing but wait.

It was a small encampment—Dominic and Minuette Courtenay, their youngest daughter, Pippa, and a dozen retainers, all armed. If Julien had been afraid of his reception by the family, he need not have worried. He had known Minuette to be beautiful when he was younger—but in his youth he had overlooked her great warmth and generosity. And perhaps Dominic had said a word or two in her ear about his suspicions of Julien's feelings. Heaven knows he'd said little enough himself, but the Duke of Exeter seemed to know how to read the quality of his silences.

In any case, he was welcomed as an ally, though Julien had no illusions: if it were between him and Lucette, they would cheerfully throw him to the wolves. At least in that, their intentions aligned perfectly.

For days now, Julien had done little but ponder his brother's astonishing betrayal. He still wasn't sure of Nicolas's motivations. Nicolas hardly spoke of politics at all—when had he come to care so much about Mary Stuart and England? Julien had thought he'd been the one keeping all the secrets these eight years. Once again, his self-absorption had blinded him.

An hour or two after sunset on the fourth day since reaching Wynfield, Dominic and his man Harrington received the scout's report of riders coming fast. Julien recognized Kit Courtenay on horseback and guessed the second rider was the other brother, Stephen.

"We've got it," Kit called as he swung off his horse, both man and beast looking utterly exhausted and soaked through from long hours of hard riding. "Stephen's got the Lord Chancellor's seal and we have the phrase from Mary."

"She is gone?" Minuette asked her oldest son. He looked like his father, but Julien thought there might be a streak of his mother's temper running through him.

"Mary Stuart?" Stephen said with contempt. "She's gone, sailed off to whoever wants her. France, I suppose. It was a French ship."

"Let me have the seal," Dominic said, and Stephen handed the velvet bag containing the symbol of England's most powerful office to his father.

"I want to go in," Kit announced.

Dominic shook his head. "You're worn-out and that's my home and my daughter."

"And Anabel!" Kit said fiercely.

With a glance at his wife, Dominic again shook his head. "I won't forget. I will get them both out."

Julien had mostly kept his own counsel, aware that he was here on sufferance, but finally he offered, "Shouldn't I come with you? I thought I was here to deal with Nicolas."

"He hasn't asked for you. I'd rather keep you in reserve till necessary."

If something went wrong, Dominic meant. If Nicolas broke his word and kept the women, or took Dominic hostage as well. Julien felt a chill along his spine. He knew perfectly well that this would only end when he and Nicolas were face-to-face.

But he was in no position to argue.

Kit had no such scruples. "Take me with you."

"No."

"Father, please, it should be me, I'm less valuable than you. If something happens—"

Surprisingly amidst all this male tension, it was Pippa who broke in. "Let Kit do it," was all she said, but it froze everyone to silence.

Minuette looked searchingly at her daughter. "Are you certain?"

"I don't think—" Dominic started, but stopped when Pippa laid a hand on his sleeve, just above his missing left hand.

"I am very certain, Father. Kit is right. Let him go."

There was something otherworldly and yet absolute about her, and the chill Julien had felt before shivered through him again. Lucette had never told him her sister was a . . . What? Seer? Visionary?

Whatever it might be called, the men in her family listened. Dominic handed the bag with the Great Seal to Kit and said grimly, "Bring them out, son."

"They're moving."

At the note in Anabel's voice, Lucette steadied herself and reluctantly returned her thoughts to the chamber she was in. She had taken to retreating in some form to pass the long days under Nicolas's razor-sharp attention. She was clever enough to hold up her end of the conversation without being wholly present, and gave thanks to Dr. Dee for teaching her how to think of more than one thing at a time.

She didn't stir from her chair, though, for she had learned by hard experience that Nicolas liked to tell her when and where to move. He went to the window where Anabel looked out and studied the landscape with her.

"I believe you're right," he said. "That does appear to be a party for parlay approaching from their encampment."

He opened the door and summoned Laurent with barked orders. Anabel and Lucette exchanged a long glance, then both looked away. As long as Anabel got out of here, Lucette would be happy. She was perfectly certain she herself would be staying behind.

Laurent took the princess, and Nicolas escorted Lucette, both of them with daggers negligently held to their sides. Lucette was under no illusions about how quickly that positioning could change. Her father had taught her several ways to bring a dagger into play and was certain these men knew even more than she did.

The four of them took up position in the rebuilt medieval hall of Wynfield Mote. Though designed along its previous lines, modern comforts and touches had been introduced when it was restored after the fire. Lucette had always loved the hall, redolent as it was of family and laughter—would she ever be able to feel that way again?

She had been expecting her father, certain he would not let anyone else do it. But perhaps Nicolas's men had been ordered to keep the elder Courtenay out, for to her surprise it was Kit who entered. Her brother had always possessed a certain grace, but his movements today spoke more of contained violence than fluid action.

His eyes went first to Anabel, and Lucette nearly caught her breath at what she saw in his face. But he was quick and shut down his feelings before they could more than briefly flash.

Did Anabel know that Kit was in love with her? Did Kit even know it before now?

"And why," Nicolas wondered aloud, "did they send the young colt?"

"Because I saw Mary Stuart board ship for France and sail away with my own eyes. I have the Lord Chancellor's seal, and your phrase."

Nicolas cocked his head impatiently. "And?"

Kit tossed him a small velvet bag, then spoke. "'The nightingale sings her freedom.'"

Kit let it linger, and Lucette felt Nicolas's satisfaction through the points where he touched her. However much he'd had his own agenda—and still had things to finish—he was truly satisfied to have freed Mary.

No one moved, though Lucette could see what it cost her brother to stand still and wait. His jaw was tight surely to the point of pain, but he would not speak first for fear of unbalancing the moment.

At last Nicolas flicked the tip of his dagger in Anabel's direction. "Let her go, Laurent," he said softly.

Like the good soldier he was, Laurent released Anabel without hesitation. She shot a glance at Lucette.

"Time to go, Princess," Nicolas said. "I think the young Courtenay boy will be only too glad to take you out."

"What about Lucie?" Kit broke in.

"You got what you came for. Take her now, or forfeit."

"Anabel, go," Kit said softly, but she reached his side and took his hand, determined to stand with him. Lucette nearly shook her head at the foolishness of both of them.

"I won't offer again," Nicolas promised.

"You said Mary's freedom for the girls."

"I promised a princess for a queen. You have her."

"And my sister?"

"Ah, a sister requires the offer of a brother."

Kit glared. "Good thing I'm standing right here."

"Not her brother, boy. Mine. I know perfectly well that Julien is just outside these walls aching to get his hands on me. Take your princess out, and send my brother in."

It was Lucette who had to order them. "Go now."

Anabel at least had sense, and more time with Nicolas to know he meant what he said. She pulled Kit with her. "Wait outside, Laurent," Nicolas said. "Bring my brother in when he arrives."

Then he turned to Lucette and caressed her cheek with the flat of his dagger blade. "The three of us have unfinished business."

————

Kit returned with the Princess of Wales. Everyone in camp had watched the two figures approach in grim silence, and waited for word from inside.

Julien didn't think anyone was surprised when told that Nicolas would not deal for Lucette until his brother had surrendered himself. Not surprised, but disappointed.

He said roughly to the princess, "Has he touched her?"

"He has not hurt her," she answered carefully.

Which was not an answer. Julien simply nodded once and began to walk toward the manor house.

Minuette stopped him, though her husband was immediately beside her. Julien expected to be told to do whatever it took, perhaps even to be careful for they were not cruel people and would not lightly see him hurt, even for Lucette's sake.

But she put her hands on his face and pulled it down to kiss him on the forehead. Like his mother used to do. "I am sorry, Julien," she whispered. "I know what it costs to confront one who has betrayed you—especially when it is someone you love."

She dropped her hands. Dominic's face looked carved in stone, but he nodded once. In approval? In resignation? Julien didn't much care. As he began the walk to Wynfield Mote, he silently spoke toward the woman inside: *Lucie mine, you're coming out of there alive and whole. Whatever it takes.*

Once across the shallow moat, he was searched thoroughly by the kind of men who would kill without thought when ordered. He had dressed plainly and casually, prepared to fight. No weapons, of course. He'd figure something out.

It was odd walking into Wynfield Mote. There were flashes of memory from his previous visit, his body remembering where buildings were: the practice yard to his right, the stables where he'd hit Nicolas for his insolence . . . and been interrupted by the fierce ten-year-old girl who'd followed his brother around like he was God. There had been a week or two this summer when he'd imagined returning to Wynfield Mote with that fierce girl—if not tamed, at least gentled to his hand, coming home to receive her parents' blessing.

He should have known better. Dreams were only that.

Felix's tutor waited for him outside the front door. Julien had never been fond of the supercilious Laurent, and now that the fanatic in him had been given free rein, Julien would cheerfully have knocked the man senseless. Instead he submitted to the tutor's search, though he did say, "You saw your men search me already. Is it that you like to feel men's bodies?"

He received the expected backhanded blow without a word. Laurent laughed grimly. "Can't wait to see you brought down, traitorous filth."

Julien, his jaw throbbing, kept his mouth shut. Better not risk too many blows before he got to Nicolas.

Laurent shoved open the door and jerked his head for Julien to precede him.

His strange sense of déjà vu continued to overlay his vision—the wide-planked floors strewn with rugs, the medieval fireplace—but the moment he locked eyes with Nicolas, all déjà vu vanished. There was nothing but an awareness, deep in his bones, that only one of them would be leaving this hall alive.

With effort, he pulled his gaze to Lucette, for it seemed dangerous to take his eyes off Nicolas for even a second. She looked back at him steadily, no colour to her face at all, dark hair hanging loose. Her gown was plain and clearly could be laced without aid. He didn't know if it made him feel better or worse that Nicolas had not insisted that she be dressed and pampered elegantly.

"Are you well?" Why did one ask that? Because to ask anything more would upset his own precarious balance, not to mention whatever balance maintained between Nicolas and Lucette at this point.

"Perfectly." If she could not control her colour, she could control her voice. Neutral, verging on bored. Seized by an insane desire to laugh, Julien nodded once, then turned his attention back to his brother.

"So, Nic, I'm here now. Whatever lies between us began long before Lucette was involved. Let her go."

"The moment she leaves, my men will be overwhelmed by her father's men and I will be seized for Walsingham's vicious questioning. I have no intention of being racked by the English. I need her to get to the coast and out of England."

"So you plan to return home as though nothing has happened, as though Father isn't going to say a word about the fact that you violated the trust and hospitality of his friends and laid violent hands on a girl he cares about for her own sake?"

"Whatever you may say about my hands on Lucette, they are never violent."

Julien took a furious step forward before he managed to restrain himself, but it was enough for Nicolas to pull Lucette against him as both warning and shield. Swallowing the bile that rose, Julien halted.

"Lucie mine," Nicolas purred, and how Julien wanted to smash his brother's face for appropriating that phrase, "why don't you wash your face and change? We should celebrate being together. It's the way I want it, you know. The three of us. Together. I've had weeks to think about it."

"I'm not changing clothes with Laurent watching me."

He managed to sound injured. "Of course not! Go on up to your chamber. We'll wait for you here."

"Aren't you afraid I'll do something rash, like jump out a window?"

Though Nicolas spoke to Lucette, it was Julien he stared at. "There is not the slightest chance in the world that you will do a single thing to jeopardize my brother's life. Knowing that he's here with me, that if you are not back in this hall in a quarter hour—

dressed and fashioned appropriately—knowing Julien will pay forfeit for whatever price I demand . . . no, Lucie mine, there's not a
chance in hell that you won't do exactly what I say."

Julien could only hope Nicolas was wrong. That Lucette would
use her head, and figure a way either to get out of the house or to
signal to her father and brothers . . . as long as she was out of reach of
Nicolas, everything could be borne.

Because this would only end when one or both of them were
dead. He knew it as surely as he knew his name. Death loomed in
Wynfield Mote's hall, waiting to pounce. All that mattered was that
Lucie be well out of death's reach.

27 August
Outside Wynfield Mote

*As soon as Julien headed for the house, Dominic and the other men
questioned Anabel closely about the state of affairs in and around
Wynfield. Bless the girl for having her mother's practicality and quick
wits! She not only did not wonder at the purpose of such questions,
but had clearly anticipated them. Her answers were prompt and clear.
The men on the outside, of which we have counted eleven, never enter
the house. The cooking, such as it is, is carried out by the tutor,
Richard Laurent. Laurent and Nicolas LeClerc are the only men in
the house. They are armed with daggers, swords, and pistols.*

*Anabel and Kit described the scene in the hall before she was
handed over. "It was the first time we were let out of my chamber,"
Anabel said. "It's possible Nicolas took Lucette straight back up when
Kit and I left."*

*"Possible," Dominic said slowly, "but also highly possible they're
still there. If he wanted a stage for the first part of the climax, he'll
most definitely want it for his confrontation with his brother. We
should proceed as though they are in the hall."*

*"Proceed how?" I asked. Mostly to force my husband to speak it
aloud for those who do not read him as quickly as I do. Though I*

imagine our sons knew what he would say—and for certain Harrington did. He had already alerted the small force of handpicked men who have been kept two miles away so no one at Wynfield might catch sight of them. Dominic had spoken privately to Julien while Kit was in the house. He knows what is coming. When it is full dark, in less than an hour, those men will be led by Dominic, Harrington, and both my sons. No matter the tiredness Dominic noted—my boys will not be left behind. And like their father, they have the necessary strength to do what must be done when it must be done. They can sleep after.

Of course, the hope is that Julien will be able to talk—if not himself—at least Lucette out of Nicolas's hands. But if she is still inside Wynfield when darkness covers all, then my men must move silently and swiftly.

While I sit with Pippa and Anabel and Carrie and pray. And wait.

There is nothing more difficult in this world than waiting.

TWENTY-FOUR

Lucette went up to her bedchamber in a dreamlike state of unreality. It was precisely as she'd left it. Covers drawn back but the bed unslept in, the gown she'd worn that last night at dinner still lying on a closed chest. Only once alone did she truly feel the tension that had stalked her these last days: the constant pressure of someone watching her, breathing in her hearing or just outside a closed door . . . Lucette gave a great shudder and felt a sudden desire wash over her to curl up in bed and sleep.

There wasn't time. She had only minutes to change her dress and prepare for whatever crisis was imminent in the hall. For that she would need a different dress, and a different hairstyle.

Someone—no doubt Laurent, as Nicolas hadn't done it and no one else came indoors—had filled the pitcher with water. Lucette quickly stripped down to her shift and washed her face and as much of herself as she could in three minutes. She was grateful for how that revived her. A clean shift helped to further restore her, and now to choose a dress.

Hopefully Nicolas hadn't meant her to come down dressed for

court or even church. Were men aware of the help required to get into such complicated layers? She imagined both brothers had done their share of removing such gowns from women … but that was not a thought to linger on at the moment. Her own requirements for what to wear were simple: she could put it on herself, and she could hide a weapon in it.

She chose a gown with cherry-red flowers on a white background that she'd often worn at Wynfield during the summers. It had belled sleeves of white lawn that gave her a certain freedom of movement. But most important, along the inside of the split overskirt that left the vivid red of the kirtle showing was a matched set of sheaths sewn in the stiff line of seaming. One on the right, one on the left, just far enough down not to interfere with sitting or walking, but perfectly placed for a quick hand to snatch out two narrow bodice daggers. Though the wicked long dagger her father had once given her had been removed from her chamber, thankfully neither Laurent nor Nicolas had thought to explore further. Her bodice daggers were where she'd left them, stored in the false bottom of her jewelry casket.

The final step was her hair. Like the dress, it couldn't be elaborate. She braided it at both her temples, then managed a single thick plait down her back. It was imperfect and no doubt crooked, but who cared? Once plaited, she wound it at the nape of her neck into a heavy bun and secured it with pins. Then, a single decoration pushed through her hair: a gold-leafed, circular ornament six inches long and with a teardrop-shaped ruby at the top.

The benefit to Nicolas's tight timeline was that she couldn't dwell on the many things that could go wrong. All she could do was utter a quick prayer for guidance and safety as she made her way back to the hall.

She was not surprised to hear Nicolas speaking as she approached, for she had become accustomed to his near-constant murmur that had at times seemed only half directed at her. Pausing to make out what she could, she caught only a few snatches: surprisingly, Nicolas seemed to be musing about how Felix was passing his time at Blanclair without his tutor.

Was he really talking about his son at such a time? As though Nicolas expected, as Julien had sarcastically pointed out, everything to go back to normal once he left Wynfield? It was that blitheness that terrified Lucette more than anything else about the last days. Nicolas might be focused and clearheaded on his own concerns, but he seemed to have no realistic grasp of what others might be feeling or planning. Lucette liked logic and mathematics because they made sense. One could not reason with a man who lacked the most basic awareness.

No time for regrets. Lucette stepped forward into the hall, stopping Nicolas's speech for a moment before he turned his words on her.

"How pretty you look! Very charming in your summer dress. I approve."

"That was the point," she said drily. She could not bring herself to flirt with him, but nor did she want to upset him. Nicolas had not let go of his dagger—Julien's dagger—and Laurent leaned against the front door with dagger in one hand and pistol in the other. The tutor's eyes never left Julien's back, and they were filled with an icy rage that scared her. Laurent hated Julien, and there were not even any ties of sibling memory to soften it.

"And now we can talk," Nicolas said cheerfully. "Anyone care to sit?"

"Talk about what?" Julien demanded. He had looked her over once, swiftly, when he'd come in and again when she'd returned to the hall. Otherwise he seemed to hardly know she was there, so tensely was he fixed on his brother.

"About the future. About how the three of us—sorry, Laurent, *four* of us—get out of England. About what happens when we reach France."

"You're not taking Lucette out of here, Nic. She's got a father and brothers and a band of very angry Englishmen just waiting for you to stick your head out the door before they take it off."

"Not if Lucie comes willingly."

She was getting tired of being talked about and around. "But I won't, so there's no need to imagine it."

"Of course you'll come willingly, *ma petite*. Otherwise, I kill Julien. You'll leave Wynfield to save him. You'll return to France to save him. And when we reach France, you will marry me . . . to save him."

"Not going to happen." Julien said it firmly, but Lucette noted the edge to his expression, coming in and out of focus through the flickering candlelight. Someone had lit the candles on the sideboard during her brief absence. It would soon be full night outside, and with all the shutters firmly closed the hall was already dark.

"Lucette is not that stupid or desperate," Julien went on. "She knows I am not worth her life."

"Such a martyr! Always ready to die for a cause, Julien. Or no, more like always ready to let someone *else* die for your cause."

"And that's the crux of all this, isn't it? What happened to you because of me. Because you went after Léonore for my sake, and in trying to help me got yourself nearly killed. That's on me, Nicolas. I know it. Don't punish this girl because once you tried to help another girl I cared for."

"You are such an idiot! How in Heaven's name have you managed all these years not to get yourself killed with your stupidity? I wasn't trying to help you. I wasn't trying to save Léonore. She was a Huguenot bitch. Good for a little fun in bed, but that little fun cost me a lot more than my life. I wasn't trying to help her, you stupid bastard—I was screwing her and got caught in the cross fire."

Julien had gone so white and so still that Lucette was afraid he would stumble or fall. "Say that again." His voice was like lead shot, dropped into her heart.

"I was caught in her damn bed when her brothers returned to the house. I imagine the mutilation they inflicted on me was just the beginning, but before they could kill me the Catholics stormed the house and tore them both to pieces."

When Nicolas smiled, it was the most terrible thing Lucette had ever seen. She wanted him to stop talking because he was going to break Julien, and she didn't know if anyone would ever be able to put the pieces back together again.

"As for the girl," Nicolas continued with remorseless pride, "I stayed conscious long enough to cut her throat myself."

For the third time in his life, Julien stood still and recognized in a single moment that his life would never again be the same. They were rare, those moments, when one could see with perfect clarity that at this point everything changed. There would be *before,* and there would be *after.*

The second time had been just over a week ago, when Dominic Courtenay told him what Nicolas had done.

The first time was the moment he'd found Léonore dead and Nicolas castrated and bleeding out.

Julien had changed everything in his life—sacrificed his family, lied to his fellow countrymen, missed his mother's deathbed—because of what he believed had happened that day. He knew that, should he get out of this house alive, he would have to deal with a crushing weight of guilt, much worse than the false guilt he'd been carrying for years.

But first he had to get out. Or, at the least, get Lucette out.

For she was the only fixed point in his world at this moment when all else hurtled into a chaos of lies and deception. She stood there staring at him, as if her gaze could keep him anchored to the world. And it did.

Julien asked simply, "How long?"

"Just the once," Nicolas answered, correctly surmising his brother's intent. "I thought for certain you'd already had her, but she was a virgin, sure enough. Your loss. But then, you always have been the romantic one. The one for whom honour is more valuable than life."

Julien blinked, and twitched his head as though shaking off a fly. He could not afford to get lost in memories just now. Focus, instead, on Laurent at his back and Nicolas facing him. Focus, also, on the quality of Lucette's gaze, and the way she flicked her eyes downward to her hands, crossed demurely below her waist.

But not just crossed—her fingertips disappeared beneath the fabric of her split-front skirt. Back in France, outside the Nightingale Inn, Lucette had produced a dagger from somewhere about her women's clothing. Could it be she had hiding places in this dress, as well?

As though she could read his mind Lucette said tentatively, "Nicolas, I'm feeling a little faint. Might I sit down?"

He cupped his hand on her cheek. "Of course. Laurent," he called over his shoulder, "place a stool for Lucette next to you."

Perfect. Laurent thudded a low-backed stool in front of the door, with just enough room for him to stand behind her. Leaving himself in easy reach of a woman he wasn't much afraid of.

His mistake.

As long as Lord Exeter's men were quick and quiet in their execution, then Nicolas would never know when his men outside were taken down and he and Laurent remained alone. Dominic had told Julien he preferred not to storm the house and risk injury to Lucette. If only they could take out Laurent and better the odds, then Julien would force her to run.

It was interesting how his mind could operate cold-bloodedly on such details while his gut roiled with bile and betrayal. But as much as he hated Nic at this moment, when he looked at his brother, he could not help seeing Felix as well. And Charlotte. And their father. And even Nicole, who might be watching her sons from Heaven.

Nicolas stopped the threat of drowning misery in its tracks. "So, brother, how would you like to share a woman in truth? Everyone keeps making such a fuss about Lucette deserving to have children of her own. Why should she not have LeClerc children?"

"You must be mad," Julien said flatly.

"To imagine she would welcome you into her bed? Not mad, brother—just perceptive. She's fond enough of me, and I'm not too proud to trade on that fondness and even pity—but it is you she wants. From the moment she laid eyes on you in Paris, it is you she has wanted to claim her."

Julien was glad that he could not clearly see Lucette.

"If you hate me so much, why offer what I want most in the world?"

"Because it is not what you want most! You want all of her. I know you, Julien. You want the priest and vows, the loyalty and the love, the days as well as the nights. You are too honourable for your own good, and that is why you lose. I am willing to throw you scraps of my wife, if only to keep you in perpetual torment."

Julien had to close his eyes against his brother's venom. When he opened them, he had himself under control. "You might read me well enough, Nic, but I'm afraid you've completely misread Lucette. She had quite other plans in coming to France, and marriage was not among them. Haven't you worked it out yet? Didn't she tell you?"

"Tell me what?"

"Walsingham sent her to spy out Nightingale. Before she left Blanclair, she knew it was one of us running it. She would have done whatever was necessary to get us both to England. She accepted your proposal because she knew I would come with you, putting whichever of us was guilty into Walsingham's reach. She would have accepted me with the same calculation. Everything she's done has been bent to her purpose."

He had shaken Nicolas; there was a sheen to his brother's face as though finally the heat of the closed-up hall was getting to him. "If you believe that, you know nothing about women. She was lost the moment she loved you. And you're too much a fool to have seen it.

"Besides," Nicolas gestured to her sitting before Laurent, "she has failed spectacularly. She followed the false trail, thinking it was Eliz-abeth's death we wanted. And in the end she brought me exactly where I needed to be—within reach of the heretic's daughter. So calculating or not, I must thank her for her service."

Nicolas sketched a mocking bow in Lucette's direction, breaking eye contact with his brother. Without turning his head, Julien could just see the moment when Lucie rose and turned in one smooth movement. The daggers she'd pulled from their hiding place had blades barely longer than her palms, but light gleamed sharp on their edges. In the same moment that Nicolas straightened, Julien tackled him and prayed that Lucie's blades met their mark.

Lucette had never plunged a blade into living flesh, and so was sur-prised at how easily she did it. The dagger in her right hand went straight through the fabric of Laurent's shirtsleeves and into his fore-arm, which made him reflexively drop the pistol he'd been holding in that hand. Her left-hand dagger did not quite so easily find a mark, skittering across the buttons of his jerkin. With a wrench, he pulled her blade out of his arm and backhanded her with the other hand.

"Bitch!"

Behind her there was the sound of scuffling, which faintly re-called the time she'd come across the brothers in Wynfield's stables, but she knew this was far more deadly. Laurent struck her again, so that her vision blackened and she fell awkwardly backward, half sit-ting on the floor. With black spots still dancing in her eyes, she watched Laurent raise his pistol.

And then a sword, knocking the pistol aside, and before she could react the blade plunged into Laurent's stomach. He fell with a ter-rible gurgling, and Lucette thought dimly that she had to get up, she couldn't keep sitting on the floor with a man dying three feet away, she must . . .

It was Nicolas who pulled her up, who ran his hands along her body. "Did he hurt you?" he asked urgently.

She shook her head, which made it ache worse, and then Julien was in her vision as well and she could breathe deeper.

His lip was split and he had a welt along his cheek, but he appeared otherwise unhurt. Beneath the relief, confusion pounded through her: Why had Nicolas killed his ally?

For her sake, apparently. "Bastard was told not to touch you. Ever." Nicolas bent to his son's former tutor, who was still twitching a bit, and studied the wound Lucette had made in his forearm. "Although I must say your provocation was extreme."

When Nicolas moved again, it was to make a clean sweep of the various weapons in the hall. Laurent's pistol and sword, Lucette's thin bodice daggers—they looked like toys in his grasp—everything except Nicolas's own sword and dagger, he locked in the silver cupboard on the wall across from the fireplace.

At last Julien moved to stand between his brother and Lucette. "Nic, let's go now. If you leave her alone, Lord Exeter will allow us through his line. We can be halfway to the coast by morning."

Nicolas seemed not to have heard him. All his attention was bent to Lucette, who met his gaze fiercely. "Little spy," he purred, and he was only partly amused. "Did I give you enough mysteries to puzzle out at Blanclair?"

"What did you do to the maids?" she threw back at him in challenge.

Julien looked bewildered, but Nicolas grasped it at once. "Was it Anise leaving that set you off? Or had you picked up on that before?"

"Before. There were four maids who left their employment at Blanclair with no more than a message left for the cook, all within the last five years. Five maids, once Anise left. Even after Anise left, you used her to send me a message naming Julien as working against me. Did you kill the others?"

"Of course not! What do you take me for? I paid the bitches well to leave without notice and with a promise not to return. With the money I paid, they would have little need to look for work for some time to come."

"Why pay them off? What did they learn about Nightingale?"

"So focused on politics—I thought women were supposed to be good at understanding the personal."

But it was Julien who spoke up in quick understanding. "You seduced them," he said flatly, "as well as you could. But when they came too near to discovering that the seduction could only go so far . . . well, you would do nearly anything to protect that secret."

"As would any man. Don't you sneer at me, Julien. What do you know of the hell those Huguenot bastards left me in? Better to die, I thought, for a long time. But then I realized that I wasn't absolutely, entirely unmanned. Did you know that, in some few cases, it's possible to feel arousal? Possible for desire to flood you body and soul until there's only one release? And when that one release is impossible . . . what then? Don't you dare mock at how I managed in the face of such provocation."

Lucette did not care to imagine the details of Nicolas's accommodations for his desire. She might once have felt sorry for him; that time was long past.

Perhaps Julien was beginning to feel the same, for there was no apology or guilt in his voice when he answered, "I don't care who you use or how you use them, except for Lucette. She's not leaving here with you. I'll kill you first."

"With no weapons? Come on, Julien, let's fight as we used to."

"You have weapons."

"And you have your manhood whole and entire," Nicolas snapped. "Seems a fair trade to me."

"Agreed," Julien said flatly.

"Julien—" It slipped out of her without warning, but Lucette managed to bite off the instinctive protest. Nothing could keep these brothers from battering one another. All she could do was try and tip the scales toward Julien. Nicolas's control was tenuous at best—she might be able to exploit that. And if not, she still had one surprise left to her.

And then, for the first time since entering Wynfield, Julien locked eyes with her and smiled as if it were only the two of them. "Lucie mine," he said, "you are the cleverest, wittiest, most exasperating woman I have ever, in my lifetime, had the good fortune to meet. Also, you are far more beautiful than your mother."

She could no more have stopped her answering smile than she could have stopped breathing. "And you are the most charming liar I've ever known."

This doesn't end here, she swore silently to herself. *I'm dragging us both out of this if it's the last thing I do.*

When Julien could no longer bear the blinding beauty of Lucette's smile, he turned deliberately to where Nicolas waited for him, sword in his right hand, Julien's dagger in his left.

The key would be to take out—or take over—one of those weapons as quickly as possible. Julien wasn't afraid to fight dirty, and he had the edge of having fought for his life more than once during the years Nicolas had stayed at Blanclair. Practice yards were one thing; fights to the death another.

The key to fighting dirty was the unexpected. Nicolas thought Julien had been left unarmed—because he didn't take into account that household items can become weapons in the hands of a creative man. When Nicolas paced him, as though they were fighting in the practice yard once more, Julien seized the first thing his hand touched. It was one of the highbacked chairs at the table, too heavy for an accurate disarming blow, but the weight of it made Nicolas stagger to the side. In that moment of unsteadiness on his feet, Julien made a grab for the candlesticks on the table, fortunately unlit, and, with one in each hand, advanced on his brother.

The silver was heavy enough to deflect the sword's thrust at his ribs, but the blow jarred clear through Julien's shoulders and he dropped one of the candlesticks. He used the remaining one to slip through Nicolas's guard and hit him on the side of the head. His brother grunted and drove the dagger up, catching Julien's arm in a long scratch that tore through fabric and drew blood.

But that move, by Nicolas's weaker hand, gave Julien the chance to elbow his brother just below his throat. When Nicolas staggered back, Julien twisted the sword out of his hand. In a continuation of that movement, he pushed the tip against the floor and brought his weight down through his boot onto the slender blade until it broke. He tossed the hilted piece across the hall and kicked away the remaining half. Lucette was already scrambling for them when Nicolas was on him in a flurry, and Julien had to concentrate to keep the dagger away from his face.

The tip caught a glancing blow to the top of an ear, but then he circled his brother's wrist with both hands and forced the dagger away. With a vicious twist, he wrenched Nicolas's wrist, but his brother would not drop the dagger.

Then Nicolas yelled, and Julien saw Lucette pulling back the blade she'd shoved into his brother's calf. Where the hell had she hidden another weapon? Then he recognized the twisted, ornamental ruby pin that had been in her hair and almost laughed. Trust Lucie to have dangerous hair ornaments.

In the chaos, Nicolas slipped out of his grasp. He dropped Julien's dagger, but only to knock Lucette's small blade away and wrap his hands around her neck. She wasn't very big; Nic's hands completely spanned her neck. His thumbs dug into her throat and Julien could hear her gasping for breath. Already he was moving, fitting his own familiar dagger into his hand.

His first strike was in Nic's upper arm, which caused a satisfying spurt of blood. Nicolas hissed in pain and, loosening his grip on Lucette's throat, grasped her loosened hair and shoved her away. She tripped over her skirts and her head hit the floor with a distinct thud.

Nicolas grinned at him with sudden, feral humor. "You're too honourable to kill me, brother."

Julien drove his dagger at Nicolas's throat, but his brother side-stepped just quick enough to avoid it. He elbowed Julien in the temple as he moved; pain blossomed behind Julien's eyes and he dropped his dagger. Almost the next moment he felt a second pain, lower down, and realized Nicolas had grabbed the falling dagger and plunged it into Julien's stomach.

The doubled pain threatened blackness, but his instincts were stronger. And so was Lucette. She was on her feet next to him and, without even looking, Julien grasped the hair ornament she held, sticky with Nic's blood.

"Not so very honourable," Julien choked, and thrust. He didn't aim to wound; the blade went straight into Nic's throat. There was an instant spray of blood, warm and thick across Julien's hands and face, and then he fell.

What a bloody waste of a life. As the words flitted across his rapidly darkening mind, Julien didn't know if he meant Nicolas or himself.

TWENTY-FIVE

14 *August 1580*
Wynfield Mote

It is over. We are restored to our home, almost . . . I nearly wrote
"almost as though nothing had happened" but that is patently
untrue. There is blood in our hall, and two bodies in the icehouse.
And in her bedchamber, Lucette sits watch over Julien LeClerc as
though her own breath is tied to his.

When Dominic and the others had silenced the men Nicolas had
surrounding the moat, they had to decide whether to storm the
house. They could hear nothing in the hall, so Dominic kept
Stephen and the men outside the front door and took Kit with him
through the study windows around back. It is a good thing Dominic
is not given to second-guessing himself or dithering, because when
he reached the hall, it was to find Lucette cradling Julien's head in
her lap. She was covered in his blood, as I saw for myself, for she
refused to wash or change or leave Julien until I promised that I
would hold his hand while Carrie helped her.

*It is a nasty wound he has—stomach wounds are always
dangerous. Carrie and I have treated him as best we can and sent
Harrington for the nearest physician. Lucette will not leave him, not
even long enough to tell us what happened. Explanations will have to
wait until Julien recovers.*

If he recovers.

Lucette had never been a chatterbox, but alone in her chamber with
Julien, she could not stop talking. She didn't even know half of what
she said—some of it was family history and some of it chess problems and some of it algebra—but she kept up a flow of words as
though if she stopped talking, Julien would stop breathing.

He wasn't unconscious, the physician said. And the wound had
been cleaned and stitched, and as far as anyone could tell Nic's dagger had missed anything vital. (The "as far as anyone could tell" was
the significant part—there were any number of things they couldn't
tell that might yet prove fatal.) Carrie herself did most of the nursing, with Lucette's stubborn and inexpert assistance.

But Julien remained out of reach. His eyes would open from time
to time, and he swallowed the liquids forced upon him, but all with
the greatest disinterest, as though his body responded instinctively
while his mind remained firmly shut to the outside world.

For two days, Lucette did not leave his side. She slept in the chair,
head resting on her arms on her bed.

"Lucie mine." His voice was rough and soft, as though it hurt to
speak.

She jerked awake, afraid for a second that she dreamed, but his
eyes were open and he was not just looking at her, but seeing her.

"Julien!"

He blinked once, painfully, then in a single word asked everything
he needed to know. "Nicolas?"

She nodded.

"I killed him." It was not a question.

She didn't know if she was glad or sorry that he remembered. "He tried to kill you. In more ways than one, and for far longer than just here in England."

Did that make it any better? She didn't think so, but she was desperate for him not to slip away from her again. "Julien, I need you. Don't go away just because it's easier. I know this world hurts, but I need you in it."

She had never dreamed he could look so vulnerable. "I don't know if I'm brave enough to live."

"Then I shall be brave for the both of us," she promised firmly.

Anne must have been watching for the royal banners, because she met Elizabeth and Walsingham half a mile outside the manor. Elizabeth almost remonstrated, in spite of the fact that Dominic and Kit had her surrounded by a dozen men, but when her daughter flew into her arms, she let herself be nothing more for a few moments than a grateful mother.

It could not last. Dominic had eleven men under arrest—and Elizabeth insisted on seeing Nicolas LeClerc's body for herself. He and his second-in-command lay in the icehouse, the August heat already working on their remains.

"Put them in the ground," she said abruptly. "Wherever you want. Unmarked. I don't want anyone to make martyrs of these criminals."

She stayed only one night at Wynfield Mote, for she needed to be back in London before the news of Mary Stuart's escape broke. Burghley would need her to settle the nerves of the populace, and they had to decide how much information to release.

Also, Elizabeth could not but feel she was not entirely welcome. Dominic had an air of wanting to tell her to get out and take her royal daughter with her so his family might not be caught in a dangerous political cross fire again. She respected the emotion, but could not afford to indulge him.

In fact, she spent an hour that evening trying to persuade Minu-ette to persuade her husband into greater service. "He is needed," she insisted to her friend. "Dominic is respected on all sides of the religious divide, and there is no man more likely to give me disinter-ested advice."

"A man who is honest when he should not be?" Minuette shook her head. "He will not play that role again, Elizabeth. And it is selfish to ask him to."

"I am queen. I am expected to be selfish."

Minuette merely fixed her with a look that made Elizabeth feel as though the last twenty-five years had never happened and they were both young and reckless and free.

In a gesture of surrender, Elizabeth shrugged. "I'll keep trying. In the meantime, your Stephen did good work at Tutbury. He is a natu-ral leader, and good at gaining confidences. Am I forbidden to speak to him as well about future service to the crown?"

"Stephen is old enough to know his own mind. And speaking of children grown old enough, I think it would be a mistake to send Ana-bel back into seclusion. She is always going to be a target, Elizabeth, and she proved herself every bit your daughter during her ordeal. Use her—and perhaps you will find you enjoy her for her own sake."

Just because she had four children to Elizabeth's one didn't mean Minuette was so much wiser. The sting of it made Elizabeth ask tartly, "And what of Lucette? I should like to speak to her before I leave. She owes me a report."

And there between them was the last twenty-five years—the se-crets that had made Elizabeth queen and Minuette subtle in defi-ance and conspiracy. "My daughter owes you nothing. I will not have her disturbed for your convenience."

They left it at that for the evening. Elizabeth spent a little time alone with Anabel before bed, and promised her daughter that she could come to court in September when the news of Mary Stuart had been absorbed. "We will see what she does next, and decide our next move from there," Elizabeth concluded.

Anabel seemed pleased at her mother's choice of pronoun.

Elizabeth rose early the next morning and dressed for departure in a gown of pale green velvet cut high at the waist to show the patterned damask kirtle of green and gold. When she opened the door, she found Lucette waiting for her in the corridor. Elizabeth raised a quizzical eyebrow. "You could have knocked," she pointed out.

"I wasn't sure I wanted to see you."

"How is your Frenchman?"

"He will live."

"Good."

Lucette stared at her as though she'd never seen the queen before.

Impatient, Elizabeth asked, "Well? Do you find you have something to say?"

"Yes, Your Majesty. You are my queen and as such you command my respect and even affection. But no more than that. I know who I am and who my parents are. I hope you will respect my family."

She sounded so much like Will when laying down the law that Elizabeth had to blink fast to keep her composure. It took a moment to realize Lucette was trying to hand her something.

"This belongs to you."

It was the necklace of enamel Tudor roses. Elizabeth felt a familiar fury tinged with an unfamiliar sense of shame. She took Lucette's hand and covered it with her own. "Keep it. As a sign of my affection for your own sake."

With that, the remote, imperious mask Lucette had assumed cracked. "You are a very great queen, Your Majesty. And yet I like you mostly for your own sake."

And that was as fine a compliment as Elizabeth had been paid in many a long year.

It was three weeks before they let Julien get out of bed. He'd been shocked to realize it was Lucette's bed they'd put him in, but as the days passed and his strength grew, he found the amusement in it. He thought of many teasing things to say to her, but found himself uncommonly tongue-tied.

Once Julien was out of immediate danger, Lucette spent only a few hours a day with him. He suspected Dominic had forbidden her more than that, and certainly no more nursing. It was one thing when a man was dying; a man halfway to being on his feet again was going to be closely supervised in Lucette's presence. But Carrie was a lenient supervisor and there were plenty of opportunities for them to hold hands or touch if they cared to.

He didn't know if Lucette cared to. And he cared so much that he was terrified to be rejected. So they were as chaste as though they were children.

The second week of September, as early autumn rain fell relentlessly against the walls of Wynfield Mote, Julien made it downstairs to the hall for dinner. The family gathered to celebrate his great accomplishment of walking down the stairs, but afterward everyone withdrew swiftly and tactfully. Even Lucette. She did not look back at him, but Kit did. He'd been studying Julien suspiciously throughout the meal, and his glance now seemed eloquent of distrust. There went a boy who would never find anyone good enough for his sisters.

Left alone with the Duke and Duchess of Exeter, Julien prayed fervently that Lucette's parents would be kinder. Surely Minuette, gentle as she was, would moderate her husband. Not that Julien expected Dominic to hurt him, not truly, but one never knew. After all, Julien had killed his brother in this chamber with Dominic's daughter caught in the middle. Who knew what the man might do?

What Dominic did first was ask him, "What next, Julien? The physician—and more importantly, both Carrie and my wife—say that you should be well enough to travel by the end of the month. Will you go?"

"I have to. You must know that."

Dominic nodded in agreement. "So perhaps the pertinent question is—will you come back?"

He looked from Dominic's stern gaze to Minuette's more sympathetic one, and back again. "If you don't mind, sir, I think that is a question Lucette should ask me first. If she cares to."

He could have sworn a smile passed across Dominic's face, but it was gone so swiftly he wasn't sure. "I suppose you're right. You may talk to her in here—with her mother and me close by, mind you."

What did Dominic think, that he would ravish Lucette in the same hall where he'd killed Nicolas? Did they think he would take her on the table? Propriety alone would stop him, not to mention the fact that he could hardly breathe deeply without pain. Ravishment was as far from his mind as could be.

Until Lucette entered the hall alone, dark hair left loose against a striped gown of cream, gold, and orange. Like sunset, or autumn leaves. Her skin glowed in the late twilight pouring through the open windows and Julien thought dizzily that the physical pain of ravishment just might be worth it after all. She sat next to him with an expectant gaze. Why was she here again? He'd had a hard time thinking clearly since being stabbed. Not that he'd ever been able to think clearly around Lucette.

"My father says there's something I'm supposed to ask you," she ventured.

Ah, right. "At the end of the month, I'll be leaving Wynfield. Your father said he would help me arrange passage home."

"You're going back to France."

"I have to. I cannot simply write to my father, not to mention Felix—" He broke off. "They deserve to hear what happened from me. You know it."

She did not deny it, but still argued. "What if the Catholics are waiting for you? Nicolas had been tracking your movements for months, what if he told them that you were a traitor? They could so easily—"

"Kill me? So they could. But I don't think he told them anything about me. I think he hoarded that information. Nic was never one to share."

"What will you tell them?"

"My father? The truth. All of it, from St. Bartholomew's Eve on. He will know how and what to tell Felix."

As still as marble, with no clue in her face or voice as to what answer she wanted, Lucette said, "So I suppose what I'm supposed to ask is: Will you come back?"

"That is for you to answer." Julien resisted the instinctive urge to tease or charm, and instead said as plainly as possible, "Shall I come back to England when I am finished, Lucie mine?"

His heart beat four times before she answered. "If you do not come back, I will hunt you the length and breadth of Europe until I string you up like a dog."

"Like father, like daughter," he laughed.

Her answering laughter was like summer rain after a drought, or the caress of soft wind beneath a blazing sun. He loved the sound. But he also did not want it to draw her parents' attention too soon, so he stopped it with a kiss.

POSTLUDE

September 1580
Madrid, Spain

Philip II of Spain waited until Cardinal Granvelle had crossed the chamber and stood behind his king, who looked out at the vista of the city he had made his center of government.

Without turning, Philip asked, "She is here?" An unnecessary question, but Granvelle, like all royal advisors, was accustomed to answering all questions, even the unnecessary ones.

"She is here."

"Show her in."

With a last, approving look at his city, Philip turned his back on the pointed arch of the stone window surround and waited where he was, hands clasped behind him. Granvelle reentered with a woman following. A woman dressed in black and white, taller than Granvelle by several inches—at nearly six feet, she was taller than most men, including Philip—with auburn hair and a regal carriage. Dowager Queen of France, disgraced Queen of Scotland, Mary Stuart approached Philip and sank into a nicely judged curtsey that managed to express appreciation and respect without forfeiting any of her innate sense of position.

Philip had had weeks to decide how to greet her. "Welcome to Spain, Your Majesty. I had thought to offer you greater, more public welcome . . . but I'm afraid the recent treatment of my daughter has left me unsettled."

Mary had also had weeks to decide how to reply. "Your Majesty, I did not know that your daughter would be offered harm. I did not know she was any part of the scheme to free me. If I had known, I should never have agreed to put an innocent in harm's way."

He did not know if he believed her. In the end it did not matter. They were playing a game, the two of them, and after all, he himself had agreed to the Nightingale Plot without knowing the details. If his Anne had been hurt, he would have had himself to blame.

But his daughter had not been injured, and the Nightingale Plot had succeeded where all others had failed. Mary Stuart was free. The problem, as it had always been, was what to do with her next?

"Madam," he said in his most formal manner, which was very formal indeed, "it is my understanding that you wish to make Spain your friend in the years ahead. Perhaps, to make us something more than friends?"

"That is as Your Majesty wishes it." What else could she say? All of Catholic Europe had marveled at Mary's escape from Protestant England, but that didn't mean they wanted her on their hands. The French queen mother loathed her onetime daughter-in-law intensely, and even Mary's de Guise relatives were in no hurry to welcome her into their homes. She had been a bad queen and a worse wife . . . but she was important in the balance of things.

Philip had considered long and hard before giving his consent to Nightingale, and once he made a decision, he did not change it lightly. He had determined his course of action months ago; it only waited now to be put into practice.

"My lady," he said, more gently than before, "it is my great wish that you will consider Spain your home. And that you will consent to adorn my kingdom with your beauty and grace. Would not the Queen of Scotland and France like also to be the Queen of Spain?"

She was too clever to gloat, but not so clever as to hide it completely. Satisfaction flickered in her eyes. "I can conceive of no greater purpose, Your Majesty, than to be your wife and to give you sons."

He could not keep half the chamber between them any longer. Crossing the marble floor, Philip kissed her lovely white hand and thought, And that, Elizabeth, is how wars begin to be won—by changing the rules of engagement.

This is a new war now.

Acknowledgments

Where to begin with my undying gratitude? How about with Tamar Rydzinski, who talked me through the perils of submitting a new project and held my hand along every step of my worried path. Tamar, I wish I could promise you that I will get less neurotic as time goes on, but I think we both know different.

Jostling for that first spot is Kate Miciak. She's the kind of editor I might sell my soul for, if it came down to it. And even then, my soul might not be enough for what she's worth! She knows instinctively what to say—from compliments to reassurances to dead-on critique of every weak spot in a manuscript. And she introduced me to Lee Child!

And then there's the Penguin Random House team. Julia Maguire has the unenviable task of reminding me of the many things I forget. Shona McCarthy, Maggie Oberrender, Abbey Cory, Angela McNally, Pamela Alders, Caroline Cunningham, Susan Zucker, Liz Shapiro, Marietta Anastassatos, and Susan Corcoran are the most dedicated, talented professionals—each of whom has made every day better since they allowed me into their world. I was visiting London when I got the news that they wanted this trilogy. I nearly burst into tears in Trafalgar Square when I realized I could continue working with all of these people—and more.

Peter Weissman is the most fabulous copy editor ever. His green pencil never (okay, almost never) freaks me out. He deserves special appreciation for this book, which he received sooner than I expected him to. For wading through my many errors, a million thanks.

An enormous thanks to the *Romantic Times* organization, especially the reviewers who have given so much love to my books. Winning Best Historical Fiction from them was the best surprise of last year—and I'm still a little afraid they're going to take it back.

And always and ever, there's my family. I have had many opportunities this last year to remember that, as much as I love my books, I love my people that little bit more. Last June our second son graduated from high school and started college three weeks later—two thousand miles away. Also in June, our beloved as-good-as-daughter graduated from college and left our house after more than two years with us.

The greatest loss last summer was my dear father-in-law. I met him when I was only seventeen and in the nearly thirty years since, his has been one of those few whose good opinion I cared for. This book is his, if for no other reason than because he helped raise his youngest son to be a person who makes every day of my life better. I chose the word "gentleman" in the dedication advisedly—because Dee Andersen was, truly, a gentle man. We miss him.

THE VIRGIN'S
DAUGHTER

Laura Andersen

A Reader's Guide

FROM THE DIARY OF MINUETTE COURTENAY

30 August 1561
Wynfield Mote

Elizabeth's summer progress has brought her to Warwick Castle for a fortnight, a visit that might very well bankrupt Ambrose Dudley. It is, of course, a mark of great favour to host the queen—but the wretched man apparently had to build an entirely new timber structure in which to house her, seeing as the castle itself is in such poor repair. Perhaps that is why our queen never chooses to stay with us at Wynfield Mote—she knows that we would not go to such lengths to impress her.

But as Warwick is only ten miles distant, Elizabeth has come to us for this one night only.

There have been rumours, of course, since almost the moment she made her wedding vows last December. But I said I would believe none of them until Elizabeth herself told me. And so she did, as we sat alone together after dinner.

"I am with child." She delivered the news as abruptly and matter-of-factly as though she were commenting on possession of a new book or piece of art. But I know her too well to be deceived.

"I am glad of it," I replied, with real pleasure. "Have you been ill? Tired? Uncomfortable?"

"I cannot afford to be ill, breeding or not."

"Philip must be pleased." I called him by name deliberately, to separate the husband and father from the King of Spain.

"Naturally he is pleased. It means he has done his duty. Now he can return to Spain for the winter."

"I do not think you are only a duty to him, Elizabeth. And nor will his child be."

But my friend has refused to be sentimental since the death of Robert Dudley. "We cannot all be as fortunate as you, Minuette, with your adoring husband and perfect brood of children. For it is no secret in this household that you are also set to deliver another before spring."

There is no such thing as perfect, I wanted to snap. What does Elizabeth know of the price Dominic and I continue to pay for our past sins? Does she know how my husband retreated to Tiverton after Stephen's birth last year and did not communicate for so many months I began to think he had left me? He loves me, I know, and he loves Lucette equally with Stephen—but love does not preclude pain.

As Elizabeth knows well.

27 February 1562
Tiverton Castle

Elizabeth is safely delivered of a daughter.

She is named Anne Isabella, for her Boleyn grandmother and her Spanish great-grandmother. If there is disappointment that the newborn is not a son, it is masked for now with relief that the queen is clearly capable of bearing healthy children. King Philip will return in the spring to meet his daughter, yes, but also to begin the business of the next child.

But I can care about Elizabeth only in brief snatches between my own joy and exhaustion. Three days ago I was also delivered, almost a month before my expected time, and gifted by God with two beautiful children. A girl and a boy. Philippa, we have called our daughter, after Dominic's mother, who died last year in blessed peace. We considered naming her twin Jonathan, after my father, but Dominic kept looking between the two babies with a crease in his forehead as he pondered.

"Christopher," he finally announced.

I blinked, somewhat surprised, for there is no Christopher in either of our *near families. But then Dominic gave one of his rare, open smiles and said, "I like the way they sound together. Pippa and Kit. What do you think?"*

I think I love you so much my heart is near to breaking, I thought.

3 May 1562
Tiverton Castle

The children and I leave for Wynfield Mote next week. Dominic will not be with us. He has been summoned to court. Elizabeth has tried summons before this, but Dominic has always ignored them. What can she threaten us with? Taking away Tiverton and the duchy of Exeter? It would be no punishment, for Dominic serves his people from duty rather than ambition.

This time, Elizabeth took another tack. Please, *she wrote to both of us,* I have great need of a friend. Not for myself. For my daughter.

The closer he came to London, the more tense Dominic Courtenay grew. He had not been anywhere near the city since his imprisonment in the Tower five years before. At least Elizabeth had sense enough not to summon him to Whitehall. Indeed, he did not actually have to enter the city at all, for the queen awaited him at Nonsuch Palace, fifteen miles southwest. The distinctive octagonal towers rising before him made Dominic catch his breath before he ruthlessly banished memories of previous visits. Visits when Elizabeth was merely Princess of Wales and William . . .

Tension made him curt, but he had never been a man of many words and Elizabeth's guards and stewards passed him along swiftly enough to the queen's privy chamber. To his surprise, she greeted him alone.

"No counselors today?" he asked her. "No clerks or ambassadors begging your attention for the great matters of state?"

"There is no matter of greater importance to me than what I am about to ask you."

"Why bring me all the way here simply to tell you no? I am finished with courts and royals, Your Majesty. You know that."

"But you are not finished with loyalty. Nor will you be so long as you draw breath."

"What do you want, Elizabeth?" If she was going to pluck at all the most painful chords of his past, he would treat her not as queen, but as the girl he'd known since childhood.

She matched his tone. "I need you, Dominic, to stand as Protector to my daughter."

All the breath left his body. He'd known a Lord Protector once, and no way in hell was he going to follow in the footsteps of George Boleyn, Lord Rochford.

Elizabeth didn't wait for his refusal. "I am not asking you to run the government, Dominic. You are entirely too honest for such a task ... although I suspect Minuette would be quite good at it."

"That is not—"

Elizabeth overrode him. "Let me be frank. My life is all that stands between security and chaos in England. My life—and now that of my infant daughter. An infant whose father would gladly seize whatever power he could in this nation."

Dominic had learned a few things from his wife, including sarcasm. "That is only occurring to you now?"

Her eyes darkened, and he realized that there was real fear beneath her royal composure. "For a man so eager to keep apart from politics, that is a rather piercing opinion to voice."

He raised a hand in conciliation. "I apologize. What is it you want from me?"

When she spoke again, it was entirely as Queen of England. "If I should die during my daughter's childhood, England will have need of a strong government during her minority. That responsibility would lie in the hands of Lord Burghley and Sir Francis Walsingham, as well as a carefully composed council of men I trust. I am not asking you to protect England in such a case—I am asking you to protect Anabel."

It was that last word that moved him, the realization that Elizabeth had given her daughter a pet name. Even though he suspected her of using sentiment against him, it worked. There was only one thing more she could try, so Dominic asked before the queen could. "May I see her?"

He followed Elizabeth to a separate suite of painted and gilded chambers attended by soft-footed ladies who looked more suited to royal feasts than caring for a baby.

Anne Isabella, the Princess of Wales, lay in a cradle beneath a cloth-of-gold canopy embroidered with her mother's personal falcon badge. The baby looked a little bigger to him than did his own twins, but the plump cheeks and finely pursed mouth were familiar childish traits. The infant had her mother's distinctive red-gold hair and stared up at him with a curious intelligence he told himself he was imagining.

"She's a pawn, Dominic," Elizabeth said softly, next to him. "A Spanish pawn. If I die young, Philip's men will spare no effort to lay hold of her. She must not fall to Spain. Promise me, Dominic. Promise me that if anything happens to me, you will take Anabel into your care. I trust few men with my government—but only one man do I trust with her life."

The last royal who trusted me with his life is dead, Dominic thought bleakly. In the end, it was the memory of Will, as much as Elizabeth's plea, that decided him.

"I will protect her, Your Majesty. As though she were my own."

QUESTIONS AND TOPICS FOR DISCUSSION

1. Discuss Elizabeth's marriage to King Philip. Can you envision any scenario in which their marriage might have survived? Or were their religious differences and political responsibilities insurmountable?

2. What do you think motivated Elizabeth's revelation about her suspicions regarding Lucette's true parentage? Was her choice political or personal? How might she have handled the situation differently? Discuss the long-term impact of her decision on Lucette and the Courtenay family.

3. Which character surprised you the most? Why?

4. In what ways are Anne Isabella and Elizabeth similar? In what ways are they different? Compare and contrast the two, both as women and as leaders.

5. Discuss the relationship between Minuette and Elizabeth. In what ways has it evolved, and in what ways has it remained the same?

6. Elizabeth plays many roles—that of wife, friend, mother, and queen most notably. Discuss these different facets of her personality. Do you see a difference in her behavior in each of these contexts, or does the monarch necessarily overshadow the other roles?

7. At one point, Lucette asks, "Should not love between spouses be absolute? How could one ever love a second person as much as the first?" Do you agree with this sentiment? Is it possible to feel romantic love for more than one person in a lifetime?

8. Renaud tells Lucette: "You are so afraid of not being wanted, you will not put it to the test, and thus create the very distance you fear." Do you agree with his assessment of Lucette? Can you think of anyone else in the book to whom this sentiment applies?

9. Discuss Julien's motives for becoming an English spy, taking into account the events of 1572. Do you find his reasons compelling?

10. Before leaving England, Philip says to Elizabeth, "I indulged myself in a dream these twenty years because I loved you and because I hoped persuasion would be of greater influence than force." What do you think his dream was? How could Elizabeth have handled the situation with Spain differently? At this point, do you think there was anything she could have done to dissuade Philip from carrying out his plan?

11. Compare and contrast Nicolas and Julien. In what ways are they similar? In what ways are they different? Did you sympathize with Nicolas at all by the end?

12. If you read The Boleyn King Trilogy, compare and contrast the relationships between Kit, Anabel, Pippa, and Lucette to those between the previous generation: Elizabeth, William, Dominic, and Minuette.

13. What did you think of the revelation at the end of the book? Any predictions for the sequel?

If you were enchanted by *The Virgin's Daughter,*

you won't want to miss

THE VIRGIN'S SPY

Laura Andersen's next dazzling installment

of The Tudor Legacy trilogy.

ONE

June 1581

Elizabeth loved weddings. At least those weddings in which she could appear the benign good fairy, generously bestowing her favor upon a couple and, as always, claiming the spotlight for herself. Most families fortunate enough to draw the queen's attention to such an occasion fell over themselves to get out of her way and let her run things the way she wanted them.

Not the Courtenay family.

At this wedding, Elizabeth was little more than a guest. For one thing, she had wanted the wedding to take place in London. As the bride was the eldest daughter of the Duke of Exeter and Elizabeth's own goddaughter, the queen had graciously offered any number of royal chapels for the ceremony, from private ones such as Hampton Court to more public parishes like St. Margaret's at Westminster.

But Lucette Courtenay had her mother's stubbornness when her own wishes were at stake, and so Elizabeth herself had to travel northwest to participate in the wedding of the English lady and her French Catholic spy.

Elizabeth did not stay at Wynfield Mote with the Courtenay family, but in Warwick Castle ten miles northeast. After the castle's forfeit to the crown upon the Duke of Northumberland's death, Elizabeth had bestowed it upon one of the duke's surviving sons, Ambrose Dudley. In gratitude for the queen's generosity, Ambrose gave her the run of the castle whenever she wished. There was no such thing for Elizabeth as a release from ruling, so she filled hours with letters and papers and in meeting with the men who rode back and forth between the monarch and Walsingham in London. Though her Lord Secretary (and chief spymaster) had once used both the bride and groom in his intelligence web, Walsingham had not been invited to the wedding.

The ceremony itself went off beautifully. Conducted at Holy Trinity Church in Stratford-upon-Avon—and in the language of the Prayer Book issued by Elizabeth's government in the first year of her reign—Lucette Courtenay and Julien LeClerc pledged themselves to love and honor, to worship with their bodies and remain loyal to their deaths. Elizabeth herself had not been married to quite those words—indeed, the working out of her marriage more than twenty years ago to Philip of Spain had required nearly a month of exhaustive debates on how precisely to balance their vows as Catholic and Protestant. But as Julien LeClerc had willingly adopted the Protestant faith for his bride, there was no trouble about words.

They at least allowed the queen to host a banquet for them afterward at Warwick Castle. Elizabeth had rather hoped that Lucette would wear the Tudor rose necklace she had once given her, but the dark-haired bride was adorned instead with another necklace familiar to the queen: pearls and sapphires, with a single filigree star pendant.

When the bride's mother joined her, Elizabeth said acerbically, "Don't tell me you have handed over your prized possession, Minuette. Whatever does Dominic say?"

Though nearly forty-five, Minuette Courtenay was recognizably still the young woman who had once captured the King of England's heart. If there were strands of gray in her honey-gold hair, they did not show and her gown of leaf-green damask fit as neatly as when she was young. There were times, looking at her friend, when Elizabeth could almost believe the last twenty-five years a dream.

Minuette returned her to the subject of the necklace. "It is only lent for now," she replied with equal tartness. "And Dominic would say that we ourselves are our prized possessions, not any material goods."

"Do you never tire of your husband's practical perfection?" Not that there wasn't a grain of envy in Elizabeth's soul at her friend's long-lived and loving marriage.

Minuette turned the conversation with the ease of a woman who had known her queen since childhood—indeed, still knew her rather better than made Elizabeth comfortable. "Anabel tells us you intend to invest her formally as Princess of Wales. She is very proud—and, to your credit, taking the responsibility seriously. Dominic says her spoken Welsh has become quite good."

Instinctively, Elizabeth darted a look to where her only child sat in merry companionship with Minuette's twins. Kit and Pippa Courtenay were either side of the princess, their matching honey-gold heads (like their mother's) bent inward as the three of them talked in no doubt scurrilous terms about the guests. The tableau tugged painfully at long-ago memories. *The Holy Quartet*, Robert Dudley had called them: Dominic, Minuette, Elizabeth . . . and her brother, William. She could only hope there was less pain in these young ones' futures.

"The investiture," Elizabeth acknowledged. "Of course it is only a formality. A ritual I never had. But it will be useful just now to remind the Welsh of our power. That is why I have chosen Ludlow Castle for the investiture, rather than simply doing it before Parliament. Anabel will make a charming figure to the Welsh."

"She says the council has invited a representative from the Duc d'Anjou to attend the investiture."

"As well as an envoy from Scotland. France is prepared to give us a large measure of what we want now that Mary Stuart has wed Philip. I will see what I can get from them, but it is Scotland that is most desperate for an alliance."

"What has Anabel to say about it?"

Elizabeth huffed in exasperation. "You know better than that, Minuette. With my divorce from Philip and his recent marriage to Mary Stuart, all Europe is on edge. Mary wants Scotland back, make no mistake, and if she can persuade my former husband to give her Spanish troops, then our island is in serious danger. If Anabel were at all prone to romance—and I'm not certain that she is—she would have to give over for hard, cold reality. England and Scotland must stand together or we will fall separately to the Catholics."

Minuette held her silence almost to the point of discomfort, but finally said, "I wasn't criticizing, Elizabeth. Not intentionally. It is only that you were my friend before you were my queen, and at times I wish you unencumbered by the burdens of ruling. You and Anabel both."

It was my choice to rule, Elizabeth thought but would never say. I just didn't have a clear idea of what it would mean, the years of weariness and care and doubt. And always, the waiting for the next crisis.

She didn't have long to wait. Before the wedding party had quite broken up, a courier arrived from London with a curt message written in Walsingham's hand, the message Elizabeth had been fearing since the Scots queen had escaped her English imprisonment last year and then married the King of Spain.

Mary Stuart is four months gone with child.

The morning after his sister's wedding, Stephen Courtenay woke late and for nearly the first time in his life was reluctant to leave

his bed. (His empty bed, at least, and at home it was always empty.)
But with Lucie's wedding out of the way, he couldn't put off what
came next. The queen had offered him a command, and would
not long await an answer.

Command was one thing—he had been raised to expect it.
Command in Ireland was something else entirely. And convincing
his parents to accept it when he himself was ambivalent? No wonder he'd rather stay in bed.

But he was twenty-one years old and could hardly hide from
trouble. So he flung himself out of bed and dressed in record time
in the belief that he might as well get unpleasant things done
quickly. If he were Kit, he would dawdle his way through, putting
it off as long as he could, but irresponsibility was not a trait an
eldest son and heir could afford. That was the province of younger
brothers.

On this particular morning, Kit was long gone on a ride with
Pippa and Anabel. Lucie and her new husband had spent the night
at their new home, Compton Wynyates, and from there meant to
spend the next few weeks in Yorkshire, since the French-born Julien thought it sounded exotic. From the way Lucie and Julien had
been looking at one another last night, Stephen supposed they
would hardly notice their surroundings, as long as they had a bed.

And that was a disturbing image. Stephen shook it off as he
swiped bread and cheese from the Wynfield Mote kitchens and
headed for the fount of all certain knowledge where his family was
concerned—Carrie Harrington.

Just turned sixty, Carrie had been in his mother's service for
twenty-five years, and in Minuette's mother's service before that.
After she'd lost her first husband and both their children to illness
early in life, she had remarried the large, silent Edward Harrington who'd served Dominic Courtenay since before he was the
Duke of Exeter. Carrie had personally delivered Stephen and each
of his siblings and could always be counted on for good advice.

And also a certain amount of mind reading.

"Looking for your parents?" she asked, squinting up at him from her comfortable chair in the sunlit solar. "Or looking to avoid them?"

Stephen smiled. "Which should it be?"

Her hair was a soft grey-brown and her face lined, but her hands were steady on her needlework. "Don't look to me to sort your problems. Go to Ireland or not—it is your decision. And that, for what it's worth, is what your parents will tell you."

"I know. Sometimes I wish they were more autocratic."

"No, you don't. You only appear submissive in comparison to your brother. If ever you are commanded against your wishes, Stephen, you will balk authority as surely as Kit does."

"Then let us hope I am never commanded against my wishes. There is only room in this family for one Kit."

"Your parents walked in the direction of the old church," Carrie said, dismissing him and returning to her sewing.

Stephen met them coming back toward the house, halfway between Wynfield Mote and the Norman church that had stood empty since Henry VIII's reformation. Dominic and Minuette Courtenay had been married in that empty chapel—married in a Catholic ceremony, surprisingly. Every now and then Stephen remembered that his parents had not only had a life before their children, but a rather complicated and dangerous life. They were so very . . . stable. But today, remembering that his father had once been enough of a rebel to land in the Tower gave Stephen courage to speak the whole of his conflicted mind.

As ever, his mother went right to the heart of the matter. "The queen is demanding an answer to Ireland, is she not? I could feel the weight of her attention on you yesterday."

"I've put her off as long as possible. If I'm taking a force to Ireland, it must be before summer's end."

"Are you seeking counsel, or approval?" his father asked.

"I'm always seeking both." Stephen smiled briefly. "Partly I feel

I don't want anything to do with the mess in Ireland—and partly I feel that very reluctance means I should go."

His mother laughed. "So like your father, making everything ten times more difficult than it need be. Go to Ireland or don't, Stephen, but stop flaying yourself alive over the decision."

But Dominic Courtenay knew his son as he knew himself, and so he added what the young man craved—an opinion. "If it were myself, I would go. I was your age when I commanded men along the March of Wales, and it was a critical experience in my life. You are a good leader with good men from your Somerset lands who will follow you. Let them. What they learn of you in Ireland will shape their lives and yours. Besides," and here he cast a rueful glance at his wife, "military service is the least demanding request a monarch can make. Be glad if that is all the queen wants of you, son."

Stephen laughed as he was meant to, and he did feel lighter when he wrote to the queen later that day to accept her offer of command in Ireland.

But beneath the lightness of a decision made was a brittle unease. Because military service was not the only thing wanted of him. His second letter was to Francis Walsingham. Though officially the Queen's principal secretary, Walsingham had never given over his role as her chief intelligencer.

I will be in Ireland by mid-August, Stephen wrote.

He expected Walsingham would have requests of his own to add to the queen's orders.

Anne Isabella, Princess of Wales, had learned from her earliest years that she could nearly always get her way. Not many people had the power to say no to the daughter of two reigning monarchs, and so nineteen-year-old Anabel, when she was being particularly honest with herself, admitted that she was a bit spoiled.

The trouble was, one only tended to realize that when one didn't get one's way. As now, with Kit Courtenay staring her down in refusal.

"What do you mean 'no'?" she demanded. "I have appointed you my Master of Horse. It wasn't a request."

"Unless you mean me to operate in chains, then I am telling you that I very kindly decline the appointment."

"What is wrong with you, Kit? You've been irritable and difficult for months."

"Because I have a mind of my own and a wish to do more with my life than follow you around and offer you compliments? 'How lovely you are today, Your Highness,'" he said in deadly mimicry of court sycophants. "'The very image of your royal mother, but is that a touch of Spanish flair in your dress?'"

Anabel's temper went from raging to white-hot in a moment. In a chilly tone reminiscent of her father's Spanish hauteur, she said, "Long acquaintance does not give you the right to insult me to my face."

Most unusually, Kit did not immediately respond. Anabel was used to his ready tongue and the quick wits that could spin any conversation a dozen dizzying directions without warning. But in the last months, his irritability had been accompanied by these bouts of reflection before speech.

Kit did not apologize; she had not expected him to. But he offered something of an explanation. "I am growing older, just as you are. I do not have a throne waiting for me, nor even a title. Stephen inherits my father's riches. I must make my own path. And I would prefer to do it without undue favoritism."

"And what of due favoritism? Do you expect me to appoint strangers to serve in my household?"

"I am not insensible of the great honour, Your Highness. But I have made other plans. The Earl of Leicester is bound for Dublin and has appointed me his secretary. I leave for Ireland in two weeks."

"You're going to Ireland with Brandon Dudley? To be a *secretary*?" Anabel laughed in disbelief. "Why not at least go as part of Stephen's forces?"

"If I'm not going to accept your favours, Anabel, I'm hardly likely to go begging to my brother."

That at least sounded like the Kit she had always known—irreverent and occasionally insolent. Although Anabel was as close to the Courtenay children as anyone, the princess occasionally studied relationships as an outsider and wondered if the pleasures of siblings outweighed the resentments.

"I don't suppose there's any chance you would reconsider?" There was a wistfulness to her plea she had not expected.

His quick, rueful grin was answer in itself. "You'll be happier with someone more biddable, Your Highness. You and I should only spend our days arguing."

But those are the best parts of my days, Anabel thought forlornly. Arguing with you.

She was still fretting about his uncharacteristic refusal that night when Pippa helped her change for bed. There were two other ladies moving silently about with her gown and kirtle and ruff, but Anabel ignored them.

"What is wrong with Kit?" she demanded of his twin.

Pippa continued to brush Anabel's hair as she answered. "Kit told you the truth. For all his mischief, he is ambitious and proud. Is it truly a surprise he should wish to make his way independently?"

Pippa had her twin's sharp cheekbones and eyes that tilted up on the outside. They both had their mother's thick, wavy hair the colour of sun-warmed honey, but Pippa had a streak of black that framed the right side of her face. It made her look—not exotic, exactly—but otherworldly. It was not the only otherworldly aspect to her character.

But at the moment Pippa did not seem interested in sharing any of her unique knowledge, so Anabel contented herself with logical argument. "Being Master of Horse for the Princess of Wales would be an independent position. I don't mean to tell him how to perform his responsibilities."

"Kit does not wish to take your gifts."

"Because he does not wish to waste time in my company?"

Pippa laid down the brush and, when Anabel made no objection, pulled a stool alongside her friend. Her voice was kind but implacable. "You know better than that. Anabel, what is truly bothering you?"

Your damned twin with his arrogance and pride and sudden wish to cut himself off from me. Kit was hers, as much as Pippa. What was the point of being royal if one could not keep hold of the people one wanted?

But not even to Pippa was she prepared to share the full turmoil of her thoughts, because beneath them lurked something that frightened her. An image—a memory—that came to her at night as she drifted between waking and sleep.

The expression in Kit's eyes when he'd walked into Wynfield Mote a year ago to negotiate her out of the hands of a violent man.

Anabel had not seen that expression in the months since. Instead, Kit had been moody and unpredictable. And now he seemed so determined to get away from her that he was willing to go to godforsaken Ireland.

When it must have become clear that Anabel would not speak further, Pippa sighed. "Someday you will have to learn to trust yourself, Your Highness. I cannot do it for you."

30 June 1581

Dearest Lucie,

When you traveled to France last year, I teased you about coming home with a Frenchman. Or half-teased. I did not know—I never know—for certain how events would play out. I knew there was dan-

ger and pain and loss all tied together with your happiness . . . but is that not the nature of life itself? One cannot untangle only the parts one wants. They are woven together too tightly.

How do I tell Anabel that? She is not prepared to admit, even to herself, that she knows perfectly well why Kit is leaving England. Having had the shock of confronting his own feelings for her so suddenly last August, Kit cannot go on taking her favours as nothing more than the friend he has always been. But nor will he press on her a love she is not prepared to accept. To serve in her household would be a daily insult to his pride, especially with the looming visits of the French and Scots representatives coming to vie for her hand. Kit knows perfectly well that Anabel is not meant for him.

What do I know? Only a tangle of paths and choices and troubles that lie ahead. England's future is no more secure than Elizabeth's or her daughter's. If I knew how it would all turn out, I would truly be the witch some might fear me of being.

But I am only a girl who knows more than I wish.

Oh dear, only days away from you and already I am slipping into melodrama. In your great happiness, Lucie, steal a few minutes away to write to me with your mix of sisterly compassion and common sense. I need it.

Love,
Pippa

5 July 1581

Pippa,

Stop being melodramatic! The world is not yours to order or decipher, only to live in as we all must do. If you had tried to tell me that I would fall in love with Julien, I would likely have refused to do so out of sheer stubbornness. There's no use fretting over Anabel and Kit—I have never known two people more certain to do precisely as they please. Getting in their way will only aggravate the issue.

I feel quite certain now that York is the most beautiful city in England. Though probably I should feel that way about Bristol or Leeds or Carlisle if I happened to be passing these days in any of those towns. It is Julien that makes all beautiful, especially at night when we can shut the door and there is nothing in this world but the two of us. And a fine cambric shift. And a bed.

It is a state I highly recommend.

Your most lovingly contented sister,
Lucie

ABOUT THE AUTHOR

LAURA ANDERSEN is married with four children, and possesses a constant sense of having forgotten something important. She has a B.A. in English (with an emphasis in British History), which she puts to use by reading everything she can lay her hands on.

www.lauraandersenbooks.com
Find Laura S. Andersen on Facebook
@LauraSAndersen

ABOUT THE TYPE

This book was set in Requiem, a typeface designed by the Hoefler Type Foundry. It is a modern typeface inspired by inscriptional capitals in Ludovico Vicentino degli Arrighi's 1523 writing manual, *Il modo de temperare le penne*. An original lowercase, a set of figures, and an italic in the chancery style that Arrighi (fl. 1522) helped popularize were created to make this adaptation of a classical design into a complete font family.

Chat.
Comment.
Connect.

Visit our online book club community at
Facebook.com/RHReadersCircle

Chat
Meet fellow book lovers and discuss what you're reading.

Comment
Post reviews of books, ask—and answer—thought-provoking
questions, or give and receive book club ideas.

Connect
Find an author on tour, visit our author blog, or invite one of
our 150 available authors to chat with your group on the phone.

Explore
Also visit our site for discussion questions, excerpts, author
interviews, videos, free books, news on the latest releases,
and more.

Books are better with buddies.
Facebook.com/RHReadersCircle

RANDOM HOUSE

RANDOM HOUSE
READER'S CIRCLE ®